RICHARD HEAD
THE WORKING MAN'S GUIDE TO THE GALAXY

United Arts Publishers Limited

THE WORKING MAN'S GUIDE TO THE GALAXY

"Bloody cheeky message if you ask me" shouted the Queen's New Zealander shoe cleaner Kevin Indiana William Illushias, "Once they know who we are they will sing a different tune." "Hang on a minute mate" responded the crown polisher, "when we get to the next gate, what's beyond that?" "Nothing of course you daft twat, just like we've seen all these millions and millions of years, absolutely bloody nothing" spouted KIWI. "I know you call it nothing, but nothing is something out here even if it means nothing to us. What I really mean is when does this space all end?"

"Yes mate, I see what you mean, we keep going through gates, travelling for millions of years until we reach a new gate. So, what's behind the last gate?" replies KIWI. "But we can't have a last gate mate, because there is no such thing as nothing, because it must be something, therefore there can't be a last gate" says the crown polisher in a worried tone. "Now hang on friend, if there is no last gate then this means that space goes on for ever?" "Yes kiddo, it means that this is eternity where it never ends even though the human brain cannot comprehend anything never ending. It's so mind bending that here we have discovered a power so great, so overwhelming, so incredible, so impossible that maybe........."

THE WORKING MAN'S GUIDE TO THE GALAXY

*First published in 1993 in Great Britain
by Londinium Press, London and Chatham.*

Copyright © Richard Head 1993
All rights reserved

*The right of Richard Head to be identified as the the author
of this work has been asserted by him in accordance with
the Copyright, Designs and Patents Act 1988*

*Cover Design and text by Tony Waterhouse,
Waterhouse Graphic Design and Visual Communications, Warwick*

*Printed in Great Britain by
Jolly & Barber Ltd. Rugby*

*British Library Cataloguing in Publication Data
Head, Richard
Working Man's Guide to the Galaxy
I. Title
823 [F]
ISBN 0-906264-09-x*

All rights reserved.
*No part of this publication may be reproduced, stored in a retrieval system
or transmitted, in any form, or by any means,
electronic, mechanical, photocopying, recording or
otherwise, without the prior permission of the publishers*

*All quotations and authors in Chapter 20 of this publication
have been created by Richard Head and are therefore subject to
Copyright restrictions*

**Londinium Press is an imprint of United Arts Publishers Limited
11 Military Road, Chatham, Kent, ME4 4JG, England**

WHY?

Writing a book is a personal achievement that involves great anguish and suffering which only the most foolhardy and dedicated should attempt to achieve. During the writing of this book I have been infected with an incurable mental virus that has led me onto a fool's paradise of disillusionment; a dark place better left alone by the silent majority.

This planet of sadness is full of disturbing conclusions relating to the endless cruelty of the human race upon itself. Cruelty as a physical activity of the barbaric mind is horrific enough, but is a mere slap on the wrist when compared with the mental cruelty dealt out by nations upon their citizens as a matter of policy.

If we don't resist such a policy and stand up to be counted then where is the future for mankind?

Publisher's Note

The Working Man's Guide To The Galaxy is a work of inspiration - it is outrageous; it is funny and occasionally sad.

Some readers may find the language offensive, but the words employed are in common use among our male population and they achieve the Author's aim by their directness.

The narrative is fiction and no reference is intended to anyone, living or dead, except for those historical figures, past, present or future, who are addressed solely to project the Author's views.

No man, having read this book, will put it aside without having exposed his mind to a shattering eruption of ideas.

In Memory

To George Wilders, one of the great Chieftains of the working class who never forgot his roots and yet achieved his greatest ambitions. A man of incredible opinions and vision who gave inspiration to all around him. His wife Sheila and their children George, Tracey and Donna, together with so many other friends, are privileged to have known and loved him.

INDEX OF CONTENTS

Chapter 1	What's it all about..1
Chapter 2	WARNING 45
Chapter 3	Pies to Democracy 63
Chapter 4	UNCLE to Eternity 117
Chapter 5	Rubber to Murder 139
Chapter 6	Authority to Hong Kong 173
Chapter 7	Sickness to losing your head 209
Chapter 8	Inventions to XXXXX 231
Chapter 9	Obenfloof to getting stuffed 253
Chapter 10	Umpteen Ethos to John Brown 273
Chapter 11	Comedy to Capitalistic Corporations 293
Chapter 12	Artless to Artful...315
Chapter 13	From Charisma to Mr. Kithbang 339
Chapter 14	From Earthly Paradise to Shite..................357
Chapter 15	Freebee to Poems 377
Chapter 16	English Language to Condom Testing 399
Chapter 17	Death's Knell 415
Chapter 18	DikHed's 20 Questions 417
Chapter 19	Beat the Ban!...421
Chapter 20	Masterful Quotations 423
Chapter 21	Because 437

Chapter 1

WHAT'S IT ALL ABOUT?

"True adventure is essential to Man's evolution on his epic voyage in search of life's continual quest for knowledge. A perpetual encyclopaedia written by artists and missionaries, to be made freely available to all mankind for common advantage and edification. A man lacking this voracious appetite for enlightenment is but an aerophobic salmon fearsome of leaping the final waterjump separating him from the upper waters where his species will multiply and survive, thus failing to reach his nostalgic destiny, never experiencing a true inner self."

President Lincoln
(written 5 minutes before he was shot)

During every millennium, a monumental event occurs on this earth of ours which is destined to change the course of mankind for ever and often for a few days longer than that. The better the idea, the longer it is used, so to speak. The Holy Bible covers all the great characters up until 0BC (including 0AD and 1992 BDH), and since then we have had the "Three Great Dicks", consisting of Moby Dick, Dick Whittington and Richard Nixon, all following in the same footsteps of greatness as their predecessors.

Albeit a pure coincidence of only a name, I now confess to being the latest "Great Dick" to join the ranks of such Godlike heroes of the earth, a new group soon to be known forthwith as the "Four Great Dicks". This new enlarged group of Godlike heroes will be so referred to until another Dick of greatness enters stage left with the sole intention of muscling in on my act. In simple to understand terms, I am pleased to inform all and sundry that Dick Head the world famous author has arrived upon the world stage carrying with him the unique ability of being able to change the life of every working class man who dares to proceed with the further reading of this published classic of literature without fear or remorse. Now let's get on with the real basis of my story and cut out the bullshite, shall we? Yes of course we shall. Begone all bullshite and let the story unfold.

I make a proposition and proffer the hand of friendship to all philanthropic friends, venomous foes and chauvinistic countrymen alike, you investors of the Queen's currency, who have speculated a large proportion of your hard earned shekels in search of a better life by patronising this publication bearing such a cretinous title. You are warmly welcomed to matriculate your moniker within this brave new world of self enlightenment where you will have the opportunity of shaking hands with your true destiny.

Such intoxicating breathless expectations are now within an underfed fly's eyebrows breadth of your sweaty and greedy grasp. No physical effort or macho actions are asked or demanded of you. All you need do is to reach out now, without wasting one iota or second more of your wasted life which you are living in chains. Take time by the forelock and join my winning team of working class folk on our biospherical revolution in mass education that is the culmination of my long held dreams.

This monumental achievement of remedial education that is finally possible by using the Dick Head ICAT (inscribed chalk and talk) technique, a primrose path upon which my working class readers and admirers can become as one with the Norse God, Odin from Valhalla. You will soon be receiving the spirits from dead heroes through your dedicated and concentrated reading of The Working Man's Guide To The Galaxy, thereafter returning at dusk to feast upon the newly found and acquired spoils offered to all of superior education. Treat me, Dick Head, as another Norse God, Valkyries, working slavishly in your service, guiding the battles yet to be fought and with the final honour of choosing the warriors to be slain for subsequent entry into Valhalla.

Since my conversion to the advancement and endless

good of the working class man, I have invested continuous unrelenting hours, manipulating such famous teachings onto cheap parchment with a multitude of pen strokes applying personally selected fluorescent green ink. This strange aquamarine writing medium essential for assisting my rapidly failing eyesight and fast depreciating inventory of cheap candles over the past years of continuous dedication. Such special incandescent pharmacopoeia, purchased on the 10th March 1973 by mail order from the Shining Knight Ink Company Limited, after seeing it advertised in the sales catalogue of the British Ink Mail Order Company of Bradford. My choice of writing medium was being offered very cheaply indeed, at a bargain basement price of only 90 pence per pint, this being cheap by anyone's understanding.

To explain how cheap this really is, you must compare it to the GQS Guinness Quantity Standard, where you will soon see that you can only buy half a pint of Guinness for the same price as one pint of ink. As I planned to write for the remainder of my creative living days, I took the decision to purchase a fifty gallon drum of this ink, which with the 15% bulk discount, £2.50 delivery charge, plus the value added tax gave a total of a mere £331.64. This amount exceeded my bank balance by £3,789.45 (as I was well overdrawn) but all was not lost because I remembered my flexible friend, VISA the king of all credit cards.

By paying only the "minimum" payments per month, the cost of this ink, as of last thursday, has now reached a trifling £794.45, including all accumulative interest charges. "In for a pen, in for a pound", I say. No investment is too great for Dick Head to complete such a worthwhile and rewarding calling in life. Only seven days after placing my order for this ink by phone with the British Ink Mail Order Catalogue Company, the AngloEurasionAfroOriental Delivery Service delivered my fifty gallon red painted drum of green ink, which had a label on the outside saying "green ink."

Ink was first used by the chinese in 2500 BC when they wrote on *Papyri* and posted a few exhibition samples to the British Museum in London where it can still be seen today. The far more famous indian ink was also originated in China (perhaps the world's oldest civilisation) and known in those times as chinese ink. In 1832, our old friend Dr. Henry Stephens perfected the blue-black ink as we know it in these modern times.

The word *pen* originates from the latin word *penna* meaning feather which is not supposed to indicate any type of sexual connotation whatsoever. So much knowledge expressed in so few words will continue to amaze and fascinate you to a point of boredom throughout this book of wonders yet to unfold.

As at 4.30 pm yesterday afternoon, about 48.85 gallons of my verdant ink remains from the original fifty gallon drum, purchased so efficiently by system post haste. This means that from every gallon of this liquid I can write over 27,000 pages of genius text inscribed in my beautiful handwriting. Solely for the motor car fanatics amongst us who are infatuated and very daft to believe in the government's forged consumption statistics, this ink usage can be translated to read that the Shining Knight brand of SK487/F/DHSI grade ink returns 2,745 miles to the imperial gallon, (610 miles/980 Kilometres per litre) under normal urban conditions.

I can therefore write for a further 134,000 miles before reordering any more green ink, or in fact ink of any other colour if I get totally pissed off with the green stuff. Reduced consumption figures can be expected in the event of using badly serviced or secondhand Portuguese pens.

Within the old Roman city walls of Rochester in Kent, I am described in many circles, including all the cheapo pubs and the castle grounds, as that rosey fingered nocturnal wordsmith called Dick Head, which is personally accepted as something of a high browed compliment. The multitude of sleepless dark hours spent burning the midnight oil, is considered but a meagre invested disbursement on the road to my zenith of literary achievement. Such a wonderful meridian resulting in the forging of a rock solid teaching doctrine especially programmed for the advancement of the working class man.

All students must now take note that the penalty for non conformity with all my instructions in this book is instant banishment to the Town of Wankie, a small habitat located in that former colony of ours, Rhodesia. I refuse to use any non Empire names in my teachings with you, even if personal abuse is forthcoming from the United Nations Committee on modern names or any other committee for screwing the colonials.

I have a special message for those two hundred and forty million quaint unwitting readers living in that country of bullshite and deprivation in North America. These protectors of the free world, living just a few miles south of six million idiotic French Canadians who cannot, and will not, speak the superior tongue.

My message to you Yankees is one of satirical rebuke for the endless method in which you gum chewing, television believers of garbage ideas, insist that you are always right and everybody else in the world is wrong. In case of emergency or an imminent election, castrate any nation that dares to cross your path or hints that you may be wrong. At least you protectors of the free world have learnt the hard way that it is easier to cut off a pair of bolox than it is to sew them back on.

Enough! enough! any more offence and they will run off with all the petrol. I'm also jumping ahead of my preplanned route and missing the point at hand. I shall not promote the feeble-minded international cause of these juvenile demented cowboys on the world's political stage any further. If I do, then next I will start recognising the gallon as anything less than an Imperial Gallon which, as everybody knows, is equivalent to approximately four and a half litres.

Imagine the crass jumped up pompous attitude of a nation wishing to introduce a new standard of liquid measurement onto the world stage when we are all already happy with the pint we've already got. As a person who is internationally recognised as being fairer than an albino snowman I will always give credit where credit is due. In the case of the Mickey Mouse gallon, this is like giving credit to an ignoramus arsehole with piles. I can now reveal for the first time why the counterfeit piddly undersized cowboy gallon is so much less in volume and value than the real full sized Imperial Gallon as recognised in all civilised countries. - da da da!. Another scoop coming up from yours truly, Dick Head.................

Up until 1873, in the land of Disney, murder for fun, fools, "have a nice day", "aha" and a reverse economy, the population of the USA was contented to utilise the civilised Imperial Gallon for liquid measure, just as all ex colonials of the British Empire should. This logical acceptance was in line with the cogent rationality of all peoples inhabiting the British Empire or living in lands stolen from the British tax payer once we had made them rich enough and powerful enough to screw us.

The British Empire, an elite microcosm where total darkness of witching time cannot possibly cover it all from coast to coast at any one and the same time. This rationale of a standard liquid measurement ceased to exist in 1873, and it all started to go wrong because - yes you've guessed it - because of the involvement of another bloody Frenchman. First millions of letters from Msr. Conopole Domincile and now this.

The infamous Frenchman responsible for cheating generations of Americans out of a full sized Imperial gallons in return for the pissy sized American gallon was christened Rodney Garlic de Wanckaire. The ludicrous actions of this gentleman brought about the offensive obscenity of calling an idiot a "Wanker" and such bad language is still used with severe effect today.

Rodney was an immigrant from the affluent city quarter of Marseille who emigrated to America, bringing with him the knowledge of brewing Irish stout beer. This skill he acquired following his six years employment at the famous stout brewery in Dublin prior to his arrival into the land of the free. Within three years of his arrival in Boston, he opened his own successful brewery which operated under the family name of Wanckaire's Beer Company Incorporated. This brewery was established within the city limits of Boston, where it produced a special very dark brown beer similar to the irish stout variety but with a more powerful effect.

Rodney had previously negotiated a marketing agreement with the B.B.C. (Bostonian Bus Company) to have huge posters advertising Wanckaire's Beer placed on the side of all of the city's 645 tramcars. It was the main slogan printed in bright red and yellow on the posters of "Voila! de Wanckaire beer de day keeps de Doctaire away" which started to upset the much pissed off protestant applecart and almost brought about Rodney's downfall. This gall and wormwood style jingle moving up and down the city streets alerted the populace to the benefits of Rodney's beer and a massive increase in sales resulted, but the twist in the tail was waiting to kick him hard.

Unluckily for Rodney, this pornographic graphic presentation of drinking stout staring out from the sides of all the city transport gave severe bouts of schizophrenic syndrome fever to the city councillors of irreproachable temperance within the chamber of local government. So powerful and influential were these incorruptible City Fathers that in an attempt to put an immediate stop to this degradation of Bostonian morals, they passed an emergency resolution effective as from the previous week. This called for all glass bottles containing products measured in Imperial measure to be manufactured and controlled by the Boston City Council under a monopoly situation unheard of since Popeye pinched all the spinach in 1645, thus causing the great spinach famine.

On page 543 of this emergency resolution, clause 37(b) 1.5, it stated that, " The supply of glass bottles in Imperial measurement can be withheld from any brewery for any reason whatsoever at the sole discretion of the Boston City Council, if in the opinion of the majority of the city council the products being sold within such containers are considered to be against the interests, or morality, of the people of Boston."

There was a huge argument that the people of Boston had no morality in the first place, but the chairman's casting vote won the day. In addition, Clause 37(b) 1.6 relating to bus companies stated, "No bus company shall exhibit advertising material on the sides of any vehicle operating within the city limits if such advertising includes the word Wanker (or any similar expression or any word that could be confused with the word wanker or tosspot), unless prior approval is obtained from the Archbishop of Nairobi at least twenty four months prior to the appearance of such advertising."

Big, big mistake my Bostonian politicians!, because as has been endemic within the cowboys and indians political scene for over 200 years, no brains had been utilised in drawing up this legislation to cover all the loopholes that were waiting to be exploited. This is why in the USA today there are more lawyers than all the doctors, nurses, teachers and postmen put together.

If the American legislatures could learn how to get all their new laws right in the first place then they wouldn't need all those lawyers would they? But as the new laws are drawn up by lawyers also in the first place, then we have one big problem...........

Rodney, with the tenacity of an infuriated golfer, first played with himself for twenty minutes whilst reading his favourite book, Not All Wankers Are French, and then eventually admitted he did have a big problem. He set about bypassing such a potentially disastrous commercial inconvenience to his business life by taking a holiday with Pierre de Balles, his homosexual cousin who lived with six lovely little boys in Mexico. His idea was to relax and fully consider the best solution to this problem of having no beer bottles for his Imperial pints of beer, whilst at the same time drink tequila by the gallon, and he didn't give a doodly shite just what size of gallon that this referred to. Rodney packed his pink suit, fluffy condoms plus six pink carnations and off he went to Mexico, complete with a family sized tin of Vaseline in his pocket, just in case.

Mexico, a population of around 80 million people, the third largest country in North America with a land mass of 1,972,547 square kilometres. The native language of Mexico is Aztec but over 50 languages are spoken with Mixtec and Zapotec being the most used today. With a 2,400 kilometre border with the USA in the north, it is bordered in the South by Guatemala and Belize. Almost half of Mexico is arid or semi-arid desert. Things today are vastly different since the Spanish Conquest by Cortes in 1519. Greed has slowly destroyed much of Mexico's rich historical culture. So endeth your first lesson on Mexico, a poor country, best left to the Indians or Dagonians.

Rodney took the Pullman stage coach down to Mexico City where he stayed at the rather tatty TobbyTacco guest house, situated in the poorer area on the East side of town where Pierre also lived with his boy friends and seventeen queer pet mice.

During his very first night in Mexico City, Rodney followed Plan A and became intoxicated after consuming unknown quantities of the local tequila hooch. In a hazy blur, he cried on Pierre's shoulder, puked chopped carrots, peed on the floor and started to cry, complete with loads of real tears. Out flowed all of Wanckaire's problems concerning the lack of beer bottle supplies and the imminent closure of his company unless God was willing to help in the not too far distant future.

On this occasion, God had little to do with the final solution to Rodney's problems, as one of Pierre's boyfriends already knew the answer to the riddle. This particular boy, wearing very attractive ladybird earrings, a tight dress and blue stockings, spoke up as a good friend always should and said, "Meester Rodneesdeey, muys coosin hees can helpiz yous!"

It turned out that his coosin was the one and only Carlos Spicco de Spanno, a short ugly man who owned and ran the largest brewery in Mexico City and permanently picked his nose with great enthusiasm - some coincidence you may be thinking? I can assure you all, that these facts, no matter how far fetched they may appear to a simple reader like yourself, are the truth, the whole truth and nothing but the truth so help me God. Without further ado about nothing in particular, Rodney thanked Pierre profusely for having such an influential and pretty boyfriend, gave him a kiss, and rushed off to see Carlos Spicco de Spanno of the Spicco de Spanno Brewery Company fame.

Meeting the queer ladybird earring lad was an omen of good fortune, of that Rodney was now fully convinced, even though he wasn't too sure about the blue stockings. If God had known more about beer bottles, maybe the story would have been different, but you cannot be an expert at everything. Picking one's nose is a filthy habit, but it's preferable to being a queer Mexican.

As I do not intend to go on for ever about this bloody silly American gallon, I can tell you that during Rodney's visit to the Spicco de Spanno brewery, he found out that the half pint and pint beer bottles being made there were in fact something well under these volumes. "Ma! bottyer dis iss nears enuffs," shouts Carlos Spicco de Spanno the owner, pissed as a dago rat.

The rest is now history, because Rodney learnt well from this meeting with the fates and Mexican nose pickers. Upon his return to Boston he started selling Wanckaire's beer in these new undersized bottles which he imported in vast quantities from Mexico. He sold his new smaller bottles at a lower price than before and the city council could do nothing about it because they were not of imperial measure and therefore were outside of the new imposed restrictions.

More beer was sold than ever before in the history of the brewery trade and all the other breweries in the area were forced by commercial competitive pressure to adopt the same bottle size. The name given to this new bottle size was Wanckaire's Pint, but this name was later changed to protect the innocent. Eventually this new undersized pint was adopted nationwide and eight new undersized pints made a new undersized gallon. So endeth your first gallon lesson.

For your second gallon lesson, the Imperial gallon was originally known as the Exchequer Ale Gallon which was used when life was simple and one gallon of water weighed ten pounds. Today in our high tech world we insist on a highly complicated life to give highly paid employment to government pricks. The Weights and Measures Department (particularly big pricks) specify the Imperial Gallon as, "The gallon is defined as the weight of air of density 0.001217 g/ml of 10lb water of density 0.998859 g/ml weighed against weights of density 8.136 g/ml^2" And I thought petrol pumps were simple.

Compare this with the US gallon which is only 0.83267 Imperial gallons. British cars give more miles to the gallon than american cars, a state of affairs which is being discussed at last in the US senate. They are seriously considering making a shorter distance mile to accommodate this difference in consumption because they hate being second best and not selling many cars to Japan. To date, the International Olympic committee have failed to reach an agreement on such a drastic proposal for a shorter mile in America. Did you know that a Tun of wine = 252 Imperial gallons = 2 pipes = 3 puncheons = 4 hogsheads? What an interesting fellow I am.

So now you know something new folks - but this has

absolutely no connection with the subject of my book, or the very green ink that I use to record my prose and verse.

Back to my ink!

With the remaining green ink left in the red painted drum (which sits next to the paraffin can in the garage), it is more likely that I shall die before needing to instigate a restocking procedure for this Argentinian made product. I also have in stock some 126,634 unused A2 sized sheets of pulchritudinous cream coloured papyrus, thus eliminating any possible danger of experiencing a supply shortage during the next twenty three years, or even longer.

Do not become confused over this vast stock of writing material, all will be revealed to you eventually my inquisitive amigos. The only point to remember so far is that you are all ignorant plebs, I have enough paper and ink, the men from pilgrim father stock are flibbertigibbet drivellers and God knows nothing about beer bottles.

Ah, I forgot about a few less important things that must be confessed before we continue any further, which by my deeply instilled code of honour forces me to do the needful and go to the botheration of declaring a total stocktake of my personal possessions. I give you this further information unguardedly, without fear of reproach, in front of the eyes of the world, thus proving once and for a million and one times that nothing is as honest as a Dick with a Head.

My other assets in stock are three 18th century quill-pens (from a long dead homosexual swan), six assorted fountain pens, two felt-tip pens in red and green, 131 cheapo biros (British made), 73 pencils of assorted lengths and condition (mostly knackered), 56 roller ball pens of assorted colours (Japanese), 144 washable "Johnies" condoms (see later chapter), a self portrait of my dog Henry licking his balls, 60 toilet rolls and a bail of straw for the horse.

Openness is one of my strongest characteristics and I

pledge myself to this number one principle until death do us part or until the end of this novel, which ever comes first, so help us God.

A single huge nagging worry that followed my every move over the past fifteen years, since first embarking upon this extravaganza of literary supposition, was whether the superintendency controlling publication of such unconventional expressionism would allow me to get away with it. With the luck of the average bisexual (the type with a preference for boys and tight arsed parrots), I am pleased to report that so far so good.

The R.S.P.C.A. are however seriously looking into the welfare of some unfortunate parrots as a matter of extreme concern, but the accused are claiming that these offences were covered by Parliamentary privilege and therefore no further action can be taken. Privileged or not, the Bird Breeders Association are furious and six Norwegian Red Nosed parrots have died of heart attack and burst blood vessels in the Members Bar during daily party time during this Parliamentary session.

Another seventy nine of the stronger willed and larger boned Giant Blue Amazon Bumster parrots, owned by a member of the shadow cabinet, have been similarly abused and are in a seriously disturbed psychological condition. All in all, these unfortunate brazillian nuts are like football fans - psychotic and with huge arseholes.

Parrots are found in the warmer parts of South America and Australia. The male species are very rarely imported into this country, some say because they play with themselves and make obscene noises. The Owl parrot from New Zealand is a flightless parrot, living on the ground but is very good at climbing trees, where most New Zealanders live. The African Grey parrot is the best talking parrot when held in captivity, but has the inbuilt bad habit of shouting out the word "shithead!" whenever he sees a red rose or a plastic raincoat.

Our fascinating pilgrimage to the terra incognita of encyclopaedic perception is available to you all, the pick of the working class bunch. Open to you sweat stained workers waiting only for the Sahara's warm air to cross the great oceans of the world, allowing you to burst into a multi-coloured academic plumage and enter a new era of achievement.

As likely as not, only a small percentage of our great unwashed vulgar herd of so called *demi-monde* women living on this planet will have the strength of character to venture with us on this insuperable trip to alter the course of history. However, any nagging, bragging, shagging, bagging and being a general pain in the arse will prohibit even these few of the lower order and weaker sex from joining us on the A team.

Notwithstanding this conditional offer to such a small minority, no matter how smart or determined you are, if your name is Janet or Lucy, then you are definitely barred from joining us on this journey to eternal learning. These God forsaken and vulgar names remind me of my mother-in-law.

First things first Dicky boy!

This prosaic variety of intellectual intoxication brought about by the mere inquisitiveness for self improvement, installed within every one of us, must be restrained within the preset guidelines yet to be divulged to you. Acting to the contrary, in a flurry of frenzied over zealous philistinic action, would certainly cause you unmitigated confusion leading to a scrambling of your brain. This disaster would occur before we even raised the anchor and set sail upon our epic voyage to mass educational paradise.

How can I expect a group of crass ignorant working class readers (I mean you - the proletarians), to keep up with my complex association of ideas located within the fast turning wheels of such an advanced train of thought? This dreaming of utopia is impossible!

It is an extremely bad and nasty habit of mine to rush ahead of myself in an attempt to reach the next station in life before I have actually purchased a valid ticket for the trip itself. Previous examples of my trail of premature embryonic starts are spread everywhere around the libraries and dole queues of the world for all to see and ridicule. I swear with all my heart and new found honesty, that further deranged behaviour of a similar nature will cease as from now on to be replaced by a thoroughly organised train of thought developed for our new civilisation. Pretty good stuff, huh?

A retrogression of literary standards was indeed a more serious problem during my early years of creating the prophetic written word. Foremost gossip writers in the educational press have already positively blamed and criticised this one single character blemish. One literary critic of the Tory press placed the spotlight upon the absolute ease in which success arrived during my apprenticeship days with the pen, whilst others struggled to be recognised.

This analysis could indeed hold some substance because my first two novels of *Simple Simon* and *The Asian* Connection sold over 3 million copies each during those heady days of 1965 when even the most crappy word turned into gold when passing through my verdant transcription. Those lusty quisling novels were written during three months of tea and lunch breaks, whilst working at Patel's Cheapo Pie Factory for a mere pittance. Such early scribblings were but an effortless and directionless flurry of exertion for Dick Head the aspiring writer, yet to receive accolades on a global scale from around the world - so to speak.

Such simplicity of creating literary masterpieces led me into a blind alley, a dark and dangerous alley full of rich but uncreative writers, plus several million dogs and two famous postmen. I was left with no escape exit, exploited up to the hilt by my publishing company, although upon reflection it was more likely my own naivety dressed in greedy clothes looking for somebody else to blame.

The Punjab Press of Southall, tricked this baby faced pie making author into signing an exclusive contract whereby they received 90% of the royalties, but I had to pay all expenses from the remaining 10% royalty. Total earnings received from these two blockbuster paperbacks was a meagre £189.65 which even on a meat pie diet and earning £27.96 a week on the pastry line (including overtime) was not a lot of money.

In anger at being diddled out of my fame and money, I blew the lot on a ten day trip to Majorca, that wonderful Balearic island where lager is on tap in all hotel bathrooms. After only three fantastic days my funds ran dry as well as my lager glass so I took a job with Spitto's Shoe Shine of Luton Limited, polishing shoes at the airport to earn extra cash. The bigger the gob, the shinier the shoes.

My pen name used for these early books was *Mato Harry*, but regrettably for me, the publishers had been very businesslike (crafty shites) and had registered this name for themselves. They therefore owned the copyright to this name and this explains why I am reduced to using my deed poll changed name of Richard Head for future publications. Such double dealing trickery has forced me to start again as an unknown writer but at least it's my name without a Harry in it.

A very short curry smelling fellow from Burma, Punrabbe Gwantimeelyba, the current tea boy at Patel's Cheapo Pie Factory, has been requisitioned by Saresh the owner to write the next Mato Harry novel. This coffee coloured tea boy cannot yet understand the English language but has purchased one of the latest electronic translation machines from Dixons for £26.70. With this tool at the ready, his first book is an almost certain blockbuster, and is to be called *Batman Eats Pies At Night*.

Never trust your manager when he says "velly goods, pleece signs he-are".

I intend to be full of mortification up to the end of this

chapter for writing such crap during these first two novels. I am sorrowful that I allowed this one blot on my escutcheon to accrue and that I cheapened my pen for such ill begotten gain and early fame. Such a capitalistic and egotistic badge of infamy is beneath the dignity and professional behaviour that is obligatory for such a leading author.

A minutiae of protocol is justifiably expected from any author placed in the world's top ten of literature's masters. I am only granted absolution from your clamjamhrie buffoonery because of the superlative quality of splendid prose that has hereinafter been created for mass reading by the working class people. Such fabolic words of wisdom being gobbled up in a ravenous stampede of unofficial consumption by the ancien regime, high society, Jones and Robinson non working class deviates seeking cultural improvement.

Who can blame even our capitalistic snobs, disguised in rags for fear of discovery by their peers, snapping up such a fearful weapon now being unleashed against their cosy lives? You will see more and more of these sheep in wolves clothing visiting the all night book stores and then creep back to their wall to wall pelmetted palaces to read The Working Man's Guide To The Galaxy in secret. Tens of thousands of people in their heated shoe boxes, located in worried conservative catchment areas, all now suffering from high tension and high taxes. Whole housing estates (sorry - developments), at present occupied by wealth grabbers now starting to feel just a single isolated chill of fear starting to appear near the base of their spines. Just read on my outdated beau monde and your balls will soon freeze solid like an antarctic football ready to be kicked harder than ever known before.

Diametrically opposite to such upper ten respect, projected by their deeply instilled fear ethos, comes the brinkmanship and role playing nature performed in self defence by the limited brain power of my target audience.

This means you!, the canaille de la galoot. You, with your inbuilt destructive nature, inbred through centuries of repression and hate for all on the social register, that blue blooded race listed in Burke's Peerage, where if you had your way you would reposition the position of all those silver spoons.

Your cup runneth over with vile thoughts through uncontrollable subconscious actions, including envy and fury at my success in the fables of literature. In justification of such hatred you devise a horrid story of self-deception which refuses to allow your memory and moral conscience to forget those long forgotten and only-begotten villainous Mato Harry books. Those low life blockbusters that flowed so quickly and wickedly from my pen during a previous lifetime that I am trying to forget, but which you will not let me forget.

Your pent up emotions of hate and jealousy are throwing you into a panic because you refuse to forgive and forget like any good Christian should. If this retrogressive attitude continues to exist within your zit infested soul, I really don't give a shite and prescribe that you get back to your de rigeur daily grind of porno books and video films and stop wasting my time - arsehole! Remember, he who casts the first stone is a DikPrik.

Some 76% of my gullible gum chewing readers have bought this book simply because it stood out from the rest of the filth and garbage that one finds standing on the bookshop shelves today. You are probably already convinced that The Working Man's Guide To The Galaxy is a reprint of an old classic, originating from William Shakespeare's stable of influence and pen. This false illusion created so successfully by my publishing company is an intentional misconception, planned by the publishers Marketing Director, the one and only (thank Christ), Adam Whunce. This bisexual (salmon-trout and ducks) gentleman is also responsible for designing the beautiful cover that protects the expensive bindings of this particular paperback version of The Working Man's

Guide To The Galaxy. Such planned deception was a necessary evil to ensure that this new Encyclopaedia DikHedia was openly available to both the common riffraff of Dole Street and to the many millions of casual readers who are at this very moment totally absorbed into this adventure. For the everyday reader who is statistically brain dead, but is constantly searching the bookshelves of the world's libraries for a guiding star to lead them to a new world - such a saviour has now arrived!

It is of little compensation to the world awaiting breathlessly for the arrival of this prophet of literature (as I have indeed created the greatest prose since Macbeth), unless we ensure that enough copies of this great book actually do end up in the hands of the needy recipients. No book - no reading, No reading - no learning, no conning - no selling, no selling - no book, No book, no reading.........and so on and so on and so on. Have you got it yet?, my off-scourings of our demi-monde society?

Some twelve months ago, the first prepublication draft copy of The Working Man's Guide To The Galaxy was being checked out by our libel lawyer, Tatum Screwall, an iconoclast dressed in an icelandic wide band maroon and white pin striped suit. His professional advice given through his skeletal sylph-like lips was, "Jesus Dick, I professionally recommend that you either burn this book or find another lawyer!" I took as much notice of this advice as that jewish bookmaker did all those years ago when he took all those huge bets on Goliath. I did however appreciate Tatum's reference to Jesus Dick which inspired me to write even greater things, my ego searching for even bigger possibilities.

All future writs will be ignored and I will not reply to any further insulting letters or phonecall abuse from fools or agnostics.

Tatum's advice was rejected with a gentle rendering from yours truly, of "bolox to you Tatum". I then fired him for giving me advice inconsistent with the views I wanted to hear. I proceeded to hire, via an ad in the Newmarket Sporting Life, a much more friendly lawyer from Dublin, named Paddy Filpatrick. This wonderful professional legal brain also owned and personally operated, "Paddy & Patrick's Green Mistletoe Bar" located in the centre of Derry in the Republic of Ireland, where they all are so merry. To be absolutely precise, most of them were permanently well pissed, as well as being very merry from Derry.

It was obvious that Paddy was a great knowledgeable international lawyer able to solve any prospective libel problem from the moment that he read the draft copy of this book. On finishing the final chapter, he looked over from his bar stool and complimented "Dick moi beautiful friend, tis a wonderful book ye has wrote for dis world of sinners- I give ye ten out of ten - let's have de drink on tit." He spoke these words as a poet would read his favourite ode, yet still carrying a beautiful red faced blind smile.

After spending ten days with Paddy on holiday last June sailing off the coast of Kinsale, it can be said without any fear of contradiction, that Paddy is the biggest drinker of Irish stout I have ever met. My God, what a bloody liar, but can he sing Danny Boy!

Following Paddy's certified anti libellous approval of this book, we carried out our first scientific market research to evaluate the exact details of how the launch should be handled, this being planned for November 1992. We appointed the London firm of Knowsy Parkers plc as launch advisers, and after charging us some £24,765.34 over a period of seven months, their market research analysis quickly showed that we had to offer the dead neck public the following goodies to be assured of success:

A thick book with lots of pages or use thick paper.

First impression must show that it is written by a world famous author. Shakespeare or Chaucer will do.

A dirty suggestive picture on the front always helps sales and increases cover price.

A worrying title to wake up the conscience of the people.

Offer a money back guarantee of some sort but be sure to cheat, otherwise your royalty will be reduced.

Yes my gullible reader, you are another one caught so easily within this marketing trap, because you now own a book written by an unknown author who will earn some 49.9p royalty from your purchase alone. You don't even have any tacky bits to read or any tits to look at - how do you feel about that Willy Prickhead Smith?

Are you an average outcast of society, complete with the average obnoxious nosy nature and a mistrusting and shitty attitude towards all men? The answer to this simple question must be surely yes, and if so I expect that you will now insist on evaluating the first few pages of this extravaganza to see if enough smut can be found to justify your investment. Your peanut sized polluted brain will be in paranoiac retreat whilst it is considering that this event could represent the first in a lifetime possibility that you may have wasted your hard earnt money and much good drinking time. Even worse, you might even be reading a book that includes no screwing, raping, murdering or indeed any other item of modern day pillage. You are racing your fishy suspicious eyes across these pages at an incredible speed of some 25 lines per second, searching for a single "fuck" or "panties" or maybe "forced entry" amongst the type face.

Please be informed, my pathetic lower class potential undergraduates, that after the previous obscenities expressed in the last sentence you will find no more of such outdated and vilesome words used in the dirt ridden context that you so desire. You therefore have no need to proceed any further with wasting or investing your time in reading this potboiler novel of learning from cover to cover, if filth and debauchery are your only aims.

Notwithstanding that you have now been shown to be a fellow of doubtful morality, do not give up this chance of finding your personal freedom and liberated life after such a few minutes of reading where you have failed to find mere cheap words inscribed onto such expensive parchment. I strongly advise you with all my heart to give this matter your further deep deep consideration.

A decision to end your reading of The Working Man's Guide to the Galaxy at this premature point in your shitty life will ensure that you will remain a common underprivileged git for the remainder of your nose picking days.

Without my assistence and guiding light during the remainder of your nostril searching and heart pumping existence, you will continue to support the Labour party and believe that institutionalised charity and television pornography is satisfaction at its best. Such a dismal decrepit outlook is not preordained by any flights of imagination, because at this precise point in time you do have the chance of making an alternative choice and to proceed further with your reading and advance on to chapter 2 and maybe even further beyond.

The world can become your oyster, with you proceeding at a rapid pace towards your true destiny in life. This destiny of your true inner self as clearly identified by Mr. Lincoln in his quotation at the beginning of this chapter.

Abraham Lincoln, who was both a unique politician and the greatest non-cowboy President of all time, a giant of a man, so tragically shot in the prime of his life by a gunman who I believe was hired by the Cardiff Short of Stature Miners Society. This was a wickedness of gigantic proportions, brought about by internal political squabbling after Abraham Lincoln refused to appoint Gwyn "Boyo" Jones (originally from Cardiff), as Undersecretary for Singing, Sheep-poking and whining.

Despite this cold blooded murder of his political enemy, Gwyn Jones still didn't get the job as he was sent to prison for twenty years for stealing some $321.87 from the coal miners strike fund and buying a bungalow in Alaska. This must be a form of hypochondria that afflicts various leaders at certain times throughout history. Such a libellous statement was originally written in more specific terms, but Paddy advised against it by saying, "Eye tink dat everybody wheel get the gist of diss as it tiz."

If after you persevere and read all of this first chapter , you still find this book of books boring or offensive, do not despair. Rome wasn't built in a day, and converting you from a sex inspired mental nutcase into a genius of minor proportions will also take some extended period of time - beyond one evening's reading. If you go forward together with our other tens of thousands of fellow students, then I can personally guarantee that you will be assured a better and more satisfying life.

If however, after forcing me to beg and grovel in such an undignified way, like a crucified worm, you then still decide not to proceed any further with your voyage to this educated freedom, then you are a Wanker, spelt with a capital double you. You cannot damage my dignity, it is only you little people who are obsessed with losing it.

For those undecided people who live a life of permanent shilly-shallying and bafflement, remember that you are entitled to read this first chapter on the "5% money back" guarantee offer as specified later on. You must be extremely careful not to mark this book in any way whatsoever, not even a minute blemish or a spit mark is acceptable, as we must be in a position to resell all returned copies at full cover price to enable us to reimburse the 5% to the original purchaser. The other 95% not refunded to you, goes towards the very high administration overheads and loss of profit experienced on the original sale.

The DikHed Publishing Company Plc will not reimburse one single penny, mark, yen, dollar, lira, krona, condom or book token to anyone who returns a book for refund if the book is marked or if you dare read it past page 24. Inscribed comments inside the book carry the same no refund conditions.

It is imperative that we communicate without delay with the slightly vexed customer who returned a deplorably marked copy of this book last week with the scrawled critique located at the bottom of the first page saying; "Dick Head, you really are a Kraut trouble maker trying to bring your united Super Race ideas into the lives of a nation of people who are quite content at being second class citizens and to be ruled by kraut prikz. Let sleeping dogs lie and pitz off back to Austria and take all your bloody cuckoo clocks with you."

If only I am able to expatiate deeper with this literary ignoramus, I feel self assured that I can evangelize this crank to enrol for the complete The Working Man's Guide To the Galaxy graduation course which he so manifestly requires to improve his attitude towards all good hearted authors. So if Mr. Bolox Toyou would kindly contact me on my home telephone number, 0634 0908012, we can discuss this exciting prospect in a more civilised manner.

I shall be pleased to fully explain the advantages of the complete course and give details of my family background to offset his hasty backbiting comments. This should be more acceptable and satisfactory to Mr. Bolox Toyou, rather than him making snap judgements after reading only the first chapter of this book. If I have spelt Mr. Bolox Toyou's name incorrectly then please accept my sincere apologies for this error but the signature scribbled underneath your message was difficult to decipher underneath the smelly brown substance that had been rubbed in over the top of the communication.

Let's get to it.

My name today is Richard Head, born and christened in 1933 as Herman Hitler, the youngest of eight sons of Karen and Klaus Fritz Hitler, my dear parents, whom I loved dearly during just a few periods of my varied life.

Confused?

I take for granted that you erudite tenderfoot remedial pupils having seen at a glance the Alpha plus qualities of joining our ranks, will demand some further epigrammatic curriculum vitae. These very personal historic facts, which you are now awaiting with bated breath, can only be fully mitigated if at the same time you allow me to salve my conscience by acquainting you with some historical facts from the year of 1781.

On the first day of April that year, King Alfred had been dead for 756 years and 127 days, having been done to death by the royal baker in a fit of great anger. Apart from the biased opinions of all master bakers and pricks in our audience, you will all eventually agree that an even more epoch-making event occurring upon this same day was that it was my great great great great grandmother Hansel Hitler's 56th birthday on the following morn.

Under normal Anglo-Austrian marital and historical standards, this unrecorded event in time would seem to be of little consequence and should have gone totally unnoticed as an unimportant and totally insignificant matter. Not so my red blooded readers, not so indeed, because da de da!, this was the exact date when the beginning of a great change upon the future direction of mankind was being caste.

My great, great, great, great, great grandfather Einrech Valter Hitler decided to change his life, and therefore subsequently mine, forever and ever and ever and ever..........We should all thank our lucky stars that Einrech married Hansel, became disenchanted with such a miserable bitch and on the 1st of April 1781 decided that birthday or not, he was leaving home forever, just like any caring teutonic tribesman should, to establish the overseas clan of Hitlers.

Without Einrech Hitler there would have been no Dick Head - without Dick Head there would be no The Working Man's Guide To The Galaxy - without The

Working Man's Guide To The Galaxy there would be no hope for you. So in effect, we all are all very thankful to Hansel for being such a miserable bitch to Einrech.

Einrech was reputed to have had the largest thighs in Austria, which is probably why he chose to walk all the way from Vienna to Dunkirk non stop. This overland trip of over 1000 kilometres he achieved unaided and on his own, except for the company of his beloved chinese poodle Dog "Pumpkin" who trotted along quite merrily by his side during those long and hard seven months.

Einrech originally bought Pumpkin from a restaurant owner in Peking for around ten pence, which was the price of the meal that Pumpkin would have made. It was not his love or pity for the dogs in the restaurant's soundproofed show case that extracted such hard earned money from Einrech, it was only that one barbecued dog cost seven pence whereas you could take two meals for the bargain price of only ten pence. Einrech's stomach and calculating mind ruled the day, so he bought two dog meals for ten pence.

He ate Pumpkins twin sister Ayeee with chop suey for lunch and took Pumpkin away in a bamboo box to eat on ship the following day as a cheap three pence meal. During the night Einrech was as sick as a dog, so to speak, and he quickly realised that Ayeee had not been skinned correctly before roasting. So now he owned one regurgitated dog with chop suey in lumps in his hammock and one screaming dog in a bamboo box. One of them had to go, so he kept Pumpkin.

Einrech's trade was cuckoo clock making, so it was natural for him to carry his cuckoo clock making equipment in a rucksack upon his back when heading out from Austria towards the western horizons of France and beyond. Why did he leave the rest of the Hitler family at home, particularly his wife Hansel on her birthday? This is still a mystery which will remain forever unsolved and yet I surmise that he was probably a mean bastard who didn't want to buy a birthday card for his miserable wife.

A different decision by Einrech could have changed the shape of history, but this useless suspension of belief can drive a man crazy if taken to extremes. When Einrech arrived at the coastal port of Dunkirk he sat on the sea wall and spoke to Pumpkin in a tired and cuckoo clock making tone, "My bloody feet ache." He then explored the town where he found a tourist shop and bought a Teutonic/French dictionary to look up the French words for toilet, toilet paper, birthday cards, postbox, clean socks and have a nice day.

Hansel eventually received three rolls of french toilet paper and a pair of old socks for her birthday with a note saying "It's the thought that counts, have a nice day, love Einrech."

Einrech stayed at a small boarding house named "Froggies" for three months, which was sufficient enough time for him to produce one large French looking cuckoo clock. This piece de resistance was a true *objet d'art,* fitted with a chiming thinggummy mechanism that warbled out a rendering of "haw haw haw" every hour on the hour, sounding like a deknackered soprano from Mozambique. He sold this weird looking and bizarre sounding timepiece to a french garlic and frog trader for some 47 french francs. This hard earned coinage enabled Einrech to visit the port area and convince a clownish French Lilliputian fisherman (who answered to the knickname of "Pierre the Short Assed Fisherman"), to transport him by boat across zee shannel to a place Heinrech described as, "Zis cuntitz verr zee Englishers lift."

Einrech took with him on this historic voyage, one seasick Pumpkin plus two bottles of the famous "Dunkirk Spirit" brandy, and naturally his cuckoo clock making gear. When stepping ashore in Ramsgate, on the south coast of England, he found a quaint and beautiful coastal fishing town, inhabited by really nice people. This just goes to show how much things can change over such a short period of time.

Dear Einrech proceeded to rent a small stone built cottage in Ramsgate where he started to practice his skills in the manufacture of a wide range of cuckoo clocks. He quickly found acceptance for his special edition of the "Einrech Hitler Cuckoo Clocks" which had tall black helmeted cuckoos marching like geese every hour across the clock face chimimg "Heil, Heil, Heil!" These clocks made him famous throughout the whole of Kent and beyond; even as far as Tilbury. This was even before the ferry from Gravesend to Tilbury went into service some 200 years later, indeed! Red Indians love cuckoo clocks but time waits for no one.

Despite my cynical suppositions regarding Einrech's desertion of Hansel, it is possible that he left his native Austria in 1781 as a direct result of the Potato and Sauerkraut famine that had held Austria and Germany in its death grip for over fifty years. This awful period of deprivation over the second rate Teutonic race was equally traumatic as it was heart rending, causing misery, death and massive hardship. Many historians, including the famous historian Luther Brown of Calthwaite, considered this famine as the prime reason why the Teutonic people are such miserable and arrogant sods.

What do I think about it? I'm a Liberal and I always say that we must all live and let live, giving all people of all races the benefit of the doubt. God knows what He's doing, just ask the Russians. All men are born equal, but it's just that the Germans learn to be clever bastards so much faster than we do.

Throughout each successive generation the Hitler family in England were taught the art and skill of cuckoo clock making, this being passed from one generation to another, from father to son. My own mein papa, Franz Hitler, was a wonderful man who spoke night and day about cuckoo clocks which drove my mother, Heidi Hitler, into fits of cuckoo clock depression. Notwithstanding the mental weaknesses of my mother, this system of keeping the skill within the family led to almost 150 years of great success for the Hitler family.

This success was so dramatic, that by the time I was born, the Hitler Cuckoo Clock Company was the leading company of cuckoo clock makers in Great Britain. Amazingly, the most successful and famous model clock was still the Einrich Hitler Cuckoo Clock which now had singing birds and German military music added to the original specification.

A large thirty six inch diameter model (and that's big even to a german) of this famous clock was purchased by the Ministry of Defence in London in 1927 where it hung over the entrance of the main reception hallway until late in 1938. Its whereabouts today is unknown and the Ministry declines to comment. There are many unsubstantiated stories relating to this clock and it is said that a Winston Churchill's game of "Crap on the Germans" included this clock in the game rules - it is reported that the clock lost on every occassion.

The company's best year for sales was in 1936, when 5,675 cuckoo clocks were sold in Great Britain and some 3,897 were sold overseas. Of the overseas sales, one huge solid gold framed cuckoo clock, weighing over 1200 kilograms was specially manufactured and delivered to the Vatican Guardhouse (the one on the right of the main square), but due to the outbreak of World War II this clock was never installed and has not been seen or heard of since. If you happen to come across it during your travels please buy it for me and I will make it well worth your while. You will recognise it immediately as it has 320 special cuckoos fitted on the dial face, all manufactured in solid gold and all with specially designed wings to make the cuckoos appear as angels. This whole flock of 320 golden angelic cuckoos fly around the clock face every hour, all chirping a beautiful rendering of the song "I stuck my finger up a woodpecker's hole"

As a clue to its whereabouts, it has been rumoured in several left wing Italian newspapers that a group of cardinals have recently been sighted, within the Vatican walls, singing in harmony with this cuckoo clock during their private party celebrations. This rendering of the woodpecker song has also apparently become very popular during the selection process of all new Pontiffs, and during important meetings with the Vatican Bank.

In 1937, the English Hitler family were invited to a party in Berlin to celebrate the wedding of one, Walter Hitler, the cousin of the most famous Adolf. Walter was to wed a huge lumberjack of a woman named Maria Mussolini, the sister of that short prick from Rome. Walter had been informed lovingly of his decision by a letter from Adolf in 1936:

Dear Walter,

Il Duche has asked me to bind the Hitler and Mussolini families together in a strong Axis alliance by finding one of us Hitlers to marry his spaghetti bashing idiot's sister Maria. After a short ballot by me, you're name has been voted the winner. Refusal to marry this fat, ugly, bitchy, Mussolini cook will carry the penalty of immediate circumcision with an unsharpened bayonet.

Congratulations on your wonderful choice.

Regards,

Adolf H.

Needless to say, my distant relative did indeed marry Maria and hence my first visit to the Fatherland. During the evening drinkee celebrations, a strange short fellow in a black uniform, looking every bit like Charlie Chaplin, came up to me and said, "I ampst dee Fuerertz oft dee Farterland - mein nametz iss Adolf!" Here I was, a seven year old boy talking to the man himself. Only seeing Christ II or Elvis reincarnated could beat this moment of history.

The very next morning Adolf and his merry men took over Austria - after he had spoken to me only a few hours beforehand. Was I responsible in any way for influencing Adolf H - could a young boy have averted world war II?

So for the Hitler family in England, everything was great until 1937, just after we returned from Berlin, when mein papa started to worry about Adolf. Only an ex corporal who was trying to imitate Charlie Chaplin and Ivan the Terrible, could cause so many ripples at Downing Street. Great Britain had no problems because we had Chamberlain the Terror in charge and were in alliance with the great French nation. Rule Britannia and *Vive la France!*

After Adolf took control of Austria, at the Austrians' request of course, the sales of Hitler cuckoo clocks in Great Britain plummeted dramatically to only 17, but exports to Germany increased to 256,879. All sales to Germany were of the new "Adolf Hitler" type that were then supplied complete with military music and a small voice box that pronounced "Heil Hitler ya ya ya!" every quarter of an hour.

We were so busy in the factory producing these clocks for Germany that we were forced by the sheer pressure of orders to employ some outside labour for the first time in the company's history. You must understand that despite the 150 years that the Hitler family had resided in Ramsgate, all of us through the generations had fully maintained our superior Teutonic origins. All family members were obliged to speak with our well known clan twang and accent.

We were taught only to use the words as passed down to us from our forefather, the pilgrim Einrech. We would say, for example; "Ziss iss verr impotantz to ownleez toos speakz likez ziss." Within our close knit family this dialect was believed to be a normal state of affairs and we even joked about the Ramzeegatz Vankers who spoke verr poshzz. The new Ramsgate employees found working for us quite amusing and very soon they gave us new adopted names of "Those German Dick Heads" and so starteth the realleth story.

By February 1938 mein papa realised that this corporal was going to ruin his business because if war broke out with Germany, who the hell would want to be seen buying a Hitler cuckoo clock in England. Exports to an enemy during a war would also cause some difficulties with the Ministry of Trade and Industry and we could all be hanged for treason.

As would be expected from a well trained capitalist with a weak neck, mein papa changed the family name by *deed poll* from Hitler to the name already given to us by the local workers in the factory; to that of "Head". He then proceeded to give all eight of his sons (me included) the first name of Richard (Dick) because similarly this name was already the name used by all the workers when talking to us and therefore the change would go unnoticed. They would never notice the difference - there would be no confusion because Dick Heads we were and Dick Heads we would be.

Mein papa explained this decision to us one Sunday morning after Church, before the beer sausage and Yorkshire pudding lunch was served. "Meinz childrenz, I haft decided toos haft zee families namesez changez to Head becaustz oft ziss blooditz Hitler vanker inz zee Fathers ladtz whos viltz haves zee voor with Engladtz. Ziss name Head iss verr poplar with zee peoples inz zee fatoriz. Sewz ziss changez vill notz be notitz becaustz ziss name off Dick Head iss verr commonz andz vill be giventz toos allz youz childrentz - iss goodtz ideaz ya? Sows weez altz nows Einglishtz, ya?"

So from that moment on my name was changed to Richard "Dick" Head, the same name as given to my seven brothers, but there is no chance of confusion because none of my brothers are famous authors.

However if you do meet anybody in this country who speaks to you and says, "Ellowz, Verr Pleatz toos meetz youtz, meintz nametz iss Dicktz Hedtz," then this will almost certainly be one of my seven brothers and I would appreciate it if you could say hello to him for me please.

Before you all shout out, "Dick Head's a Kraut tosspot," I wish to remind you that ever since Einrech arrived in Ramsgate during 1781 the Hitlers have only married good English maidens, never anyone Krautish or with Kraut blood in their veins. Therefore I have only 0.78125% Austrian blood inside me and consider myself more British than most of the citizens that walk the streets of our cities today, normally on the way to the dole queue or race track.

Compare my Englishness to that of the rest of our mixed race and you will see that I am one of the top ten people challenging for the purist English blood award. How English is our next king of England or mayor of Bradford?

When war was declared in 1939, following "peace in our time" (what a prick he was), the British Hitler family was interned into a camp located just outside Meopham in Kent. The great British government decided that we were aliens and that as such we should be kept in atrocious conditions until 1945 when we were allowed to continue our lives as British citizens. I was more British than the royal family, and yet here I was placed in prison whilst the royals lived in luxury.

Mein Papas accent and attitude did nothing to help our plight during our early days in the camp; "Ziss ist a notz possibalzt antz Ice shalstz contactzt mein relationstz inzst Bearlinstz ifst we arse notzt releazt immediatzelist!"

The internment of our entire family with 99% English blood seemed unwarranted but this blot on our lives will be omitted from my book as self pity is not in my nature and only leads to a spate of negative and vengeful thinking - Don't get mad, get even.

During my time in the camp, I secretly took elocution

lessons from a kind old lady, Mrs McCreary, a teacher who gave up her time to the children in the camp to make them ready for the world of equal rights that would exist once this war to end all wars was finished. By the time I entered the free world again in 1946, I could speak English better than any of the car workers at the Morris factory in Oxford. Brown cows or not, I could speak good and perfect English.

After the war, my father's mind and brain went for a permanent walk back to Vienna and he refused to speak to anyone in real English (as though he could anyway). He kept writing to the King insisting that his cuckoo clocks be used for timing devices on the delayed action bombs being dropped on Berlin - to confuse the Germans. "Ziss vill bees verr confusink becoss zee dispossall squadz vill thinkz zis iss a Germanz bombzt vitz ziss typz off cuckoos clockstz timertz! P.S. Neffer trustz zee juice." He was eventually committed to the "Ramsgate Clinic for Insane Fishermen & Cuckoo Clock Makers" where he continued to make cuckoo clocks until his death - once a cuckoo clock maker, always a cuckoo clock maker.

In 1947 he sent a booby trapped cuckoo clock by post, with the package marked, Herr Hitler, Berlin, Germany. This clock was stuffed full of home made explosives ready to blow the long burnt and dead Adolf Hitler to kingdom come. After this huge success of ending the war single handed, mein papa thought he would be sure to be released from this awful hospital by royal pardon as a royal sign of gratitude, but even the best laid plans can go astray.

The Post Office sorter handling this package, had a bloody good laugh when he picked up this obvious practical joke parcel and after sharing his amusement with all of his his mates, he marked the parcel "return to sender." Mein Papa was so happy to receive such a wonderful return gift direct from his distant relation, Herr Hitler himself, that he was laughing like a Welsh constipated hyena as he blew himself and his precious cuckoo clocks all over the Ramsgate beach and golf club. Never again did a Hitler or a Head make a cuckoo clock.

So now you know; my legal name is Richard Head, generally referred to as "good old Dick Head" by my friends and "that XXXXXXX Dick Head!" by my enemies; of which there are many. Envy is the scourge of the uneducated world.

The real turning point in my life, which pointed me in the direction of stardom, came some nine years after the war on Christmas day in 1953. It happened just after Ma Ma had finished off her bottle, of what she always described as "Me Christmas Gin". This was a one litre bottle of Gordons Gin which she bought every Christmas since mein papa and his cuckoo clock were blew to pieces at the seaside.

The drinking of "Me Christmas Gin" started at 2 pm every Christmas day so that, as ma put it, "I prefer to be smashed before She gives Her speech on the telly." I can assure everybody listening or reading this book, that she always achieved her target by about 2.45pm or often much earlier, and was generally unconscious by the time the speech started. She of course missed nothing of importance or if she did I didn't catch it either. Regretfully, this was to be the last Christmas that Ma and the eight Head brothers would be all together because at 2.53 pm on that holy day, she collapsed onto the unwashed kitchen lino floor and died of "natural causes".

The undertaker commented on how well preserved her body was. From that tragic moment, I promised myself that I must go out into this fine green land of democracy from whence I shall rise from the ashes of this life of cuckoo clock making and thumping football fans. As Ma was being buried, I spoke out at the wake in a bold fashion as befitting a future star of the written word, "I shall become knowledgeable and I will be recognised as a person to be reckoned with; to such an extent that in the future you will hear across this planet's surface, from Cleethorpes to Bombay, the words of respect and envy from millions of people, all full of utmost praise. There will come a time when all people will expound - "There goes that clever Dick Head." How right they will be.

Have you caught the gist of my story yet, my dubious confused pilgrims in search of knowledge?

On the 3rd. January 1954, I joined Patel's Cheapo Pie Factory as an assistant meat processing hand and the change in the direction of my life continued. This job was only a temporary one as I knew that eventually after great sacrifices and study, I would qualify as an open heart surgeon, or as a fighter pilot (to shoot old Jerry out of those blue English skies during World war 3), or even as a leading business executive looking after lots of money in the City of London. Concerning the job in the city, this would be taken only providing that I can wear my own style of hat, or indeed no hat at all.

From the passing of Ma Ma, I have now read 31,986 books from the local library, books of every imaginable subject, written by experts in virtually every field of knowledge. My photographic memory is a unique phenomenon, with the ability of instant recall on any subject I have ever read. I am therefore able to talk with authority on any subject available to mankind. I have just finished reading *Migration of amphibious mice from the Steppes to the Himalayas, A Chromosome study of the Pigmy race,* and a double reading of *A complete study of personal hygiene habits of Prehistoric animals.* Oh, I forgot to also include my favourite children's books on Child abuse fully explained and *Don't get caught shoplifting whilst playing truant.*

The relationship I have developed with my working class colleagues at the pie factory has fast become more desperate over the past eight years because, for example, how can I talk to them about the reasons why an eccentric gang of mickey mice are stupid enough to walk and swim 3,000 miles every 5 years, or the why pigmies are so short, or details about how dinosaurs cleaned their teeth. Also it is embarrassing to explain the reasons why parents knock seven bells of shite out of their kids or how the kids keep bringing home stereos and compact disc players which they are lucky enough to win every week in the school raffle.

Stop blabbering Dick Head and get to the point!

To get to the central point is not quite so easy as you might think. For example you probably already have a high respect for me as a reader of specialised books, who has dedicated himself to reading so intently over the last 15 years of his life. Or you might think simply "Dick Head by name, Dick head by nature - Imagine how somebody can waste his time reading 31,986 books!"

I must point out at this early stage of my teachings that all personal abuse is futile as it has no effect on me whatsoever, and only lowers my opinion of you to a point where you will be described as a sarcastic arsehole. Any educated person should reserve criticism and judgement until after all the facts are presented. Be a little more patient you fellows of literature and you will realise after finishing this book that anyone who can work at Patel's Cheapo Pie Factory for the past 35 years, 56 days and..and...and, "when you hear the third beep the time spent at the Patel's Cheapo Pie Factory as sponsored by DikTime is 35 years, 56 days , 3 hours, 37 minutes and 50 seconds precisely...beep...beep....beep."

There you are folks you now can be on the same time scale as your benefactor. At regular intervals, I shall be giving you further electronic time checks to assist those of you that would like to follow my timing schedule throughout this complete dictum. DikTime will be used throughout all 61 publications planned for this complete education programme.

Devoted Dick Head undergraduates can check with Yellow Pages to locate the nearest watch shop that stocks the special DikTime range of digital wristwatches with integral alarm. This exclusive wrist mounted timepiece, once set accurately from my next time check, will allow you to be in total synchronisation with my exclusive DikTime. You will be one of the chosen few who will never miss a Dick Head lesson and will be recognised as such by other less fortunate and affluent folk.

Special preset DikTime watches can also be purchased direct from the Taiwan Emporium in Grimsby at a price of £176.53 (including VAT) but unfortunately no mail order service is available; personal shoppers only.

So, What's it all about? You still haven't caught on?

Quite simply put, the more I read and learn, the more I have moved away from the acceptance of being an over exploited working class Joe Soap, controlled by Authority with no possibility of leading an independent life. We are the backbone of this country; did we not fight two world wars to protect democracy and to have a country fit for the ordinary people to live in? Yes, we did fight and spill our guts out, but the result was different than we had hoped for. Even after the millions of human sacrifices, we still have the same gang of city slickers owning all the money whilst, we the working class people, do all the work.

Do you rabble realise that swell money moguls in London, Zurich, New York, Tokyo and Hong Kong can increase the price of bread in our shops by simply deciding to sell Pounds and buy Dollars. This taking of bread from the mouths of our children by these greedy patricians and uncaring governments leaves no room for moral ethics within their public account. Your working life is in the hands of the vicious government accountants my friends. All governments are good if they are afraid of losing an election but in between time they work to improve their own egos and chances of knighthoods.

Only a dictatorship could correct these problems and improve our government's performance but this common sense answer is undemocratic and in any case would require a royal commission to research the idea first. By the time this commission sat, the dictator in waiting would have been shot dead and democracy would be back. How is it that governments can fool the majority of the people for the majority of the time?

Why does God choose such horrible people to be rich and nice people like me to be poor?

The Midas well-heeled jet-set retain their position on the top rung of the money tree picking ladder by firstly owning the ladder, and secondly by subjugating all of the humble folk and holding them shackled. We are all locked up inside an inbuilt inferiority complex, further extenuated by planned control of the nation resources to prevent the rising up of these masses to equality where sharing of wealth would be a disaster. In other words, these rich guys can only remain rich if they keep the working class people poor. They can only keep them poor by keeping them as working class.

This is a well worked and successful scheme that has now been uncovered and is about to meet its doom, once the millions of Dick Head graduates start rolling off the "Galaxy" production line.

Now you understand everything. Now you know what's it all about!

This theorem forms the basis for The Working Man's Guide To The Galaxy's exciting investigative study into fighting this common oppression by bringing my revolution of education into your lives by any means at my disposal. Within this first book, the main function is simply to awaken your dormant minds and to start making you operate with independent aspirations. No my friends, in this, and the following sixty books of the "Galaxy" series we shall dissect and challenge all aspects of your stymied existence in a professional and fastidious way, thus covering the complete 360 degree spectrum of the freedom cycle.

By studying together, we shall increase our combined working class power, leading to a richness in both knowledge and possessions. I will also teach you so many other wonders of life; from integrity to happiness and satisfaction to self control. Such cherished riches of humanity that have been kept under wraps and hidden underground for thousands of years - these riches that are rightfully yours.

It all became as plain as a pikestaff, or the nose on your face, whilst talking to Boiler Bill, the day before Good Friday (Good Thursday?) in 1965. Boiler Bill from his side of this epic repartee, seemed somewhat bemused vis-a-vis the reasons behind my more recent points of discussion. He looked completely hacked off and totally bored, whilst I went on in my monotone lecturing about the perseverance of those marathon mice.

I also spouted on about Squirt, a pygmy friend of mine, who with a different combination of Amazon chromosomes, could have been seven feet tall and could also have won the heavyweight boxing championship of the world even though he could then not sweep chimneys any more. Boiler Bill looked up from reading his newspaper and after listening to this mass of cultural advice, replied in crabbit and gnashing fashion, "Very interesting Dick but my God you are so bloody boring, please please piss off and leave me alone to read my Sun and eat my meat pie in peace. Tell Squirt he's a microdot prick who should stay up the chimney."

Boiler Bill's views are his own personal opinion and are not binding upon any other member of the Dick Head team. Life's too short for.........................sorry!

The Dick Head horoscope identifies my true destiny, which is shining out in silver luminance dust amongst the stars bright above, intermingled as one forever with those great ancient Hindu Gods of Ganesha the luckgiver, Indra for thunder and Lakshmi for wealth and fortune. Egyptian God Nut of the Sky, Ma'at of truth and Imhotep for peace. Nordic Gods of Thor of thunder, Bragi of poetry and Mimir the guardian of the spring of wisdom. Celtic Gods of Dagda, Magog, Nudd and the love of Creirwy. Aztec Gods of Quetzalcoat for culture, Huitzilopochti the warrior and Mixcoatl of the sky. And now we have Dick

Head the first God of the new civilisation of twentieth century common folk, twinkling as a sparkling star within the unlimited bounds of eternity.

If the under privileged wage earners are unable to learn real knowledge due to the previous generations of abusive exploitation by the grandee twice born, then it is my lifetime duty to bring about a transmigration of these souls. This sea change of opportunity can only be successful providing that the solution is in a monolithic form which is simple enough for our variety of down-and-outs to absorb.

Today's top drawer of upper crust ruling class won't help them, the present education system fails them, the government are incapable (and owned by the rich anyway), so it's all up to me, Dick Head, to turn this world the right way up and to put the rich on their asses and give it all to the deserving nation. Got it folks!

Now you do understand what's it all about!

Do not become despondent about this challenge just because your school grades were disgusting or if you have lost your self respect for being a thick head. For you bottom of the barrel Tony Lumkins, help is at hand in the form of my Dick Head's Dictionary in which, any word not fully understood from The Working Man's Guide to the Galaxy is explained with the benefit of full colour cartoon pictures that clearly explain everything. Not satisfied with this achievement, we have also included free of charge, a ten pack compact audio cassette set which allows the more agile keep fit readers to both aerobically dance and listen to the story unfolding at the same time.

This "DikRobik aerobics with background education" module and the "DikShunnary with colour pictures" is available at a combined price of £164,97 and can be obtained from Charlies Far Eastern Imports in Inverness but please note they are closed on Sundays.

The Working Man's Guide to the Galaxy has been

written using experiences taken from my actual life combined with those of my many dear close friends who have now disowned me. They really were good friends at the time. On many, many, occasions I felt like packing away my pens, pouring the green ink down the drain and burning my special parchment, but when such thoughts crossed my mind an even stronger urge always took hold of me during these periods of excessive drinking.

It is a wonderful and satisfying inner feeling to know that the course of the good ship Galaxy is now complete and will, like the Arks sailing before me, lead you all to safety from a great disaster. When the waters ebb, you will step ashore as new human beings, but this time you'll know you're alive.

Every moment will bring a new enjoyment of Joy itself, Pleasurableness, Content, Relief, Cheerfulness, Rejoicing, Amusement, Wit, Beauty, Beautification, Ornamentation, Good taste, Fashion, Affection, Hope, Courage, Caution, Desire, Fastidiousness, Wonder, Repute, Nobility, Pride, vanity, modesty, celebration, friendship, sociality, courtesy, congratulation, endearment, favourite, benevolence, philanthropy, pity, gratitude and forgiveness, These wonders of our life are given to us free with our naturally born right to accept and take them.

Not all life is fun, and the strength of a man is how he handles the difficult times of suffering, painfulness, discontent, aggravation, dejection, lamentation, tedium, dullness, ugliness, blemish, bad taste, ridiculousness, hopelessness, fear, cowardice, rashness, caution, indifference, dislike, satiety, lack of wonder, disrepute, commonality, humility, ostentation, boasting, insolence, servility, enmity, unsocialability, discourtesy, hatred, resentment, irascibility, sullenness, marriage(!), celibacy, divorce, malediction, threat, misanthropy, pity, pitilessness, ingratitude, revenge, jealousy and envy. These wonders of life are also given free but are more difficult to take and live with.

When you can accept the good and the bad, you are part of the way towards being a real human being.

To be absolutely certain that the world will treat this book as a watershed in literary advancement, I have taken the liberty of referring to a Thesaurus book to find complicated words to describe ordinary things. Normally, this conversion of easily understood wordeology into confusing crapeology is essential for a writer who dreams of being recognised as an author of distinction and respected by the publishing world.

Now you wiil recognise that all those books that you have struggled in vain to read and understand over the past twenty years are just ordinary but confusing words. Interesting maybe, but crap nevertheless, converted into confusing upper class reading material by the simple application of Thesaurusism.

Please purchase your own copy of a Thesaurus from any major book store at around £5.00 or obtain a specially signed copy direct from us at £76.65 including VAT. The choice is yours but my personally signed copy adds about £70 profit which goes directly into my bank account.

Some may call me a thief for such gross profiteering, but your Thesaurus will give you a choice of also calling me a crook, artful dodger, light fingers, sticky fingers, kleptomaniac, stealer, lifter, filcher, purloiner, pilferer, petty thief, larcenist, sneak thief, shoplifter, pickpocket, pickpocket, highjacker, pirate, robber, brigand, bandit, outlaw, Robin Hood, footpad, highwayman, Dick Turpin, racketeer, freebooter, plunderer, defrauder, embezzler, fiddler, diddler, fraudster, swindler, sharper, cheat, shark, con man, trickster, tosspot or genius.

You see just how variable and colourful is our unique English language; giving us a word for each inflection or degree of meaning. I knew all these words beforehand, except for Kleptomaniac which I always thought meant a man with twenty seven different types of venereal disease. So, armed with your thesaurus, we continue.

In this first of my 61 publications to educate the ignorant masses of ordinary working folk in this great land of the free, I have found it an essential ingredient to use various swear words and other forms of curses. Without these expletives it would not be possible to transfer my message in such a short book, but the language will greatly improve by the time we reach book 14, *Wizard Tactics*. I make no excuse for this language, because if you are offended, then you are not of the class that should be reading this book anyhow.

Now my working class comrades, stop for one last breath and deep thought, before you embark upon this adventure that will change your life forever. Be completely and absolutely sure that you wish to leave the comfort of ignorance within the working class life-style in which you have become comfortable and impaled.

Never start reading this book before discussing the implications with your partner unless you wish to leave your partner like a dried fig in the desert or like a nagging bitch on the doorstep. If you wish to stay together with your partner then you must read each page together! If you decide to proceed after these warnings, then good luck to you all, you are entering a zone from which there is no return - you can never be the same again. Let's go folks and conquer the world!

Ten, nine, eight, seven, six, five, four, three, two, one ......We have ignition! We have lift off! ...

The Galaxy is on its way... ......
God bless all who fly with her.

A new life form begins...

Chapter 2

WARNING!

"A time bomb is only dangerous if you are not aware of when it is due to explode."

> Harry Hancock (deceased)
> Bomb disposal expert

READ THIS BEFORE STARTING CHAPTER 3.

Most governments of the developed world extract a major part of their spending money from the tobacco smoking community by applying huge taxes on cigarettes, cigars and pipe tobacco. As a democrat with full democratic principles of free speech inbred into my very bone structure, I cannot disagree with such an equitable way of raising the dosh, even though a high proportion of this money is spent on Trident nuclear arms which will blow us all to kingdom come one day.

Over the past few decades, governments have been under great pressure from various scientific organisations (mostly American inspired) in a concerted effort to ban tobacco smoking completely because it is dangerous for our general health and will kill us all eventually. This popular belief therefore demanded urgent government action to keep such influential pressure groups quiet and to convince Joe Public that he was not going to die of lung cancer by merely visiting his local pub for a pint of cheapo stout.

A satisfied Joe Public means votes for the satisfiers.

The governments of our free world now ban tobacco advertising from the TV screen and demand that health warnings be printed on our fag packets despite the fact that over 87% of our people cannot read what is written in the first place. I am surprised that the ethnic pressure groups in this country have not forced the government to increase the cigarette packet to the size of a Spanish orange box to allow sufficient space for the health warning to be written in twenty six languages and six hundred and thirty two dialects that I believe are spoken in Bradford alone.

Apart from these useless warnings printed on the packet, as a further deterrent, governments also increase the taxation levels on these products but the sales drop as a consequence and therefore we have less dosh in the coffers which means more taxes for the masses to make up the deficit. As a true democrat, my policy would be to encourage these stupid gits to smoke even more tobacco by printing an encouraging message on the packet such as "Smoking these macho cigarettes can make you look a tough and handsome prick". We would then sell more cigarettes and we would all pay less in taxes - now that's what I call democratically equitable.

What I fail to understand is that if tobacco smoking kills you, then why on earth is it even allowed to be sold in the first place? Smoking in public really is a filthy habit for all the company present and it defies logic that even intelligent keep fit fanatics still take the weed, knowing that it will kill them eventually.

If you search deep enough, then there is danger lurking around every corner and at nine out of ten take away curry shops in the country. Bearing this thought in mind, I feel morally obliged to give you a warning concerning the contents of this book. This warning is aimed at the following class of people living so smugly within our superior minded society of conceited fools:

Upper classes, upper ten, upper crust, top layer, top drawer, first families, the quality, best people, better sort, chosen few, elite, high society, social register, high life, fashionable world, beau monde, ruling class, the twice-born, the Establishment, high-ups, Olympians, the haves, salaried class, salariat, patrician, aristocrat, person of high caste, Brahman, thoroughbred, senator, magnate, dignitary, don, grandee, caballero, hidalgo, gentleman, squire, laird, boyar, Junker, emperor, king, queen, prince, sovereign, snob, swell, gent, toff, panjandrum, superior person, bigwig, titled person, noble. nobleman, noble lord, seigneur, princeling, lordling, aristolordship, milord, peer, hereditary peer, life peer, peer of the realm, prince of Wales, princess royal, duke, grand duke, archduke, duchess, marquis, margravine, count, countess, contessa, earl, belted earl, viscount, viscountess, baron, baroness, thane, baronet, knight, banneret, knight-batchelor, knight-banneret, rajah, bey, nawab, begum, emir, khan, sheikh, potentate, governor, aristocratic gits, rich arseholes, very rich arseholes and all variations and shapes of wankers.

Take note you of the quoted classes - do not ignore this warning!

A horrible fate is awaiting our satin smooth world of velvety nobility living out their lives of *embarras de richesses* amongst such a shrivelled and dried out morality. All these participants of privilege looking inwards with a sly smirk, upon the hard core of our sweat laden society, feeling transcendental and beyond compare in this great world of want. Retaining and ever increasing their inherited wealth for personal and egotistic gain without a care or even a meagre thought for the future of so great a nation's future. Not even a nod of recognition or appreciation to any of us, the working class fodder, that inhabits and cultivates this land for their everlasting good.

Sell, sell, sell! those pounds - buy, buy, buy! those Swiss francs. After the pound falls in value, due to the legal manipulation of international currencies by those ferocious velvety gloved hands in Zurich London, Tokyo and New York we have - sell, sell, sell! those Swiss francs - buy, buy, buy! those pounds. These tyrannical bankers making millions in profits by simple manipulation of a computer screen, yet producing nothing for the good of mankind. They live in sheer affluent luxury, complete with every conceivable extra that the fat cat Riley can supply, and yet not being able to fit an electrical plug onto a new toaster. These currency and commodity profiteers living on easy street, quite content to increase inflation and lower the standard of living of the poor, providing the milk and honey continues to pour into their elastic coffers.

The sick joke of it all is that these vampires of the Earth's riches don't even think, realise or care one jot about such fiscal immorality, because their inbuilt morality has been sold and washed away by their forefathers many years before they were born. They don't give one monkey's toss or butterfly's fart about us, the common folk in any way or form whatsoever because we don't matter - that is up until now (or at the very least by page 78) - da, da, da!

My vonderbar papa once gave me a great piece of advice, vich eyes shaltz nowts past ontz toos yooz vankertz:

"Vitchart mein suntz, iftz zee jobtz iss vorth dootzing zenz itz mutts bees donz propertzleez!" Gos bless mein papa for this critical advice and for all his Hitler cuckoo clocks that sailed with him.

During the juvenescent springtime days of my pent up youth, mein papa instilled within my fast developing morality an epoch making basis for living a good life. I can describe his secret ingredient as an all weather direction finder which is now located deep within my soul, guiding me unswervingly through the assault course that I have experienced over these past few short years.

Thus, papa, by laying down the law with his unshakeable opinion was definitely, for sure, to be sure, with no shadow of a doubt, doubtless, indubitably, as sure as anything, as sure as eggs is eggs, as sure as God made little green apples, as night follows day, of course, as a matter of course, no question, no two ways about it, no ifs or buts, without fail, sink or swim, rain or shine, come hell or high water, come what may, whatever happens, he was always right and completely pissed everybody off as only a real pisser offer can achieve.

Pissing offing or not, he certainly guaranteed that in all personal matters and business dealings that I developed a perfect character which ensured that I could never be accused of being less than perfect. A large majority of my very few critics, who were mostly from the upper echelons of the aristocracy (rich arseholes), are probably now sniggering into their glasses of 1962 Chateau de Crumptoise red vino from Tesco's. All smirking with the mental image of just how worldly wise and earth-shakingly indispensable they are to this galaxy full of plonkers.

It is part of the make up of these lampooners and poison pen hatchet men that they specialise in the single expediency of besmirching the very people they most admire, in an attempt to reduce the social standing of these national heroes to a lower level in their vain attempt of achieving personal recognition and glory. The latest smear campaign launched by these prikopositivo comic cretins is aimed directly at showing Joe Public at large just how insignificant that idiotic low class jumped up nazi author fellow Dick Head is.

We should allow these dingbats a few remaining moments of smugness and superiority during their remaining few months in power, because after graduation day my laughingstock muddleheaded burblers, the ceiling comes crashing down upon ye without pity or favour. After all, my friendly wimps, isn't this exactly what this Dick Head graduate course is actually all about?

My advice to you wine drinkers from Kensington and Berkeley Square is for you to visit your local Spa Minimarket immediately and buy a large three litre plastic bottle of Tizer, the bottles must be recyclable of course. You must lay off those expensive gin and tonics. Start your practice drinking sessions now (using your large collection of free glasses obtained by collecting ESSO coupons) several times per day. Such creditable practice will put you at an advantage over all other ex rich arseholes in your future life of poverty and degradation. For extra training, try peeing in a rusty bucket or jogging in Brixton at pub closing time.

It was in honour of my mother and father's memory that made it so very very very very important for me to complete this first book in my planned 61 book educational series. I also had to ensure that all the books in the series were suitable for the purpose for which they were written. This basic requisite, as expected from a writer of outstanding repute, is imperative to avoid any conflict with the local Weights And Measures Department office which is occupied by several mentally degenerate prats and several hundred pricks. Distinguishing the difference between these two breeds of inferior beings is of course an impossibility.

Obeying the laws of the land and keeping away from the Wanckaire habits is the very least that my students would expect from me, if utmost respect is going to be maintained. Solving the questions of book weight, quality and quantity of content became a very complicated calculation, requiring all three areas of concern to be ruled upon and authorised by the local prats (or was it the pricks?).

Upon contacting these jolly fellows abiding at The Weights and Measures Department, they spoke in some foreign tongue and proceeded to send my publishers a form with a printed reference of "type 876WM/782345/books/UK/rev3" supplemented by the heading "Weights and Measures Check for Book Quality & Quantity 1965 (revised 1989 sub section 145(a)". With the help of three local gospel singers and a lamplighter from Putney, it took us some three weeks to complete this 176 page form. Upon completion, we then had to sign it on each page in the presence of an Irish priest or a protestant archbishop, as we found it impossible to find a Chinese nun.

To end it all, this bloody form had to be finally endorsed by a Unigate milkman with a big pair of balls and a handlebar moustache.

We eventually found a castrated milkman, who answered to the name of Oliver Twist, who worked for Presto Dairies and was as bald as a coot with no facial hair whatsoever. With the inducement of a counterfeit £20 note he was more than happy to exaggerate the truth and sign where indicated at the bottom of the form. To protect ourselves from future blackmail from such a bald headed bollockless milkman, we then proceeded to threaten to cut off his limp cock if he ever dared repudiate this signed statement at any time in the future.

Complete cooperation was now assured and the form "type 876WM/782345/books/UK/rev3" was returned to Pratsville together with ten copies of the book, none of them with my signature. These ten copies were required because they were to be read by "ten expert government officials" on the basis that the form stated that we "agreed to abide by the majority decision of these multi-racial government readers".

As is usually the case with Authority, there could be be no appeal against their final decision. Nice and democratic as usual; but we knew our onions and were confident in the quality of our classical writings. On the 17th October last year we received the news from Pratsville in letter form as follows:

Dear Mr. Head,

876WM/782345/books/UK/rev3
WORKING MAN'S GUIDE TO THE GALAXY

Following your recent submission of form 876WM/782345/books/UK/rev3 to this office, we can now confirm that the results of your application are as follows:

(1) WORD NUMBERS

You claimed a total number of words as 367,238 and from the ten inspectors involved with this count we can give you the following results:

- *(a) Inspector Mr. Sankarintorumba ..Agreed*
- *(b) Inspector Mr. Ching......................Lost count*
- *(c) Inspector Mr. Roma.......................Ran away*
- *(d) Inspector Mr. Obistso. ....Abstained*
- *(e) Inspector Mr. Jubuntolo...............Lost*
- *(f) Inspector Mr. Kasiwanki..............Still counting*
- *(g) Inspector Mr. Birtwhistle.............On holiday*
- *(i) Inspector Mr. Crumpole...............Unknown*
- *(j) Inspector Mr. Harso.....................Invalided*
- *(k) Inspector Mr. Kinnock..................Welsh*

By the majority of Mr. Sankarintorumba this count is passed as correct.

(2) WEIGHT OF BOOK

Concerning the officially declared weight of this, as specified on the front cover as "Nett weight 1 lb", we have discovered a small problem which must be quickly rectified to avoid prosecution under Section 5467 (b) Sub Section 6543(g) 1991 edition. After careful testing on one group (10) of your book using the latest atomic weighing scales (1992 edition), the total weight of these ten books came out to be 10.20lbs, thus giving a mean average weight of 1.02 lbs per copy.

According to the mean average weights legislation

now in force, it is an offence to give overweight as well as underweight on any published commodity. According to our standard deviation charts, the maximum weight that is allowable for this book is 1.009 lbs. Therefore you must reduce the thickness of paper being used or write less words to ensure that you conform with the full letter of the law - which we will ensure that you do!

By using a pro rata calculation, we have assessed that by reducing the book by only six pages, then this publication would come within the legal weight limits. As this would only delete some 429 words from such a large publication, we suggest that a 3.5% reduction in your swear word content would hardly be missed and would be a big enough reduction to meet these requirements.

(3) QUALITY OF PROSE

Regarding the quality of the prose aspect within your publication, if it was solely my choice then your publication would be banned worldwide and you would be jailed for perversion of the working class minds. However, as we live in a free and democratic society then we must give you the benefit of any doubt.

All of my reading inspectors thoroughly enjoyed the chapters about homosexuals, the peeking ducks and the queers in slingback shoes to such an extent that the quality level of The Working Man's Guide To The Galaxy has been unanimously approved, providing you remove six of the "shites" and eleven of the "boloxes" from the overall text forthwith. You may add as many "queers" or "brown hatters" to the book as you feel is appropriate to maintain the same shock level and sexual climate.

During our interview with a Mr. Oliver Twist, we must say that this man seems somewhat deranged and specifically denies any knowledge of either you or your book. We noticed that he had shaved off all of his hair (moustache included), had a metal dustbin lid strapped over his balls and carried a huge double barrelled shotgun with him at all times. He refused to allow us to measure his balls, even after we all agreed to take our trousers off whilst carrying out this delicate task. As a God fearing man, I hope that you fall on a spiky fence and get hoisted off by your balls with your own petard, never to write your book number 2 or beyond.

Yours sincerely,

W.C. Paypa
Chief Inspector

PS: Dick Head with no balls sounds great to me, you satanistic anti-hero.

So my undergraduates, here you see another example of the attempted suppression of this book - but like all other attempts it is of no avail as the Dick Head steamroller moves on and on, no matter the amount of pressure applied from my critics.

Being a fair man throughout this fruitful God given life has been my trait and trademark since the tender age of twelve, when my favourite sweet was Barratts Sherbet Dip and I picked my nose regularly. It was at this age that I first helped an old lady across the road in Peckham, whilst she screamed out "bleedin' leave me alone you shitty little prick."

With this inbuilt armour of morality and respect for the aged, I decided to research the view of the working class man regarding this great book, The Working Man's Guide To The Galaxy, that I planned to create. I organised a pre-publication run of some 5000 copies which were sold in the bookshops at Esher and Walton-on-Thames main line railway stations.

These two specific locations were chosen because our market research study highlighted that the common folk in these areas were shat upon at a greater height than in even the poorest areas such as Fulham or Brixton. This market research was thought to be essential to find out if I was giving full value for money to the right people. This matter had to be checked before I gave the go ahead for the publishers to print the full 20,000,000 first edition copies that had been planned.

The results of this market research exercise were by necessity going to be very complicated and only by using the Rotherhyde Statistical Analysis Formulation Programme could the results be accurately analysed. We arranged for this programme to be installed onto a very expensive and multi-megabyte computer system installed with a large frozen fish and chip company in Cleethorpes.

This crappy frozen food company is owned by my dear and beloved publisher whose name is Pietro Roberto Indiana Campari. The funny thing about raw fish is the way in which the fishy smell lingers on for ever and ever and ever - and that's a fucking long time indeed, so much so, that the computer print outs covering this research exercise still reek of rotten fish, some 3 years after the event, but the good thing is that they are easy to locate when required.

Poor old Pietro has recently been divorced by his scouse wife Kathleen who accused him of mental torture, which she claims was caused by Pietro stinking of rotten fish on a permanent basis. Poor old Pietro was so distraught after she left with their six miserable children that he drank a bottle of duty free vermouth and fell asleep in the freezer room where he froze to death together with the fish he loved so much.

Before his unhappy passing away to the other side of our blue yonder, Pietro did take the trouble of reading this famous book of mine and complimented me on just how superb a publication he thought it was. "Dick my friend, this book should be read by every working class man and every fish packer in the world. Indeed, I am so enlightened and encouraged by its content that my life has positively changed for the better."

The next day he slept with the cod and God, which made him feel so much batter.

Death is but a part of our short life cycle which rotates at great speed between conception and eternity. Whatever we think about our eventual death at this moment in time, it is infinitely better that Pietro is the one who has frozen to death rather than it having been me. The fishy computer did eventually digest all the data fed into it regarding the sales results experienced during our prepublication trial in Walton-on-Thames and Esher and after some whirring noises, it spat out some very disturbing results.

After reading this laser printed assessment of my prepublication launch, my blood boiled over like liquid nitrogen inside a volcano. Of the 3000 copies placed for sale at the British Rail stations in both towns, all were snapped up between 7.00 am and 9.15am by London commuters on the first day of release, and not by the common folk for whom they were intended - Disaster! Now my know-all friends, you may say that this result indicates a huge impending success leading to a potential national sale of some 43,765,400 copies of my book during the first day of release. You are of course correct in your dumb headed way, but you would be missing the central point of the argument that I am trying very hard to explain to you all.

The wrong people bought my bloody book!

I did not spend over 20 years of my life devoted to writing such an important epic for world education of the working class man to have all these prepublication market research copies hogged by city slickers that drink real ale or gin and tonic (with ice and lemon). This book must be made available for the exclusive benefit of the 22,657,987 members of our downtrodden working class people (taken from government statistics as at 03.33.45 on the 18th December last year).

Allowing this book to be read by other classes can be dangerous for their health and will give them an advance warning of their fast approaching fate, thus allowing them to erect defences against our taking over their empire of wealth. If those snobbies buy all the books, there will be no copies left for you working class sweaty people. If you can't read it in the first place, how can you learn to be a better fellow and join my revolution?

To avoid such an awful possibility taking place, I must ask all working class readers to please contact me by letter, enclosing a money order for £63.82 and we shall send you a rubber printing stamp and a DikPad of special invisible ink, plus a pair of DikSpeks. The ink, which is invisible to the naked eye, can be clearly seen in a rich red crimson colour when viewed through your personal DikSpeks, thus enabling all of the working class to easily indentify the rich and unworthy people reading my book.

Now pay attention all punchy readers. Carefully look around you and identify the nobility that are reading this book of ours and trying to be smart. Once you have spotted these spies in our midst, carefully ink the stamp on the DikPad and gently press the ink stamp softly onto the side of their arm. It may very well be the person sitting next to you who is illegally reading our book, but whoever it is, print quickly on their arm with the DikStamp. The words from the stamp read "Rich arsehole beware!" and these words of warning can only be seen through your DikSpeks. This will allow us to identify the enemy that is within and thus take corrective measures for resolving such underhand spying tactics.

DikSpeks are available in red or blue, or for an extra £2.90 they are available in a sparkling brown/silver mixture intended for homosexuals or sex deviates only. The pink covered edition of this book entitled, The Working Man's Guide to the Galaxy for Queers" is also available at a special price of £84.89 including sales tax and is sent complete with a list of all names and addresses of other people buying this special edition (we try to be as helpful as we can). Please order the correct type of DikSpeks and book style to match your sexual habits, taking note that we are not responsible for any unsolicited mail or male you may receive, but we do hope that you have fun.

I must warn all spies and trouble makers from middle and upper class backgrounds that have a destructive reason for buying this book of educational freedom. Beware you tories, liberals, queers and other parties that are depriving the working class - we are out to get you all - we want your jobs - we want your posh houses - we want your mistresses - we want to vote tory - we want to wear pinstriped suits - we want to be healthy - we want your fur lined condoms - we want everything that you've got that is rightfully ours!

No amount of sabotage, subversion or withholding of financial support already agreed with the National Frontdoor Bank of Guildford will stop us now. You can't stop this tide of freedom sweeping across our divided land. Soon all men and a few women will be equal, so look out you hoarders of the workers' wealth, we're coming to get you! Our attack will be based upon absolute knowledge - from banking to the stock exchange, from car dealing to carpet fitting, from dispensing to drug production and from doctors to surgeons, from A to B. Yes, all will be open to you my educated Dick Head students.

Imagine my band of over 22,000,000 new Dick Head Graduates - not only fully educated, but with a complete experience of all aspects of life. They will understand all problems and therefore will have no need to speak down to customers as is the norm today. No more crap like "I understand Mr. Head, but........." Bank managers with no cupboards to hide in, lawyers that win cases, doctors that understand why they give you antibiotics, policemen that tell the truth, scouse tory MPs, traffic wardens that smile, train drivers not pissed, honest taxi drivers, athletes without drugs, fresh foods, teachers that teach, a National Health service that works and endless more, but still unfortunately a weird Labour Party leader

At this present moment in time, some of you (40% tory blues), are mumbling quietly, "bloody Dick Head, I'm not one of those rich bastards, I'm an understanding middle class fellow - leave me alone prickhead." Well my lovey Dovey blue squeaky arsed friends, you are equally entitled to legally read my book (even after reading this warning).

Maybe after you have read the entire book, you will change your pattern of life - it's great living amongst the tenement squalor in Glasgow where you have the chance of going out to get "blotto" (you will soon call it "pissed") and to puke carrot lumps over the pub wall. Why not try it for a year or so, I can promise you a definite change in your thinking pattern and you'll still remain different from those working class people you have been forced to mix with.

Notwithstanding these yet to be forthcoming experiences in life, you'll still be the biggest twat cat in town. Indeed some things never change.

For those local councils in Surrey and Hampshire, where at this very moment they are trying their hardest to ban this book from all schools and libraries hard luck chaps! I can tell you that your resistance to change is a total waste of time and local tax payers money. The "Screw the Rich Society" in Basingstoke, has just purchased 234,000 copies of this book in the paperback version and will be distributing these free of charge on a door to door basis to all council houses (and ex council houses) within their county boundaries.

The Society has ordered 180 special book vans from which to hand out copies free of charge outside all of the schools in these areas of suppression, together with free Coke and Condoms. We invite reports of similar restrictions applied by any other Authority in any area of the country so that similar action can be taken to defeat these outdated twats. You see how easily money and power controls everything my sons of the Earth?

For existing nobility, fat cats: bank managers, lawyers, doctors, property tycoons, city slickers, etc. please take this warning seriously, READING DICK HEAD'S BOOK CAN DAMAGE YOUR MENTAL HEALTH. You should not read this publication of mine because it is too great a cultural shock that may affect your life support system. Until my graduates are ready to take over this great land of the *Magna Carta* and *Bodmin's Treaty,* we must keep you healthy and maintain services as usual.

You endangered species can look forward to reading my book entitled *Fat cats Survival in an equal society* which will be published as book number 58 in the series. This publication predicts where you'll all be in five years time my scared bunnies - deep in the proverbial shite.

Last Monday as I was throwing stones at Buckingham Palace, I was approached by a kerb crawler riding in the back of a golden carriage drawn by eight white stallions with two fully dressed footmen standing at the rear. This weird looking fellow with a corgi hat on his head, leaned out of the window wearing a ridiculous false beard which reminded me of an out of work actor practising a part in *Cinderella's Father is a Dirty old Bugger.*

"My man! It is most appropriate for his Royal Highness to request a sample copy of your publication with six sets of pink DikSpeks thrown in - and make it quick before my flowers become lonely." At this he threw me a velvet bag full of golden sovereigns, grabbed a book and six sets of pink DikSpeks and shouted up to the fully liveried driver, "Tallyho Jeeves!, back to the jolly old ranch." The Old Vic I've heard of but...........in any case he forgot his invisible ink DikPad.

If any of you people out there in the real world see a man driving around in such strange dress or being transported by such affluent transport, please stop the carriage and inform him that his DikPad of invisible ink has been left at the left luggage department in Kings Cross Station marked for the attention of "Twat in Coach" in locker number 1568. He can get the key from the station master by using the password, "I'm a royal prat to catch a mackerel."

The sovereigns have realised £387.87 at Spinks in London, so a twat or a prat he may be, but a rich fat cat prat twat at that with a corgi hat is OK by me.

The grammar and language I have felt obliged to use in this first book of learning has distressed me during the final editing, which was completed whilst in the bath reading the Daily Mail. However, the language level has been lowered to meet the needs of teaching such a large group of IQless students, where mere good language alone would not suffice.

In subsequent later publications, the language will improve quite dramatically, to match the increasing IQ level of my students, which is assured after each book study tutorial. Remember, it is not the language you use that places you in society, but the intellect which you have developed that changes you into a leader of society. This is a position that is yours to take if you follow my lead.

So, for those less ambitious fools, not proceeding with any further reading for fear of a complete breakdown in their central nervous system, please give your copy of The Working Man's Guide To The Galaxy to the next working class man that you set your eyes upon. You will be giving this lucky fellow the chance of a lifetime.

Please note that people wearing spectacles with the words DikSpeks on the front will already have a copy of this book. If you have chosen the homosexual edition of the book complete with sparkling DikSpeks, please be very selective in your choice of person to whom you give this book. I cannot be held responsible for any bashed in faces or kicked in knackers if you choose unwisely.

If you see people wearing the DikSpeks in the wrong place where it may offer some offence, will you be kind enough to explain the true use of this tool of our trade. This request follows the unfortunate and very embarrassing arrest of two homosexual readers accused of indecent exposure in Hyde Park last month. They were found unconscious after walking into a tree with their eyes closed and their trousers off.

After recovering consciousness in the police cell at Westminster Abbey police station, Cuthbert said to Clarence, "Mmm ducky, I told you that it wasn't your Dick that it referred to on the glasses my darling, but I enjoyed it anyway." They were bound together to keep the peace for twelve months but the judge kept the DikSpeks and has since purchased five copies of the pink book for his friends - "just to get the feel of things".

Thanks a lot for listening to this warning you hunted fat cats, even though I expect you all to be smug enough to disbelieve that your end is nigh. We'll no doubt see you in book 58, but I strongly suggest that you should immediately start worrying about your future, because you are going to be replaced my friends.

Start being really nice and playing up to everybody and everyone from the working class people that you now look down upon, particularly if they are wearing DikSpeks. If your assistant is wearing the sparkly DikSpeks and reading the pink book version, be careful, but still make the effort with this gay capitalist of the future. Ven vun doors shutz anothertz doors closez. So said Adam to the ant on the Queen's birthday.

For true Dick Head undergraduates from the working class masses, my message is clear, The Earth is ours, we only need take it!................Nobility, your sand of time is flowing in a downwards direction.

Get on your horses and shove off to other lands.

Chapter 3

FROM PIES TO DEMOCRACY?

"A healthy nation develops a flexible integration policy to guarantee equality of all of its cultures and religions, together with the forced feeding of working class lives with a range of nutritional and inexpensive meat pies."

> Saresh Patel
> Oscar Presentation Ceremony (1987)

On the 1st June 31 BD (1958 AD) at precisely 11.49 WDT (World Dik Time), a critical and key moment in the history of mankind was about to unfold its mysterious story. This eternal moment would prove to be a major and fateful turning point, destined to dramatically affect the lives and general welfare of all meat pie chefs, stray dogs, rats and meat pie consumers alike, living within the realms and borders of both Great Britain and The Isle of Wight.

Before proceeding any further with this history lesson in Asian culture and gourmet mass production cooking, I insist on lodging my official complaint to the British Government for allowing the puritanical and virginal English word of Wight to be misappropriated with such a crappy dirty island that is infested with such a miserable and conceited bunch of anti British prima classe prudes.

This poxy island should be renamed as Browne Cowes Resort. Wight (or white) is a literal term thus describing purity of an absolute virginal nature that reflects the blessed goodness in the human race, not to be confused with the mongrel acceptance of modern day man.

Should ever any sane, insane or disloyal British

subject dare to visit this supercilious and puffed-up snob ridden land of dinghy posers, then they should be castrated on disembarkation. At the very least we must express our utter disapproval and hoot, boo, bay, heckle, hiss, whistle, give a slow handclap, give the bird, hand out brickbats, throw mud, throw rotten eggs, throw bricks and stones, make a face, grimace, spit, look black, look daggers, fault find, pick holes, niggle, cavil, carp, nitpick, deprecate, run down, belittle, slate, lambaste, put the boot in, cry shame, call names, gird, rail, revile, abuse, pour vitriol, objurgate, execrate, curse, vilify, blacken, denigrate, defame, stigmatize, pillory, denounce, sneer, twit, taunt, reprove, reprehend, reproach, rebuke, snub, rebuff, send away with a flea in the ear, wag one's finger, read the Riot Act, censure, reprimand, take to task, rap over the knuckles, tick off, have one's head for, remonstrate, expostulate, admonish, castigate, chide, correct, inveigh against, bawl out, scold, tongue-lash, give the rough edge of one's tongue, rail in good set terms against, give one a piece of one's mind, give one what for, let it rip and generally piss over anybody with even the slightest connection with such a putrid, nauseating and shitty lump of God's earth.

Within God's house-trained world of uncivilised citizens only New York city and Naples can be described as equally obnoxious centres of crass humanity in drag as bad as that Browne Cowes Resort.

Now that this truth of truths is despatched from my hairy and muscle bound chest at the speed of light, I really feel so incredibly much better within myself. I am so proud of this verbal achievement that I could at this moment in time be described as being as sprightly as an olympic high jumping spring chicken on drugs. No matter how fast this gold medal winning spring chicken can run, his future is destined to be very dim indeed.

The average life of a chicken in Kentucky is forty three days from hatching date. It takes a further sixteen days for all cocks to be processed, frozen, despatched, defrosted, baked and gobbled up. This equates to a cock life of just fifty nine days from hatching to regurgitation. It is interesting to note that only cocks are short lived in the chicken kingdom, because the crumpet chickens (hens) are kept in concentration camps for the continuous breeding and hatching of the replacement cocks for human consumption. I have a much better future in mind for myself, and my cocks, which excludes being stuffed with a large spanish onion by a wise man from the East. I am so light headed with ecstatic euphoria and universal confidence, that even Herman the german, the famous blond gas meter reader from Reading, could not upset me now. I am in a special moment of absolute bliss. I wonder who thought up the slogan "That's the beauty of gas", "High speed gas" and "gastroenteritis"?

Talking about wise men from the East, reminds me of the very true story concerning another virgin Mary from Basingstoke, who visited her local doctor with severe stomach pains. Following a full and comprehensive medical examination the doctor congratulated Mary on her future motherhood and after which he received a huge smack around the face, plus delicate feminine words from Mary of, "You filthy shithead, I'm a fucking virgin and have never been with a fucking man in my life. Been with a fucking woman? - yes, but with fucking men, definitely no!"

I must point out that Mary had indeed failed her English language and biology exams at school and could therefore be partly excused for her foul mouth and ignorance. This lack of education was not recorded on Mary's medical records and it was therefore understandable when our calm Doctor Joseph walked over to his large medicine cupboard, situated alongside the large picture window, removed a large powerful set of binoculars from the top shelf and proceeded to scan the horizon with great enthusiasm whilst reciting the Lord's prayer.

After some five minutes of searching in muted

silence, our most agitated non poked virgin Mary, became more than a wee fractionally bit irritated with the constant binocular searching by kind doctor Joseph. in her usual gutter snipe manner spoke out boldly the words, "What the fuck are you searching for you daft old coot?, because my tits are bloody frozen here fully undressed you dirty old fart."

In response to this question, dear old Doctor Joseph looked up from his binocular watching and in an amused irish lilt replied gleefully "My dear Mary, the last time that this type of wonderful virgin miracle happened on this earth of ours, there were three wise men seen coming from the east, and I'm certainly not going to miss seeing them this time around."

Let's continue, without further ado and without even a few extra seconds delay, even whilst I take time off to scratch that itchy spot on my bum. Why is it that we are permanently embarrassed to bum scratch even when we are lumbered with the itchiest of itches? Society at large is appalled and disgusted if a mere flick of any human hand crosses the rectum crevice in an effort to obtain a modicum of itch relief even when you are being chased by millions and billions of queer mosquitoes.

This is incomprehensible when you consider that we actually witness our highest and most respected autocrats and TV prats being seemingly proud and free to scratch their stupid heads at any time of the day or night, even when there is no itch (and sometimes no head) present? Rumour has it on good authority (via a Sunday newspaper reporter) that even Solomon was allowed to scratch his head and balls when acting the fool and whilst digging deep inside his gold mine. Therefore at the very least we should allow our infantile politicians to scratch their bums without criticism whilst they act the giddy goat as a natural part of their egotistical political lives.

After all, they spend their lives sitting on and talking from them, so an itch or two requiring a good old fashioned scratch is to be expected from time to time.

Stop it Dick!, you are yet again jumping ahead into subjects that are far too complicated and rude for these first book students. Back to the epic history in the making, which started its journey into the lives of all mankind for ever more at precisely 11.49 WDT on the 1st June 31 BD. Amen, so help us God.

The dramatic and titanic changes to man's way of life, brought about at this momentous moment in time, could have been averted if only the good ship *Vellygood* had managed to sensibly hit any huge iceberg, or some other type of partially submerged frozen lettuce, whilst on its precarious voyage from the Indian continent, heading for the centre of culture for all of mankind.

This sinking of the Vellygood with no survivors (that didn't take place), should have taken place at any time prior to 11.49 WDT on the 1st June in 31BD, but after 08.56 WDT on the 16th May of the same year, whilst our future pie making disciple in the making was on board. Such useless daydreaming and poetic imagination is a fanciful delirium experienced by those fortunates so comfortably established in the rhapsodist world of Utopia or Ruritania.

Such vapourware and absurdity is the jabberwocky that feeds the minds of all space odyssey believers supported by their fanciful dream of having a queer Narnian cuckoo piloting a high flying castle through thick clouds over Madrid whilst eating meat pies and smoking a pipedream. Good times are a coming my boys, but beware, skiamachy is still reserved only for the dreamers and lovers lurking within our midst.

If this figment of the imagination had become fact, then a block busting new movie film entitled *The Sinking of the Vellygood* would be released in the very near future. This film would naturally require the use of sub titles in English for the benefit of the few English speaking people still remaining in this great country of ours. To be filmed in the Indian Ocean, a huge number of massive ice making machines would be required to assist the shooting of the final sinking scene to represent a truthful re enactment of such a tragic event.

It has been calculated that at least 256,000,000 tonnes of ice would be required for the grand finale of this film. The need for such a huge quantity is giving the ice making machinery companies a big problem to produce, even on their largest custom made machinery.

The latest quotation from The Iceberg Ice Making Company Corporation of Alaska showed a total cost of £234 million to cover the supply of this specialised equipment. This figure was thought to be rather excessive by the film's producer, Gary Cooper Ghandi, a very short fellow who was compelled to stand on an orange box during filming.

Fibre Glass replicas of the iceberg to save on this high cost has been ruled out following some test runs carried out at at sea on a prototype glass fibre unit. It was found that upon impact between the Vellygood and the glass fibre iceberg, the iceberg sank whilst the good ship Vellygood remained afloat, thus defeating the object lesson of the script.

Finally the answer was found, but not without the cooperation of the United Nations in the process. Yes my friends, our international policemen in blue berets agreed to tow a small 300,000,000 tonne lump of the Arctic ice cap by sea, direct to the Indian Ocean ready for the filming - hey presto, all is solved because we've got a real bastard great iceberg to play with.

Lateral thinking is a sly, yet smart, way of looking at many situations, but on this occasion such objective criticism is unjustified. It had been agreed that after the filming was finished, the remaining lump of frozen arctic ice cap should be transported to North Africa where it would be wrapped in recycled plastic bin liners to stop evaporation of the ice by the raging suns of the Sahara.

This first voyage of over 60 billion gallons of arctic unpolluted frozen water would be just the start of such iceberg projects, for moving H2O from the north to the south of the world map in an effort to save millions of lives and to improve racial harmony everywhere.

This humane project, was first thought up in the town of Ollyvood (near Bombay) and then fully endorsed by the United Nations Iceberg Committee in a concerted effort to help solve the world's drought crisis. An ever present drought crisis has always existed in those arid areas of the world where millions of human beings perish every year whilst we eat caviar, smoked salmon and dump millions of tons of food into the ocean.

Humanity, if it costs nothing, should be practised by all budding film stars, business men and United Nations autocrats alike - it's good for their ego and improves their chances for re election.

Nothing good evolves without bitter suffering by someone somewhere. In this case it involved some 600,000 totally fed up penguins from the Arctic Circle, who were now being forced to live in glass fibre icebergs which made them all as sweaty as the woman in that antiperspirant advertisement on TV where she's chasing Batman. In this particular case, all the penguins were marching up and down the iceless pavements and holding placards up in the air reading *Who the fuck's pinched all the fuckin' ice?*

Alas, the good ship Vellygood did not sink, the ice cube did not reach North Africa, the film was not made, the penguins are still freezing their balls off in their ice houses and water is still scarce in North Africa. Please excuse these meanderings taking place inside the head of such a constructive genius whilst at the same time I tread along my dreamland road of perfectionism which should have no place within the greedy hands of mankind.

The British and other inferior races can now be informed that Dick Head has ensured that you have not been left alone to carry on as unfettered slaves, subjugated and oppressed by an Authority that controls your lives totally all the way from the womb to the furnace.

Without this book, The Working Man's Guide To The Galaxy, all you unfortunate readers would have continued to consume your daily ration of British lard, black pudding, plus gristle and potato pie for ever (until death or the tax man do us part), or at least until Rochester United won the European soccer championship three years in a row whilst employing a one legged castrated pigmy as their goalkeeper.

Candy is dandy, but sex rots your teeth.

There is no need to search endlessly for this poor bollockless short arsed goalkeeper because it has been reported that he has recently moved into the brightly coloured pig sty located at the back of Rochester United Football Club toilets. All the above information is pure supposition based upon the good ship Vellygood sinking, but, as we all know, it did not unfortunately sink or even come anywhere near to sinking.

Despite this non event not taking place, if you do happen to meet a crippled soprano voiced pigmy goalkeeper from Rochester, please, please, please sympathise with him. He cannot speak any English but answers to the name of Big Joe, or more usually prefers being referred to as "You Short Arsed One Legged Useless Awkward Bastard from Peru". Warning: Do not upset him in any way because he carries with him a blow pipe that shoots very sharp and painful darts which have had their tips dipped into the excreta of a Nigerian masturbating frog.

It is too pornographic for me to give you a fully detailed description of the change in your social habits that take place once you are hit by a pigmy dart with the extra crappy ingredient, but take it from me these changes are very dramatic indeed. It is obvious to most people in the know that Big Joe has somehow entered and fired his darts inside Buckingham Palace and the Houses of Parliament on various occasions over the past few years.

As I was saying, on the 1st June 31 BD (1958 AD) at

precisely 11.49 WDT (World DikTime), a critical and key moment in the history of mankind was about to unfold its mysterious story as the good ship Vellygood entered British territorial waters.

With this exhilarating sighting of the English shores, a momentous occasion in history was being confirmed by my customised DikTime wrist mounted gold plated chronometer because a new disciple had reached landfall. This marine vehicle's arrival from the Indian continent heralded the genesis of a new meat pie age for over fifty million people.

A new leader of men, an ethnic visitor from a far off land, was about to place his bare feet onto the dirty sods of English soil where thereafter nothing would ever be the same again and kidneys would tremble for ever more. Just as a butterfly flying in China can affect the breeding habits of white mice in Sardinia, so this simple uneducated man from Asia was fated by our God of the Circles, and of all church collections, to develop a whole new world of nutritional support for the good of the ordinary class folk on Joe Bloggs Street.

Sitting alone with his thoughts of kebabs and bajees, here indeed was a modern day Darwinian disciple, a poor man dressed in rags to successfully disguise himself as a dishevelled crappy and grotty looking native from India, hiding his real underhand nature from the local Essex populace. The crafty way he spoke out the words of wisdom, "mees velly scuffy ant velly smelly barsturd" always worked wonders in those early days of mass immigration and brought enough local sympathy for him to get by on, and a fair bit more on the side.

This wayfaring bird of passage was coming home to roost into the same cosy nest as his imperial past masters, albeit he looked a far different cry from our other hero Darwin, that famous *illuminati pedagogue* who laid the roots of some very serious monkey business. Dearest Darwin, this doubter of Alpha and Omega, involving himself with contentious debates in years long past, concerning himself unnecessarily with the evolution and development of mankind.

What fury he caused by accusing the Old Testament of being a comic book full of much doubtful matter.

To shorten the contentious and endless argument created by Darwin, I can now inform all of you that we definitely have two completely different types of men. One type of man was created by God and is therefore directly related to Adam and Eve. The other type of man in our midst is a direct descendant of that horrible huge monkey that is now well stuffed and exhibited at the Natural History Museum in London.

After just carefully studying the crowd around you now, you should quickly be able to say with a clarity of mind, "he's from a monkey" - to describe some sixty percent of them, or you may say "he's from old Adam the ant."

Indeed, this hypothesis of etymology and heritage can be no better illustrated in all its hereditary glory than when the Prime Minister takes all members of Parliament, no matter their party leanings, on their yearly outing to London zoo for party line reclassification. The monkeys at the zoo really look forward to this reunification with their closely related family; so much so that when they see these hundreds of blustering limp-pricks walking by, they become sexually excited and all scream in chorus, "Get 'em off, get 'em off, get 'em off!"

They are never disappointed about the getting them off bit of the proceedings, but it's at this point that things can start to go dreadfully wrong.

Every year at least one hundred and fifty of our legislative genii stay the night at the zoo, and not at the local Bates Hotel where the manager has recently banned bed shitting monkeys from their executive rooms. Now, this situation is the final proof of uncle Darwin's theory of evolution, don't you think?

Indeed, many a fierce fight has taken place over the past few years amongst a large proportion of these animal loving Members of Parliament, caused by the general sex driven panic to grab a pretty one and not being left with one of the ugly monkeys with bad breath. You can get some really ugly looking monkeys that even ten pints of Guinness fail to improve - and that's what I call really ugly. Incidentally, three of the resultant cross breeds have the same father, Samuel, a deformed midget bishop turned politician, who has a first class hem and ha cleft pallet defect.

Do not mock the afflicted.

Until the conception of Samuel's first primate bastard child at the Zoo in 1986, this unfortunate man stammered so badly that he took over two hours to complete the Lord's Prayer during Sunday service. He now completes his Sunday service in four and a half minutes flat without a single stammer and with a huge grin on his face. Last March this cloaked follower of the faith came second place in the speaking race competition held at the Pinkokiss Chapel in San Francisco, beaten only by a pink nosed canary from Barbados.

The Church of England was very proud of this oratorio achievement by one of their own bishops, but they still refused to christen his offspring in St. Paul's Cathedral. Samuel was recently given the primateship of Westminster and upon enquiry with a representative of the Archbishop of Canterbury, I was assured that there was nothing vindictive in the decision of the Church in giving Samuel this post.

All primates in the Westminster area are fully satisfied with this inter racial appointment and Samuel has been given the Keys to Regents Park zoo providing he remains faithful to his common law anthropoid wife. The Queen is said to have been highly amused but Prince Philip is reported to have been extremely upset and is taking out his frustrations on his kids (all of them) and the drey horses.

By accepting without question or hindrance the new

fully substantiated Dikonian theory of Evolution, we can keep everybody happy all of the time, and not just a few of the egg heads and prick heads unhappy just some of the time. Thus we are allowing all of the natural history museums and churches around the world to continue selling their ideas and taking entrance fees, without fear of contradiction or living in the deep worry of receiving writs for libel from Adam supporters or old fashioned freaks who believe in The Holy Bible.

Why try to shoot down a long held theory when it is much easier to accept my Dikonian theory that allows you to get on with your own personal life, without threat to yourself or your fellow men? That's my idea of a stress free life, far away from the influence of toss head know alls and tosspots. Many monkeys have made strong objections to some of the more dramatic theories that I have put forward in this book, but it is interesting to note that these particular primate agitators are always the ugly ones who are obviously looking for extra attention.

My 1,867 page publication of *Dikonian Compromises* has become the standard authoritative textbook read and studied within the walls and bedrooms of all the red brick universities of our modern day world. This published wonder of lateral thinking fully explains the answers to some 1,645 previously unexplained points of contention and doubt, each one explained with the support of my usual standard of absolute irrefutable proof.

All theories are fully documented and jointly approved by an Archbishop and a museum director. One major subject of a very serious nature required a higher authority and is signed by the Pope, Queen Elizabeth, twenty seven racing drivers and seventeen ski instructors - all this to alleviate any doubt from your minds that the disclosures are anti-royalty.

This book covers subjects as far diverse as How Stonehenge Was Built In A Day to Why All Frenchman Are Wankers, and much, much more. Available from all university book shops at only £389.76, or better still direct from Mario's Ski School in Cloisters at $500 each, including postage and a set of secret photographs. The very secretive parts of this publication, written only for the eyes of us common workers of the land, is printed in special DikInk requiring a pair of DikSpeks to read it in all of its pornographic glory.

Without your original pair of DikSpeks you will only see and read a copy of the Old Testament written in ancient Greek, plus sixteen thousand swear words from ancient Rome which are inserted to confuse old Greek and Italian people who think they are ultra clever. Think again my friends.

Back to our Darwinian apprentice in rags who was waiting to join the British people on the 1st June 31 BD (1958 AD) at precisely 11.49 WDT (World Dik Time). God, I do wander around the houses and zoos of the world whilst creating this wonder of literature.

Monkey business aside, steak and kidney, and chicken and mushroom pies were unknown commodities yet to taint the nostrils or cross the gullet threshold of this shiny coffee skinned immigrant of such futuristic magnitude. Here was our future food production hero, Saresh Telforsih Patel, dressed in smelly thin cotton clothes, looking out of a ship's porthole, totally oblivious to the root and branch mutation of this honourable sector of the food industry which he was to carve out in future years.

This reconstruction and rape of the meat pie market, to be achieved by the surgical thoroughness of his application of Machiavellian manoeuvring schemes wherever his shadow was set to fall was not yet even a dream. His total lack of business morality was to become world famous as being consistently unbending during non sunny days and also during the night time, including weekends, bank holidays and whenever it poured down with rain.

On a few rare occasions, such as during the eclipse of

the sun on Friday 13th (part II) during a leap year, Saresh would soon be seen to imitate politer gestures towards his suppliers in an effort to get things done, but he still never reverted to telling the truth. These creeping lying requests to all suppliers were to become folklore within the Bradford and Coventry communities, where such ethics are today described as *Saresh's Greek Gifts from a Trojan Horse full of bullshite.*

But despite being a tricky bastard (oh dear, now I've actually said it), Saresh had a lovely smile, a beautiful set of teeth, a pocket full of money and could his respectful wife Pinda make wonderful hot Pindaloo curry - could she ever!

These future accolades were unknown to this poor immigrant as he dreamed philosophically, with the patience of Job, awaiting instructions to disembark. From the filth infested porthole he stared out in wonder at this new world of riches, spreading his glistening eyes across such a modern waterfront where such well dressed human ants were locked static in all departments, because they were in fact on strike. At last!, the antiquated squeaky tannoy located in the ceiling of his dingy cabin screamed its urgent message of "action stations, action stations - dive bomber attack!"

Ha, ha, ha! this is only a joke for my remedial pupils and to find out if you are fully awake and giving this chapter your unmitigated attention. If you see any students reading my book, wearing DikSpeks and diving for cover, then please inform these attentive scholars that the bomb warning is all a false alarm. Dick Head is very impressed by their efficiency and quick movements but thinks that they are a bunch of real gullible fools.

No, my friends, the tannoy actually squealed out, "All passengers may go ashore now!" This was the message that Saresh had been waiting for during these past seven weeks at sea - it was time to go. He commenced to disembark from the good ship Vellygood, a rusting hulk of bygone Tyneside history.

The customs officers were on strike as already anticipated, and the weather on this epic day was typical for such a time of year in the grimy industrial south east of England; it was bucketing down hard with rain. The Australians were thrashing us at cricket, Austin made reliable cars, lemonade powder tasted great, morality existed, a condom was called a rubber johny and Saresh was bloody freezing cold. But fortunately for humanity at large, as yet Saresh knew not the inside or the outside of a meat pie.

Gripping a bunch of British passports in his sweaty left hand, and his bag of belongings in his right hand, he proceeded nervously with his regiment and family down the rather slippery gangplank, where he stepped ashore onto the black smelly tarmac of Mother England. Saresh T Patel and gang had arrived!, as but a speck amongst the hundreds of thousands of immigrants from India, bringing with him his entire belongings inside a wrapped up bundle which he carried across his sunburned shoulders.

He eventually arrived at Passportland, which once satisfied of his rights they would allow him to head westwards, where a vast fortune was awaiting him on the roads of London - cat or no cat. The British people were such a fair minded race, openly inviting him, and many like him, to come into their country and take their jobs away from them.

Taking the very bread out of their mouths to feed these new brothers and sisters from India is true charity indeed - God bless the Queen, the British people, the Social Security Office and the Empire of opportunity. Stupid nitwits.

As is a common trend with impoverished people, surviving on the breadline or just below, Saresh quickly learnt his rights and how to obtain the maximum remuneration for the minimum of work and effort. If this kindly government, controlling his new homeland publishes books to show him how to claim money for no work, and also employs people to hand out social security money free of charge, you would be foolish to refuse it, wouldn't you? he thought.

He loved the idea that the more children in his family, then the more money they paid to him and the bigger the house he was given. This fantastic attitude increased his sexual ardour and appetite to such an extent that Pinda his wife felt obliged to inform him, "No matter how hard you try Saresh, we can't speed up the process!" His thinking was carried out in an Indian native dialect as the speaking of the English language was limited to the simple profitable phrases of "please sir, velly good sir" and "thank you sir, velly good" - but he always accompanied this English speaking with a great big cheesey smile spread across five and a quarter acres of teeth and gums.

Saresh was entitled to permanent abode in Great Britain because he was born as a citizen of the British Empire and this was his right as outlined by our government of the time and governments before them. It's funny how governments and attitudes change though. Why they change is a subject for my book No.77 entitled *Politicians are Backstabbers*.

Within a few days of arriving into this tax evasion heaven on earth, Saresh knew that all the stories being told back in India were more than true concerning the money one received here for old indian rope tricks. For almost no work you could earn fantastic amounts of money by carrying out simple uncomplicated jobs that the natives of England refused to do.

By just applying to the Local Borough Council in Gravesend he was immediately offered a top class well paid job as a road sweeper that paid him the huge sum of £5.15s.8d. per week - not per year as back in India.

If you are smart enough and can convert this amount into modern day currency then you are either an old knackered tosser or a smug mathematician. I required the use of a cheapo digital calculator to work this out. My cheapo figure box was given away free when I purchased 5 litres of motor oil at the local BRITTO petrol station. I will never ever require the five litres of oil, but the calculator was free of charge and after all, my company was paying the expenses.

The characteristics of being an Einstein mathemetician or an old knackered tosser are equally objectional to me and classifies you within the five star DipDik class. In fact, to stop you being any one of these sodding prats, I will tell all of you readers now, without further ado, that £5.15s.8d equates to £5.78333333333333333333333 and a bit more in today's UK decimal currency. In ECU's well it's..............Uh, well who gives a shite anyway?

All Saresh had to do was to turn up for work at 8.00 am each morning, collect a barrow and broom, push it slowly around the streets and occasionally also do a weenie bit of sweeping up for a few minutes per day. The one golden rule laid down by the workforce was the minimum of work whilst looking busy at all times.

The rules of work had been set out by previous local native workers which limited exactly the amount of work that could be done in a single shift. If there are as many fairy Godmothers in India as there are golden teeth within Indians sweeping the streets of Britain, then there were certainly tens of millions of very happy Godmothers grinning through their jewellery shop munchers in Bombay.

After some eight years of slowly sweeping the streets of Gravesend, he eventually finished his first three mile circuit and started on his second round. Working eight hours per day, six days per week and fifty weeks per year, this equates to Saresh sweeping one yard of the street every three hours and thirty eight minutes. For the European metric minded fools amongst us, this equates to one metre of sweeping every three hours and fifty six minutes.

This does not mean that European roadsweepers

work harder than their British counterparts. Despite this lacklustre performance, Saresh always looked busy and sold bottles of Coke as a profitable sideline from a small chest freezer which was hidden away inside his rubbish barrow.

Saresh began to have a weight problem, putting on over forty-five pounds due to this permanent life of luxury and lack of physical exertion. Life was never dull, because during his working hours he had smiling conversations with the Anglo Saxon boys from the local schools who doubted his parentage but understood the colour of his skin. How nice for the young folk of a foreign country to take all this trouble to make him feel so welcome.

Life was wonderful, albeit slightly overfed, and he definitely would never stare a gift horse in the mouth when you could pinch the saddle at the same time. By being a generally mean person, Saresh managed to save the princely sum of £687.64. within his first five years in England. This vast fortune he held in a deposit account at the local branch of Barclays Bank, where the employees did not abuse him whilst he was facing the counter and appeared so pleasant and multi-racial - that's what handling money does for you.

It goes to show that white employees of Barclays Bank are velly good at race relations but not too velly good at loaning money to South America or me.

This also goes to prove that not all of my white brothers are anti racial pricks all of the time, it's just that some of them hate to be seen to be nice pricks at any of the time when they are supposed to be bad pricks all of the time. And there rests me case, me lord.

The Asian people had no colour prejudice against anybody during that early period of their take over of the commercial life of this country, and fully supported the Pedigree Pet Food Company and all that it stood for. It stood for feeding the animals in Britain better quality food every day than people in India had to eat every year of their lives.

This was justified to the Asian community and Battersea Dogs Home by explaining that our domestic pets had rights too you know and Ghandi never came to fight over here anyway. In any case our pets were here first. Do you know where the saying it's raining cats and dogs comes from? The first correct answer will receive a lorry load of pilchard and horsemeat tinned pate with coconut brandy. This excellent first prize is being supplied direct to the winner from the factory in Bombay. My judgement will be final regarding selection of the winner and inducements will be accepted in cash only (no indian or pakistanian currency accepted).

Saresh eventually decided to make a move to a new home, a position of stardom where he would surely achieve better things for himself, his wife and seven children. He knew he could easily compete with all these crazy lazy white slobs who controlled the inefficient businesses that employed equally lazy workers who in turn were controlled by marxist trade unions who didn't know what they were doing.

With capitalistic ideology now ingrained under his brown skin, Saresh bought a very old and noisy pink coloured Ford Transit van from Pete's Motor Mart in Dartford for the bargain price of £16.50. The vehicle was supplied without a warranty of any kind but sounded very noisy, just like a sports car. He loaded up all of his possessions into this smoke infested and unroadworthy vehicle and proceeded on a permanent move to the city of Coventry. He took with him his wife, six brothers, six sister in laws, thirty one children and lots of ambition. He took no cats, dogs, parrots or perverts of any kind.

Once located in Coventry he joined up with two of his brothers in the buying of a large detached house situated in one of the less desirable suburbs of the city. Within 5 years, these three brothers had acquired 27 houses and converted them into 158 bedsit apartments which brought in the amazing income of £57,498 per year. This income, combined with the explosion in property prices at that time, made all three brothers millionaires by 1968.

There were several worrying investigations by various government organisations concerning tax evasion, housing grant frauds, fire regulation contraventions, gas meter frauds, tenant intimidation, illegal immigration, planning regulations etc. During these times, Saresh and his brothers suddenly could no longer speak English velly well. By luck, a genuine non english speaking Mr. Singh suddenly turned up and volunteered to take all the blame for these serious offences, for which he received 3 years imprisonment for such voluntary efforts.

After only fourteen months spent inside a soft open type prison near Bristol, this Mr. Singh was released on parole and the Patel brothers, feeling so velly sorry for him, gave him free of charge a seven bedroomed mansion and a cheque for £150,000. Such is life when you have a criminal record and nice generous friends of the same faith. I have personally not found the average Asian business person quite so generous towards me as the Patel brothers were on this occasion towards Mr. Singh.

Insinuations of fraud apart, Saresh Patel now proceeded into industry and purchased THE ECONOMIC PIE COMPANY LIMITED as a bankrupt operation from the official receiver. By pure coincidence the receiver involved with this disposal also had the name of Mr. Singh and just happened to be the brother of the other Mr. Singh of fraud fame. The buying price for this pie factory was a meagre £20,000 which turned out to be a real bargain when one considers that the buildings alone were worth over £400,000.

This receiver, Mr. Singh, became the second lucky Mr. Singh in Coventry that year because he won £90,000 betting on the horses the day after contracts for the ECONOMIC PIE COMPANY were signed. By coincidence he had placed his bet at Saresh's brother's betting shop named Patel's Flutters. He then proceeded to purchase for "cash" one of the houses owned by Saresh Patel at only £20,000 when the market value was more than £110,000. Such are the coincidences and fortunate breaks when you are a lucky man with the name of Singh and take the opportunities offered at each junction of opportunity that you reach in life and when you meet a man named Saresh Patel.

Take the left junction and it leads to a dead end leading to nowhere, but take the right junction and it leads you to the evergreen pastures of lucky opportunity where millions of Singhs and Patels live. This is a lesson that all my Dick Head undergraduates must learn before you can graduate at the end of this course of social engineering for the working class. From entrepreneur millionaires to bank robbers in Pentonville jail, all have reached their junction in life and made this vital decision.

They have equally chosen the right hand track, thus heading for the land of the Singhing Patels and lifelong opportunity. If you're the smart one, you'll get away with it and you become an entrepreneur, but if you are less smart and get caught then you end up in jail as a convicted villain.

A good friend of mine, Frank Shakespeare, once wrote a famous line which is now part of our country's literary heritage, "Better to take the road of adventure to experience full achievement than take the road of safety and boredom to remain a prick forever". Frank is directly related to Willy and it shows very clearly by the pure poetry in motion within this literary quotation of his.

To start off his new aquisition, Saresh changed the company's name to PATEL'S CHEAPO PIE FACTORY LIMITED and created his new sales slogan of, *nice pies at the right size and price.* This slogan was signwritten in purple and orange paint, by another Mr. Singh for a fee of £50 in cash and no receipt required. This huge hoarding was placed over the front entrance of the factory.

The remainder of the factory was painted, using a

bright pink paint, by a gang of six Mr. Singhs at a cost of only £500 paid in cash with no receipt required. Saresh luckily bought some 500 gallons of this bankrupt pink paint from The Homosexual Immigrants' Retraining Centre in Tilbury just after it was closed down for sterilising. Things and people being as they are, at the last count there were some 1405 Mark II Ford Cortinas and 986 Toyotas plus 875 houses and one postbox painted bright pink within the Tilbury area using this very same paint.

Across the river in Gravesend, the figures are much less, but the numbers are still sufficient to give an added burst of colour to the landscape. Personally I love pink roses and also I drink Mateus Rose wine served very cold in very large glasses.

This bargain priced paint is still on sale today at the AngloPakIndian market stall in Southall for only £1.00 per pint milk bottle full. On the side of these paint bottles is printed "This bottle is the sole property of Richards Dairy and must be returned after use". We must now issue a health warning to readers. Please do not - I repeat do not - return any milk bottles to Richards Dairy if they have been used for containing this paint.

These paint contaminated bottles should be destroyed after use to avoid any further bottle washing machines at Richards being clogged up with dried paint in the water filters. Please smash these bottles to ensure health and safety is assured for the populace at large. It has been found that young children in the Greenwich area have been searching the garbage dumps for these paint infested Richards milk bottles and taking them back for the 5p deposit refund.

Richards have tried using these paint infected bottles for strawberry flavoured yoghurt-milk so that it blends in with the paint colour, but even this has been classified as a marketing failure following some serious genital defects and penis blockages suffered at the local boys school. Paint stripper and pipe cleaners are being prescribed as a cure by the school doctor, but it hurts like hell and there is a small chance that one or both of the recipients balls will drop off.

By bringing in many new production procedures and savings (low wages or no wages at all), that Saresh had learnt a long time ago in Bombay, he strove to turn this factory of animal carnage into a profitable line of business for the good of all mankind and his bank balance. Saresh had selected the right hand junction in life's course of opportunity, where his good fortune and rapid brain now kept some three hundred and seventy-six of his family employed producing meat pies, or pies that were called meat pies.

I often wondered if Saresh Patel ever knew that India had produced Rabindranath Tagore, one of the world's great writers. However, to my knowledge, Rabindranath Tagore never created a story about pies of any kind.

This is where I come into the story and where the real interest for you all begins to take some logical pattern. Patience is a virtue but virtue is not a patience unless you are a virgin tortoise. This is yet another important lesson for all Dick Head undergraduates to absorb.

I joined Patel's Cheapo Pie Factory as one of their first Anglo-Saxon employees and quickly learnt many things, all relating to the life of working alongside average working class mates of low mentality but kind hearts. Quickly I found out that democracy for the common people did not exist and was just a joke being played out by the rich over the poor.

Don't start shouting! Please bear with me whilst we tread through this minefield of discussion, and if you than still cannot understand my irrefutable logic then by all means climb on your roof and shout out "Dick Head's another left wing agitator!"

Just imagine my old mate Fingers, real name Peter Ivan Samuel Smith, God bless his thick bald head, sweeping the factory floors inside the tripe processing area at the pie factory, day in and day out for the last 11 years, give or take a few days or so. Now this nickname Fingers did not derive from his rude gestures of which there were many, or because he continuously had his fingers scratching the crevices of his back side just before lunch.

No my friends, rude gestures and bum scratching apart, Fingers obtained this nickname because he was short of three fingers from his left hand which had been left behind in an automatic chipping machine in Frankfurt. He lost contact with these three poking digits forever whilst he was serving his national service with the Royal Catering Corps in Germany during 1953.

Because I love chips, chips of all types, I felt obliged to ask him one bright and sunny day whilst the birds were chirping in the wind swept trees, "Fingers old mate, it's a lovely sunny day out there, but what did you do with the bucket of fingers and chips after your accident?" He turned the colour of an overripe tomato and replied with more than a sign of fierce irritation and not some little venom, "Sympathy costs you nothing Dick Head but Sarcasm will one day cost you dear. I should have tipped the contents into the incinerator, but I couldn't carry the bucket. I may lack three fingers, but I don't lack sincerity!"

With threats like that, you may wonder why our friendship flourished, as indeed it did, but you must understand just how good it is to have me as a friend. Lost body parts or not, he really was a miserable old codger when you took the piss out of him over his three missing fingers and bucket of chips.

The most strange characteristic I learnt about Fingers was that every day at exactly 12.30 pm he would sit on the floor within the production area, with his head in his hands, and go into a strange trance, mumbling continuously "watch out for the the poxy chipping machine, it eats people"

This weird action would go on for a minimum of twenty minutes whilst at the same time he would go into a hot sweat and start crying. After another five minutes or so, he would get up and start running around in circles pushing his bristleless broom before him like a wheelbarrow with no wheels. Another strange feature was that at every tea break, he collected his mug of tea in his single finger and thumb left hand and, as you and I would expect, he proceeded to spill the contents of his mug down his trousers, because naturally he couldn't hold the mug.

This continuously spilt tea, combined with several months of crushed in dried tripe juice, created a smell similar to the worst smell one could imagine, something like very bad shite. Many people permanently ridiculed old Fingers for this gross lack of personal hygiene, but who am I to teach an old fingerless soldier new tricks, even if he did smell like crap from a very constipated donkey with clap.

More critical people, with less understanding than me, living in this wonderful democracy of ours would wonder if Fingers had perhaps lost just a few of his marbles at the same time as he lost his fingers. I have always allowed him the benefit of the doubt, which is the only fair thing to do when you think that this sacrifice was made whilst he was serving in the service of our Queen, country and Trade Unions.

Many of his other workmates were less sympathetic and before each tea break would start to sing a very wicked song every time he spilt his tea, "one finger, one thumb, keep on a moving, one finger, one thumb, keep on a moving...." - Rotten bastards!

Fingers' five carat gold wedding ring from Woolworths was also lost during his military accident and it must have ended up inside the same chip bucket in Germany, together with his fingers and chips. He was, as would be expected from a man in love with three lost fingers and no wedding ring, very distraught at such a heart rending personal loss.

Today he has also recovered his composure

following the further sad event that took place on the 10th March last year.

On this piscean misaligned day, Fingers' very ugly, smelly and overweight wife named Mabel (or "fat cow", as the case may be) cooked as normal her daily lunch of three eggs, four slices of bacon, black pudding, four sausages, baked beans, tomatoes, fried bread (three pieces) and a bucketful of mushrooms. Whenever the fat in the huge frying pan spat or sizzleed, Fingers would become extremely nervous and mumble "Watch out for your fucking fingers Mabel!"

On the seventh rendering of this warning, our dearest Mabel who has such a pleasant personality, went totally nuts and shouted out "Peter, you stupid bastard, you're as nutty as an overweight squirrel and twice as bleedin' daft. I wish you'd also left your stupid poxy head inside that bloody chippin' machine in Germany." She then tipped her lunch all over Fingers' head and rushed out in a less than charitable mood, screaming "I'm leaving you to find a man with all his brains, fingers and balls!"

With bright undercooked runny yellow egg dripping down his nose and a pork sausage stuck behind his ear, Fingers started to cry. Runny eggs are dangerous and should be avoided at all costs to prevent salmonella and egg infested hair.

In this wonderful world inhabited by one Italian hero, cowards, Robert Maxwell's business ethics and Oz, we must remember that life is always more difficult than it first appears to be. We must always give credit where credit is due, and a great deal of credit was most certainly well overdue at that moment in Fingers' life when he found out that runny eggs were all the rage. Mere ordinary people and sane mortals, plus every Irishman I've ever known, would have reacted with a degree of physical violence against Mabel at that sad moment of food wastage time.

Probably any other completely finger endowed person would have knocked seven bells of crap out of her, plus some more to bring fairness onto a more even keel. But despite such provocation, there was no such violent reaction from sad yellow faced Fingers who merely reacted like the thick dick prick that he was and still is to this very day.

He calmly looked up from his sitting position on the kitchen floor, where he was fully engrossed in self pity (including crying and scratching his itchy balls), and said to Mabel with a sobbing voice, "OK Mabel (sob), best of luck (sob, sob) to you luv with your new man (sob, sob, sob, sob) with fingers and brains my love, but tell him to be careful with the chippy machine (oh dear! sobbbbbbb), and I do hope he has a big pair of balls (Ohhhh! sobbbbbbbbbbbbbbb!)."

To this heart rending response came a further aggressive and uncalled for abusive remark from Mabel, in words similar to those used when the leader of the Labour Party is losing another argument at Prime Ministers Question Time....."Peter you stupid bleedin'........" (the remainder of her comment has been omitted in an effort to maintain the literary standards of this book). Mabel then left the house and Fingers for ever and ever and ever and ever, never to return to the family home again.

Peace be with you Mabel, you fat, ugly and horrible deserting bitch.

Time like a faithful doctor is a great healer, and although his fingers are still missing, Fingers no longer misses Mabel or his long lost gold ring, but he wishes to have his three fingers back when finger transplants become available on the National Health Service at some later date.

Not all is bad when you have a reduced number of digits, because he greatly benefits from the saving in time that he now experiences by not taking so long in cutting his finger nails, but holding the scissors to cut the nails of his right hand does cause a few problems. Fingers does not make any constructive use of this six minutes per month saving in finger nail cutting time because he just stays longer in bed instead.

This acceptance by Fingers of 'what is, must be' is just as well, because even if the British army was able to find his long lost five carat gold Woolworths ring inside some long forgotten latrine filter in Germany, how could Fingers wear it when it was returned?

Even if he purchased artificial fingers from Cadburys, onto which he could fit the ring (which is doubtful to the extreme as the National Health Service also refuses to buy Cadburys spare fingers), how could he then live a pleasant life when the ring had such an obnoxious and shitty smell.

No my readers, it is better that we all pray in unison and all together that the old gold shitty smelling cheapo ring is never found. Let sleeping dogs lie and rotten smelly rings stay where they are with all the other crap in Germany. Another problem is solved by Dick Head.

Mabel did not return to Fingers because she married an Afro-Belgium pickle maker and they are now living happily in a dilapidated council caravan which is parked on the seafront at Cleethorpes. They breed chickens for a living and have a great love of boiled or fried eggs, eating at least eighty per per week each. They really must love each other a great deal.

I've just learnt that there are now more fairy Godfathers in this country than fairy Godmothers or fairy soap.

From this sad story about Fingers, you can understand that based on the United Kingdom National IQ Assessment Chart, Fingers would not quite make it into the top ninety nine percent, but he could possibly qualify as a support player somewhat below my parrot Betsy. To be fair to Fingers, Betsy would only be above him on the IQ chart because she has a better speech pattern and a higher standard of pronunciation than he has. We are convinced that Betsy's spelling is also superior to that of Fingers, but such a claim is difficult to prove because Fingers cannot hold a pen or pencil in his writing hand and refuses to use his feet or mouth to prove otherwise.

Despite his low level of IQ assessment, there are certain times when Finger's amazes even me with his ability to understand things that one would normally consider to be well above his ability in life. One tries not to have a cheap laugh at the expense of others of a less fortunate nature (especially the real pricks), because this is unjust to one's fellow man, but I recall a true story that happened on voting day at the last general election that must be retold.

On this particular election day, after looking and dribbling at the tits on page three of his newspaper during the morning tea break, Fingers noticed that the main headlines on the front page read "Tories heading for sure defeat" and underneath it read "2:1 on Labour win". He became a maniac, jumping and shouting out like a castrated monkfish, "Yippee! and off he ran to the local voting station.

Still laughing like a Chinese drain, he grabbed a voting paper, rushed into the secret voting area where he thought that his future wealth was awaiting him. In the sanctum of such democratic secrecy, he put a cross against the Labour candidate's name and in the blank space at the bottom he scribbled "£100 to win". He wrapped five twenty pound notes inside the ballot paper and posted it into the little black box on his way out.

How could he lose? No sir, today he was the winner - he would prove just where he should really be on the IQ chart - up there with those other clever friends and pisstakers working at the old pie factory. Thank Christ, plus some help from Dennis, Maggie decided to declare war on Argentina and thus the Conservatives won the election. Otherwise, at 12.30 every day, we would have heard over and over again in that horrible shrieking monotone voice, "First me fucking fingers, then Mabel and now me fucking 'undred quid."

Being thick is no disgrace, but many people in this strife torn world find that other people being thick is a reason for making them the subject of permanent derision and criticism. My father once told me, many years ago, "Yoos mustz listentz toos alstz zee peoples becostz yoos cantz learntz fromptz altz zee peoples iftz yoos listendtz fortz longstz enuftz."

Now my father's advice is not an original quotation but it is advice that all of my clever clogs readers should bear in mind at all times during their life. This statement does not of course apply to any Members of Parliament who have separate rules covering derision and criticism which is just part of their profession.

Televised Parliament is something which has recently been allowed by Authority for the working class to watch and listen to during working hours when they cannot watch it anyway without getting the sack. By allowing this stupidity to exist, Authority is assured that the thick get thicker, the rich get richer, the politicians keep on playing with themselves and Bob's your uncle.

Certainly Fingers is not alone with a zero IQ classification because during my four years engaged in the statistical studies of the average working man's intelligence, even I was amazed at the final results. By using an AMSTRAD personal computer (solid disc drive of 40 Megabyte) I was able to accurately assess that 17.98% of the whole population of the UK had an IQ level of between zero and seven.

To put this in its true perspective, you must remember that this is a very sad state of affairs indeed for the future of mankind and in particular for this great country of ours. An IQ level of seven means that these people would find tremendous difficulty in opening a tin of baked beans in less than two hours or of writing "bolox" on the toilet room doors in Kings Cross Station within a whole day.

This difficulty in loo graffiti ability is not improved by any measurable amount, even when we give them a sample writing of this word on a children's learning card and a bottle of Scotch whisky. Most of these recipients became totally smashed on the whisky and proceeded to punch the nearest policeman or traffic warden they could find. If you are one of these unfortunate thickheads, longing to write obscene words onto the bog door at your local railway station (or in fact on any craphouse door), do not despair - Dick is here!

Just send me a £50 note and a stamp addressed envelope with "crapwords" written on the front of the envelope, and I will send you a rubber printing stamp (self inking type) that guarantees to give you 100,000 impressions of "I am a wanker and bolox to you", each one perfectly reproduced in bright scarlet print.

This ink is guaranteed to be impossible to remove from any toilet door that has yet ever been produced by man. Your words of wisdom will remain for ever my friends.

As a matter of interest you can purchase a copy of the software that I wrote especially for this project and subsequently used on my AMSTRAD brain box, entitled, *Programme for the Statistical IQ Analysis of the General Population of Working Class Nincompoops*. It is available at a special price of only £49.56 but unfortunately, the DikChek spellchecker on this version 1.4.9 does not include the mutated spelling of bolox as often used within this book and is therefore quickly becoming the preferred way to spell this word in this country.

However, to make up for this one omission, the DikChek spellchecker does include the standard spelling of bollocks as used by all the rich people, directory enquiries and the army recruitment office. This software is available to personal callers only from: The Asian Bargain Basement Replicas Limited, Flat 6b, 37th Floor, Withering Heights, Anglesey. Weekdays only.

Version 1.4.10 of DikChek with all the latest swear words included will soon be available - I will keep you informed on issue dates and prices. A further development for Windows and 486 processors will be available once I understand just what the bloody hell it all means.

Enjoying singing or whistling whilst you work keeps you very merry and with this theory in mind, Mixer Dick would try every alternative to win first prize in the World Championship Whistling Competition. This most stupid of competitions is held in Cardiff Town Hall on the Friday evening before every Welsh rugby international played between Wales and England in Wales.

The winner of the whistling competition receives a free three year residential course at Cardiff university to learn Welsh which I can see would be a really lovely experience indeed. All the runners up in this competition are given tickets for the rugby match itself, where they have the honour of sitting next to our Welsh political heroes from Westminster.

Everybody at the match sings that stupid irritating song (I refuse to give this song any stature by giving its name), singing in full voice only if Wales are winning by 50 points or more, which happened in 1921 when playing Panama. It is a far different story when they are losing by 50 points and you witness an empty stadium at half time. Great sportsmanship with the Welsh even if they are all short in stature and prefer to teach than work hard.

If you are at one of these matches and support the opposition, it is advisable for you not to applaud any scores against Wales, because any Welsh wonder boyo may punch you in the teeth as he is prone to do when annoyed by any other race. Still, broken teeth apart, this aggressive approach to sport does show a certain type of strength that could be used in a better way, like the growing of large onions.

Due to the complicated rules for the above competition, the Association of Welsh Whistlers have released a new book called, *Teach Yourself Whistling and Understand the Rules*. I have no further details at this moment in time, but you can telephone the Welsh

Embassy in LLydrollthyledome for further information, but I must warn you that only the welsh language is spoken.

Our Mixer Dick operates the famous all-in-one mixer installed at Patel's Cheapo Pie Factory and hence how he derived the name of Mixer Dick - quite easy to understand really, don't you think, yes? If you don't understand the reasons for this name being used, then you are an ignorant pleb and you must discontinue reading this book immediately to stop wasting any more of my time.

The word "meat" in Patel's "meat pie" is not a truthful description of the product and one that should be taken with a pinch of salt and vast quantities of stomach pills. To avoid explaining the full recipe used for producing this "meat", my advice to all of you is to definitely stop eating these meat pies.

Just where Saresh Patel buys his "meat" from is an interesting subject for conjecture (and a huge worry) in view of the fact that he arranges for it to be delivered at around four o'clock each morning; which I consider is a strange hour for meat deliveries. Saresh claims that this special night time delivery arrangement is to avoid the rush hour traffic, thus keeping the meat fresher by having less delays?

Delivery is made by means of a non refrigerated van that has the words "WOOFO'S DOG AND CAT REFUGE" painted onto the side panels of this very old and squeaky Russian vehicle. The driver of this obscene smelling vehicle is quite obviously a red brigade terrorist from Greece, who answers to the name of Andreas or "you there". He has a strange sideways looking twitch in his eyes and a massive red and blue scar running some 20 inches across his face at an angle of roughly 45 degrees, continuing down until it goes out of sight past his filthy shirt collar and then one assumes, further down his neck, presumably down as far as his balls.

Saresh must obtain a big discount for making it

worthwhile for him to pay this supplier in used five pound bank notes, because he always hands over a large stack of this flexible currency in a brown envelope to our greek partisan after each delivery. This is a strange situation for Saresh, as we all know how he hates to pay anybody, let alone immediately and in cash.

A bouncing cheque, yes, but hard cash on the nail - never. Strangely enough, after taking the cash and stuffing it into his inside poachers pocket, Andreas leaves without giving Saresh a receipt of any kind. I've thought about this strange business procedure over the years and have come to the conclusion that maybe Saresh has made a special arrangement with the inland revenue and local VAT office for such cash payments to be made without any proof of purchase being required whatsoever tax purposes.

Hopefully in the interests of hygiene, Andreas will earn enough money from his wholesale butchers business to allow him in the very near future to wash off all of that congealed dried blood from his overalls because it really does give his company a bad name and reputation. In fact a complete new set of overalls are called for to replace these disgusting ones which he always wears with *Dog Catcher* printed on the front breast pocket.

During each of these night time deliveries, carcasses of very weird shapes and sizes are quickly unloaded and transported directly into the deboning area of the factory. This is a special room that is permanently locked, where Saresh's three cousins work nightwork so that the other employees never see this weird flesh until it is delivered to the cooking area as minced meat before the regular morning shift begins.

I must admit to some considerable doubt and worry regarding this part of the company's activities, because recently after the cousins threw out a bag of leftover bones and other body pieces from this secret department, I spotted a sparkling metal disc attached to a leather strap. Intrigued like any other working class nosy bastard would be, I picked up this strap with very little effort indeed, thinking of using it to bundle up firewood for the poor people in Rochester. I then found that this silver disc was beautifully engraved with the wording of "My name is Rover, If you find me lost please phone 0111 333 REWARD GUARANTEED". Strange name and message for a cow, chicken or a mushroom.

Being generally a very inquisitive and somewhat a very greedy person, I telephoned the number as shown on the shiny disc and after only two rings, a female Brummy voice answered: "Hello" she said, I then responded with, "Hello" and she re responded with, "OK buster, what the fuck do you want!"

Here was I, a man of charitable intentions being spoken to as though I was a common pervert. This is not a nice response to a charitable deed, albeit in greed. "Good morning, my name is Dick Head, and I'm calling about your cow Rover." I responded with ironic annoyance which must have showed up by my agitated speech pattern. The voice at the other end of the line softened up a little and said, "My God! you've found Rover; I'm sorry for being so rude but I've been very upset lately. Where is my lovey dovey Rover?"

Being more than a trifle baffled at this excitement concerning a processed cow, I replied hesitantly, "Well, Rover is now very very dead, deboned, minced, mixed, boiled, put into pies, baked, distributed and by now eaten by about two thousand midland idiots. But to set your mind at ease regarding Rover's quality of taste, I can assure you that Rover tasted very nice this morning and the bones are now helping to glue reproduction furniture in High Wycombe. Waste not, want not is what I always say."

After a few seconds enlightened pause being given to this confusing conversation, the response from the cow's owner was a horrible screaming of "AghhhhhhHHH Yewwwww Fuckkkkkkkkkkkkkkkkkk, Barrrrrrrrrrrr Starreddddddddddddddddd!!"

Now I became very angry indeed and shouted down the phone with real working class venom, "Look you swindling bloody cow farmer, you say on the tag REWARD GUARANTEED and that's what I want, reward fucking guaranteed!" At that I smashed the phone back into its Telecom cradle and kicked the table in a furious mood.

To help relieve my pent up emotions, I ordered six taxis from six different taxi firms to take the James family from next door on a two hundred mile trip from Gravesend to Manchester airport, "And make it snappy please," I instructed. The superb punch up that followed, between six agrieved taxi drivers and the three James boys, did drastically reduce my anger level relating to Rover's promised reward. By the time the ambulance had arrived to collect the casualties, I was back to my normal creative self and in full control of my most innermost emotions.

In the following week's Gravesend and Dartford Reporter rag was printed the sad headlines, *Loss of dog causes woman to go crazy and burn down 20 pie and chip shops.* I have still not received any reward but will contact this pyrotechnic inclined arsonist if she is ever released from the Fire & Brimstone mental institution which is located on Browne Cowes Resort.

Ever since my futile slamming down of the telephone in such an adolescent fit of temper during the Rover story, my British Telecom plastic and crappo telephone has not worked correctly. This goes to show that doing a good deed for an angry owner of a dead cow can completely fuck up your telephone with nothing to show for it as a reward.

Each day's work in the mixing room at Patel's consisted of mixing the previous night's delivery of "special tenderised meat" together with an assortment of other very dark frozen meat that is delivered regularly from BANGLADESH FRESH FROZEN IMPORTS. All this horrible mixture is steam cooked in a special steam cooker and when ready, Mixer Dick shovels the resultant product into the mixing machine.

This machine has a one off unique smell, unlike anything else experienced, ever since dinosaurs stopped crapping. To this awful stinking mixture we add a small quantity of a black powdered substance as instructed by the well established pie recipe. This pitch black substance is delivered in huge plastic drums with labels on the side saying, "WONG'S TENDERISING COMPOUND - made in Hong Kong". Finally, we add a few pints of essence from another large drum, marked "JOSEPH'S NATURAL ESSENCES - made in Israel - contains dried pigs blood".

Everything is now ready for the 20 times per day ritual - The raising of the mixing bowl into the mixing machine! It is during this very touching ceremony that we all sing in loud vocal accord, "here we go here we go here we go....." Happiness at work is the natural right of all lazy men.

PATEL'S CHEAPO PIE FACTORY produced 11,560,789 meat pies last year and each pie sold for an average of 28p at the wholesale level, giving Saresh a turnover of over £3 million - not bad for an ex road sweeper. All of the meat in these pies was mixed by Mixer Dick, who had not been a road sweeper on his way up the commercial ladder to meat pie fame. This just goes to prove that an ex road sweeper from India has a better chance of owning a meat pie factory than does a thick headed git who answers to the name of Mixer Dick.

Incidentally, the local Health Department is at the moment trying to halt all production of these meat pies, claiming that they contain some certain illegal ingredients which are making all the local children hyperactive and punchy.

Over the past two months, these pies have been served at the local football ground on match days and the police claim that there has been an 870% increase in violent crime including seven murders and two rapes involving police dogs. The dogs are no longer fed these meat pies. The police feel that there is a link worth investigating between these serious crimes and the steak and kidney pies sold from our factory. Another complaint claims that small pieces of chipped teeth, resembling those from small constipated kittens, have been found in several batches of the chicken and mushroom pies.

Saresh being an honest and a most confident businessman was not afraid to face the press after these ridiculous and scandalous accusations were made. He believed that when you are in deep trouble you should attack the problem head on. With this principal in mind, he called a press conference where the new managing director, no other than Cuthbert Ulyses Nicholas Twist was appointed as spokesman for Patel's.

At the Press conference, he spoke out with his B.B.C. trained voice, " Gentlemen, thank you for coming to discuss these false and scandalous accusations. We have sold over one hundred and thirty five million meat pies over a period of ten years and have never before received such a ridiculous complaint. In fact our pies have been the standard diet for a complete generation of midland children and have become an institution within our society. They contain fully balanced nutrition, this being checked continuously by our food scientists and quality control managers on our modern hygienic production lines. Indeed gentlemen, you can quote me on the following new company slogan, *One of Patel's Cheapo Meat Pies per day keeps malnutrition away."*

Not bad eh? for a transvestite liberal councillor from Peckam.

Personally I found his speech very enlightening because now we all know why we have a complete generation of idiotic and hyperactive punchy Midland kids to contend with. Please see Spot the Brainy Brummy Competition in book number 6. The winner will receive a gold DikTime watch and a pair of gold plated DikSpeks complete with an imitation alligator skin case.

Over the past thirty seven years there has been no winner of the "spot a brainy Brummy" competition but we are still hoping and searching the horizon for a winner. There are also no recent sightings of any female virgins in Birmingham since 1937.

Working alongside Mixer Dick is our crippled limping colleague Scrappy Ken, real name Peter Richard Ivanhoe Colin Kennedy, whose official title is that of Meat and Pastry Scrap Collector. This lengthy job description is as printed out at the top of his wage slip as issued every week by the company's £120,000 computer system installed within the wages and tax evasion department.

This computer could with all probability send a rocket to the lunar surface and back, but finds it totally impossible to correctly calculate my overtime and bonus pay correctly at any time. As this electronic wizard always manages to only underpay me, then maybe it's not so stupid after all. However we must not digress from our story about democracy (forgotten already?).

Scrappy Ken has a very special scrap trolley nicknamed the *Never Walk Alone Trolley*, or to the more crude workers in our midst it is rudely called *The Crap Can*. It takes all kinds of language to make a World and therefore we should continue our adventure into educational bliss without a debate on descriptive language used within this publication to highlight a shitty piece of equipment.

All day and every day, Scrappy Ken pushes his trolley alongside the production lines collecting from the floor and machines alike the scraps of meat, pastry and the 11.6% oil and other debris that is scattered during the day. Now it is curious, you may think, for me as a simple author, to be so precise about exactly the 11.6% oils and other debris that ends up in The Crap Can. Less accurate and meticulous people will be mumbling to themselves, "why not just say about 11.5%?"

I will explain once and only once the exact reasons

why approximations in my life are not adequate enough for a leader of men.

To some degree, in some measure, to a certain extent, to some extent, somehow, after a fashion, sort of, in a kind of way, in a manner of speaking, all but, within an ace of, within an inch of, on the brink of, on the verge of, within sight of, in a fair way to, close upon, pretty near, just short of, more or less, near enough, roughly around, somewhere around, in the region of, hereabouts, thereabouts, circa, closely, hard on, close on, well nigh, as good as, or, on the way to, ARE THE EXCUSES OF WAFFLERS.

Let no waffle cross my tongue, or I should be struck down with a very blunt axe wielded in anger by a hero hating waffle eater with the trots and no toilet paper. Need I say any more about the accuracy of my writings?

Approximations are for the general ignorant mass of average thick punters in our midst. A major lesson in life is to learn that accuracy always scores goals whilst sloppiness gives away penalties. The goal scorer is a hero and earns big bucks, whilst the regular penalty giver is a tosser who is fired without compensation and ends up as a wino in the London tube network.

To learn more about this particular subject of accuracy and not approximations, just look out for my editorial on *Statistical Analysis of Crap in Meat Pies* which is being included in next month's release of the International Meat Trades Analysis and Test Reports, available in all European, Arabic and Asian languages. Please specify your language preference and send an annual subscription of £489.56 to World Trading Corporation, c/o DikHed Publications, PO Box 999, Angola. Delivery cannot be guaranteed and money back conditions cannot be offered.

One strange and puzzling item found during my research carried out whilst preparing this editorial report was the 1.6% rubber compound found in one of the study cases. This non toxic rubber compound was found inside a batch of "luxury Christmas turkey and meat pies" which had been produced during the evening shift on December 17th last year, the shift following our company's Christmas lunch function.

The company carried out an internal hygiene investigation in a vain attempt to track down the source of such contamination during which several eye witness reports confirmed a strange phenomenon. This involved many fully corroborated reports from the supervisors that there had been permanent smiles on the faces of all the production staff during the entire evening shift when these meat pies with rubber bits in them had been produced.

As we are all aware, all women normally look as miserable as sin when working together in a production environment and their being so happy caused great worry to the management. The conclusion was that perhaps rubber has a very special effect upon the working habits of the female employee - I must study this theory in greater depth in a later publication. Stop, stop, stop! enough of this Dick, we are entering a field that is not becoming of us.

As a prologue to this rubber and meat pie story, these particular pies sold very well in all areas of the country. Some people did complain of a chewy texture which had a familiar smell, but nobody died (as far as we know) and no writs were issued.

However, many of the consumers of these extra chewy meat pies have since been compelled to seek anal surgery in an effort to remove the several layers of rubber that had subsequently formed as lumps in the anal passage. This rubber formed itself into huge balloons during each farting motion, an action accentuated by the meat pie itself.

One unlucky consumer, decided to use his Swiss penknife to burst his anal balloon during such a severe farting session, whilst at the same time he was smoking a cigarette. This foolhardy action caused a massive explosion when the escaping methane gas met the glowing cigarette. Both his balls were sent up his nostrils and expelled in a distorted form out of his ears.

This not being bad enough for this poor unfortunate victim, the resultant flash fire burnt off all of the hair on his head and melted his ears. He is reported as saying "I'm not eating any more of those bloody meat pies. I for one don't blame him, because he did after all buy the pie in good faith and look what good this did for him.

A well known government health warning does specify that smoking can damage your health.

What was I was leading up to before discussing condoms in our food production system? Oh yes, every day Scrappy Ken shovels up the "crap scrap" into the "never walk alone" trolley and then wheels it up to the meat steaming area where all is included for recooking. Just as he pours this "rework" into the cooker he can be heard rendering a chinese version of the famous working man's song of "ho, ho, ho, hum, hum, hum, hello crap here it comes" - and all the gunge goes splashing together with various other ingredients into the cooking bowl.

Once this bubbling and gurgling meat pie mixture has had its last camouflage of flavours and colours added by Mixer Dick, it is then pumped into a storage hopper which is located above our fantastic German pie making machine. As this witches brew spew comes out of the pipe, all of the "Cheapo Boys Choir" sing in unison, "God save our gracious crap, long live our noble crap..............etc" until all is ready for the pie making process itself! Da, de, da!

Pie making is an art form, and this is where Pastry Pete, real name Peter Ilia Shane Syriaca, comes in and joins our cause for the feeding of mankind. Pastry Pete was born in Bangladesh during a serious famine, the son of a tall ginger haired father and a very short and fat foul tongued mother. Standing over six feet, six inches (about two metres) tall, Pastry Pete has medium brown skin, very bright red hair and sings Bangladeshi songs to himself all day. One popular ditty he repeats over and over again sounds something like, "Hi La Mar!" after each shout he jumps up high into the air swinging his arms enthusiastically all around him.

He has been instructed that his very long bright red beard must be covered with a special hair net as specified by the "quality control executive" from one of our biggest customers, Food for the Poor Corporation, based in Westminster, London. This attempt at controlling Pete's hygiene standards was to no avail as he always insisted on using the same net cover given to him some eight years before. When I try to talk to him about the health risk, he replies with enthusiasm, "I like dis vun, it tis velly cunt-fart-orrible."

You can't teach an old pastry mixer new tricks no matter what the health risks are.

"Minimum effort with maximum wages" is a concept originally invented by Pastry Pete and is vouched for with his permanent performance of being a real lazy bastard which he has really honed to perfection.

Our German pie making machine from PERFEKT PYENFABRIK MACHINEN of Hamburg, requires one bowl of mixed pastry every 30 minutes, thus giving a total requirement of 8 x 2 = 16 batches per day. But, and this is the biggest BUT, the pie making machine must have fresh pastry which must be at a temperature of no more that 10 degrees centigrade and no older than 45 minutes before it is used.

Achieving this fine balance is not a problem for any German, but is a huge problem for a simple dedicated man from Bangladesh, particularly as he had no intention of working all day. An entrepreneur in the convenience store business cannot be held back from his well laid expansion plans by the needs of a German pie making machine and being forced to work in the pie factory when he should be selling newspapers and cigarettes in his shop.

When Pastry Pete arrived for work each morning, he

mixed up the full days pastry requirements of 16 batches within the first half an hour of production time. He then put each batch into a separate trolley and arranged to have all of these filled trolleys hidden by "Boiler Bill" inside the boiler house and behind the coal stacks. To stop lumps of unwanted coal falling into the Cheapo pastry mix, Boiler Bill covered the trolleys with some tarpaulins borrowed from Turner Tom in the engineering shop. This ingenious application of labour then allowed Pastry Pete to go out of the factory to efficiently opearate his three newsagents and two minimarts during the day time hours.

He paid Boiler Bill a lucrative £30 per week for this assistance, which was really no effort at all, and everybody was happy - in fact everybody gained. How about the temperature of the pastry? Well this still remained the one big problem that Pastry Pete had yet to solve, but he worked on this brain teaser very hard during his spare time when not serving newspapers or tins of baked beans. Remember, nothing's perfect in this imperfect world.

Watcher Will, real name William Arthur Nicholas Keithly, is a man amongst men, a man to respect, even though he is not a true working class man like us. He is the time and motion officer in charge of company output efficiency. He has found life has become a nightmare with the PERFEKT PYENFABRIK MACHINE pie machine over the past years and subsequently his life at home must be extremely problematic.

His time and motion studying starts in a happy mood at 8 am each day when the efficiency on the pie lines is a good acceptable 107.5%. At about 8.30 am the efficiency drops to 101.54%, and then a half hour later drops to 75.23% and so on downwards as the pastry gets older and hotter, but Pete gets richer. Finally the efficiency drops to 6.34% by 3 pm when Watcher Will is quivering in a spasmodic way and orders the pie machine to stop production.

This German creation from the Fatherland refuses to

make good meat pies anymore and me thinks zap zip is snots goodtz enutz mine fuerer. The particular area of problem for Herman's pie maker is in the pastry moulding section, where the overaged and overheated pastry is causing all sorts of problems.

Watcher Will has tried with all his might to isolate this sticky problem, but alas to no avail. His previously admired head of thick black hair has gone the same way as home made custard, and now Watcher Will is as bald as a coot with worry lumps all over this shiny cootish skull. Such decrepitation in the biological human function of this poor bastard has only occurred over the past couple of years. He has developed a terrible stammer but now speaks really good fluent german.

Despite this increase in his linguistic achievements, the pie making machine is still inefficient and has to be stopped every afternoon by pressing "zee halten" red button which is now wearing out fast. For Watcher Will, what makes this situation even worse is that during each monthly managers meeting, he must admit to not knowing the reason for these problems. After each month's meeting he then sends a fax (in pure Teutonic tongue) to the machine manufacturers in Hamburg, saying (translated into English for my readers benefit),

Attention: Herr Harold Heinz Zuppen
Reference:Pie Maker number: 54327864/GHFDSON/56
Type: hgtd-987/JKY/876-io

Despite the tests last month carried out by your pie machine specialist Herr Belointment, we still have same continuous drop in output efficiency during each days production. Please send Herr Belointment over again as a matter of urgency to correct this problem.

We understand perfectly well that all these problems are our own fault as they could not possibly be the fault of the PERFEKT PYENFABRIK MACHINEN pie machine or you as the manufacturers. We understand that we must pay all costs as per the PERFEKT PYENFABRIK

MACHINEN service rates as specified on your service tariff. We apologise to the PERFEKT PYENFABRIK MACHINEN company for these problems. We don't know how you lost the war. God save the German Mark.

Sorry to have troubled you,

Your humble servant.

Within four hours of receiving this fax, the PYENSTORMTRUPPEN brigade arrives by parachute, carrying enough gear to invade China. And why not?

We all (including Pastry Pete) fully understand that you cannot fool the Master Race with a simple pastry problem. With this in mind, Pastry Pete leaves his wife to run the shops on her own for a day, so that he can produce fresh pastry every thirty minutes as per the company procedure dictates whilst Herman's gang are around.

Perfect pastry means perfect pies, which means a perfectly running Perfekt Pyenfabrik Machinen - yes indeed it does. Yet again the universal expertise strikes gold and the production line runs at 132.87% efficiency all day without fail.

Watcher Will sees a glimmer of hope rising above the ashes of his shattered life; hope which is ready to be smashed the day after the PYENSTORMTRUPPEN returns to within the borders of the superior Fatherland. They do not go back by parachute.

Probably by now you are considering that the workers of Patel's Cheapo Pie Factory, including me, Dick Head the author of great tidings, as the users of the people, a rabid clan with few moral ethics and a bunch of real miserable sons of a bitches. You are also feeling sad and sorry for our colleague Watcher Will as he is being put through the unfresh warm pastry confidence trick.

You are extremely angry at our inconsiderate and mean distortion of the truth which takes place entirely for the benefit of our own financial gains. What pricks you all are.

I am not in this part of your learning describing you as spikes, piercers, borers, corers, gimlets, corkscrews, augers, drills, braces, lancets, lances, bodkins, needles, awls, bradawls, pins, nails, broaches, stilettoes, punches, picks, skewers, spits, punctures, tattoos, probes, stabs, pokes, injects, perforates, holes, riddles, peppers, honeycombs, punches, bores, drills, trepans, burrows, tunnels, mines or penetrates.

No my friends, all of you wishing to graduate with me Dick Head the author, when I call you all pricks, then it is pricks you all are. This is spelt pee are eye see kay ess - got it?

So now you understand how wrong you all are with your self indulgent and egotistical protectionism of the german speaking Watcher Will of pie crust fame.

Why should I lead you liberals in an effort to release Watcher Will from his nightmares on pie street? Please stop for some moments to allow yourselves some group reflection regarding this delicate subject before shooting off your mouths any further. Listen to Dick, my uneducated children; remember the one very important and essential asset that is essential for the success and growth of any loving fraternity. What is this secret asset necessary for any B.Sc (Dick Head)?

It is that long forgotten factum which is that of true and genuine loyalty. Often also described as constancy, devotion, fidelity, faithfulness, good faith, allegiance and fealty. Whatever your personal choice of words, I choose the word loyalty. I had loyalty at school, loyalty to the Chelsea gang, loyalty to Hitler cuckoo clocks, loyalty to Saresh and now loyalty to my friends at the pie factory.

This current very serious loyalty must of course include equal loyalty to Mixer Dick, Scrappy Ken, Boiler Bill, and many others including Rover if only we could find him alive. Indeed, this deeply instilled loyalty also extends even to our subject matter at hand. Yes, even to

Watcher Will, this sad man of the world, who would no longer be needed by the pie factory, and would be made redundant by the company, if the pastry problem was solved. Also on the plus side is that Watcher Will can now speak fluent guttural german, enjoys sauerkraut with boiled beer sausage and marches his kids the six miles to school every day.

Children get used to any type of discipline in their horrid victimised lives, but Watcher Will's children only become embarrassed when they must give the Nazi salute when saying goodbye to that jack booted man wearing a black coloured S.S. uniform and helmet to whom they refer to as Mein Dadtz.

Enough about meat pies and all who sail in her.

Getting back to the subject of true democracy within this British land of free men and far too many conceited bloody women who charge far too much. Democracy is but another word for deception of you unbeknowing ignorant souls of poor upbringing, wishing to believe in equality for all men and one man, one vote. Before we continue further along this delicate trail,

I must point out that with any type of democracy, we cannot live with it when it exists and we cannot live without it when it is dead. This is something like a blind castrated man being married to a nymphomaniac guide dog with sharp teeth.

Comparisons apart, it is imperative and vital for all of you to understand the exact meaning of democracy within our so called free society. If we don't understand democracy, then how can we criticise it? And if we don't understand democracy, then we may just be stupid enough to vote for the Labour Party and all their promises obtained from a bottle of blended Welsh whisky. The exact blend is 90% bullshite and 10% sweat.

Democracy in the United Kingdom is explained by Dick Head as: "The governing of our nation by a bunch of self centred conceited pricks, who are voted into power by a minority of the nation, whose majority are even bigger pricks"

Democracy in the rest of the E.E.C. states and Northern Ireland is more democratic than for us here in the UK (home of democracy) because they have proportional representation and we do not. Proportional representation is so logical to everybody, except to the pricks, that it leaves you bewildered at the prickedness of not implementing this same democratic democracy within the United Kingdom.

But who am I, a plebeian constructor of the written form, to sit here and dictate just how this country should be governed? If it was my choice to put things right, I would become a dedicated dictator against all pricks, and become one of the dreaded enemies of all free and democratically minded society.

The people would be given a better life style under my rule and the wealth of the nation would be redistributed to help the good of all mankind, plus I would help the................enough!!! you sound just like one of those long haired flower power dreamers of the 1960's, those nice guys that are either now all dead or are teaching the next generation of degenerate children how to be equally lazy ignorant pricks as they are themselves.

Make love not war they cried.
Screw the war and fuck the flowers.

Let's look at the pathetic state of affairs that exists with us in the home of democracy. Firstly, we have a massive number of our populace (poor pricks) that are really thick and committed to always vote for the Labour Party. Similarly we have a huge number of the privileged people (rich pricks) that are really fearful of losing what they have got, so they always vote for the Conservative party. Apart from these two mainstream clubs, we have our happy band of weirdo liberals made up from Volvo owners, men with beards, teachers, tossheads and a few wankers thrown in.

The worst type of liberal is a Volvo driver tosshead teacher with a beard, wearing a plastic raincoat, who masturbates all day whilst playing a mouth organ. The total number of this type of homosexual liberalist is increasing at the same rate as the spreading of Aids, but I make no libellist claims as to there being any connection existing between the two.

If there is a connection then maybe it's this combination that attracts them to the liberal fold - maybe I should try it when I get older and buy a plastic rain mac and a blow up doll which I have decided to christen Arthur Pederson III.

Politics in the United Kingdom? It's all very simplistic really. People vote generally in the way they were brought up, or for the party that offers enough bribes to assist their class of people at the expense of somebody else. No matter what arguments you put to any type of voter, explaining that they are wrong, you will finally surrender to the illogical mentality that is endemic with all pricks.

After talking for some two hours or more, explaining your point of view, they will reply, "it's all right for you to vote that way, but I'm voting for............, no matter what you think, you twat!"

The policies of governments are so complex that when eventually the political parties issue their manifestos, your IQ rating needs to be in the top 0.078% (totalling 76,867 people) to stand any chance of understanding these complicated pieces of political bull shite. From this total of 76,867 privileged people that are capable of understanding just what the hell we are voting for, there are only .7534% (totalling 569 people) that can then calculate whether the proposed policies make any sense or whether it is total and absolute bullshit.

From these 569 people, you have 398 working for the Civil Service that created this deception, 143 in prison for fraud, 25 charity organisation operators, 2 postmen and me. The remainder of the populace have no idea whether or not our government is offering the right things for them or their country or not. Quite frankly they don't give a single extended shite anyway.

How on earth can we reach a situation where the two major parties can't agree upon the cost to the country for their policies? For Christ's sake, surely somebody can count up the cost so that these pricks in government are able to inform the ignorant masses of the mere costs of their follies. "What will it cost?" seems a fair question to me.

My suggestion is that we, the people of the United Kingdom, set up a "people's logic centre" where the logic and costs of all political bull shite is calculated in a sensible way. No more crap such as, "It will be paid for from increased productivity", or as we often hear, "We'll pay for it from increased tax on the rich". If you overtax the rich, they just pick up their bank balances and bugger off to lower tax lands and you achieve nothing, except venting some of your anger against those rich bastards.

No, my friends, you and I can easily add up the money being paid to the exchequer on one side and then assess the true expenditure on the other side - without the need of creative accounting procedures that even the government don't understand. In this way life becomes easy and we get the things that we vote for, at the right cost.

My latest study entitled *Voting habits of twats* shows a figure of 28.564% of the population will always vote tory and only 26.765% will always vote labour, with another 8.675% who don't even understand my question. On the basis that 42% of the vote will bring either major party to power, this means that the Tory snots only need an extra 13.236% and the Labour hoodlums only an extra 15.235% of the undecided voters to gain power over this democratic land.

Are you with me so far lads and lasses? If not, get a piece of paper, pencil and cheapo calculator.

Well one of my areas of deep study has been the

level of human IQ, of which there are several examples given in this chapter, with my friends at PATEL'S CHEAPO PIE FACTORY, this being typical of the average factory in the United Kingdom.

I have some further 4587 individual case histories of varying IQ projects to draw upon and from this complete list my book number 32 *Voters IQ Statistically Analysed* has been based. The final results of this international study bear out our previous assumptions, in that some 27.564% of our nation have IQ's below 27.

In everyday easy to understand language, this means that these people believe that the Labour party are a gang of queer midwives and that the Conservatives are a group of crooked waiters. These misunderstandings apart, they are under our democratic laws entitled to a vote - remember, one man, one vote - even if they are thick, stupid and drink beer that is brewed in the midlands. No midland thicko will drink bitter before eleven o'clock each morning.

So, if either major party can offer enough bribes to convince about 15% of this idiotic variable voting wankforce to vote for them, then in power they will go. It doesn't matter if the political party making these ludicrous promises has no intention of keeping them, because they have achieved their aim of getting into power.

We, the stupid and foolish electorate, cannot do anything about it for five years, which is of little interest after the event.

Our idiotic voters will forget all about the promises some 45 minutes after the pubs open the next day. The people with an IQ of less than 27 are in fact the lucky ones amongst us. They must direct all their energies to remembering their birthday, the date of Christmas and when the toilet roll runs out. Remembering and worrying about a few lies in five years time is dangerous to their health and also totally unimportant to these vegetables of humanity (arseholes).

Come on you jolly old parliamentary candidates, let's hear it again, just for us, the voters:

* *We will reduce taxes for the working class.*
* *We shall increase old age pensions.*
* *We will spend more on the National Health service.*
* *More investment to expand business*
* *We will eliminate unemployment within 12 months.*
* *We will reduce pollution to zero*
* *More money for the railways.*
* *Bigger and better motorways.*
* *Halve mortgage rates within 6 months.*
* *Cleaner water supplies.*
* *Better law and order.*
* *Above all we will screw the rich!*

And any other bullshite that they can extract from the best selling book in the Parliament book shop, entitled *Tell them anything providing you win*. This publication has been used as a political guide to all parties alike for over 50 years since it was written in 1939 by Armhed Forsessis an Arab silk trader from Morocco.

A batch of 12,000 copies of this book was once sent to Wales for one of our famous Welsh wizards in Parliament to distribute throughout the local party and trade union offices.

The increase in the bullshite level has risen dramatically since these books were available, this being most noticeable on TV during the latest Labour Party conference. They have learnt the lesson of offering our people everything free, screw the rich and get rid of the Americans very well indeed. All great stuff for such a party where I thought all Labour supporters could only punch and not read; how wrong can you be?

So, we have a democracy in which a minority of the voters vote into power a majority government, of which about 15% of these 42% have an IQ under 27 and don't understand what they are voting for anyway, but can be easily bribed.

In short thrift, we can make the following thirteen democratic commandments.

1. *True democracy is but a dream*
2. *Slick politicians are too clever for a prickhead public*
3. *Don't elect the clever people, they might do something*
4. *Democracy requires discussion before autocracy prevails*
5. *Good men and true fight for democracy but die alone*
6. *If democracy is the will of the people, hang the killers!*
7. *They can't control their own lives, but vote to control mine*
8. *One political party can never agree with another*
9. *Where are the other 590 MPs on a Friday afternoon?*
10. *Democracy is where the pissed upon cannot see the pissers*
11. *Freedom of speech in a democracy is occasionally allowed*
12. *More money buys you more democratic rights*
13. *Democracy in heaven would be a strange thing*

If Great Britain is the home of democracy then God help the rest of the World. The trouble about this gawd awful democratic system of ours is that it works very badly but it does however work, unlike all other alternatives in existence today. Never mind about this dent in your faith folks, once you accept this truth about undemocratic democracy, you must keep it to yourself or dispose of it immediately.

Somebody once told me, "Democracy cannot defend democracy", I hope this guy was wrong!

Chapter 4

FROM UNCLE TO ETERNITY

"If I am to understand all things, then I cannot believe in God."

Peter Pumpkin (1904)

Do you believe in a Greater Being?

Just answer me this simple question with a simple yes or an equally simple no! Don't start your fart arse answer with your usual piss poor excuses that you hope will leave you with an escape route into heaven if indeed there is a God after all.

I cannot think of anything worse than not believing in God, even if I have to pretend that I do, because when I die I do not want to have my departing soul racing helterskelter down a hill covered in broken glass heading towards a blazing inferno of hell with the sign at the black hole entrance saying *Welcome all non believing atheists*.

I see this realistic dreaded future within my worst nightmares, such horrors that normally follow a drink of Welsh crappo bitter or French cheapo wine. As I head towards this fiery end, God mocks my pathetic black soul by sending a group of pure white Tory laughing pricks racing past me heading in the opposite direction towards *The Pearly Gate* pub, which is a free house situated in Heaven above. Those conceited blue souls shouting sarcastic and purist comments such as "Have a great time down there - hope you don't catch a cold you Prick Head!"

The wickedness and sarcasm of mankind does not end even when my body is cold and ceases to function.

I often wonder whether dreams are a sign of our inner desires or of the evil things inside us that cannot be contained under the relaxed sub conscious state of sleep when our defensive shield is at its weakest. How often do we experience things in life that we have previously dreamt about only a few nights before the actual happening?

For me this is a frequent occurrence and one that can leave me with some worrying conclusions. Only last night, I dreamt that I had actually died and gone to heaven, but the gatekeeper would not let me enter the Golden Kingdom due to some clerical error in the transition department.

No clear reason was given for this soul destroying rejection other than an aggressive response of "Dick Head, you were a pain in the arse to the world below when you were alive, and you're a fucking big nuisance up here now that you're dead. Most people find it very convenient to die when they are supposed to die but you've decided to die two weeks before you were supposed to pass this way. Following the recent typhoon in India, we're completely overworked with scheduled bookings and therefore you must await your correct turn in the queue - now piss off and come back later!"

To a mere ordinary soul, without the experience afforded me as a famous author during my hugely successful time on the living side of eternity, this rejection at the very moment of entry into Heaven would have been awful and unbearable. I took such a setback in my stride as usual and decided to approach this death or life challenge head on (so to speak).

I stood up tall and replied to this translucent apparition in pink and silver high heeled shoes "Excuse me Charlie Angel, but I can assure you that my death had very little to do with me, as I preferred it down there with polite friends, than up here with a rude bastard servant of Him like you.

Now just what the hell (oops!) do you expect me to do for the next two weeks until the time comes for my official passing over from this side to the bright side? In other words mate, if I'm dead then I'm fucking dead, and if I'm dead then you've got to let me in now. Got that my old Angie boy?"

A lesson you can learn from this tough approach to stupidity is that justified aggression works just as well with angels as it does with traffic wardens that you punch on the nose. Angie boy looked extremely embarrassed and took me to one side of the gates before whispering in my ear "Dick old boy, you're right about this, but I cannot let you in today, because it would be more than my job was worth. It is not easy getting a job as an angel wearing pink high heeled shoes and therefore to make up for our mistake and your two weeks loss of life, you can go back to earth for two weeks. Obviously we cannot allow you to return in your original human form as this could upset the delicate balance of the churches and their beliefs, but you can choose any other form in which to return. You must swear violently on the Bible that you will return here in two weeks time or go to hell as a consequence."

That's what I call a jackpot bonanza, and all because I gave the guy a little bit of aggro. Now I could make love to all those fantastic women that I missed out on whilst saving the moral fibre of the working class population over the past twenty seven years and sixty one educational blockbuster publications. Angie boy carried on discussing this fantastic possibility of a lifetime, or maybe we should describe it as a fantastic possibility of a deathtime. "So, how would you like to go back to Earth for two wonderful weeks, as an eagle, Olympic champion, jumping salmon, priest or maybe as something completely different Dick?" spoke out our nervous Angie boy.

Pretending to think of all these possible options, I eventually burst out in a lustful laugh and whilst partially sneering (to my everlasting disgrace) I answered in a sexually perverted way "Angie boy, I want to go back to earth as the best black stud in America!" Ghosts don't need condoms, do they?, and they certainly can't die of Aids in only two weeks.

Everything faded in my mind as Angie boy agreed to this lusty request and he pressed a few buttons located on his huge glowing computer console. I was transported back to earth with a flash of lightning which lit up the heavens above but there was no thunder to follow, which I thought was very strange indeed. Within what appeared as only a few seconds, I screamed out in horrific pain as my backside was scorched and torn by pain and agony caused by what I thought was a homosexual red hot poker - my God what on earth is happening to me and my rectum at this very moment when I should be Dicking the girls? I opened my eyes and saw in horror the words in big black letters written above me of SR 401 SPORTS HS. Jesus Christ, I was a rubber stud on a fucking Michelin tyre on a Chevrolet car in Cleveland! Never trust an angel bearing gifts in Heaven even if you do end up doing 50,000 miles without a retread.

Don't start to cringe and berate me you non believers out there in this world full of evil and evil doers. Dick Head is not yet converted to the standard Faith as spouted by the various thousands of different churches and religions located around the world. Each one being convinced beyond any possible doubt, but within their bank balances, that their faith is the true faith, the whole faith and nothing but the faith, so help me God.

Many churches have opposing views to other churches which is a sure indication that these churches can't all be right in their beliefs. If in any other part of our lives we had traders selling us goods with opposing claims of usefulness, some of them untrue, then the untruthful ones would be put out of business in a very short period of time. But the differences between the churches cannot be quantified or decided upon by mere mortal man. If it's in the Bible and this fits the churches view then it's true, unless of course the church decides otherwise. Got it? With these guidelines for running a business, even I could give it a good shout.

My own belief is that as the churches can't even

agree with each other on how the Faith should be interpreted and explained to us mere mortals ("punters" as expressed in some lower church circles), then how on earth can they even try to convince us to believe in any faith. So, my thinking is that the United Nations should arrange for a special International Church Summit Meeting which should be held in Tokyo, where a declaration of unity should be signed by all churches once and for all.

This agreement would put an end to all the inter church bickering that goes on every day of our unchristian lives. With only one church to support and believe in, we can then sell off all of the vast excess of churches that would no longer be required in return for billions of lovely greenbacks. At last the social workers will be in heaven (so to speak) and will be given all those lovely billions of dollars to spend on housing and food for the poor throughout the world. We could name this new church the United New Church Loving Everybody which would be commonly called U.N.C.L.E.

A new world headquarters, known as W.H.U.N.C.L.E would be necessary to replace all the other old centres of religion that could now be converted into football stadiums or scrap car tips. For pure convenience and because I think it is a good idea, W.H.U.N.C.L.E would be located inside a huge 50,000 seater aircraft hangar adjoining terminal 4 in Heathrow airport, London. This hangar is an obvious choice for the location of W.H.U.N.C.L.E because London airport allows easy access for all the people of the world to congregate.

The hangar should have direct overhead access for all visitors and could be made into an international zone thereby allowing visitors to avoid having the alligator alley glares of passing through the green customs channel where the leading arseholes of the British Empire are employed. Indeed, this new unified single church could train a new breed of social workers to visit the poor of every country in the world to ensure that poverty and deprivation were eliminated forever and made a thing from the past.

By the year 2500 AD, the word poverty would be obsolete and deleted from the Oxford dictionary. When you hear a message from a man from U.N.C.L.E, you now know that it means goodness with plenty to eat.

With U.N.C.L.E we shall have just one holy book to read, this being called *The Only Holy Book* which will be printed in every language under the sun. Every language that is, except latin, because only doctors and people over 1800 years old ever understand what is being said during these church services held in latin. Alternatively, U.N.C.L.E may decide to have compulsory latin lessons of six hours per week for all the people in the world to assist the common folk to understand just what is being spouted by the top man during latin church services.

The economy of scale that would result by printing The Only Holy Book in latin only would give cost benefits resulting in substantial savings which would be passed down by U.N.C.L.E to the poor and needy. This extra hand out would only be required until the year 2000AD and thereafter, when poverty had been eradicated, it would be given to the Save The Whales fund instead.

Some of the less progressive more spendthrift wasteful believers amongst us may unjustifiably say "Why must we go to all the effort to learn the latin language just so that we can understand the church services? Why doesn't each country give services in its own language so that people understand what's being said?" A simple question you may think, but as I am a man prepared to bow to superior knowledge, I accept that there must be a strong and powerful reason why this is not so. Maybe the service is Holier than thou when held in latin or maybe there are things being said that we wouldn't like to understand.

Notwithstanding these possibilities, the use of latin in

church services does baffle me very deeply indeed and I need you all to assist me to comprehend this subject much more. Please send your own thoughts and ideas on this to: Dick Head's Latin Competition, c/o Charlie Chester, P.O. Box 6543, Taiwan, Tasmania. The ten best comments will receive a free signed copy of my book No. 46 entitled *The Coming of U.N.C.L.E.*

U.N.C.L.E would sell all its expensive cathedrals, churches, properties, gold, etc and move into new inexpensive utility complexes around the globe where other activities, including bowls, keep fit, squash, snooker, darts, etc., could also be carried on in unison with the church. In fact, if a council estate type pub was also installed in each complex, U.N.C.L.E's membership would escalate and funds would be proportional to the number of barrels of Guinness drunk on a Sunday.

All that lovely lolly used to save millions of more lives throughout that unified world of ours. After all, surely this can be the only reason for the churches to have collected all their vast wealth over the centuries - for the day when it can all be spent in helping other people. If you have faith in the church, then you cannot believe that they have all this vast wealth for any other purpose such as prestige or ego - surely not!

God would support my radical ideas because they are purely for the total good of mankind. Did Jesus Christ spend his life on earth telling us to go out and collect great wealth and then lock it away in the name of the church whilst people starved to death around the world? No sir, indeed he did not!

Let's ask each church, "Excuse me, but could you tell me how much is the present day commercial value of your church and its other assets. Do you think it would be a good idea to start spending some of this wealth on the people, particularly those people that will be dead next week unless we give them a few pennies worth of food."

The response would be a wringing of hands, a solemn look and *We in the church are doing everything we possibly.................... Amen.*

No, my friends, nothing will change, because the church is run by people, mere human beings, who are brain washed into believing they are for the GOOD and that people against them are for the BAD. We need the churches more than ever today to revitalise our rotting moral standards and yet this would seem to be an impossibility.

What in fact do the churches do?; they support the very opposite values on many occasions so that people are alienated against them. Just imagine the respect we would give to the Archbishop of Canterbury if he called a press conference just prior to the televised Liverpool V Manchester United soccer game on Boxing Day and spoke out "I am speaking to all of you today to condemn all kinds of homosexuality, perversity, sex before marriage, divorce, swearing, bad driving, long hair, frenchmen, poll tax, labour party fools cognac and Japanese undersized condoms.

"All these things I condemn because they are not written of and therefore not approved in the Bible. Even more important is that I don't like them or use them. All these things will send you to hell. Long live the reds. Amen."

The church should join in the people's sporting pleasures such as forming a Church of England rugby team to play in top class games. We could name this team the Modern Athletic Disciples so that their bus loads of church supporters could chant "Come on you M.A.D. lot". Every church in the land could arrange a bus outing each Saturday afternoon to support the M.A.D. team, charging £2 each which could go towards supporting the needy. Old age pensioners could travel to these rugby games free of charge and would feel part of the community and of the human race again. Give it a go you Archbishops, join in with the working class.

In the near future I will be setting up a school to teach young boys between three and fifteen years old some special new lessons called *You can really trust a queer priest*. These lessons will be handled by teachers with a minimum of one wife, six mistresses and fifteen children. A book with the same title will be printed and will be offered free of charge in all churches where the Church of England decides to install homosexual priests.

I have nothing against homosexuals, providing they don't teach my children, grandchildren or any child that I love and care for. "You're a totally biased pervert Dick Head", all the queens are shouting. "How dare you discriminate against a minority faction - this is what causes all the problems in our society". With respect my lovies, everybody should have a free choice as with whom they place the safeguard of their young children, and I personally don't consider this the case with a queer priest, no matter how nice he looks and speaks, or how soft his hands are.

In conclusion, the Church of England should open up and fully advertise in the Yellow Pages a full range of regional Churches for Homosexuals where homosexual men, ladies that adore homosexuals and others of a similar wish can worship their faith to their total satisfaction. This solution will allow homosexuals and normal people to remain separate if they so desire, or worship together if that is their choice and preference. Maybe our homosexual friends will end up with an even bigger congregation than before this separation scheme was introduced - what do you think?

Have you noticed how the middle class (ex working class) living in the villages are very religious and attend church every week, always just prior to the Sunday lunch? Whereas, the working class fellows living on 1948 style council estates are not religious and spend every Sunday lunch in the pub getting pissed and ready to thump the wife. Now why do you think this is?

I have carried out a five year research study on this holy subject and can briefly share a few of my conclusions with you, my wondrous cynical mob:

(1) Villages have holier air to breathe
(2) Village pubs are boring
(3) Village churches have better presentation
(4) Only holy people move to villages
(5) Easier car parking at village churches
(6) Council estates have unholy air
(7) No car parking at the council estate church
(8 Council estate pubs are very exciting
(9) Only unholy people live in council houses
(10) Council estate pubs sell Carling Black Label and bad gin
(11) Village pubs sell real ale

For full details of this unique research programme, please purchase my book number 54 entitled Churches versus Pubs - a modern Holy War available only from The Knackered Chicken pub, located on the Dirty Mersey council estate in Bootle, Merseyside @ £25.78, (cash only) for personal callers only - no mail order available. Suggest you call before closing time to avoid physical abuse. PS: Don't wear any misleading clothes; donkey jackets and jeans are the safest.

So, do you believe in God? Answer now or forever hold your tongue.

Now, I wonder with amazement just what individual thought up such an irrelevant saying as speak up or forever hold your tongue? If this command was to become a legal requirement within our society then we would have at least 49,879,564 people plus two postmen permanently living out their lives whilst permanently holding their tongues.

These two postmen amongst the masses would find it an almost impossible task to forever hold their tongue and at the same time deliver letters and parcels. Because of this impossibility, you can be sure that the Post Office Union of Tongue Holding Postmen would get a labour government grant to investigate the possibility of inventing an inexpensive, yet effective, socialist mechanical tongue holder, thus allowing their members to go about their job unhindered by sticky fingers and sore tongues.

One must take into consideration that our average Mr. postman Pat has had no previous training in the art of tongue holding and therefore it is unreasonable of the Post Office to expect them to do so, AND deliver the post at the same time.

"Either I deliver letters or I hold my fucking tongue" shouted postman Pat at a recent union meeting held in Swansea. Despite the fact that all of the existing tongue holding Welsh postmen are first class wankers giving a second class postal delivery service, you can understand the complaint.

You could of course be highly delighted at such a state of affairs, because the logical conclusion is that whilst postman Pat was indeed holding his tongue and delivering the post, then he could not play with himself at the same time.

Could this be the cure for all wanking Welsh postmen, we might ask ourselves? Only more tongue holding will give us a positive result if we could get them to stop such unsocial habits. A recent national opinion poll carried out by WWP Association gave the following results:

	yes	*no*	*undecided*

Would you prefer to hold your tongue than speak up:

	19%	*5%*	*76%*

Would you prefer to speak up than hold your tongue:

	5%	*19%*	*76%*

Would you prefer not to have to hold your tongue & be able to speak up at any time

	2%	*3%*	*95%*

Would you prefer to forget all this crap and carry on wanking as usual

	98%	*0%*	*2%*

God I do go on about insignificant things.

If a problem arises, then the ingenuity of mankind will never cease to amaze us in the way that inventions are invented to solve even the most complicated problem. And so it came to pass one blustery winter's day that the Welsh Tongue Holding Double Clip Peg Device came into being, created by a Welsh sheep farmer whilst tending his herd of radioactive sheep.

This device is now manufactured in bulk in a modern factory located just outside Swansea and has solved the tongue holding problem forever. These Welsh wanking tongue holding postmen now also look like real pricks when they use this huge plastic clip that links their tongue to the lower part of the nose by a bloody great red plastic connector. You see this new Welsh Tongue Holding Double Clip Peg Device is similar to using two clothes pegs that are joined together at right angles.

A right angle is ninety degrees as measured in geometry and has absolutely nothing to do with boiling a kettle or a bath of water. A right angle is also the correct position for one dog to poke another dog. If you drink twenty pints of Guinness and jump from the observation tower of the Sears Building in Chicago, you will also land at right angles onto the sidewalk below. Here endeth my lesson on right angles.

So, the Welsh Tongue Holding Double Clip Peg Device was simple to operate, so simple that even postmen could use it - you clipped one peg to your nose and the other to your tongue and - voila! - you forever held your tongue. When I say forever, I really don't mean forever, because what I really mean is it is forever until you realised just what a prick you looked and decided that speaking up was a far better proposition after all.

I have recently purchased the patent rights for this device and have renamed it as the new *DikPeg*. I fully expect to be inundated with enquiries for this new DikPeg double peg device which is now available in the usual range of colour choices as with all DIK products - to suit all sexual and perverted bents, including the pink and silver unit for our students of special inclinations.

Please do not share your DikPeg with any other person, even if they have decided not to speak up and deserve to hold their tongues. This forbidden exchange habit carries the risk of passing on infectious diseases and therefore a high temperature dishwasher wash is essential before you share DikPegs even with your near and dearest trusted loved ones. Soaking in medical spirit or ten year old scotch whisky is also a safe sterilising process and gives a great flavour during use.

At this moment in time, DikPegs cannot be worn on any international flights, except on Aer Lingus flights to Derry, but we are working hard to get them approved for all airlines. Our approach is that the banning of DikPegs on international flights is a restriction of civil rights under the 1967 United Nations Charter.

It is reported that a spokesman for British Airways, a Mr. Salumani Rustikin Copochi, states that DikPegs had been banned on their flights following multiple complaints from fellow passengers who found the permanent dribbling and squeezing out of huge numbers of nose bogeys very disturbing and unhygienic. Also, the air stewardesses were recently in a state of permanent laughter when confronting a group of six tongue holding wanking Welsh postmen on a flight to Bombay. These six men were arrested for obscene behaviour on the flight but this has not been used as a further excuse for banning DikPegs.

For air travellers who are converted people determined to forever hold their tongues rather than speaking up, I have some very good news for you. We can now supply the optional DikMask which covers the entire face, including the offending DikPeg device and any runny bogeys. These DikMasks are available in the following design versions: Batman, Spiderman, The Queen happy, The Queen unhappy, A talking flower, Fergie, Racing Driver, Mick Jagger, Mars Bar, Elvis Presley and Betsy the Parrot.

Now that the question of holding your tongue has been clarified, we must get back to our beliefs.

Who or what is God?

Is God looking after us all (or at least me)?

No, God cannot be looking after us all because of all the tragedy we see in this world during every day of our lives. Maybe, as it is God's Will, this explains everything - certainly I, Dick Head, cannot help you on the do's or don'ts on how to keep on the good side of God, but certainly I believe in some Power that is so fantastic and great that no mere mortal will ever understand it.

My own simple logical thinking way of understanding that there is a greater Power seems so positive to me that I am disturbed that a similar discussion is not standard practice in our schools and churches. Why not? this is a very interesting question my dubious adventurers. More about this later - yes you have to wait longer.

How long can mankind survive on this polluted chunk of rock that is spinning endlessly around a glowing sun in a space vacuum? Will mankind end itself by its greed and inability to control this greed, turning this massive house of mankind into a spinning ball of shite covered rock, so polluted that life as we know it will no longer be possible? Maybe, through further natural selection and evolution, a different type of human being will evolve, or be created by our loving scientists, which will probably be a hybrid mix between a maggot, sewer rat, bat, blow fly and a man from Peru.

In this way our new human based creatures can live by eating up all of the crap that we are now creating, so that within about 50 Billion years these new guys and gals will have eaten up all this gorgeous food so kindly being produced by us. At that time, they will eventually only be left with useless things like fresh air, clean seas, fertile earth, rain forests, clean beaches, wild flowers, etc.

All those things that they cannot live on.

At that time, the present human race can be resurrected by unfreezing the 5 million millionaires and their 25 million mistresses that were frozen in liquid nitrogen in 1999 for a payment of $4 million each when the going started to get really tough for them on Earth. These people would have a great time making profits in the new world of endless resources without any competition and plenty of space for pollution again - no green parties here my friends.

So don't worry folks of lesser faith, whatever happens in the future, life goes on. However, if you wish to take five mistresses with you, it would be just as well to save up $24 million by the 31st December 1999. For the less affluent folk this huge sum would not be possible, but for a measly $8 million but you can still be frozen but with only one mistress.

If even $8 million is too much, then find a friend and both pay $6 million each and freeze one mistress between two of you. The choice is yours! What a wonderful thing is our capitalist society.

Now my friends of the Earth, if you think that collecting this type of cash may be somewhat delicate in such a short period of time, do not panic because as the end beckons nigh for the poor ordinary working class punters, some other capitalist will start building a huge fleet of people movers to take a few of us to a brave new world within a different solar system where crap is yet unknown.

These huge space ships will be named Peoples Interstellar Solar System Official Fleet Flights, commonly known as P.I.S.S.O.F.F.s and each one will be self sufficient for an indefinite period of space travel.

No doubt some cynics within the working class will start a slogan misusing and mispronouncing the P.I.S.S.O.F.F.s name and this is not really acceptable when one considers that this vehicle is for the salvation of mankind.

As any Bible reader would expect, two of each surviving animal species will also be taken aboard the special P.I.S.S.O.F.F. zoo ships, but at the present rate of animal extinction, this will probably mean two of the Royal corgis, two goldfish and two sheep with a mad brain disease.

However, our scientists are working on the D.N.A. system to such an extent that maybe we might only need to take with us a computer, a big freezer, a few buckets, rubber gloves, laboratory equipment and a couple of scientists.

The wonders of science never cease to amaze me and it's just as well that all scientists have solid moral ethics as otherwise how could we trust them?

It is anticipated that you will be able to choose either first or second class accommodation on all P.I.S.S.O.F.F. flights, but to obtain first class accommodation, you must qualify in three of the following sections:

(1) Be a close relation to the Queen.
(2) Really like Di and Fergie
(3) Be an Archbishop
(4) Have a degree in outer space navigation
(5) Know Captain Kirk personally
(6) Guarantee never to be ill
(7) Have attended a top Public school
(8) Be above the rank of major in the Coldstream Guards
(9) Be a member of Parliament who doesn't drink alcohol
(10) Be a civil servant who smiles

However, the P.I.S.S.O.F.F.s owners have specifically stated that all working class people must travel as second class passengers to avoid offending the upper class passengers. It is feared that some drunken working class person will make a pass at a royal princess during dinner and then get involved in semi-nude photographs to embarrass the Queen.

If there are any people that qualify for a first class cabin based upon the above preset qualification list, but they also live in a council or rented house, then they must be demoted to second class accommodation. All qualified zoo keepers, Scrappy Ken and Saresh's two brothers at present working in the meat processing department at Patel's Cheapo Pie Factory must travel in the zoo ships where they may go free of charge

At one second into the year 2000 AD (still yet to be re scheduled as 1AP (1st year after P.I.S.S.O.F.F.s), all 47,978 of these special sleek craft blast off from the Earth's surface from the special launching sites situated just outside Eccles. They soar majestically up into the beautiful sunlit blue skies of home heading for a new world and without much hope of ever returning to see this Mother Earth again.

Imagine the varying feelings on board these Arks of the future and from the people being left behind.

Those billions of people being left to rot would be fully justified in saying "it's all right for them lucky bastards just getting into a P.I.S.S.O.F.F. and pissing off, but how about us left down here in all this shite?"

Quite a reasonable question to be put, a question which was at that very moment being answered by a special new year's edition of the Queen's Speech being transmitted from 329,000 miles out in space:

"My people, I am pleased to be able to speak to you from this new palace of mine in the sky where I would like to wish everybody a most happy and prosperous new year. Now some of you may wonder why the whole Royal Family and the Conservative party have joined me on this adventure into space. Yes, I can explain this, it is because we can now rule the country from up here without the risk of death and disease, thus giving you the satisfaction of knowing that whatever happens in the future on Earth, your Royal Family and Conservative government will be with you until the end. The changing of the guard at Buckingham Palace will continue as normal until further notice.

"It is the deepest wish for my husband and myself to have brought you all with us, but space would not allow this. The Prime Minister also wishes to express great concern over the plight you are in. Once we have found our new home, to be called DikStar, we shall send all the P.I.S.S.O.F.F.s back to Earth to collect more people, providing that we consider that DikStar is big enough for all of us.

"Throughout history the British people have proved to the world that they are a charitable nation, so much so that I know that your message to us will be good luck and God go with you all. I also wish you all on Earth the very best of luck and God go with you. Each year, I will transmit an equally cheering Royal message to you for as long as life as we know it continues on earth. This is to show you just how much we care for you all.

"God and a lot of good luck be with you - now let's all sing together Auld Lang Syne followed by God save the Queen."

God bless the Queen!

So whilst the poor mortals on Earth rot, the privileged few fly on into unchallenged space, and far beyond, into a mysterious black space, seeking a new land, a new planet to re-establish a new future. What mystique, what fear of anticipation, what luck to be on board instead of rotting to death back on Earth. God, how everything smells shitty down there.

After 25 years of travel through permanent darkness, an amazing phenomenon becomes apparent (yes even to the conservative MPs), nobody was getting any older! Also, no matter what happened, not one of the females on board was becoming pregnant. We have a situation on board where a stagnant nation is now travelling through endless space. After a further 2,876 years in space, the divorce rate increased to such a level that a law was passed stating that you could only marry the same woman 18 times within a 500 year period.

By the year 3,400 AP it was calculated that every man had married every woman an average of four times, except in the Royal family where divorce was forbidden. Unfortunately all members of the Royal family had long since stopped speaking to each other for the past 2,754 years and still counting.

All things come to an end and sure enough, on 1st April in year 5,768 AP the P.I.S.S.O.F.F. fleet is forced to slow down as they reach a gatehouse in space with a sign that reads "Stop at Barrier for inspection". Not wishing to risk the wrath of this new civilisation in space, the leading ship pulls up alongside where he sees another sign "Switch off all engines", which he obeys immediately and the engines stop with a stutter.

Captain Ruffus Arthur Peters looks out of his flight deck window and sees a red button marked "ring for attention", so he presses the bell for a few seconds. Immediately, a frog shaped creature comes out, wearing a peaked cap and shouts out "Ogreasf jutyd moitgfd jikklre!" which from our single copy of the book "Languages from outer space" we found meant "Stop that bloody noise!"

"Sorry about the noise" said Captain R.A. Peters, "but can you direct me to a planet similar to Earth but uninhabited, where we can land and take over?" By now Froghead with peaked cap had switched a control on the front of his tunic that read "multi-lingual translation device" and replied rather abruptly, "Sorry but you must go back from whence you came, everything past this gate house is already owned by my people, the Frogomats, and we do not permit trespassers."

Taken aback by this rebuff, Captain R.A. Peters responded "Look here my man, we have travelled 5768 years from Earth and we must find a new planet soon. Surely one teenee weenee planet out there could be sold to us." Froghead replied harshly, "I won't tell you again, now piss off!"

With the only other choice of travelling back 5678 years to Earth to live on a planet covered in twenty feet of assorted crap and weird creatures as neighbours, Captain R.A. Peters blew off froghead's head with a sawn off ray gun and gave the message on the intercom to all the P.I.S.S.O.F.F.s "Tally ho chaps, let's go!" and off they set at warp speed 15, heading further into the unknown, deeper into dark space, past the frequent signs saying "redgjoiu poingfd erdfcou nhgfds oiujn!" which when translated meant "All trespassers will have legs removed for cooking in garlic butter in Frogomat restaurants!" Uncivilised bastards.

So, my readers in wonder, even out in space some 5678 miles from home, the human reaction is to knock seven bells out of anybody who wants us to stop what we are doing. That frog was only carrying out his orders and we blew off his green slimy head.

At last, 8765 years after leaving crappy Earth, a bright sun was sighted in the far far distance, and around this sun revolved several planets. "Yes!", shouted Prime Minister John Major, "not long now Norman, we shall soon have zero inflation, fixed exchange rates, low income tax, local property tax and value added tax again. You've had it easy for 8765 years but all good things must change, including love scenes with film stars."

Unfortunately all these planets around the sun were visited and were found to have surface temperatures of minus 150 degrees centigrade, too cold even for the royal princesses hearts. So onward they must travel, further and further and further and further and further..............until crash!, yes the lead ship crashed into a pair of iron gates, but luckily no serious damage resulted.

On the gates was another notice (which I have translated to save you the problem) "End of space - no further travel possible - turn around and go home". Now what would you do my fellow space addicts? The Government sat together with the Queen and some others from the Royal family and discussed in great depth this problem. The result? yes, you've guessed, the commando squad blew up the gates and the P.I.S.S.O.F.F. fleet made a run for it , passing a multitude of signs all saying "You are now lost in eternity forever".

After a further 34,876,987,456,765, years travelling through eternity with nobody getting any older and everybody marrying everybody else every six weeks, life starts to become really boring. Finally, the Prime Minister calls in the Home Secretary and shouts out "Home Secretary!, you call yourself a bloody Home Secretary! What bloody use are you in finding us a home in this eternal place? You're fired!"

With more than a glimmer of relief in his voice, the Home Secretary replied "Thank you very much indeed Prime Minister, it was becoming quite a frustrating job and worried me a great deal also."

As each million years passes by with total darkness outside, everybody becomes even more bored, but eventually the great day arrives when they see a bright light out in the far distance yonder. "What can this be?" said the navigator, Fred Ivan Neville Davidson, in a high pitched squeaky voice. After a further 567,895 years they reached this bright light which was placed over the top of a set of gates with the sign "You didn't listen chums, now you will travel even further into eternity".

"Bloody cheeky message if you ask me" shouted the Queen's New Zealander shoe cleaner Kevin Indiana William Illushias, "Once they know who we are they will sing a different tune." "Hang on a minute mate" responded the crown polisher, "when we get to the next gate, what's beyond that?" "Nothing of course you daft twat, just like we've seen all these millions and millions of years, absolutely bloody nothing" spouted KIWI. "I know you call it nothing, but nothing is something out here even if it means nothing to us. What I really mean is when does this space all end?"

"Yes mate, I see what you mean, we keep going through gates, travelling for millions of years until we reach a new gate. So, what's behind the last gate?" replies KIWI. "But we can't have a last gate mate, because there is no such thing as nothing, because it must be something, therefore there can't be a last gate" says the crown polisher in a worried tone. "Now hang on friend, if there is no last gate then this means that space goes on for ever?" "Yes kiddo, it means that this is eternity where it never ends even though the human brain cannot comprehend anything never ending. It's so mind bending that here we have discovered a power so great, so overwhelming, so incredible, so impossible that maybe this power is actually what we call God."

This is the God that I believe in Amen

Chapter 5

FROM RUBBER TO MURDER

"Democratic evolution continues to mutate and distort natural justice under an authoritative disguise to gain popular support from the masses but with no regard for the real good of Mankind."

Bishop Zalumpo
World Child Care Conference 1984

On the 10th March 1941, during an above average noisy night for that time of the year, a multitude of bombs (some very big and some not so big) were cascading down from the sky above in huge numbers over the south east of England including London. This particular day was during the Battle of Britain, a unique conflict where a "few" pilots from the heroic Royal Air Force flying Spitfires, the last line of defence of the free world in Europe, were fighting against great odds to protect the future for generations of children yet to come.

Such incredible bravery was taking place whilst various nations in Europe remained neutral and felt that Adolf Hitler was not such a bad guy after all. It was obvious to all people living in these countries that once Adolf and his lovely cronies took over and occupied Great Britain, he would then disband his army and leave them alone to brew beer and remain permanently pissed.

Notwithstanding this crass stupidity of utmost faith, it was whilst the British alone were defending the freedom of the world for all mankind, and the bombs were raining down upon London on the 10th March 1941 that an everyday act was taking place that would have its own small but everlasting impact upon the progress of mankind.

Thousands of petrified civilians were huddled together deep down inside the bowels of the earth in comparative safety on the Northern Line platform of

Kings Cross Underground station. This particular part of the tube network was being utilised that night, as indeed it was used on every blitz night, as an air raid shelter for protecting innocent citizens from the callous bombing of the night borne killers from the land of the superior race. That gang of blond haired arrogant wankers who chose civilian targets instead of military ones in their vain attempt to snuff out our brave people's resistance and Churchill's cigar.

These teutonic morons should have realised that if you are a race of people strong stomached enough to eat black pudding and faggots, then a few bombs could not break our resolve. Now please switch on your compact disc player and play a rendering of Rule Britannia played by Arthur Daley, salute the Union Jack and shout out the window, "Fuck the Germans".

Salvo after salvo of incendiary bombs cascaded down upon London, the centre of world democracy from some three hundred bombers flying at 15,000 feet above the earth's crust. Like gentle silver confetti these bombs of death and destruction slithered out from the bowels of these black coated death machines to burst like silver stars upon the deserted streets below.

Thousands upon thousands of destructive detonations, destroying a nation's inheritance and highlighting London's skyline so totally dominated by the sheen of reflected white stone of St. Paul's Cathedral. St. Paul's Cathedral, that centre of holy strength and invisible power that miraculously survived the German mighty onslaught to clearly signify to the surviving world the puny inability of human wrath within a greater sense of being.

At exactly midnight, corporal Peter Palmer of the Royal Engineers was holding tightly onto his beloved girlfriend, Jane Huntley, the youngest daughter of Lord Huntley of Reading, thinking that this could be their last few moments alive on earth. He was wrong.

With the incessant huge explosions reverberating

through the 500 feet of solid earth and concrete separating the platform of Kings Cross underground from the London pavements above, these two loving children, Peter and Jane, came together in a natural act of lovemaking that has ensured and maintained the continuation of mankind ever since Adam was an ant.

This coupling process was accidentally completed to its full glory due to the arrival of a 1000lb bomb that landed and exploded directly above their position of love making as the final malt vinegar stroke was struck. Such a tremendous impact from this huge bomb made normal reaction and withdrawal by Peter an impossibility and thus occurred the conception of the one and only Joan Huntly-Palmer just as Big Ben struck its twelfth stroke.

In everything bad you will find something good because if it had not been for a nutty bomber pilot who was recognised under the name of Herman Allballstz by his crew, or zat bastart vanker by his family and friends, then this beautiful baby girl would never have been conceived and a future saviour would have been consigned as yet another wasted ejaculated sperm batch to the rubbish heap of life.

So my undergraduates striving for absolute knowledge, your first lesson to be learnt from this chapter is to abstain from love making or playing with yourself during any bombing raid, unless your name is Herman and you are dropping the bombs from 15000 feet.

Peter and Jane were married the very next month, a very quiet affair, held at the express request of the bride's father who was not amused. A few seconds after he was informed by Jane "I have some great news for you daddy, you are going to be a grandfather." Lord Huntley looked up with horrendous bulging eyes and promptly started to choke on his glass of vintage port, which was his seventeenth of the afternoon.

After choking for more than three minutes, he then proceeded to spew out a mixture of well chewed extra mature stilton cheese thoroughly regurgitated and mixed with a full bottle of 1920 vintage port that had cost £120 per case only last week. The subsequent smell in the room was was most vile, but at the time was considered irrelevant to the assembly of family present as his lordship shouted out "I'll kill the dirty little common prick!"

Our nervous corporal thought that there would be no real advantage in explaining to his lordship that it was not the size of his prick that was important in such a situation, so he remained silent, as any underling should. His lordship eventually calmed down and decided that things could be organised quickly and quietly to maintain the family reputation and tradition to avoid any unnecessary scandal. He still persisted in calling his future son in law a little prick.

The happy couple were married the very next Saturday at Lands End registry office where sadly only a few close friends attended this beautiful ceremony. In fact a total of only seven people were present to witness the marriage vows, these seven personally tranported to the registry office by Lord Huntley.

This miniscule audience was a great disappointment to Laura, as she had sent invitations to a total of one hundred and sixteen relatives and friends of the family. It turned out that the other one hundred and nine got lost on their way down from London because they followed the directions given by Lord Huntley, who was greatly hoping that nobody would find their way to avoid further shame.

By following the instructions given, most of these guests arrived in Newcastle upon Tyne the very next day, which is some 400 miles from Lands End and in the opposite direction. This mass loss of waying was very distressing for the bride who naturally thought that the missing guests had not turned up because they thought she was a cheap dirty slut for being voluntarily screwed on a railway station and thence put in the club by a pox ridden bloody soldier from common stock who had a small prick to boot.

She was completely misguided in having such awful thoughts about these poor folk because they had in fact become very very lost by being given the wrong directions. Things were made doubly worse because all road signs had been removed in 1939 under government order just in case the Germans invaded.

No point in showing any invading Germans the directions to where they wanted to go, because if we could be sure that they would get lost whilst heading for where they wanted to go then they wouldn't get there at all would they? If they can't get there in the first place, they can't do what they were going to do if they could get there and therefore if we take down all the signs then they will all get lost and won't get there........

Now don't talk to me about maps! If I'd had my way, I'd have sent free one way tickets to to all the German army and then had our Home Guard put up misleading signs to send these Germans round and round in circles. Once the whole German army became knackered by driving round and round in circles for three weeks, then the Home Guard could have simply moved in and mopped up these teutonic fools and the war would have been over within a few days.

Unfortunately I was only a lad during this period of the second world war, living in an internment camp in Kent and my ideas held little credence with the War Office. We now know the consequences of ignoring the Dick Head factor of war planning, don't we? We had to invade France and come in contact yet again with those garlic puffing queers who also drank German beer.

To this day, Lord Huntley's brother, Cuthbert Huntley and his dog Henry have never been found, after they were last seen just outside Exeter thumbing a lift (clever dog) back to London after the Bentley ran out of petrol. The Bentley is also missing presumed dead and sixty seven guests have never returned from Newcastle.

Lord Huntley was so furious about this marriage of

his daughter to a commoner with a name like Palmer. Fuming every day, he spat out venomous comments such as "Sounds just like a bar of bloody soap!"

After several weeks of acid indigestion, which automatically followed his consumption of liberal quantities of vintage port, Lord Huntley decided that his daughter must change her married name to Huntley-Palmer. If Laura refused her father's wishes then she would be disinherited from his will, or against his will. Such family bickering was greatly helped and relieved by the convenient demise of the much abused corporal husband, who was killed during the D day landings when he stepped onto a banana skin and broke his neck as clean as a whistle.

This was an unusual death at that particular time because he was the only one to have slipped and broken his neck on the only banana skin seen on the beach during the D Day landings. Lord Huntley assumed that this was poetic justice and reflected God's revenge against Peter's poor withdrawal symptoms experienced at Kings Cross Station. Such withdrawal problems no longer presented the same danger, no matter the minuscule size of his prick.

Whatever the reason for our poor corporal's demise, such a sad passing away on just an unfortunate slip-up, conveniently resolved any arguments concerning the child's name - Lady Laura Huntley-Palmer it would be. After the ending of this bloody war, the newly named Huntley-Palmer family became furious at dinner parties they attended around the locality when the local gentry made common jokes about a local biscuit factory in Reading, which they had absolutely no connection with whatsoever. I personally hate custard creams.

The beautiful baby Laura proceeded to be brought up as the granddaughter of a Lord and received only the very best education and training that money could buy. Not for her the stupidity of progressive socialist learning techniques that allowed you to leave school knowing how to slash tyres but not being able to add up your dole money accurately.

Laura was eventually allowed to attend Lancaster University to take an Honours Economics degree where she learnt much more about the real life that existed outside her previous life of Lordly manors and the Sloane crowd. After three years she passed her honours degree with the highest marks ever achieved in this course which highlighted the fame she would eventually achieve later in life.

Today you can still see the plaque mounted above the entrance foyer of the main reception office of the university which reads, "Laura Huntley-Palmer 1985, achieved a 100% pass mark in her Final Economics Honours exams, she really takes the biscuit". Now you start to realise just how annoying these jokes can become.

Since Laura learnt at the age of three how to draw pictures depicting the behaviour of sex mad rabbits, she decided after leaving university that her vocation in life was to use her skills to help the poor people of the world have a better choice of how to lead their lives.

Many of the rabbits posing for her pictures became very upset and annoyed at having Laura watching and sketching them screwing away (as rabbits do) in their burrows at night and they started to mislead her by committing unnatural sexual acts with some field mice who would in any case sleep with anyone.

Laura was heartbroken in 1987 when Walt Disney refused to accept her rabbit pictures as entries for the "Cartoon character for the future" competition but her milkman Pat paid £5 for each one of the now famous scribblings. Pat the dairy produce vendor is now serving six years imprisonment for raping a horse during Horse Guards parade last year.

Laura was unfortunately in Spain on holiday at that particular time and was very upset at missing out on such a spectacle - what a painting that would have made. It was quite astounding the amount of horse shite that this particular horse dropped during this sex attack by Pat. It may have hurt the horse, but surely the horse could have controlled its natural functions of life and not have unloaded unwanted fruits in front of the Royal Family.

The Royal Family never did understand exactly what happened that day to bring about it's fruity dropping episode, but it is rumoured that they have requested the same entertainment repeated next year, but without the same big pile of shite.

A repeat event can be arranged but it must be with a different horse in the major starring role. This is because the original "cocking horse" suffered serious internal damage thus putting paid to any repeat performance this year. The "cocking horse" has decided to employ his expertise and experience in a diversified and more profitable field, and is now the star of a new blockbuster film, "They screw horses, don't they?"

So successful is this first film that a follow up film "The milkman rides again" is already being pencilled in for shooting next year. Rehearsals for the horse in this new movie are being kept to a minimum at the particular request of the horse who is walking very badly indeed and really hates Pat the milkman.

Exactly a year ago, next Wednesday, Laura took up her first appointment in the commercial world as assistant publicity manager at a large rubber processing factory. This company, originally named Poke's Rubber Band Factory Limited, had its main (and only) factory situated alongside the River Thames at Putney for over 100 years.

When the demand for Poke's rubber bands died down during the beginning of the rock and roll years, the company had its name changed to Poke's Condom Factory Limited and they proceeded to design a new programme of condom products. These multi coloured items were produced for the new liberated society which discovered that screwing around with anybody was OK after all, providing it wasn't with your wife.

Poke's began an advertising campaign based upon an

existing insurance company's successful slogan *Get the strength of a Poke's Condom Company around you.* Such forthright and pseudo-pornographic messages caused an absolute uproar in 1987, which was a long time before satellite television showed us what televised sexually orientated films were really all about.

Poke's were taken to court by the local Women's Institute and the judge fined them £12,000 for corrupting the minds of the nation whilst the people's cocks were thoroughly disturbed. Such an expensive slap on the wrist made them take a more gentle approach to selling these items of family planning and they modified their corporate slogan to *Don't have a Poke without a Poke,* which again unfortunately missed the whole point of the exercise.

Four years ago, when the condom recession hit the industry as a whole and sales dropped by some 73.76%, it almost caused Poke's to close its doors to all rubber lovers alike. The company's owner, old Joe Poke aged 87 with gout, became very worried about the health of the nation as he could not be convinced that it was Poke's condom sales alone that had dropped by 73.76%.

He ranted on about the need for more sex education at an earlier age and blamed the actual lack of poking as the root cause of his business problems. "But my friends, nobody has a poke without a poke - look at our advertising campaign, it confirms it." Peter Punch, the advertising manager, being totally fed up with this old fart's stupid ideas for the many stressful years he had worked for the company, reacted somewhat aggressively at this point of the meeting by saying "Mr. Poke, Poke your pokey pokes right up where queers poke without pokes."

Poke's now have a new advertising manager.

This is the reason why Laura was promoted to advertising manager after only eight hours in the job as assistant manager - this indicating a real a rising star in the poking industry no less. Peter Punch is now an ex advertising manager, taking hard drugs whilst living with an Ethiopian Jewish woman in a shoe box located just alongside Euston Station.

Oh. how the mighty can fall. Never tell a Poke how to poke if you want to keep your job.

Laura went to work on this new challenge with great gusto, intent on finding a new marketing approach to increase the sales and profitability of this ailing rubber factory. Within a few years Laura planned that whenever you thought of poking, you would only think of headaches and Poke's. She thoroughly researched the subject and found that business had fallen drastically, taking a turn for the worse, since the launch of the dishwashable condoms produced by their main rivals *Johnies Rubber Company.*

These people had a wonderful television advertising campaign which incorporated that famous Italian WallyWash dishwasher manufacturer and the Zappaz powder with the new improved blue biological fabric conditioner and sperm remover. This had proved to be an incredibly successful promotional campaign, screened six times nightly at times when most people's dreams go to condoms. Not only did it promote a superior condom to that of Poke's, but it was also fully dishwashable, using an advanced dishwasher and washing powder that avoided the silt build up problems normally associated with washing this type of product.

On television you would see a beautiful model simply stating to the viewing nation "New Zappaz powder with new improved blue biological fabric conditioner and sperm remover is the only powder recommended by the WallyWash turbo dishwasher which comes complete with special spunk extraction system making it ideal for washing the everlasting Johnies dishwashable condom with built in pussy fur lining."

This advertising was a tremendous success and helped to sell over four million Johnies dishwashable condoms at £103.60 each in the UK alone during the first year of launch. Each one was sold with a free packet of Zappaz powder and a coupon giving 6p off the next Giant sized 50Kg bulk pack which guaranteed to give over six thousand washes.

The Johnies dishwashable condom could also cleverly be purchased on instalments over a period of 20 years at a cost of only 14p per week.

Using government statistics, this weekly cost gives a unit cost of only 2.7374 pence for each average usage, a very cheap rate compared with the cost of some 22 pence for the old fashioned disposable type item. With this huge saving in the purchase of a necessary commodity, complete with a free lifetime guarantee, how could you go wrong?

Indeed on the condom box of the new "Johnies Dishwashable Life Policy Condom" was printed,

Lifetime Guarantee Conditions

We are so confident of our condoms absolute protection that we guarantee to pay £50,000 insurance if the Dishwashable Life Policy Condom fails and pregnancy results. Please send pregnancy test results together with unwashed condom and proof of intercourse to our research department, address on the back of this package

Personalisation

To offset objections being made by spouses and/or lovers, the Johnies Rubber Company is now offering a free printing service to print personalised names onto our Dishwashable Life Policy products in bold print across the head of the condom. This will allow the spouse and/or lover to quickly make a visual check prior to penetration to ensure that their own named personal condom is being used. We understand the personal nature of such items and wish to assist our clients and their partners achieve total satisfaction.

This printing service quickly became a powerful

marketing tool, so to speak, and within a few days of its TV launch, multiple purchases were being made by the majority of customers. Remarkable as it may sound, some 47% of all purchases of this printed condom were supplied with men's names printed in pink or silver ink. Indeed, over 19% chose the name of Arnold.

Of particular interest was an order from a traffic warden who requested several condoms with the names of Rupert, Lassie, Auntie, Minister, Polly the parrot and Goldie the fish.

A fish!? Well, maybe there is a new market for blow up fish dolls.

A special part exchange deal is at present being promoted in local newspapers stating:

Don't let your partner embarrass your sex life!

Part exchange your washables for only £45.63

The idea here was very smart. Once you finished with one partner, it would be very embarrassing to have Judy printed on the end when your new love of your life was called Jack. The job is the same, but the name has been changed to protect the innocent. What happens to the old condoms sent back in part exchange? I've got no idea folks, but if you request a new one with the name of Bigfellow and you receive it with teeth marks in the side, start becoming suspicious - I can't divulge any more I'm afraid without my readers becoming aware of my sexual traits and preferences.

So, how could Poke's change from being a loser to a winner in the face of such organised competition? Indeed, was such a turnabout even possible when one looks at the general market reaction to Poke's existing product line? Maintaining one's customer loyalty was not the name of the game in this particular trade because most of Poke's customers were now dead or growing onions.

This was the serious dilemma that Laura had to face, not without some traumatic trembles during breakfast time each day. After all, she couldn't even be sure if the product she was about to unfold would be satisfactory for her clients as she she would have to rely upon somebody else to do the testing. Now we all know how big a liar a condom tester can be, don't we?

Her first action was to organise a full market research programme by taking a sample of some 2 million people which necessitated the use of 670 market researchers. These researchers were strategically placed at the entrance of all the tube stations in London, dole queues, public toilets, doctors surgeries, VD clinics, parks and barbers shops.

Over three months were spent completing this massive in-depth market research test. During this period, 164 of the female researchers were arrested for prostitution and 43 of the male researchers were punched in the face or kicked in the balls by indignant clients being questioned. Sadly, one of the poor transvestite researchers was kicked to death by a mob of Chelsea football fans as he asked the question "Do you use condoms during your homosexual relationships?"

Armed with their printed questionnaires and dressed in bright yellow suits with the huge words of POKE'S CONDOM SURVEY written on the back of their jackets these zealous and greatly enthusiastic army of researchers headed off every day to their special pitch as part of the campaign to revolutionise the protection of pricks. Just try answering the questions of this survey yourselves, it's easy folks:

CONDOM SURVEY

We would be grateful if you could answer honestly the following questions where your answers will assist us develop a new type of condom to greatly advance the comfort of mankind. Your name will remain confidential to us but if you tick the box "reward" then we will send you a free box of standard Poke's in appreciation of your assistance on this survey.

Section 1 - Sex preferences

a. Are you normal as understood by the Bible yes/no
(Please ask for explanation if you are not aware of the Bible)

b. *Are you queer?* yes/no

c. *Are you a bit of each (AC/DC)?* yes/no

d. *You cannot decide?* yes/no

e. *Do you have a full set of (2) balls?* yes/no

(If "no", please specify how you lost it/them in full detail)

Section 2 - safety procedures

a. *Do you use condoms?* yes/no
 If yes, please specify brand name and model type?

b. *Do you just leave it to God's will?* yes/no

c. *No problem because it's too limp anyway?* yes/no

d. *You just don't give a shite?* yes/no

Section 3 - Preferences

a. *Prefer a washable condom?* yes/no

b. *Would you wash with the crockery?* yes/no

c. *Wash with the bed linen?* yes/no

d. *Hand wash for perfection?* yes/no

Any other comments on re-usable condoms:

..

Name:...............................Age:......................

Nationality:.........................Place of Birth:............

Would you like your reward sent?....yes/no

Laura arranged for all of this data to be fed into a

giant IBM computer which had been specially programmed for this research project, and it came to the following conclusions:

> *Re-usable condoms were cheap to use*
>
> *Re-usable condoms were messy to clean*
>
> *Re-usable condoms were banned at the launderette.*
>
> *Hotels refused to clean them under "Room Service"*
>
> *Bylaws in Conservative controlled council areas banned these re-usable condoms from public display on washing lines*
>
> *In Labour controlled council areas it was dangerous to leave re-usable condoms on washing lines as they would certainly be stolen.*
>
> *Re-usable condoms useless for the randy four times a night couples - ardour grew less awaiting the washing machine to complete its cycle.*
>
> *Most washing machines left a fine residue of detergent on the inside of the re-useable condom and "Jesus Chriiiiiiisstttt!" that hurts.*
>
> *Breakfast cereal tastes strange in households where re-useable condoms are employed.*

Laura realised immediately, and said "It's so bloody obvious - da de da!" The Johnies Rubber Rubber Company had sold these millions of re-usable condoms because nobody discussed the problems in public! Hey Presto, the answer is nigh, let's go and finish off these Johnies once and for all.

"Identifying the problem is the difficult part of solving the same problem" is a quotation made famous by the exploits of Willy Wonker when he built his famous chocolate factory during the last century. He found that throwing live chickens into hot chocolate just gave him shitty tasting chocolate and no chocolate eggs. I learnt recently that if farmers were to plough their land during the hours of darkness then the weeds would not grow, this being due to the non germination of the weeds without daylight. With this knowledge in my pocket, I could reduce weed killer usage by some 537,000,000 tons per year worldwide and increase the sale of infrared night glasses from 12,800 to 45,876,400 per year if only I can convince the world's farmers to only work at night.

For those of us that know farmers well, we only need to offer these miserable bastards a grant of 30% towards these infrared glasses together with a bonus of 3p on every ton less of weedkiller they use, to get them to dress in black and work at night for the rest of their lives. What a lovely thought to consider; all farmers so knackered during the day that they would stay away from the village pubs and leave it all to us normal happy folk. Farmers wives would be also extremely grateful to me for such a move.

Laura took action! She arranged for the following advertisement to be placed in EVERY newspaper in the land saying:

BUY A REAL CONDOM!
No mess, no trouble
Are you fed up with the burnt rubber smells and strange foreign lumps in your cornflakes? Do you have red irritation regularly? Do your family complain of stomach pains the day after your saturday night romp?
We know the answer is YES to all these questions! Now face the real truth and say to the world, "A Johnies Condom is a no Con Dom". Get back to the old fashioned traditional way - get yourself some ORIGINAL POKES CONDOMS - no mess, no gut pains, just performance.

Boy oh boy, did this work the oracle.

Within a few days, the classified ad columns of all the national and local newspapers were flooded with small ads as per the following random selection.

"Going cheap! 3 (three) little used (345 performances each) Johnies reusable condoms for sale, printed with the names of TOM, DICK and HARRY. These

bright pink condoms are for sale as a job lot for only £50 - buyer collects. Alternatively we can exchange for 5 gross of the new POKES ORIGINALS"

"Giant sized specially made JOHNIES RE-USABLE condom with FRANK printed on the end tip. 4 years old but only used once. For sale at £56 or will exchange for night out with any blonde haired fellow between 12 and 89 years old. I am prepared to experiment and I will pay for dinner."

"Ex stockist of JOHNIES RE-USABLE condoms has vast stock of over 35,000 units now being offered for rent at £3.00 per night. You use we clean. Also over 30 tons of the special Zappaz detergent powder in 100Kg sacks at only £12 per sack. Any offer considered for the lot"

Yes Siree! Laura had cracked the problem and obtained the golden egg within her first year with Poke's and to make matters even better she increased sales even more by renaming the product as POKES COCK-A-HOOP ORIGINAL CONDOMS. Using the latest projected sales figures, Poke's are on target for selling over 200,000,000 condoms this year, which equates to the amount of rubber extracted from 25,876,432 rubber trees - thank God for Mother Nature.

With every success story comes another loser and in this case the Flamebrick Tyre Company is rather pissed off at not being able to get enough rubber for their tyre production. Laura phoned their marketing director to explain that it is understandable that the public would always put their pricks before their cars - or indeed would rather get the bus than have fourteen screaming kids and a flabby wife. Such is the result of our capitalist society.

Laura's next experience was to fall in love with the production director of the company, a tall ex carpet layer who went by the name of "Red" but whose real name was Patrick Percival Curry. He came from a rich background in Bradford, where they still run an Indian food canning factory supplying products to over 43 countries all across the world. As a young man, Red did not consider that

Indian food making suited his character or his sense of smell, so he opened up "Reds Skins" which was a specialised company for laying carpets, linos, wood block flooring etc. In 1985 he completed a huge contract for fitting out the Taja Temple in Southall with carpet costing some £287,000, but alas when it came to collecting payment, a dispute of some considerable magnitude arose.

Although the order specified "carpet of many colours", upon inspection of this beautiful carpet, it was observed that it depicted a scene of Christ's crucifixion which was considered by many within the temple as somewhat off the mark as far as "suitable for the job for which it was intended" clause specified on the official purchase order was concerned.

Red did a runner and applied for the job of Production Director at Poke's which he obtained after informing the company at the interview that his family owned 43% of Pokes stock and if he didn't get the job then they would buy a further 8% of the stock and fire them all. With this rich incentive, they gave him the job at which he proved to be a first class, albeit a rich and complete wanker - hardly the profession for a company with such a product line .

Laura found that by convincing Red that they should continually test the company's products together that life was not quite so boring after all. On one particular occasion, the evening was progressing towards another testing session when the third bottle of Barolo Italian red wine was produced to celebrate something - of which I know not what.

This most potent of Italian grape extraction did it's dirty deed and allowed them both to become completely smashed so that the testing commenced without the subject to be tested being fitted in it's correct location - they were bareback riding so to speak. As is poetic justice in such a live situation, the Joker from the big church above rang the liberty bell and Laura was fertilised perfectly. Pregnancy would slow up most people, but not for Laura the condom Queen.

"For God's sake Peter, I know you're the father and you love me and the baby, very deeply, but I've a career to think about which I'm not going to ruin just to give you the pleasure of having your own child. You should have been more careful, particularly after drinking three bottles of wine - after all it's you that's supposed to wear these bloody things, not me! I'm going to get rid of it!"

With paternal tears running down his carpet laying cheeks, Peter sobbed a heartbroken plea, "Laura my love, you can keep your career and have the baby as well because Poke's has a wonderful child nursery to look after the babies and young children of the staff. We can get married immediately my love."

"Peter, Jesus Christ! can you imagine the permanent jokes and humiliation that would be a constant feature for me if it became known that I was pregnant whilst working at Poke's. Here I am the advertising manager - soon to become the marketing director of a company selling condoms, and I become pregnant! Our competitors will photograph me fully impregnated and use this photograph in a worldwide promotional campaign with the headlines 'Poke's director gets poked to show how good Poke's are!'. No Peter I cannot live a life of permanent ridicule working with my peers. I'd love to have a child; in about fifteen years time, but in the meantime this unwanted little troublesome brat must go. I do not want to be impregnated, pregnant, enceinte, gravid, in an interesting condition, in a delicate condition, heavy with, big with, expecting, expecting a happy event, expectant, carrying, with child, in the family way, up the pole, up the spout, in the club, have a bun in the oven, fallen preggers, parturient or obstetric. Got it!"

I must admit that Laura had definitely not left much doubt in my mind about her feelings.

Peter tried even harder to convince Laura of the grave error of having an abortion over the following few weeks, but to no avail, and she furthermore started becoming paranoiac about being found out by her fellow executives. "You must promise me Peter not to tell a living soul" she would repeat over and over and over again.

Beset with grief, Peter decided to embark upon a very daring and dangerous plan of action to halt this impending murder. His plan became a personal crusade based upon the value he placed on the unborn life form containing his own flesh and blood, so soon to be done away with and incinerated, unless he took this direct positive action. The Lone Ranger rides again.

The following weekend, he secretly drove to the secluded village of Leekypryd in North Wales, where he rented a small ex pit worker's cottage for £15.00 per week, on a six month tenancy agreement. Inside this stone dwelling, which had been built during the coal rush of the 1880's, you could actually feel the community spirit that must have existed within this hard working, and tightly knit community that survived such in-depth poverty of the day.

Unless you were a short arsed Welshman, you had the problem of continually banging your head as you walked through each tiny doorway separating the minuscule rooms, but this particular cottage ideally suited Peter's future planned needs because it was situated in a completely isolated position some half a mile from any other building in the village and was fully surrounded by a multitude of Welsh Elm trees. These trees were also equally stocky and short of stature.

For the next three weeks, Peter spent all of his spare time fitting out this cottage specifically for the task ahead, to save his unborn child from the gallows! No fear of ridicule towards Laura by other people in this world was going to be responsible for the murder of his first offspring, even if the potential murderer did work for a condom factory. Peter visited the local village pub, "The Wanky Welshman" three times per day for his breakfast, lunch and dinner where the daily special dish was always leek soup which sold at 10p a pint.

To accompany this vile steaming brew was also always a lump of Coalminers bread which consisted of pure bran and a few lumps of coal dust for luck. The process of consuming this leek soup caused a big strain on Peter's thighs because of the necessity to kneel down on the floor whilst spooning up this bowl of Clwyd steaming crap.

Such kneeling was essential because the table height was too short for normal eating, thus prohibiting the possibility of accommodating a normal height Englishman with his longer legged skeletal pattern and larger brain. Despite this culinary deprivation of the worst kind, Peter managed to absorb enough calories to complete his task at hand and to be ready to save this one precious unborn human life having his same DNA pattern.

"Joan, I'm sorry about my selfishness a few weeks ago, I can now fully understand your feelings and you were right and the baby must go. To show you just how wrong and how very sorry I am to have been so unreasonable, I've arranged for my old college friend Dr. Kidclip, who is the foremost abortion specialist at Leekypool hospital to perform the operation this coming weekend. With his new technique of using liquid nitrogen to freeze the foetus into a hard ball and then using a standard corkscrew to remove it - just like a cork from a wine bottle - the operation will take only twenty minutes. He is so confident of a perfectly simple extraction that we can still then go to see the *Babes in the Wood* Christmas pantomime in the evening".

Laura was totally overwhelmed at Peter's change of heart and felt a tumultuous rush of gratitude towards him for his new understanding and perfect planning of the abortion, even if she was somewhat apprehensive about the corkscrew. She would not even have to miss any days at work and therefore nobody would find out. Pokes reputation would remain intact. Also, she would still see her favourite pantomime and she would be non impregnated when she went to visit her cousin Cecilia and her six children for the Christmas holidays.

Sure enough, Peter drove to Laura's house in his Ford Granada estate car to collect her on the following Saturday morning, at 6.45 am ready for the plot to begin. This coincided with a fantastic fiery sunrise which flooded red light across Poke's Condom Factory roofline and whilst several thousand pigeons were crapping, as only pigeons can crap, all over Trafalgar Square. Nelson's column was completely encrusted with this pigeon dung, but Peter was far past worrying about such indelicacies hanging onto Horatio's marble penis.

The first sea-gulls of the day could also be heard screeching and chasing their way towards the endless garbage that polluted the grey and black surface gleam of that old man river Thames, she just keeps rolling along. If we really do have the new strident salmon now reappearing within the upper reaches of the river Thames then we should quickly study the make up of this hardy and very stupid fish.

By understanding their ability to survive within a sewer for part of their lives, we may still yet learn how to survive ourselves during the forthcoming nuclear fusing of this planet's surface structure which will most surely occur once pollution takes over everything.

Peter chatted away to Laura in the car as they drove west on the M4 motorway, towards bloody Wales, as if nothing was out of place - after all it's not everyday you get the chance of being screwed by a corkscrew and have an abortion at the same time, is it? At midday, he pulled into a Little Chef roadside fast food restaurant to have a snack before completing the long trip to the land of choirs. They both ordered American Breakfasts with toast and coffee.

The food was good but have you tried getting comfortable sitting in one of those unbelievably stupid fixed chairs they use and have the nerve to describe as seating? I would like to meet the person who designed these seats and explain to him that not all people are small, squat and have backsides like small saucepan lids. Despite the seating pain, Peter considered that all was going to plan.

Right on cue, Laura visited the ladies room prior to starting her breakfast. Peter quickly without any sign of panic, added 25cc of the undetectable drug DownAndOut to Laura's coffee to start the clever plot. I must explain now that the drug DownAndOut is produced in Colombia by the TacoDrug Company and is regarded as an illegal substance in all countries in the world excepting Italy, Papua New Guinea and the Falkland Islands. It has a massive black market in the rest of the world for doping horses, young boys and British politicians. It is suspected that Winston Churchill's war cabinet took this drug.

The next time Laura knew anything was when she awoke some six hours later in a windowless cellar which was located below the rented cottage in Leekypryd. With a terrible headache and in total confusion, she blurted out "What's happening Peter!" in absolute panic, which is understandable as she probably thought that they had just lost the corkscrew. "It's terrible Laura! A nuclear bomb has been dropped on London and we are at war with China!" he shouted with such devastating effect that Laura had no hesitation in believing his every word of doom.

She cried out, "How about Poke's Condom Factory, is that also destroyed by the bomb?" At this question, if Peter ever did feel any guilt over his plot to save his unborn child then this guilt was now washed away for ever. My undergraduates must accept that Laura was indeed a very selfish person to worry about a condom factory when we are at nuclear war with China.

"But are we safe Peter?" she cried out in panic with tears trickling down her bemused face. "Yes my love, I heard the warning on the car radio as we crossed the

Severn Bridge and managed to reach this basement flat. Fortunately this flat is owned by my friend "Tit Rubbing Williams" who runs the *Big Breast Club* in Mayfair which specialises in personal services for retired executives and generally for any other type of rich dirty bastard. If you've got the money you can feel the goods - is his motto".

I can confirm that it did indeed start to rain as Peter reached the halfway mark across the Servern bridge.

"The BBC has informed us that the country is under martial law and that everyone must stay indoors for their own safety for at least 10 weeks until the radioactive fallout has been washed away by the rains or blown away by the winds. We shall be informed by the BBC when it is safe to go outside and they will give us twice daily reports covering the current situation. China has been mostly destroyed by American retaliatory strikes and no further bombs are expected to drop on us. It is indeed a world disaster, but with care and patience we will live to fight another day and produce another condom."

Peter then switched on the radio and the BBC news repeated a similar story to confirm the disaster reported by Peter, or so Laura thought. In fact, Peter had taken a recording of the radio play, *Chinky Destruction,* which had several BBC news broadcasts as part of the screenplay and had arranged a very clever series of news programmes of farcical proportions. It is difficult to fool all the people all of the time, but you can fool anybody during a nuclear war.

As incredible as this plot sounds, it was made easier for Peter to pull off due to the influence of the drug Stupefy which Peter fed to Laura as part of his plot. Stupefy is a hallucinatory drug used by politicians before they appear on TV chat shows, particularly on Sunday mornings. Peter added this drug to Laura's tea and coffee in minute doses - God bless him.

To cut a long story short, this illusion of a world nuclear holocaust was continued for just over ten weeks without any serious problems, and would have carried on for a longer period of time except for carelessness of the confidence trickster.

On the Sunday morning during their tenth week hiding from the radiation poisoning, Laura woke up much earlier than her drug induced sleep should have permitted, and heard Peter closing the front door of the flat. This opening and closing of doors during a nuclear aftermath seemed somewhat difficult to comprehend bearing in mind that your balls could drop off as a result, and one knows just how much Peter thinks of his balls.

She crept out of the bedroom and moved as quiet as a starved mouse wearing foam soled slippers into the kitchen where Peter was drinking a glass of fresh milk and reading the Mail on Sunday. Fresh milk, Sunday newspaper?????

Peter was completely taken aback that his super plan had hiccupped very badly over a mere glass of milk and the right to a free press, and in any case why the hell wasn't she asleep as arranged? Being a professional carpet layer, having sold christian carpets to moslems, had previously taught him the benefit of instant reply as the most effective way to overcome loose carpet edges.

He reacted with an air of love and pleasure as he asked "My darling, are you feeling better this morning? Let me get you a nice cup of coffee." He then proceeded to explain that twice a week the army delivered milk and newspapers in special anti radioactive trucks and left them outside the houses in plastic bags. This was of course an off the cuff response and a real crappy excuse because the game was up, but not quite yet.

Laura returned to the lounge where she sat down to think about this train of confusing events and to Peter's annoyance refused to take any of the wide variety of drug laced drinks being offered to her. Without drugs inside her system she heard a noise at 11.00 am that sounded like millions of tortured hyenas with their balls being cut off screaming for help. This noise was not of course from a band of castrated cats, but was in fact the local welsh chapel choir giving their interpretation of singing a choral rendering of some crappy song. During the aftermath of a nuclear war you did not get welsh choirs, chapel or not, singing amongst the nuclear fall out!

As a final but vain attempt at covering up his dirty deeds, Peter tried to convince Laura that this awful noise was caused by a band of mutated renegades from Bootle infected with radiation poisoning going on a looting spree. Great answer for a kids film, but not good enough for a wiz kid from Poke's Condom Factory now unaffected by any dose of Stupefy drug. "You bastard Peter, now I realise what the fucking hell is going on, you want to stop me having that bloody abortion!!!!"

Ten weeks late in finding out, but a very accurate assessment of the current status.

The job was done, the game was up and they returned to London where they both found that a nation wide police search had been in existence for over six weeks looking for the "Long Lost Condom Couple" as the newspapers put it. When they explained that they had been kidnapped by people they didn't know and held at a place they didn't know and released for a reason they didn't know, the police quickly lost interest.

Why didn't Laura speak up and tell the police the truth? Well, she couldn't allow the full true story to be made public because the ridicule would be international and absolute, so she went along with this lie. To make everything look even better, she informed her friends that whilst held in captivity she was forced to have sex with Peter for the amusement of the kidnappers and she was now very much pregnant.

Indeed she stated to the world that if anything good could be taken from this horrifying experience then it was that she and Peter would soon be getting married and having this love child which had been conceived under such difficult conditions. Little did she know that Peter had much different ideas. Peter now knew that for the rest of his life he would never look at another bowl of leek soup.

A beautiful son was born to Laura on the 25th December that year and this innocence of humanity was immediately given up for adoption to Peter's sister, Maria, who was married to a Jewish tailor named Joe Zeus. The newborn adopted son was named George Zeus and was brought up under strict Jewish standards including the skin removal operation. Just why do they do that?

At the age of 18 he entered the Rome School for Medical Research where within ten years he was to become recognised as the world's greatest medical scientist. By the age of 45 he would have won the Nobel prize no less than fourteen times. His greatest achievement was his "molecule conversion" theory which allowed human excreta (shite) to be converted into a liquid fuel that replaced the need to use petrol in internal combustion engines, yet once burnt left absolutely no destructive gases within the atmosphere.

This development alone saved the bacon of the ozone layer which had almost been destroyed by man's lack of caring and greed. It also stopped the ice caps melting, eliminated air pollution and ensured that no more jungles were killed by acid rain. The only side effect to this huge advancement for mankind was that the whole world smelt like shite.

All the buildings everywhere throughout the world were covered with a sticky grimy brown coating which dropped down from the atmosphere like brown hail stones as a direct result of burning this new fuel called Shitrol.

The people living in Wales never noticed the difference but the Queen complained bitterly and spoke about it on the David Crust programme by saying: "No monarch in history has ever had to live in so much excreta (shite) and why should she!" Prince Charles spoke angrily to his sunflowers shouting: "Don't you start talking behind my back concerning how I always now smell like excreta (shite). Remember if I have to live in excreta (shite), then so do you!"

The Prime Minister spoke to the House of Commons during the "Pollution or Shite" campaign saying, "We the Conservative party, fully support the humane developments given to mankind by the brilliance of our Anglo-Jewish scientist Mr. G. Zeus who has showed us the way forward in saving the destruction of this planet. Living with excreta (shite) and having to bear this awful permanent smell (shitty smell) is no new experience to us. We the Conservative party have had to bear the same smell ever since the Labour party (working class dictatorship) was formed." One of the Trade Union sponsored Members jumped up and shouted, "I'll punch anybody who accuses me of having made love to a Conservative little boy!"

So "Gee-Zeus" as he became known, was accepted as the second coming together as he had the answers to save mankind from himself?

Other developments by Gee-Zeus:

A range of tablets to turn any skin colour into the colour of your choice. Racial tension no more.

Personal pocket sized blow up aeroplanes.

A tunnel from London to Sydney via the centre of the earth. water would be pumped both ways to take the heat away from the molten lava and to power our generating stations.

The GEE-ZEUS WATCH to analyse al1.

This watch was the greatest invention of all times as it allowed a constant analysis and monitoring of a person's character. Restriction of common liberty laws prevented the governments of the world enforcing compulsory wearing of this miracle from Gee-Zeus.

Once strapped onto the wrist it was programmed to analyse everything about you and every time you pressed the red button, it would analyse you from one or more of the following characteristics:

Normal - Queer - AC/DC - Flasher - Rapist - Child molester
Animal molester - murderer - German Vanker - Italian hero
Wanker - Tosser - Mad - Liar - Arsehole - Complete arsehole
Nice - Great - Fantastic - As good as Dick Head - God

A special additional programme has been added to the Labour party EUROTWATCH version which screams out "FOUL!" if any of these people dare to become reasonable in their approach on any issue or if they oppose the party line concerning Europe.

So far this message has been heard only once, whilst the EUROTWATCH was on the wrist of a shadow minister on a visit to Brussels but he has since been liquidated. Some further 300 of these EUROTWATCHES have just been ordered by the Labour Party Central Office, but to save constant embarrassment the programmes analysing "arsehole", "child molester", "Wanker", "Queer" and "Complete arsehole" have been deleted from this special edition.

In response to various critical comments made recently concerning the leader of the labour party (ie: He's a complete Scottish twit), an additional programme has been installed to operate every ten seconds saying in a Glaswegian working class dialect "My name may be a common Smith but I'm going to be the greatest leader since Stalin".

Great thinkers the Labour party. Why is it we have so many blinking Scotsmen holding power in government and the unions?

Gee-Zeus was eventually invited to speak at both Houses of Parliament, which he kindly accepted and where he presented a most awe inspiring performance, outlining his thoughts for the future of the world. At the end of this epic occasion he gave out free personally signed EUROTWATCHES as a gesture of his kindness to all members present. After only two days the Speaker in the House of Commons had to ban the wearing of these watches because all day long some 650 of these EUROTWATCHES were shouting out their programmed analyses of "wanker" (431 members), "Arsehole" (127 members), "Complete arsehole" (92 members).

As the programme on the EUROTWATCH allowed more than one analysis, there was a continual chorus of electronic voices shouting with the voice of thousands of "Queer", "AC/DC", "Flasher", "Child molester" and other vulgar descriptions. Now, my students, the truth hurts but not as much as when it is shouted out by 650 maniac watches with a Hong Kong accent. So yet again democracy is suppressed under the guise of the necessity of protecting democracy.

In the year 2064, Adolf Lenin, the President General of the United Nations spoke at a special meeting in aid of world peace. He started with, "Gee-Zeus is the greatest member of mankind to exist on the face of this now trouble free globe, since his namesake arrived some 2064 years ago. This compliment is despite the fact that to get us out of the shite (excreta) he has been forced to make us all smell like excreta (shite). It is a far better thing for us to live smelling like excreta (shite) than being all dead." Amen to that my friends.

I am sure that most of my undergraduates, and yes indeed even my postgraduates, studying the advanced master's degree course, are disgusted with me (your tutor), the Honourable Dick Head. You are probably shouting personal abuse from your pollution ridden roof tops of your council estates against my lack of decorum on this subject.

Never doubt my ability to predict the future, particularly on this occasion after I have spoken to a Mr. Fox who confirms all is true. Mr. Fox actually witnessed these happenings whilst he was travelling by stainless steel car to his next screen set in 2300 AD last month.

Seeing is believing my doubting dicks, back to the future.

If you have learnt anything from this piece of futuristic history then you should have learnt how to become a millionaire by utilising any information that can be used for your financial advancement. No doubt many of you are now completely confused and feeling somewhat inferior at being incapable of grabbing hold of such rare chances in life.

Remember Herman's advice, *Ven vun doors shutz anothertz doors closetz* even though it has no connection with what we are now discussing. Without further ado, I will divulge the secret of making financial gain from the knowledge of the future I have written about above. Da da da!.........

All entrepreneurs within my student intake should now withdraw all of your savings and sell all possible possessions to fully liquidate your funds - all to be used to ensure that you will surely become some of the first Dick Millionaires who will live in perpetual gratitude following my advice. I have future plans to build a castle house in Windsor where we shall establish a private Dick Head's Millionaires Club with a membership charge of £1 Million per year per person. Many of you will be saying, "that robbin' bleedin' bastard!" but you would be so wrong to criticise me you ignorant bleedin' people - let me explain more before you go off your head again.

Once the DHMC is formed, then all members will receive extra Dick Head financial advice on a daily basis which will guarantee an extra income that will far exceed the £1 Million membership fee per year. This is the way the city slickers of today operate my friends. Oh, and why should I be paid so much money? Well my friends, to maintain my standing in the international community and to keep your utmost respect, it is entirely appropriate for me to elevate my financial bank balance in a considerable manner - and bolox to what the rest of you bleeders think!

However, enough of future plans because if I keep talking about all the wonderful things we are going to do once we have 100 Dick Head Millionaires, then it won't give me enough time to inform you of how to become a Dick Head Millionaire in the first place. This would be defeating the whole point of wanting to let you in on my secret and stopping me making a great deal of cash as well.

So, the few entrepreneurs with liquidated cash who are taking my advice should now proceed to install huge plastic storage tanks in their gardens and also on their allotments. You should now store huge quantities of standard shite inside these storage tanks. There is no limit to the amount you should store, because by the year 2001, once Gee-Zeus develops his new fuel, your stored product may stink badly, but it will sell for £53,478.76 per gallon (£278.67 at todays prices based upon a variable inflation rate). This quoted price is for the genuine "British Crude" whereas for students in the middle east and India you would receive a lower price for the "Gulf & Eastern Crude". Just calculate how rich you will be, all because of Gee-Zeus.

The central point of this very true story is to emphasise that Laura Huntley-Palmer wanted badly to have the unborn life form of Gee-Zeus destroyed, as easy as cracking a walnut. Easy, no effort, no conscience, uncaring and quickly forgotten. In Laura's case it was because she wanted to avoid ridicule, but for other people in a similar circumstances maybe it is to avoid social problems, or "we can't afford it!"

Our current laws allow the mother to achieve this murderess status on the assumption that it is taking the needs and wishes of mankind into account. I wonder how many unborn members of the human race have been murdered without any care in the world or any conscious thought. All these human beings killed under the protection of the laws ruling us at that moment in time and in the name of progress.

Who on earth has the right of deciding to pronounce the death sentence upon a creature of God? We don't as yet understand the relationship between the human race and God - so how we make this type of decision is beyond me. Maybe the real reason is that life is made more "convenient" for everybody to screw around and then when necessary simply place the results of their screwing into a black garbage bag ready for the incinerator as though it had never existed.

It should be compulsory for all women who wish to incinerate their unborn offspring to personally witness their act of murder. They should look into the eyes of their child, this beautiful human being full of innocence, whilst its life is being snuffed out before being allowed to take its first breath of air. These babies should be stuffed and placed upon the mother's sideboard as a permanent reminder of their actions, with an engraved plate stating, "I decided to legally murder this child", or maybe a word from the child itself such as, "I would have loved you mummy".

Wouldn't that be great! Under my new proposed laws, I guarantee that 99% of women would not agree to this murdering of their unborn children if they had to witness the execution. Well, as for parading these children like stuffed animals on a sideboard?

No my hypocritical Nazis, it's perfectly OK and twee if the unborn child gets murdered (legally of course?) providing you don't have to see it carried out - just put it in a plastic bag with all the shit and bandages - I feel better now.

How about the morality of the medical profession? the subject of my publication No. 46 entitled: *Hitler's Doctors Were Murderers But Were All Great.*

The women's rights mob are made up of lesbian

fanatics and liberal voters with left wing tendencies, no tits but including social workers, teachers, film stars, media writers and quite a few tight arseholes to boot. They're all shouting out furiously "You idiot Dick Head, what about the deformed babies."

My answer to that is simple, no matter what excuses you make my darlings, you do not have the right to murder an unborn child. Any other arguments are amongst yourselves and not with God. You are making progressive excuses for a progressive society with a retrogressive morality.

From rubber to murder?

Good night.

Chapter 6

AUTHORITY TO HONG KONG

"Authority in liberal minds cannot be enforced, whereas if placed in strong hands will exceed its mandate thereby leading to repression of the very people for which such authority was originally introduced to protect."

Franklin Peterson
(Brontis Peace Prize winner 1907)

Authority comes under many disguises including; power, powers that be, "they", the Establishment, ruling class, master, the Government, the Administration, Whitehall, right divine, royal prerogative, law, rightful power, legislative assembly, Parliament, regency, committee, power behind the throne, management, politics, constitutionalism, rule of law, high office, magistratacy, mayoralty, aldermanship, presidency, overlordship, superintendency, inspectorship, Big Brother, seat of Government, instructions, manifesto, rules, regulations, code of practice, brief, directive, order, warning, final demand and thousands of other ways of controlling our lives.

It is not possible for an individual to live a simple life free of Authority.

Authority from its very conception is disguised to exude a misleading embryonic lustiness to the subservient citizen of our democratic society, giving him the mistaken belief that such additional control of our lives actually deregulates previous aristocratic rule. This feeling of liberalism and personal security which is based upon absolute trust of central authority is the basis by which the perversion of civil liberties against the individual is made such a simple affair.

Authority is directed by those sub human creatures that spend their entire careers devoted to the destruction of fellow human beings' lives, including tax officers, local government, traffic wardens, policemen, bank managers, etc.

These people are the invisible "suits" employed in positions of authority that control the very life blood of the working class man, hiding behind their rule books to an excessive point where only they understand exactly what is going on inside our society. These city servants are non accessible turds, locked safely inside their slick city hall offices where we, the ordinary tax paying folk, cannot get at them, see them, kick them or question the bastard computer that continuously spews out piles of figures printed on reams of paper informing us of how much money we still owe but cannot afford to pay.

This totem pole of tribal authority, employing unseen quiet slithery non elected chieftains has quickly found out how easy it is to manipulate the masses. This situation is worrying to a point where they become total dictators over almost every aspect of our lives. Remember Herr Hitler and Brother Lenin? It couldn't happen in good old England could it, because we are a democratic country?

This all powerful authority creeps upon us, piece by piece, until we believe that such an organised control by authority is actually the way in which we want to live our lives within "free society". Beware my undergraduates, this freedom is nothing but an illusion of distant hope that never materialises, a promise never fulfilled yet always on the horizon of dreams. Big Daddy is watching over us at all times, tightening the screw should any one of us become too independent from the greater central control.

Today's Britisher has now reached a critical breaking point of conflicting emotions where living inside this democratic life of constant authority equates to spending more time doing things that we don't like than doing things that we do like.

Authority knows no bounds and is a heartless satanic theology, without soul but with a viciousness that is unrelated to human decency.

You can believe every word that I'm telling you on this subject my friends because it is spoken and written by a future knight of the realm, Dick Head the Younger, your leader fighting a lone campaign of attrition against the arseholes at city hall.

This constant authority syndrome is not unique to only the twentieth century, because it has been with us in one form or another since the beginning of the human race. Adam found that he could do as he wished with Eve providing he took an authoritarian approach to sex and buggery by using a whip and a firm hand.

I anticipate that a few disgruntled readers with very low academic abilities will now send written complaints to my publishers, claiming that this particular chapter has been written in an over complicated way and is completely biased towards the intelligentsia class. I refute this attack upon my integrity and in my self defence would point out just how really thick you must be for not being able to understand such basic theory. However, as a man who has refused to rise to any intimidation in my past life, I have decided to further explain some of the points enclosed within this chapter in a much simpler way.

The main trouble experienced by our unfortunate imbeciles of lesser understanding is for them to comprehend the individual human degradation caused by the AAS (arsehole authority syndrome) and it's overall effect upon society at large. Further explanation of this AAS will allow my thick head readership to keep up with their graduation studies without any need of attending holiday camp for extra tuition at my fully owned DikFik Royal School for Remedial Pupils, located in Wapping.

The DikFik Royal School for Remedial Pupils (RSRP) is a privately owned further educational establishment, centrally located in Wapping high street next to Westbury's the butchers and Wong's chinese cuisine centre, just a stone's throw from the Citizen's Advice Bureau. The 4876 red doubledecker bus from

Marble Arch stops directly outside the main reception area of the DikFik RSRP and a return ticket costs a mere 48 pence on production of your DikPass students travel permit.

If despite all you read in this chapter, you still consider yourself too thick to understand AAS, even with my simplistic examples, then please feel free to request an application form for attending the DikFik RSRP for one of next summer's sessions. Each session contains three weeks of total immersion study and a nominal fee of £568.76 is charged to cover tutorial fees and basic accommodation.

There is an additional single bed supplement of £137.56 per person per session if required, as otherwise eight students share a room which includes a king sized bed with two hot water bottles and an electric vibrating toothbrush.

I have gone to a great deal of extra trouble (at no additional charge to my readers), to find an example of such extreme AAS behaviour so that you people of a thicker persuasion can absorb and adapt to this AAS technology without the need of being even a fraction bit clever. Such an example was not easy to find, but during my visits to the libraries of the world it was quite by accident, and with a great deal of exhilaration, that I finally came across the answer to my prayers.

No, this example did not depict a picture book of The Holy Bible printed in Dublin, it was in fact a rare English translation of an ancient publication specialising in the secret and private life of Nero the emperor of Rome. This leather bound book having a gold embossed title of "Nero's most pissed off moments" was a joy to behold. The main story related primarily to how very upset this crazy Italian nutter became when he could not get his own crazy ways and the resultant massacres that followed his childish bouts of temper.

A prime example of his eccentricity is highlighted in concentrated detail throughout 213 pages of chapter 345, where the writing flows so smoothly that it is easy to imagine that you have travelled in a Japanese time machine (with CD player and air conditioning) and are actually experiencing the events as they took place during Nero's 30th birthday party celebrations.

These intricate details graphically describe just how Nero's authority and bad temper got the better of him and thus caused the death of so many innocent bystanders and various worn out prostitutes. Let me give my AAS readers an abridged version of this strange saga and thereby allow them to catch up with their backlog of study without getting too bored in the process.

Every year in Rome, the centurions of the city garrison would meet at the Screw a Slave beer house, an upper class public house (hereinafter referred to as a "pub"), located just a spit's distance from the Coliseum, to discuss and arrange the fine details of Nero's impending birthday celebrations.

Nero loved birthdays and unless he received a big surprise party every year he became more than a little bit agitated and would amuse himself by abusing others of a less fortunate ilk. This abusing of others he achieved by selecting five centurions at random, have birthday cake candles hammered into their oil soaked heads and make them run around the arena until the lit candles eventually turned the oil soaked hair into a firework display which could be seen clearly from the seven hills of Rome.

This is how Roman candles first came into being and obtained their notorious reputation and why it was considered infinitely better to amuse Nero's infantile needs that being made into a Roman candle. What do you think?

On this thirtieth birthday year, the leading centurions at the Screw a Slave pub were asked, in order of seniority, to put forward their suggestions to the assembled throng of warlike centurions. These suggestions were always very difficult to present in an organised manner because most of the watching crowd were intoxicated on the local

NeroWeiser brew of beer, whilst at the same time jeered and whistled as each suggestion was being presented. The assembly both presented and judged these drunken proposals and consisted of one hundred centurions who were described in the local press as the Centurions of the Round Table.

They sat around a very large round table which had been built sixty years before in the small town of Manhertz, Austria, by a very polite carpenter who made mangers in his spare time and today produces carry cots. Some of the suggestions put forward by the centurions were as follows:

From centurion Gobbyus: "We should take one thousand Jewish virgins, place them naked in the arena and thereafter set the two hundred royal castrated lions loose to tear them apart. Nero loves virgins, hates Jews but loves blood." The whole assembly agreed that this was certainly a most fantastic idea that would, under normal circumstances, be their first choice.

They summoned the city virgin warden, Signor Tightfinger, to investigate such a possibility. This proposal from centurion Gobbyus was sadly rejected after Signor Tightfinger confirmed that it was an impossible task to find more than three Jewish virgins in all of Rome. Even these three were under the age of seven and anyway they were already spoken for by Alexander.

From centurion Homosybius: "We should import five thousand Wajadoin Pigmies together with poisonous blow pipes from Central Africa and let them fight two hundred football hooligans from that backwoods called England." This brilliant idea was applauded by the whole congregation but after studying press reports covering the latest European cup exploits of the British football (soccer) supporters, the judging committee decided that this suggestion must be rejected due to the unfair competition rule.

This rule protected minority groups and insisted that all short arsed Pigmies must be given a fair chance in any conflict as otherwise they would end up with having their blow pipes shoved up their arses. *Rectum Blopipis Fukhirtis.*

From centurion Constipatius: "I declare that we take five hundred Germans, tie them to stakes upside down by their arms and make them die of laughing by tickling their feet with Canadian ducks feathers." A huge roar of approval greeted this idea, with the chairman shouting out in glee "Fantastic!, Goebbels will have no balls at all!"

The senator responsible for German culture was called and asked to comment on this most popular of suggestions. He read from the single page book called The complete works of German culture before giving his opinion to such brilliant verbiage.

After studying this book for two minutes, he had to inform the cheering throng that there was no chance of this far fetched idea being a success because the last time that any German had approached anything near what could be described as laughing was over four hundred years ago. (PS: My publisher has forced me to delete further details of this famous event which occurred in 1591 when a German winkle boilerman was publicly hung, drawn and quartered for laughing in public).

The senator declared that we couldn't be so lucky to find a humorous German a second time around, even with five hundred of them in the arena, or if we let them win the soccer world cup as an extra incentive. Ven vuns dortz shutz, anothertz dortz clothesetz!

Stop Press!!!! The German Mark has been revalued by 35% this morning as a retaliatory action following the publication of this anti German propaganda. The British Government stated immediately afterwards that "This is good news for the British people as it makes the pound in our pockets worth that much more".

Following some ten hours of further drunken discussion and equally negative ideas being put forward, it was time for the last and the most junior of the centurions, centurion Testiscrotum, to present his proposals. Testiscrotum walked with a distinct limp up to the rostrum and presented his proposals in a positive way, far above his position as the most insignificant centurion in all of Rome.

"Fellow centurions, I believe a simple example of absolute blood lust is called for this year, so simple that even our head banging nutter emperor can understand and thoroughly enjoy. I suggest that we take BrunoArry, the tallest African slave in all of Rome, and bury him in the centre of the arena with only his head sticking out of the ground. We then place a freshly cooked McChicken sandwich on top of his head before we release Pussy, the biggest lion in all of Rome, into the arena for the blood lust action. Pussy loves McChicken sandwiches and will rip off BrunoArry's head to get to his favourite lunch. Before we set Pussy free to cause havoc to Brunoarry's welfare, we must fill BrunoArry with Grappa (paint stripping fluid) until he's doo lally pissed as a fart and sings: 'Happy birthday to you, happy birthday to you.' Nero will love it!"

When the applause had quietened down, Testiscrotum was given a merit award, shaped like an oval laxative tablet, and sent away to teach BrunoArry the happy birthday song. Everything must be perfect on Nero's birthday, even down to the perfect rendering of the birthday song. A slave was sent running to the state owned chariot paint shop in Torino to collect fifty litres of Grappa paint stripping liquid - all must be ready for the big occasion.

One must always carefully plan ahead to guarantee success in all sections of life and this occasion was no exception to this prime rule. This planning ahead was very important, particularly if you preferred not to be a Roman candle.

On the morning of Nero's birthday the people thronged into the Coliseum to see Pussy live in action. The management committee of the Coliseum had been very clever when advertising this event because under normal circumstances nobody in Rome would wish to celebrate that "crazy bastard's" birthday, let alone waste a hot day in the process.

Normal civilised Roman gentry would much prefer to be out in the oat fields with their maids in waiting trying very hard to stop them waiting too long.

To ensure a full house for this extraordinary event, the management placed billboards outside every pub and brothel in Rome advertising: *Free Pussy show at the Coliseum on Nero's birthday - free entry and free participation with the Pussy if you wish.* This deceit worked a treat, which just goes to show how many people will travel miles and miles for a bit of free pussy.

Four hours before opening time, the Coliseum was already full to the brim, with some 150,000 other pussy lovers locked outside the gates, complaining like hell that they had been cheated. Such was the interest shown in this event by the feline lovers of Rome.

Throughout history, many well laid plans have come to a very sticky end, despite the careful planners taking all possible precautions to avoid such catastrophes.

The first recorded catastrophic and man inspired balls-up occurred when the ARK II hit an iceberg just off the coast of Jamaica. This disaster happened four days after the beginning of the great flood, when Nobee (Noah's half brother) and his ARK II set sail on a southerly course together with ARK 1, which was later in history to be known as Noah's Ark.

As ARK II sunk below the black water's surface with all manner of animals aboard screaming in panic, Noah shouted in anger at his careless half brother "Serves you right you careless crazy bastard, I hope you bloody well drown!" - and he did. With the benefit of hindsight, such unchristian comments given in anger appear to be rather harsh statements made to a half brother in distress, who was after all only trying to establish a place for himself in history but ended up drowning.

It is horrifying to think that had there been any third

party witnesses to this horrible language, then this blasphemy could have ended up within The Holy Bible.

The original publisher of The Holy Bible was informed of this non brotherly conversation between Nobee and Noah, but considered the language too horrifying for inclusion within this famous book. This decision was confirmed after further consultation with their sponsors. It was decided that only Noah's Ark was to be recorded as the saviour of the animal kingdom during the great flood and that Nobee was to die as a forgotten man, albeit full of fraternal hatred. He must be left to oblivion, far away from the written word, dying a painful death together with the only two remaining dinosaurs, pegususes (or is it pegusi?), Spidermen, Batmen, Central African Soup Worms and three thousand other species of today's extinct creatures of God.

So now you all know the secret of what happened to the dinosaurs my prehistoric historians. It is possible that a fossilised Nobee will one day be found in the chalk pits of Kent, but even then, his luck is such that he will be turned into cement. Life can be so unfair when you are not the chosen one.

The sole survivors of this maritime tragedy were two Icelandic Fuzzy Flying Sheep that escaped the sinking and managed to remain airborne for over six weeks, achieving a world record flight of over five thousand miles. Eventually they were lucky enough to spot a large unoccupied floating hawks nest on which they landed and made their temporary home until the floods subsided. One morning during their third year in this nest home, they awoke and as usual cast out a fishing line to catch some salmon for breakfast, expecting to hear "plop" but instead they heard a new sound of "Splut".

Yes!, the water had subsided and they had survived the great flood. Stepping out of their rickety boathouse, they both kissed the ground with relief and kissed the old hawks nest in gratitude for taking them to the safety of this muddy sticky stinking crappy land - need I say more?

No matter that it looked like the worst piece of real estate that they had ever set their eyes upon and it smelt like shite, one must be thankful for small mercies.

They decided that in honour of the boat that had saved their lives, they would name this spot of land as Hawkland, and because of the abundance of shitey little newts and eels they found in the mud, they would name their new country Newteelsland. Fortunately the fuzzy flying sheep is an hermaphrodite, similar to a Labour Party Member of Parliament, and this allowed them to merrily screw themselves for a few millions years, building up their population until the British Empire came along to ruin everything. I must point out that unlike our considerate fuzzy flying sheep, the Labour Party also screws everybody else as well.

Back to Nero's birthday celebrations.

BrunoArry walked across the sand after having voluntarily drunk four litres of La Gotcha brand of grappa paint stripper, which he happily consumed after being promised the freedom of Rome if he completed this little singogram jaunt. "All you have to do, my friend, is to sing the happy birthday song to Nero in a voice full of happiness, sit in that hole in the ground covered in sand, balance a McChicken sandwich on your head and freedom is yours!"

BrunoArry's singing was not of Harry's quality, but was at a level far beyond what could have been expected from a slave under such circumstances.

BrunoArry's singing was both awe inspiring and hearty to such an extent that Nero applauded in joy, whilst shouting out "great singing my African slave, but where's the pussy and the bloody blood!" This aggressive comment coming from the lips of the mad-hatter himself had a detrimental effect upon the crowd's behaviour inside the Coliseum, which was pussy mad already.

Such mass hysteria was fully encouraged and increased by the liberal consumption of the free grappa being passed around by the anti Roman candle centurions who were wearing asbestos head gear. The crowd was now in a sexual fervour and began chanting in an aggressive riotous manner "We want pussy, we want pussy, we want pussy!" After a few minutes of such uproar, Nero joined in with this same chanting because he was totally nuts and totally pissed with his trousers off.

BrunoArry laughed and shouted "freedom in our time" as he jumped into the custom dug hole which had been carefully made to suit his exact size. Once inside the hole his fellow slaves filled up all around him with sand so that his whole body was covered except for his gleaming head that now sticks above the ground and resembles a black coconut at the fairground. Hero of the day, Testiscrotum, brings out a freshly cooked McChicken sandwich and tries to balance it on BrunoArry's head but no matter how hard he tries, it keeps falling off.

Not to be beaten by this small temporary set-back, Testiscrotum requests the presence of a carpenter who sets about solving this problem by attaching the McChicken sandwich to BrunoArry's head with the help of two huge nails and some blows from a very large hammer. This act of brutality against Brunoarry's skull further excites Nero who now believes that this is actually part of the planned celebrations. He stands up and roars "Get some bigger nails and a bigger bloody hammer - no get two bloody great hammers!"

BrunoArry screams in agony for a few minutes before realising that if freedom is worth having, then what's a little pain caused by two massive nails being bashed into your skull with a bloody great hammer? - he continues with his singing duties, "Happy birthday to you, happy birthday to you.............."

Somebody amongst the organisers should have studied my book number 39 entitled *Dick Head's Solutions In Case Of A Riot,* because the crowd had definitely not waited all day, sitting in the hot sun, just to see their nutty emperor acting like a daft prat and watch some African prick sitting in a hole and singing the happy birthday song.

By now the people were becoming absolutely out of their tiny drunken minds, chanting "Pussy! we want pussy! pussy! we want pussy, where's the poxy pussy, where's the poxy pussy!" This further excited Nero to a point where he started to fully undress in view of the crowd and it was evident that his three female slaves began to look very edgy indeed.

To save the day from complete disaster and a public riot, dear old giant Pussy the lion was at last brought into the arena, just in the nick of time. I accept that Pussy is a strange name for a lion but they treated names differently in those days.

Throughout history it is a well documented fact that a captive lion does not take kindly to being manhandled by short Italian wankers, a feeling that Pussy confirmed during these birthday celebrations. He had been very happy sitting in his cage, sunbathing and dreaming of a big titted lioness, when a group of six short arsed Italian tosspots interrupted these thoughts. They moved him out of the cage and forced him into the centre of the Coliseum arena with the added help of six spears which they had stuck up his rectum passage. This multiple poking of the bum brought a great hush to the rioting crowd and more than a few tears from Pussy. Yes this forthcoming spectacle was something new, something not to miss, something to tell the grandchildren and the new mistress with big knockers.

Pussy stalked around the arena hissing at the crowd in anger, "hiss, hiss, hiss, hiss, hiss!" thinking that this was not his lucky day, and wondering why he always ended up with spears stuck up his rear end just to please that nutter up there in the royal box!

Suddenly his jungle super senses came into their splendid own as they indicated a better life ahead, surely he couldn't smell a McChicken sandwich?, not in this place of all places? After further sniffing, Pussy knew there was no mistaken identity being given out by the King of the jungle's smelling senses.

He could definitely smell a McChicken sandwich complete with salad and dressing (with no fries) - and it's somewhere in this arena! Following his unbelievable and legendary sense of smell, he stalked to the centre of the arena where yes! yes! yes! here was the McChicken sandwich sitting on top of a black man's head. Immediately Pussy sees that the man underneath the McChicken sandwich is moving and a voice is singing the happy birthday song - is this another cruel human trick to allow even more spears to be put up his arse?

Natural greed is often our worst enemy and this day was to prove no exception to this golden rule. Pussy decided that he must have the McChicken Sandwich immediately, even if it did result in a few more spears being stuck in the wrong places. Planning his angle of attack was easy peasy jananeasy, he would suddenly jump on top of the McChicken sandwich with both sets of claws aimed at grabbing the food from the top of the black man's head.

This simple plan of attack was no problem for a King of the jungle, even if he did look rather ridiculous with all those spears sticking out of his back passage. He casually walked up to within two feet of his future dish of the day and leapt directly at the McChicken sandwich, it really was going to taste good, oh yea, yea, yea! As he jumps, BrunoArry sees this vicious animal arriving with the sole intent of removing his head and in an instant he ducks his head rapidly and very quickly to his left.

Pussy overshoots the intended target and hits the ground, mouth first, and ends up eating a mouthful of sand tainted with the indelicate taste of elephants urine, which is not what he expected.

Angry as hell, he turns around thinking "If that's how you wanna play it buster!" and without further planning leaps to the left position where BrunoArry ducked during the previous attack.

BrunoArry sees this twat cat coming at him again, but this time diving to his left side, so he obviously ducks his head fast to the right and Pussy overshoots him again, ending up with taking another mouthful of sand, but this time the sand is mixed with some rabbits droppings which turns Pussy into a very hot and dangerous Pussy.

Like you, I have no idea what on earth they were doing to the rabbits in the arena on previous occasions to get so many droppings in the sand. Notwithstanding any question mark that still lurks over this rabbits shite, Pussy turns again to face BrunoArry but now intends to carefully plan his attack before leaping again - for what he is confident will be the third and successful time. His plan is simple, he will leap upon the McChicken sandwich in such a way as to cover the whole target area, one killer paw to the left and one killer paw to the right and his huge jaws in the centre.

BrunoArry, with the razor sharp reflexes developed and sharpened by his past ability to catch carnivore bats in mid air flight under pitch dark conditions, saw Pussy's tactics immediately and countered this clever attack with the tactical skill of Pele. As Pussy jumped, Brunoarry leaned his head back as far as possible almost reaching a horizontal position, Pussy flew overhead and missed the target with both fangs and paws.

Not only did Pussy get a third mouthful of sand tasting of German sweat, but as he leaped over the top, BrunoArry lifted up his head and bit off both of Pussy's balls. Nero was beside himself in fury in the royal box and jumped up in anger, shouting out at Pussy "Play fair you cruel bastard!"

So my students of history, nothing corrupts people quite as much as power and the above lesser known moment in history illustrates this point perfectly. Dictators become unreasonable, whether this relates to Nero or the civil servants that control every aspect of our lives. "It can't happen here" shout all the supporters of

Militant Tendency (those fellows with gold earrings) and the town hall wasters. You are already brain washed into believing that we have total freedom. YOU ARE WRONG MY FRIENDS, YOU ARE ALL SLAVES TO AUTHORITY.

Take any idiot who is daft enough to wear those black uniforms complete with the mandatory peaked caps, and you have instantly created the common trooper that works for Authority to suppress the masses at grass roots level every day of the week. We start with the yellow shirts, craftily given the name of traffic wardens, but this is only up until the day of the revolution.

These yellow shirts spend their entire working lives terrorising us, the motorist, ensuring that we cannot do the things we want to do when innocently driving our cars in peace and tranquillity. Every day millions of motorists drive around and around in a futile and pointless search for that twenty foot piece of road space that authority has dictated we can park on, but for not more than thirty minutes you motorist swine!

Traffic jams are formed solely because motorists are searching for this rare and privileged space, each motorist following the same cars around and around and around and around, with the yellow shirts glaring and smirking whilst they see you have conformed with their Authority. "What about the 95% of the road with no cars parked on it" you may cry in vain. "Why don't you park there?" the visitor from Mars would ask in puzzlement.

I can easily answer this question for you, my friends from the chocolate factory, because if Authority allowed you to park anywhere you pleased, then they would relinquish some of the Authority that took generations to achieve. This loss of non elected power is never allowed because they have no pressure applied by anybody to force them to do so.

Authority only grows in a geometric way, it never shrinks. In a town consisting of 10,000 car owners we have all the motorists controlled by only six or seven yellow shirts acting in the name of Authority. You may take a risk and park on yellow lines, run like a bastard to collect the special medicine to save old auntie Ethel's life, run back exhausted to the car, but too late!, the yellow shirts have got you.

You, the law breaking motorist, dared to flout Authority and park on the yellow lines whilst you get life saving medicine. How dare you flout Authority! You get a £12 fine and no chance of appeal because the motorist is guilty until he can prove himself innocent. Still I suppose that when I think back to this event, auntie Ethel wasn't really worth £12 whilst she was alive whereas after she died recently she left me her entire estate, totalling £123,768.98 after death duties. But the traffic warden didn't know this at the time.

In a special paperback publication of mine entitled *Evolution, From The Monkey To The Motorist,* I discuss how both the monkey and the motorist operate and live in a very similar fashion, even to the point of squabbling and fighting over a parking place. The traffic warden is our animal warden, controlling and frustrating us, the monkeys, in very similar ways as employed by a zoo keeper. In fact, the monkey would not put up with such treatment because he would shite on the floor and scratch his balls in public as an expression of discontent and disapproval.

At last!, you've found a parking space after only forty three minutes driving around and around the streets consuming two gallons of that cheaper lead free petrol that's better for the ozone layer - aren't you the lucky one. As you step out of your car, a yellow shirt glowers at you as she (I say she, because the female yellows are the worst) walks over to the rear of your car and takes a note of your number plate and after making sure you see her looking at her watch, writes down the time at which you parked.

Panic! panic!, Jesus Christ, you don't have change for the meter, your blood pressure rises and your heart pounds. Sweating like a demented volcano rat, you gingerly approach the yellow shirt with a slimy, creepy grin on your face. "Is it OK if I just go over to the bank and get some change for the meter?" you ask this thin, miserable and very ugly yellow shirt. Like Hitler's widow she responds "You should pay more attention to bringing the correct change in the future you silly man, but on just this one occasion I will allow you to park here for two minutes before I book you!" and starts looking at her watch.

Like a scalded child you run across the road in panic to the bank to get some change, you then you run back to the meter after you obtain the change. "You were very lucky this time because you were away for over four minutes and I was about to write you a ticket!" she barks, and you feel thankful for this small mercy - my God what is the world coming to? Just think how these situations are becoming an accepted part of our everyday life where we are totally controlled by Authority.

Until the revolution comes, we ordinary people can fight back without fear of being shot, but please be sure to have your air tickets booked for when the revolution approaches because Authority never forgets. Dick Head is marked down as the first writer to be liquidated by the New People's Courts after the bloody revolution takes place.

The judges in these New People's Courts will be the same union leaders, shop stewards, traffic wardens, Militant Tendency yobs, etc. that exist today. Alternatively, on the first day of the revolution, you could try unrolling a huge red flag (that you should always keep in reserve in the loft), run down the street and start shouting "Power to the people, Freedom to the people!"

This action will probably be sufficient to impress the red guards to the extent that you will be appointed to the People's Committee, a position that includes obligatory wearing of a demob suit with red lapels. Power to the people!

Do not be misled into thinking that everything is now OK because the Soviet Union is breaking up - Do not be that foolish - please.

Being the hero that I am to the working class people of this great land, I have invented a system of fighting back against the yellow perils and not to just sit back and take the everlasting abuse against my personal liberty. This ingenious scheme is based upon the passive resistance theory as first introduced by Ghandi, even though this brave Indian trooper was not a Guinness drinker during his lifetime. I was finally angered to breaking point and forced into forming this resistance movement last year when I received a parking ticket at exactly 5.59 pm (just one minute before free parking was allowed) outside St.Cromwells Church on 24th December.

Authority has no heart, is anti Christian, and moves against us relentlessly even on the holy days of Christmas. Apart from the lack of Christian good will to all men and motorists, this ticket happened to be my fiftieth for the year, which meant that I had accumulated a total of over £1,000 in parking tickets for this same period. This is an outrageous situation and it was time to fight back, time to give power back to the common victimised motorist.

On the 2nd January this year, I attempted to enter the Guinness book of records with regards to liquid consumption within a limited period of time which took place at the The Beheaded Sparrow pub in Harrow. This drinking establishment has a condom dispenser in the men's room which takes your money but never delivers the goods, no matter how desperate is your need. Rubber problem apart, this favourite pub of mine serves the best pint of Irish Black Gold in the town.

I failed by a whisker to have my name entered into this worldwide publication of world records, but can fully assure my readers that it was not for the lack of trying. I also had a really enjoyable day out with the boys.

It was during my record attempting session that the Sink The Yellow Peril Charter was written and approved by all of the boys who took an oath, swearing that this would be the start of the motorists fight back to recover our liberty. Fifteen of us moved out of the unlucky sparrow and walked slowly down to the town centre, singing a grand rendering of Danny Boy as a first start in our fight back against the yellow shirts.

Fortunately for our morale, the first yellow shirt spotted by our band of freedom fighters was typical, consisting of a short male, 5ft 5 inches in height, picking his nose, sporting a small thin moustache and speaking with an Austrian/German accent. I have nothing against German accents, short people or moustaches, but history fully illustrates that a combination of all three of these features usually forms the basis of a dangerous dictator or a queer politician.

I do in any case object to our public servants picking their noses whilst on duty.

We followed closely behind Herr Hitler Youth until he found his next motorist victim, one who had dared to allow a parking meter to read Excess Charge; how dare this motorist break the law. Smiling like a constipated lizard, yellow shirt started to write out a fixed penalty parking ticket, not knowing that whilst he worked we formed an arm linked half circle around him.

I switched on Bert's cassette player and the beautiful sound of Yellow Submarine bellowed forth, to which we added our vocal to further support this most famous of Beatle's songs. I am informed by several independent observers listening to this rendering of Ringo's Jingo, that the final result sounded quite disgusting. Song is to the beholder, and I behold that it sounded like the Dublin Cheesemakers Choir at their most mature best.

We repeated this street entertainment for a further hour or so until a crowd of some 5000 strong came to join us in this street jamboree. Our permanent ridicule of this little yellow shite was fast turning him into a very nervous little yellow shite. The swelling crowd was in high spirits and roared with delight every time another ticket was written out and Ringo's Dingo was rendered with our most heartfelt vocal chords.

A bully never likes receiving similar medicine, and this cross between a German SS corporal and an Italian midget decided to cut his losses and run for the cover of the local police station, to the howls of delight from the crowd.

All twenty three parking tickets written out by yellow peril that afternoon were collected from the vehicles to which they had been attached, stuffed inside a half full tin of Golden Syrup and sent for the attention of the German Immigration Department at the local nick.

Thereafter, at 9.00 am every day a group of at least 500 people would meet in the town centre to continue the festivities of yellow peril baiting as described in our Yellow Bellied Resistance Fighters news sheet, now on free issue to anybody who joined our cause.

The whole town eventually took part in this very amusing charade and people in shops, homes and offices, wildly cheered each time the ever increasing crowd started singing with Ringo's Jingo. People took portable chairs, vacuum flasks, cheese sandwiches, video cameras, etc to make a real good day of it.

The local Salvation Army band turned up wearing mock traffic wardens uniforms on Saturday mornings and played Yellow Submarine in tune with Bert's cassette recording and the crowd's singing.

The national newspapers printed front page stories of "Motorists fight back at last!" or "Labour threatens to send in the troops!" or my favourite "Dick Head Magic!"

In the music magazines the amazing headlines appeared of "Yellow Submarine is Number One for the thirtieth consecutive week!" Just think of the level of royalties on these unexpected sales for the record company. I feel sure that a large cheque will be forthcoming very soon from the record company, the cheque made out to our campaign fund within the next few days.

No decent record company would wish to profit at the expense of us the freedom fighters, would they?

Some three months later, life is now much less exciting as the yellow shirts have dived for cover and we only have one of them left on the streets. Out of the original fourteen yellow shirts in Harrow, seven are in the local asylum forming themselves into a pop group, six have joined the navy and have volunteered for nuclear submarine work, leaving the lone female survivor now nicknamed Japanese Jill.

I must say that we cannot feel entirely defeated by our efforts upon this strange surviving lady, because she has now painted her entire council house a fluorescent yellow colour both inside and out, the yellow being a very close match to the yellow paint used for painting road lines - I wonder?

For her personal protection she has purchased an old secondhand troop carrier from the Ministry of Defence which is also painted this same horrible yellow colour. For the last three weeks, Japanese Jill now walks backwards from her troop carrier to each illegally parked car singing the song "I don't care if the sun don't shine", whilst she writes out the unenforceable parking tickets on yellow toilet paper.

All is not well with this lady, no indeed not all is well at all.

The next level up from trooper level in Authority is that of the black shirts (or is it blue?) - our beloved police force - the true regiment of law enforcers. This subject is briefly covered in earlier chapters, but to cover all aspects requires a dedicated book of its own and this is available in my publication number 53, entitled *How bent is a Bobby?* Advance publication copies will be available at a special price of £142.60 and further details will be made available at a later date concerning the collection points for my dedicated readers.

We must inconvenience you by changing the location of these collection points at least five times per day to ensure that the police are not in a position to make a bust where they will probably find a quantity of drugs with the books just to make sure the charges stick. It's only fair really, because how would it look if they busted us just for printing books?

All profits from this publication will go to the Victims of False Imprisonment Association which has an increasing membership every year. We must remember that not all Bobbies are bad because we have Bobby Moore, Bobby Charlton, Bobby Robson, Bobby Gentry..............the list goes on and on.

Next we come to the S.S. level of Authority, more formally known as Super Shites. These non elected weasels are everywhere, in high positions with Authority, such success achieved by a concerted squirming and lying process. Once in position, they are never to be removed except by shooting or being given a good dose of Afghanistani clap.

These top level S.S. officers include bank managers, tax inspectors, union leaders, lawyers, magistrates, etc. These are all the arseholes that take us for a ride, yet pretend that they are serving the people whilst actually professionally screwing the ordinary citizen in aid of supporting Authority.

Did you know that a senior tax inspector, who is a non elected civil servant, has unbelievable powers to screw you if he feels so inclined? Under certain conditions, he can screw you for extra tax if "In the opinion of the tax inspector you owe this tax", no matter that no proof exists that you do not owe the tax. Yet again my graduates of democracy, you are guilty until you can prove your innocence.

How many good ordinary people have had their lives and families destroyed because some wanking tax inspector decides that "In my opinion you owe this tax" and enforces the law which he is free to interpret, based upon his personal feeling at that moment in time? Imagine that his girl friend has just informed him that very same morning that she has a good solid dose of Aids and then your tax papers are his next case - watch out my friends!

You may have no right of appeal and you must then pay up or declare yourself a bankrupt. What a nice friendly and democratic land we live in. Does our S.S. tax inspector lose sleep because he destroys you and your family based upon the results of his opinion only? No indeed he does not, because he is too busy earning his brownie points to ensure he gets promoted to the top level of the S.S.S.S. brigade which is commonly known as Senior Super Shite Shiteheads.

"Don't tell me how you're innocent Dick Head; if I say you're guilty then you're guilty, even if you're really innocent!" However, not even Authority has priority on Aids cures, not yet anyway, so life is a great leveller after all.

Bank managers are the friendly S.S. officers placed in this position of power to ensure that none of us can ever reach a position of profit and therefore have influence within society and affect the power of Authority. We must all work full time to pay back the interest on the money we have been encouraged or forced to borrow, so that we cannot cause trouble because we are too busy working to repay this interest.

In Russia, they have the same theory but keep you queuing for food instead. Different subject, same theory.

As a start, the banks through their fully owned credit card companies, issue credit cards to all and sundry to ensure that everybody is captured in the credit card trap. Don't let the people borrow money at only 3% over base rate when we can con them into borrowing money, via a credit card, at 20% over base rate - even an idiot can tell you that this is better business for the banks.

Does your bank manager suggest to you "Dick Head, don't pay these stupid interest rates on credit cards, let me arrange an overdraft for you at much lower rates?" Does he hell. He is part of Authority with the one aim in life to grab all the money you can possibly earn, by charging excessive interest rates and applying exorbitant service charges.

One well known credit card company goes even further with this deceit of S.T.A.O.O.Y (you work it out) by really hitting below the belt to get even higher interest rates from you. If this company sends you your monthly statement, which for example reads total outstanding as £1,234.89 with a minimum payment required as £67.78 then you would understand what this means, I think. How about if you paid off £1,234.88 you would expect to pay interest on 1p?

Unlucky for you my stupid credit card holder, these honest holders of the nations money will still charge you the full interest on £1,234.89! Not a bad scam even for a leading crook, but a sad state of affairs for one of our leading banks. How do they justify it? Why not write and ask them; the bullshite reply should be interesting. My publisher has deleted the references made originally that identified these guys for fear of aggressive response.

High Street Banks are moneylenders that borrow money from investors at $x\%$ and then loan out money at $x + y\%$, the value of y being based upon whatever they feel is appropriate, and what the other leading banks agree to within the power of market forces. I am told that we do not have a price ring between the leading banks and that the reason why the interest rates of all of them are almost identical is simply down to competition.

I can believe anything if the information is given to me by an honest man. In any case, my graduate economists, the reason why the biggest buildings in London are owned by the financial institutions is that they are bought with your money; the investors money. The bank managers and their snobby staff are employed and paid for by your money, the funds of the investor.

No matter that they gave billions of your pounds to

the bankrupt South American governments (who now refuse to repay these loans) and lots of crooked businessmen, nobody is fired, because the losses are only losses of your invested money.

The suits worn by the banking staff are the same quality and they still drive executive cars paid for from your money.

We have a different story when the banks are asked to back a new British enterprise by investing your money to make billions for the British economy, because then it becomes their money; Ho Ho Ho! I recently went to visit my bank manager in his cupboard, this cupboard turning out to be a £57,600 per year rental matchbox office in a high rise building in London.

After being made to wait the statutory ten minutes, just to be sure that you really know your place in life, Mr. Rupert Wayne-Jones rushes through and says "I hope you haven't been waiting too long Mr. Head?" I answered calmly, "Well Rupert, I have been waiting for ten minutes, in fact I have been waiting since I arrived ten minutes ago and since your secretary informed you that Mr. Dick Head had arrived on time for his prearranged appointment." Rupert is not listening to me but replies but says, "Just so, Mr. Head, please come into my office."

"OK Mr. Head, how can the bank help you today?"

I answered easily, "Rupert, how relaxed it is to discuss company growth with an understanding bank manager. I need to borrow £100,000 to finance my new exciting project of launching the TURD, The Unified Reactor Driver machine on which we have world patents and fully proven data showing that this revolutionary machine will convert shite into aids free blood at a price cheaper than burying people. There is no doubt that every hospital in the world will buy one of our TURDs. Your latest National advertising campaign in the national press and TV promoting 'Venture Capital - No strings attached' looks the ideal way of progressing this new project Rupert and this is the way we would like to go."

Rupert straightens his tie very slowly, looks at a computer screen for a few seconds and replies, "Very interesting Mr. Head, but after reading through your business plan covering the TURD project it does appear that the risk of this venture is still substantial. You still have to produce odour free blood that is acceptable to the United Nations study group on artificial blood. I see on page 67 of your business plan that they have rejected the first sample based upon both smell and the deep brown colour of the product and also report that all of the human trials of the finished article have left the recipients of your product smelling like shite for the rest of their lives. Under these circumstances, our ' No strings attached finance' is not available" but we can offer you secured finance to help you with this project,"

With a big smile I respond, "To me Rupert, I believe that people would rather smell like shite than be dead. However, please give me the conditions being offered by the bank for this secured finance."

Rupert the magnificent is now up and away on common ground which he can cope with with his eyes closed. Closing his eyes, he begins, " Yes Mr head, (Cough!), we can specify the secured finance as follows:

1. *We can give you an overdraft of £45,000 on your current account initially to see how the project develops. If everything is OK and good red non smelling blood is made from crap, then a further £60,000 is available.*
2. *We will charge you 5% over base rate for this overdraft.*
3. *We must take a charge on your fixed and floating assets*
4. *We must take a charge on your personal property.*
5. *You must take out a key man life insurance for £100,000 assigned to the bank.*

It's as easy as that Mr. Head!"

"Very good Rupert, so you give me £40,000 and in return I give you 5% over base rate for the privilege, you take a charge on £260,000 of buildings and about £130,000 of stock, plus you want a charge on my personal property worth £180,000 and then just in case this is not enough, I must take out an insurance for £100,000? Why not just loan me £100,000 based upon the same security at 3% over base rate?" Dear old Rupert answered nervously, "Quite so Mr. Head"......."Rupert - Fuck off!"

The South American governments are still defaulting on all of their loans and some of our magnates of industry are being exposed as fraudsters and costing the banks billions. Maybe one day I will understand.

Moving on to the deepest ingrained and hidden S.S.S.S's, we must look at some of the union leaders, complete with ill fitting suits and pretending to care and help the workers - some hope! Before my socialist readers start a bonfire using this book as fuel and start rioting outside my publishers factory in Wapping, I must give you some basic information.

How much good have your union bosses achieved for you, the worker, since 1945 when the British worker was the best paid in Europe? Despite endless strikes called by the fat, well fed union barons over the past 45 years, what have they achieved for you my socialist readers? I will tell you what they have achieved my brain washed men of red, they have taken you from the top to the bottom of the pile in Europe!

All Europe has, or will, overtake you in all aspects of income, standard of living, education, training and quality of life. After 45 years of sacrifice during endless political strikes, you have been taken to the garbage heap my comrades. These are facts that even the psychopathic flying pickets can't change.

"It's all the fault of the bloody management, they couldn't arrange a decent screw in a brothel" you are all screaming, whilst sitting around the coke fire on the picket line. How sad it is for the unions that Russia is becoming a democratic country after the failure of communism. What new song will be sung in the future at the Bugs Bunny Show of the T.U.C. conference?

What will the farce of block votes vote for this year? What industry will get screwed up this year? What daft law will be passed by the next Labour government to bribe the T.U.C. to keep paying the bills? We shall now see a quick change act of these same extremists to suit the occasion and mood in the country, but have no fear my militancy readers, at the right time the Red Blood will flow again very soon. "We shall overcome................"

Stop shouting those daft chants of "here we go, here we go, here we go......." and start thinking for yourself just once in your lifetime. To pass your final Dick Head's graduation exam, you must illustrate at least some individual thinking, and this is positively lacking in your heads at the moment. Start now........ Profitable industries don't normally close down but unprofitable industries most certainly will. Facts to note and remember, facts that won't be changed by violence on the picket lines or killing people by throwing rocks from motorway bridges.

Violence won't change the truth no matter how hard you hit my bully boys. You may not be locked up as you should be for these killings and acts of violence, but one thing is certain; you won't have a job unless you make a profit for your company - whether you like your employer or not. You will find that it will not make one iota of difference whether you like the fellow behind the counter at the front of the dole queue, you'll act differently then my lads and you'll take the money - that's the way to learn my lads.

Start thinking for yourselves; is it worth going on strike for four months to get an extra 1.5% increase over the offer being made by the company. "They made £21,000,000 profit last year and we want our fair share!" the union leaders shout, and the workers listen.

Let's look at this thinking in a more educated light.

Did your same union leaders in 1986 say "Look lads the company lost £34,000,000 we must take a wage cut of 14% to cover it!" No they did not say anything of the sort, but they demanded the usual above inflation wage increase which the managers in charge of the company, in fear of a strike which would be the last nail in the coffin of the already financially troubled company, reluctantly agreed to.

Management can take some of the blame for our industrial decline, but when dealing with industrial bullies that will enforce strikes to obtain unreasonable wage settlements on companies that are already in financial trouble, then just what can they do? Not many of the management I know are members of a political organisation awaiting the day of the revolution.

After being on strike for twenty weeks for an extra £2.80 per week your well fed, fully paid, union executives make a deal with the company for a compromise deal for £1.80 extra per week. After this "defeat of the company" the union calls a press conference and spouts, "We have won our fight for the wages deserved by our members and the management have surrendered to our demands. Tomorrow in an open ballot in the car park we shall recommend for our members to accept this well earnt victory. Our success has been achieved despite the violence of the fascist police against our members."

A poof reporter from the magazine "Right wing Rights" asked Bill Bailey, spokesman for the Bridge Painters Union, "Mr. Bailey, how can you call this a victory for your members when they must now work for a further eighteen years to get back the money they have lost by being on strike. Surely you are only pleased at the political victory and don't care about your members cash gain."

A full bottle of Pewksburg German pils lager propelled at 46.56 miles per hour impacting with a soft human skull, just above the left ear, really is a dangerous thing and Mr. Blueberry is now a very sad Mr. Blueberry, suffering from a fractured skull, deafness in his left ear and a headache. He is said to be very annoyed at receiving no reply to his question but relieved that his right ear is OK and he is not going to be deaf.

Without conflict and strife to keep the workers busy, they might just start asking questions about the suitability of the union leaders to lead them to the promised land. It is a well proven tactic used by dictators throughout history that by creating external strife, you deflect attention away from internal strife and your own inability to deliver the goods.

Just listen to the ex scouse somebody (he must be from the shop floor level) giving his speech to the T.U.C. conference, "Brovers, comrades, I'm 'ere today to propose a change in 'ow this rotten government treats our unemployed comrades on the dole. Brovers, I propose that all people on the dole should get 90% of the average wage of the workers in the country. I know money don't grow on bloody trees, but we gotta get it back by taxing all the rich geezers. I do propose, thank you brovers."

Brilliant! Guaranteed to be passed by congress, which is no problem because it's never going to happen anyway.

Comrades, you are all in one single team, including owners, managers and workers alike, with one aim in life, to make a profitable company so that all can share in that wealth. Don't destroy the company that feeds you. Build it up and fight the shop stewards who are attempting to use you, the workers, to enforce their union dogma and their prick mentality by looking for aggression at every turn. The more radical a shop steward, the more he is noticed and therefore the more likely he will be promoted to national level with a big pay check and recognition.

A shop steward who prefers to negotiate and settle disputes is as rare as the Virgin Mary, because such a liberal will not get promotion in the union by making these easy settlements. Therefore, he will take you out on strike to create the smoke that will assist his promotion and eventual path to glory. Got the picture yet my brothers?

One day we shall appoint well educated union officials, similar to the system being adopted in other more efficient countries that are ahead of us in all aspects of working class qualities. This approach is to help both the workers and the company at the same time. People must understand that a balance sheet is more than just a rain cover for the weighbridge outside the gatehouse - it's survival of the company and the good life for all. Let's sing a new song, "Keep the flag of industry flying".

Maggie Thatcher was sent down to us by God. How about Thatchianity?

When it comes to the individual working class man wishing to defend and clear his name, we enter an area of incredibility if you believe in British justice. Without riches, British justice does not exist for us, the ordinary man in the street. Imagine you have grown a third giant testicle, your head has swollen to three times its normal size and your feet are changing into hoofs; all due to the chemicals used in making those "peking duck & cauliflower" sausages that you love so much.

What can you do, apart from selling photographs of your balls to the Institute of Pawnbrokers for their Christmas annual joke competition, buying a bigger hat or entering the St. Leger? You can do absolutely bloody nothing unless you are prepared to lose everything you own and fight on for five years to do so. If you have lots of money my Lord, everything is so different according to British Justice. The one exception to this rule is for the man who is destitute and can can claim legal aid - then the other party gets no justice.

There was a recent libel case held at the Old Bailey which lasted for 128 weeks, a record for a libel case of this type. The case was brought by Lord Mytee following a front page article in the Sunday Labour Titebites which made serious libellous accusations as follows:

" Our investigative reporter Richard Barton, can now reveal the results of his three year undercover research into the double life of Lord Alan Mytee, more commonly known as Lord 'Al' Mytee, Master of a Rolls Royce. This gentleman has been a nightly visitor and customer at the 'Aristocratic Knocking Shop', an up market sauna and relaxing club located in the exclusive area of Barclays Oval. Verified statements are in our possession from one hundred and sixty two of the girls employed by this establishment confirming they have all sold their personal services to the Lord over a period of three years.

Statements also taken from sixty three young boys under the age of ten make serious allegations relating to serious sexual abuse.

We also have photographic evidence showing Lord 'Al' Mytee sitting in strange positions with six naked women, plus two donkeys stabled in the stable boudoir located in the rear garden of the same premises. A total of seventy four hours of video film taken from hidden cameras further illustrates the depravities to which this lord lowered himself to.

We have copies of credit card slips totalling £182,642.60 over this same three year period signed by the Lord, all of which read 'for services rendered'. We call for a full government enquiry and suggest that the Lord 'Al' Mytee be strung up by his balls!"

Lord Al Mytee issued a writ for libel against this newspaper the case being judged at the High Court. Lord Al Mytee using all the power at his disposal spent a total of £4,325,987.65 in defence costs. which was like a drop of ice in the Atlantic Ocean to him. He had personal assets totalling over fifty billion pounds inherited from his late father, the previous Lord Gott Al Mytee, who originated from the German side of the family.

Lord Al Mytee's barristers gave the following evidence in his defence:

(1) Lord Al Mytee was never aware that the Aristocratic Knocking Shop was anything more than a well established gentleman's club and was astonished to hear that it was used for prostitution.

(2) Yes Lord Al Mytee could remember talking to a large number of girls, but had no memory of having sex with them. If this was true he would sue them for rape.

(3) As for the sixty three boys in question, Lord Al Mytee's investigators had confirmed that these boys had all attended the same church school that employed twenty seven homosexual teachers. Obviously these boys experienced mass hysteria, confusing events with the lessons taught in school.

(4) Lord Al Mytee had never ridden a donkey up until he went to the donkey riding school associated with the club. He may have taken up unusual positions during these lessons, but it was not the first time that a member of the aristocracy rode animals in the nude with females in their presence just in case you fell off the donkey.

(5) The champagne was bloody good vintage and you have to pay good money for good products.

(6) Video films cannot be entered as evidence.

After the final summary the jury took only six minutes to find in favour of Lord Al Mytee and afterwards the judge, Lord Lord (yes, his surname was Lord) spoke out in his poker up his rectum accent:

"I find the accusations made by the Sunday Labour Titebites are a disgrace to the newspaper profession and are entirely based upon hearsay evidence from people of ill repute. Only the words of pussy for sale whores have been given in evidence together with accusations made by hysterical boys taught by queer priests. Lord Al Mytee innocently took riding lessons undressed on two donkeys to cool off from a hot day at the House of Lords and you make accusations trying to prove that he had perverse intentions with these donkeys. It is also not entirely unknown for the landed gentry to ride animals fully naked with six naked women giving a hand. As for the non admissible video film, this is confiscated and will be kept in my personal safe at my home.

"I agree entirely with the jury's verdict and for this gross libel, I grant the Lord Al Mytee the sum of £25,000,000 damages plus full costs against the defendants. Let that be a lesson to you to only tell the truth and nothing but the truth, so help you God. God save the Queen."

After judgement, the Sunday Labour Titebites with assets totalling only £133.78 were forced into liquidation and Lord Al Mytee eventually received £12.98 out of the awarded damages of £25,000,000. It is the principle that counts and not the money. Richard Barton, the unemployed investigative reporter who started all the fuss, has recently written a book describing this event which he called Lord Al Mytee Wins Again, which has now sold eight million copies worldwide and earned him over £2,000,000 in royalties - such is the final justice of a capitalist society.

'The Sunday Labour Titebites' has now reopened its doors under new ownership with the new title of *The Sunday Truth* and their new investigative reporter, Father Umberto Kirton Ussetti, has a new revelation being printed next week entitled The Rich Get Richer, now ain't that the truth.

However father dear father, watch out for the Hong Kong Chinese!

Chapter 7

SICKNESS TO LOSING YOUR HEAD

"If medicine is stronger than prayer then where shall I go to find God."

Archbishop Aspirino (1895)

Death is but a great coal-black vulture hovering in anticipation over my front doorstep, ready to pounce once my throbbing heart refuses to operate according to the commands given from my brain. My life is ebbing away fast, my temperature is steaming at around 456.89 degrees fahrenheit and my head is ready to become a nuclear supanova once superheat conditions are reached.

I have at last contracted a severe dose of the SHITS (Something Horribly Internally Twisted Syndrome), a debilitating disease from which there is no known quick cure. Following some recent generic fingerprinting research, the origin of this disease has been traced back to a British Rail porter who worked on Victoria station in 1987, but has since passed on.

There is no known cure for this valetudinarianism, a type of kwashiorker affliction that resembles myxomatosis in rabbits, and yet the painful side effects can be minimised if my train to London arrives on time just once in a week. After living in hope for six years, this morning I've at last given up such hopeless dreaming and resorted to the more traditional medical remedies for alleviating this pain.

I have consumed three packets of Rennies, four spoons of Andrews liver salts, three aspirins, a cup of thick black coffee and I then burnt the British Rail timetable.

Success is not achieved as a result of taking these remedies and my brain goes into spasmodic tremors every few seconds, during which affliction I see a huge number of masturbating black spiders crawling across my eyes every time I blink.

An average human being blinks twenty times per minute and this translates to one hell of a lot of wanking spiders for me to put up with every day if I remain ill forever. I would prefer to have an immediate head amputation because every time I lift my unshaven brain damaged skull too fast, a red hot poker passes from one ear to the other, taking the shortest possible route, resulting in such excruciating pain that my fear of spiders is momentarily forgotten.

Life should be so beautiful for any close relative of Adolf Hitler, instead I am living out my last moments being tortured like a medieval traitor of the crown. I want to live for tomorrow and for tomorrow's tomorrow and not to die here in a sordid bachelor's pad all alone and scared with only a group of disgusting spiders as company. And why should I die whilst so young, handsome and desirable to the opposite sex? I belong to the largest and most famous health insurance scheme in the world, The National Health Service of Great Britain no less and deserve a better fate.

My cure is at hand, da da da! I only need pick up the telephone and call my doctor, the one and only Doctor Kenya, to obtain immediate medical service and a life saving cure for my illness on the good old reliable N.H.S. health insurance scheme. Doctor Kenya will rush around by emergency ambulance to offer his medical assistance - my future survival is now assured and I shall survive for another day - Da Da Da! Fuck the spiders.

Feeling far more confident about the future, particularly about seeing Arsenal play Liverpool this afternoon, I pick up my flash new red telephone which I bought from Dixons last year. This wonderful example of modern technology is complete with ten automatically stored numbers and push button automatic redial of the last number facility.

It being such a new toy, no numbers had yet been

programmed into this micro chipped wonder of communications and therefore I manually dialled Doctor Kenya's surgery. It is a well hidden secret that the automatic dialling of last numbers was a feature enforced upon the manufacturers of all electronic style telephones by the democratically elected Government of Great Britain in June 1987.

This new law was passed following forty eight years of constant lobbying by an organisation known as W.N.C.B.A. which translates from *Wrong Numbers Causes Boils Association* which started with an initial membership of only 134 members in 1942, but boasts that this total is now 6,890,678 as of 23rd January last year.

I have thought and debated for hours on how there could have been 134 members of this association in 1942, a time when electronic telephones with automatic dialling hadn't yet been invented. Putting aside my dilemma on this issue, we must all pursue and understand the seriousness of the boils on dialling finger problem.

To wipe the smile off of the faces of those amongst us that consider this as a laughing matter, I command you to go out now into your nearest shopping street and study the huge number of people who you will see are wearing boil plasters on their telephone dialling fingers. Many within our population will be seen trying the latest cover up job of wearing gloves, these people are from the upper class of our society where being seen in the street wearing common boil plasters is something of a disgrace.

It has been estimated by the Cost of Boils to the Nation Department in Westminster that it has cost us an amazing £2,456,897,345.78 in lost output last year due to people who could not attend work because of bloody great finger boils.

The root cause of all these boily fingers off work problems is that we all continuously get wrong numbers when using the telephone and the latest automatic dialling of the last number device has not yet been fitted to most telephones.

By the year 2000 AD, when over 99% of all telephones will have been replaced by these new devices, it is reckoned that the membership of W.N.C.B.A. will have dropped back to 589 and the total lost production costs will fall to about £2,356,897.06. Now my doubtful readers, I didn't calculate these figures, THEY did and if you have any queries then please do not write to me, but send your snotty correspondence direct to: The Right Honourable Arthur Dobbins, The Cost of Boils to the Nation Department, 31st Floor, 10 Downing Street, London. No stamp is required.

Telephone complaints on this issue can be attempted by calling Dobbo direct on 081 001 0001 but don't expect any reply because his line is always engaged, even at 2 o'clock in the morning.

Back to my story about my dying. I telephoned the doctor's surgery and can anybody guess what happened next? Yes, my attentive experienced students of learning, the line is of course engaged, but that's what comes of giving cheap medical insurance to everybody because when it's free everybody wants it. We should increase the premiums on the NHS medical health care policies to such a high level that only a few people, including me, can afford the payments to alleviate the busy telephone line factor.

With such a savage increase in costs, we would have a drop of ninety six percent in the total number of NHS policy holders, which means that I would get through to my GP at the first time of dialling. This dreaming is getting me nowhere as I must keep trying to get through, but because my doctor's number is not programmed into the A.R.O.L.N. device, I must dial the number with a very sore finger, becoming sorer by the dial.

After forty three minutes I win the raffle - yes I hear the long lost and almost forgotten sound - "beep! beep!............" This ringing carries on for exactly fifty two seconds until a voice from doom watch answers

"Doctors surgery" and nothing else is uttered, just like talking to a devil in the night. Dare I invite a speedier death by having vocal association with Madam Mortuary or will I chicken out and return home to my normal remedy of a large brandy to cure this something "ytus" disease?

Many things I can be accused of, but cowardice and chicken shitedness is not part of my repertoire of failings, so I answer "Hello doctor's surgery, I'm dying and urgently require medical assistance under the terms of my National Health Service insurance policy. Please rush a doctor here immediately." Not bad huh?

Whilst still complimenting myself on such a smart arsed answer, a cold chill and frost emerged from the telephone headset and a voice from satan uttered, "Do what? If you need private medical care we are not the right people buddy!" She then slams down the phone whilst I scream crazy obscenities down the disconnected line like a castrated parrot. Such obscenities are really not essential for me to repeat within this book of learning.

I have brought this crisis upon myself by trying to take the piss out of an overworked telephonist who probably has huge bursting boils on the tips of all of her fingers. Quite obviously I made a basic error of judgement by trying to converse with her in a tone of voice and level of intelligence that proved totally beyond the Maid of Death's comprehension.

I must try again, but this time being very careful and polite; and yes, even to the point of sounding like a real creep - I must make sure that help is only a short moment away to halt the spreading of this terminal illness spreading rapidly within bursting head. Indeed I must act like anybody else requiring help from the good old faithful N.H.S. - I must crawl and beg.

If I live through this illness I shall always add seven apples to my weekly shopping list and then we can all stuff the N.H.S..

With the luck of a lobster not yet in the boiling pot, I

succeeded in getting through again after only twelve minutes of dialling, and the same nightmare voice answered, "Doctors surgery." I responded with the respect of a Pope. "Good morning I wonder if it is possible for me to see the doctor sometime today because I think I'm dying."

Mortuary maid replies "I'm afraid that Doctor Osmand Kenya is tied up with appointments all day, the earliest time for an appointment is 12.15 pm tomorrow" and the telephone line then goes silent. I restrained my natural impulse to be cocky and replied "But by then I will be dead and then the doctor cannot help me. I need help today - please!"

With a substantial increase in her octave level she starts lecturing me. "There is no need to shout at me young man, if you promise to be polite and be here by 11.00 this morning, I will see what I can do for you!" She then slams down the phone, not even bothering to take a note of my name or wishing me a nice day. Such instant criticism under bad health conditions is probably unjustified because maybe she's never visited Florida. By not obtaining my personal details on the telephone, she is either a telephonic psychic medium with powers of knowing a person's name by just holding a telephone in her hand and conversing with them, or she has simply written down "Right Rude Bastard" in the appropriate column of the appointment book.

Either answer is acceptable to me because when I feel like S.H.I.T. I am prepared to accept help from wherever or from whomever it is being offered. It's only 8.30 am and I have plenty of time.

I dragged myself from my bed at exactly 9.00 am and listened to the world news as I attempted to shave off a two day old beard and half of my face. This cropping of human stubble proved to be more difficult than described by Gillette on the razor blade package, a failure due to my very shaky hands not coordinating as they should. I had much greater success in shaving off half of my face.

My giddiness increasing substantially after losing three pints of valuable blood down the sink.

It became obvious that if I didn't stop this effort of self destruction by attempting to shave, then Dracula would soon be arriving to take his final revenge. Bolox to the shaving, I'll just programme in old Doctor Kenya's number into the automatic dialling programme under "0" so that in future I just dial 0 for doctor. This automatic dialling facility will ensure that I avoid the danger of getting finger boils the next time I'm ill and require medical assistance.

On the subject of automatic widgets for telephones, an old school colleague of mine, now living in California, sent me a copy of the "Widget Gadgets for Midgets" magazine that included details of a telephone that will dial to a voice command. Originally designed for use by Japanese midgets working in large American corporate offices, this telephone is now very popular with large Americans working for Japanese corporate offices.

This "KommandFone" saves you even moving your arse to call a number, let alone your fingers - pretty smart these electronic guys. Where will it all end? "KommandFone" can even be programmed to accept two different voice commands at the same time, which is very useful for the majority of my drunken friends of learning.

If you buy one of these amazing units, be sure to programme in two different ways - once when you are fully sober and again when you are smashed out of your tiny mind. Such doppio perfecto preplanning will allow you to summon medical help or a prostitute when you are sober and also when your heart is giving out due to an over indulgence with Johny Walker's Black Label.

I return without further ado to my medical story.

Whilst getting ready to go out to see the doc and be cured of my ailments, I sit sat back to reflect upon the ability of good old Doc Kenya whom I met for the first time some eight years ago.

When entering his surgery for the first time I asked

"Doctor Kenya, I have masses of little black crawling insects living and breeding under the skin in the strangest of places on my body. They are very itchy, annoying and embarrassing to my wife and recently the milkman is also showing undue concern. Surely they can't be normal?"

After scratching his filthy head and picking his nose for a few moments, Doctor Kenya formed his beautiful set of white teeth into a wonderful monkey type grin and replied, "Mitter Dicko Heady, no neet to vully about dis, I haf some velly goot med sin for dis. All vill be velly okey dokey." He then gives me a jam jar full of an evil smelling mysterious looking liquid at which I expressed some concern but he reassures me. "Mitter Dicko Heady, Dis Po shon iss velly goot and you must rub in your skin all ofer you. All crawley buggers vill go avay velly soon."

A confident man our Doc, so I went away to try the velly good po shon and I did indeed rub it in all over my body even though it smelt like shite and dead rats combined. Within a matter of five days I returned to see the Doc and told him, "Doctor the insects have gone but I'm now growing a big hard tit out of the centre of my forehead and I think the last po shon you gave me was the cause of this."

In absolute surprise he responded "Dis not a tit Mitter Dicko Heady becoss I did mix wit de po shon much male hoe mon to be quite sure all okey dokey."

After examining this very large hard lump on my forehead he smiled and said "Mitter Dicko Heado dis needs much betta po shon wid estra velly strong anti botika" and he handed me a tube of Bombay Spot Remover for which he charged £7.50. With this reassurance

I went away happy and rubbed this new cream onto the hard lump on my forehead every four hours. After a further six weeks, I started to worry even further when this lump grew out of my head to a length of ten inches.

I returned to see Doctor Kenya in less than a charitable mood and as I walked into his surgery I said

"Doctor, I've now got an even bigger tit sticking out of my bloody heady - now what on earth can you do to get rid of it?"

People who can look calm and smile under adversity will always be the biggest winners in a crisis. With this theory in mind, Doctor Kenya looked at my large protruding tit and after a few minutes reading a reference book on *Growths and Things* he gave me his medical opinion. "Mitter Dicko Heady, dis lump iss nots a tits cos dis iss a growth hor mone skin growth and diss iz nothing toos vorry abouts."

He then proceeds to give me a huge injection of antibiotics direct into my big hormone titty lump and confidently predicts, "Mitter Dicko Heado dis lump vill bees gone avays buys nest veek - ifs not ven plees come back to sees mees."

The hormone titty lumpy did not go away as predicted by our confident medical practitioner Doctor Kenya, it grew longer up to a length of fourteen inches by the following Monday and was becoming a big embarrassment to me. In anger I steamed into the doctor's surgery, "Just look at this poxy hormone titty lumpy now, I thought you said it would go away in a few days!"

Still smiling he looked carefully at this extended growth and the smile dropped off of his face. "Mitter Dicko Heady yoos mut goes now toos dee ospital toos gets full checko." After collecting a referal letter from his shaking hands, I rush off to the hospital to see a fully qualified specialist Mr. Gonkirenaminpata who must have attended the same charm school as Doctor Kenya.

He took sample cuts of my large hormone lump and told me in his Oxford accent that I should go back to see Doctor Kenya tomorrow at 10.00 am for the results. I am a worried man with a big lump on my head.

I arrived early to see Doctor Kenya, who was kind enough to keep me waiting only a mere thirty seven minutes past my appointment time. As I walked into his surgery I was confronted by Doctor Kenya and six other

Polaroid camera toting doctors in white coats, everyone laughing profusely and garbling away in various foreign tongues.

Whilst they continued laughing and taking endless photographs of my head, Doctor Kenya commented, "Amazing Mitter Dicko heady, I tink you need some diff rent po shon wit hor mones of dee girley type to cure did problem." Not fully satisfied with this explanation of my very embarrassing growth, I asked him in a rather bad tempered way, "Doctor, what the hell is wrong with me and can you ask this crazy gang to piss off?"

Looking very excited, Doctor Kenya replied to my outburst by saying, "dee tests at dee ospital shows dat Dicko heado, you are dee onlees person evers to have a second penis, and dis is growing out offer yours head!"

Jesus Christ, I had a second prick growing out of my head and this doctor and his laughing crew think it's a great discovery. I panicked, like anyone else who had just been told that he had two pricks, and demanded that he gets me to a hospital rapidly to have this second penis removed from my forehead post haste and without delay.

"Unfortunately Dicko heado dis is not posibully cause if one prick on head dies then dee other prick down dare dies and yous dies. Vee tink dat yous should get a big hat to vear overs dee top off dis prick."

My God, I've got to live with two pricks forever and cover the top one up with a big hat! I cried and mumbled to him, "Are you telling me that every morning when I get out of bed and look out of my bedroom window to look at the ducks on my pond, all I'm going to see is a big prick sticking down?"

Doctor Kenya smiles sympathetically and replies "Dis iss no problem Dicko Heady because you will not see dis biggo pricko cos yous havtz two big hairy balls covering your eyes." I really hate humorous doctors when I've got a big lump on my head.

I hate such sick humour from anybody, let alone a highly paid National Health doctor who should show more moderation when treating patients with nervous tendencies. After gritting my teeth at having to absorb such ridicule, without being able to punch him in the teeth, I learnt very quickly that there was indeed a cure for having twin dicks. He gave me a huge half gallon bottle of a new po shon to rub in as instructed and I am relieved to report that this second penis is now shrinking rapidly, but the side affect is that all the hairs are falling off of my body. Still I suppose I must be satisfied with the positive things in life.

Now the first person to say Dick Head by name, dick head by nature will be expelled from the course

Notwithstanding these mild worries that I had concerning Doctor Kenya's ability as a medical practitioner, I also read recently in the "Indonesian Potion Mart" magazine that he was now under investigation for alleged malpractice of a very serious and strange type. To explain this in detail, it is first important to understand that the Doc has also owned a very large greyhound breeding kennels in Windsor for the past six years, but no one has ever seen any greyhounds leaving these premises as either pets or racing animals.

Three years ago he installed a large deep freezer store next to the kennel area and bought a delivery van with *Body Parts* signwritten on the side of this refrigerated vehicle. An investigation was carried out by the *Royal Society For the Protection Of Dogs Being Used As Spare Parts For Human Transplant Operations* over a period of six months and subsequently some very convincing circumstantial evidence was found to prove that some of these greyhounds were being bred for such a diabolical use human.

Since this revelation the kennels have erected a ten foot high electrified fence around the premises to stop further snoopers getting in. The side of the refrigerated delivery van now reads "Doctor Kenya's International Trading Company". This scandal in itself was not a real problem for Doctor Kenya until it became known that he also owned *D.O.K.'s Organ Transplant Supplies International plc* which supplied all types of frozen organs for transplant operations to hospitals in Indonesia, where they had virtually no regulations controlling this type of sale.

The scheme started going wrong in a big way following the results of the Asian Games held in Indonesia last year when all the track medals were won by Indonesian athletes in incredibly fast times. We had results that included the 1500 metres in 1 minute 45.8 seconds, 1000 metres in 1 minute 12.34 seconds, 400 metres in 27.89 seconds and the 100 metres in 6.98 seconds. Even more suspicious was the indonesian 10,000 metres race winner who finished in 13 minutes 24.78 seconds and lapped the previous world record holder twice.

This remarkable athlete named Wong Ho has experienced some difficulties in standing upright over these past few months and last week his parents renamed him Bonzo to save further embarrassment. Despite our suspicions, a man is innocent until proven guilty and this also applies to our dear Doc.

My goodness, it's 10.46 am and I'm sitting hear daydreaming about Doctor Kenya and now I've only got fifteen minutes to get to the surgery for my appointment. I dress quickly in my usual attire of jeans and tee shirt, the shirt printed with a new slogan of mine I am a Dick Head just in case I get lost in the big city. I jump into my clapped out Morris Minor and drive at breakneck speed to meet my appointment with a possible prediction of impending death.

Upon arrival at the surgery car park, I parked across the entrance and place my best sign on the windscreen saying "Back in 5 minutes". I also employ one of my latest techniques of covering both door handles with magic glue to catch any would be car thieves. Have you noticed how it's the real twats in this world that become indignant and bullish at the slightest encouragement?

It's like placing a strip of fly paper in the kitchen where you are sure to catch the big headed bastards first.

I entered the surgery reception area and struggled up to the counter, feeling as ill as any Charlton Athletic football player. Waiting a lifetime at the counter without any vocal response from anyone is annoying in itself, but waiting whilst an enormous and really ugly woman speaks to her mother on the phone about how she would sort out her husband Wally when he arrives home is a very pissing off situation.

After listening to the ugly sister for a further ten minutes, I espied an old brass bell sitting quietly at the end of the counter with a stained dirty sign sitting alongside it reading "Ring for Attention". Not one to ignore instructions from a member of Authority, I rang this bell as requested, every three or four seconds for about three minutes, causing a great deal of amusement to the people dying in the adjacent waiting room.

Further ringing then became an impossibility because this antique ringing device disintegrated into being a bell of many pieces to ring no more; in fact all of the pieces fell over the floor causing a great deal of noise and consternation. Such a loud disturbance combined with great laughter from my very ill friends in the waiting room, brought about some instant attention from the Ice Queen. "You've broken our bloody bell, what do you think you're doing?!"

At last a recognition of my existence, so I responded positively, "Well, I would love to help you with your Wally and his girlfriend problem, but Dick Head is dying and needs urgent attention!" In a surging voice she shouted back at me "Don't you swear at me you little rude man, what is your name!"

"Dick Head!" I responded with less than a little venom, even though I felt very ill and wanted to vomit on top of the broken bell pieces.

"You disgusting man, get out of here or I shall call the police and have you arrested for abusive behaviour!"

she shouted at me unnecessarily. To calm things down, I responded kindly, "My dearest lovey dovey, my name really is Dick Head, I am dying of the incurable highly infectious Namibian Clappytitus of the testicles disease, please get me the doctor immediately."

Before she could react, I scratched my balls and held her hand in my ball scratching hand and coughed over her to achieve the maximum scared as shite impact. I am pleased to report that it worked like a treat.

So another lesson to learn - when being ignored by an ugly woman, go on the attack, break the bell and make a loud noise.

Being ignored by a pretty woman with big tits requires a different approach.

She screamed in terror and rushed to the wash room where frantic scrubbing could be heard for some three minutes or so. When she reappeared from the wash room she was dressed in a man from Mars suit, a plastic dungaree set obviously made for coping with the Aids scare in the operating theatre. "Follow me please Mr. Head" she croaked through a breathing mask.

I followed her and said "When you finish with me, could you see if somebody could move the car blocking the car park so that I can go home straight afterwards." With a nod of her plastic covered head she led me into the doctor's surgery and introduced me to my doctor, "Mr. Head, doctor." Doctor Kenya smiled and asked first about my past and present problems, "Ello Mitter Dicky Heady, how iss your crabbies and your supa new willy?"

I replied "Well doctor, all these problems are now cured and the head dicky has gone away but I am now losing all of my hair as a result of your po chon cure. However, I am here today to inform you that I must have a new po shon to cure me of my drinking problem because the wicked drink is killing me."

With an even bigger smile he laughed and said, "Mr. Dicky Heady, you are a velly lucky man as I haf a velly new po shon just for dis problem!"

To cut a long story short, the new po shon has cured me of my drinking habits but there is a very dangerous side effect to this cure. During full moons I experience horrible hallucinations where evil spirits chase me into a fiery furnace with glasses of cognac and large guns in their hands. I see these spirits loading the guns, all the bullets with the name of Dick Head printed on them. What can this mean?

What about the magic glue? Ah, I though you'd all forgotten about this anti theft system of mine. By the time I emerged from the doctor's surgery after over one hour of trying to understand just what he was saying to me, I am please to report that I had caught two culprits on the DikStik anti thief device.

Alongside my car were two police cars, one ambulance and a fire engine, all with blue lights flashing. Stuck to the offside door handle was a yellow peril traffic warden (25 points) and yes my admirers, stuck to the nearside handle was Queen Death herself - the one and only doom watch doctor's receptionist crying like a fat constipated turkey.

Despite this success with DikStik, trouble could creep up upon Dick Head unless brains and cunning were whipped into action as a matter of some urgency.

I rushed up to the Death Queen, grabbed her in an embrace and shouted "Thank you for helping with my Aids, the doctor says I have four weeks to live." She immediately fainted and the three policemen had serious problems holding her up whilst a fireman completed his hacksaw job of cutting off my door handle which remained stuck to her hand.

I then walked around to the other side of the car and commented to yellow peril, "This is what happens when you can't control those writing fingers of yours my love - have a nice day." Just to be sure of total innocence in the eyes of the law, I approached the police officer who appeared to be in charge of this disturbance and asked "Did you catch the car thief trying to steal my car officer?

Why are these people vandalising my vehicle officer?" Fools get stuck where others fear to tread.

The Doc has now left this country to live and practice in Bolivia where he runs an athletics clinic specialising in performance training. He has a large number of clients from the Eastern countries, all of whom have since broken world records and married alsatians. And what happened to Lassie?

Well, this is a very sad story because the deformity of Lassie's back bone has now become so bad that he must walk on two hands and two feet. This feature allowed the International Athletics Association to ban him from competing in future events by bringing in a new rule that specifies that all athletes must run on their own two feet and must not snarl or bark at fellow competitors.

Lassie came fourth at Crufts last year and would have won the premier prize if during the close inspection stages he hadn't told one of the female judges to "piss off you bitch" when this judge commented on his oriental looks. Lassie has just married a sheep dog from New Zealand and we all wish them a very happy and contented life. A dog's life is better than no life at all, but living in New Zealand is another question.

I must speak some more about our dear doctors, the overworked and under paid elite in our midst, the elegant trained savers of life that we treat with total respect and awe. These dedicated guys living just to help the afflicted are just like all of The Professional Class such as lawyers, bank managers, Archbishops, Queens, Prime Ministers, etc. These professionals are never wrong and can never be proven to be wrong because they hide away the secrets of their success far away from common folk (normally in a big hole).

This is quite understandable as otherwise if they taught everybody to do these professional jobs and allowed us to understand the rules, we could end up with a ludicrous situation where we had a Pope in every town, and what value religion then?

The human being is a stupid animal when it comes to health, life and death. We close our mind to the realities of life and don't want to think about the true state of affairs regarding our health care. When we visit our doctor with any ailment, we are asking an overworked man to try to analyse the most complex machine ever invented which is fitted with billions of components that can go wrong at any time. Your overworked and very tired doctor was probably trained 20 years ago and has virtually no time to read and study the medical advances that have taken place over the last twenty years.

In all walks of life, we have our very clever genii and we have the not so clever arseholes; the same applies to doctors. Here you are, telling him about your problems and he has a schedule that allows him to give you fifteen minutes of his time. Are you with me so far my medical fanatics?

The doctor thinks that he is trying his best, but this is not the case. Self interest in the profession is obvious and is very dangerous to his customers - yes, I refer to us the medical fodder.

In any other walk of competitive professional life where instant diagnosis of millions of facts is required, do you think you have one man in an office where in fifteen minutes he can find the right solution? Within NATO, do you think that situations are considered by one man for fifteen minutes?

"Excuse me sir, can you let me know within fifteen minutes whether you think we should fire the nuclear missiles on Russia or not?" No, indeed not because in 1945 the computer was invented and today it should be compulsory for all GP's to have a terminal in their consulting rooms to check all symptoms against a centralised data bank.

I would feel much happier knowing that my symptoms are being checked by a computer that has all the medical knowledge known to mankind programmed into it rather than a few words from a kindly old man saying, "Take these antibiotics Mr. Head and if the growth doesn't go away within two weeks then come back and see me again."

The present system is guesswork medicine that should not be accepted by any civilised society today. Of course doctors do a good job and many of them work very hard, but so does a horse pulling a cart - but personally I prefer to fly to Milan than be pulled by a cart. This subject is discussed in full depth in my publication Number 7, *Doctors Byte Back?*

Whenever I'm ill and my doctor gives me the magical antibiotics, I always think of the Royal family and I wonder if the Queen or the happy Duke (stories in overseas publications are untrue) are given the same story in fifteen minutes by the Royal Physician.

Does the royal quack push a big cart around the palace with a sign on the side saying Antibiotics - by appointment to H.R.H. Queen Elizabeth II - for royal use only. You can visualise a typical consultation: "Doctor, I am very ill, please cure me or you will be beheaded or forced to go shooting with the Prince."

After a few moments of bowing, the royal doctor responds "Excuse me Your Royal Highness, I must go and get the cart of 'by appointment antibiotics' so that you only take medicine that you have previously approved of. If you don't improve after taking these antibiotics, I'll call back with a different wheelbarrow next week and we'll try something different."

Or maybe They (Royals) still believe in and use only natural medicines, such as the mixture of boiled brains of the arctic pelican and the extract of green frogs semen that the Family eat for stiff muscle problems. I don't believe that this remedy really cures these ailments, but it could explain some of the weird walking habits of the Family.

If these Royal natural medicines are so great why does the royal family keep them such a secret? Why don't they share this knowledge with their loyal subjects? why?

why? why? Maybe these natural potions help make you into a Royal and only potential Royals are allowed access to the secret potions. The medicine has unfortunately had some dramatic failures with a few Royal Princesses lately.

You can probably earn far more royalties from writing a new book on *Remedies from Buckingham Palace* than in writing kiddies books about helicopters. If any Royal decides to steal my idea and does write a book on natural medicine then I do not wish to take any of the Royal royalties which are better utilised for employing some full time Royal marriage guidance counsellors.

I must ask for certain of the remedies that cure you quickly but make you start talking to flowers and cabbages to be clearly marked with an asterisk on the label. These talked to plants may grow faster, but one can imagine the social problems that would be caused by having several thousand people inside Kew gardens holding mass discussions with the plants.

Imagine sitting in your front garden on a sunny Sunday morning, reciting The Holy Bible to the daffodils in front of your neighbour's house. "Just look at Dick Head over there, he has at last lost his bloody marbles, he's reading The Holy Bible to those bloody daffodils, Ho! Ho! Ho!"

Mock not ye non believers, when our judgement day comes we shall see who is right.

No my Royal supporters of Queen and country, I actually believe that the Royal family has a better medical care service than does the working class man. Despite the flower power remedies, royalty get better treatment than ordinary folk, even though it is disguised so that we don't know about it.

To prove my point, I cannot ever remember reading that a member of the Royal family had to wait three years to have a wart on the side of the nose removed or to wait two and a half years for a simple operation. Definitely they have more than a suspicion of privileged medical services, far beyond the services that are possible for us to obtain.

This is a proven fact my subjected students of the Royal family, despite thinking how unfair this could be perceived by the sick pensioners needing medical help. It is understandable that some priority is essential when you're a very royal person, even if your subjects are suffering whilst you take up their hospital bed. We must remember that even royalty are human and humans can become very ill like the rest of us.

In 1976 I had a curious dream in which our royal family experienced a most embarrassing and politically disastrous crisis when the Queen was forced to attend a state function in Iceland in less than first class medical condition. She had a big burst boil on the end of her nose, four front teeth missing, both ears swollen with *Dukes fury* and a dose of *Tibetian crazy fever*, that most contagious of all asian skin rashes.

She was also finding it difficult to talk as she had contracted a debilitating form of distemper from the palace corgis just before she left London, which meant that even croaking was difficult to achieve. It is not known what Prince Philip thought about all of this but he did seem in a much better frame of mind during this crisis.

How impossible it was for The Queen, the country and the empire to look so ugly and sound so awful whilst representing the nation as our head of state at such an important conference. A Royal Family crisis meeting was called to discuss the best solution to such a serious and dangerous problem which could result in armed conflict if things went really wrong.

What should The Queen do? Stay and struggle through the meeting or let Prince Philip or some other family member take her place?

A vote amongst all family members was taken and the result was most surprising, even though each Royal was also allowed to vote for themselves:

The Queen:.................1 vote
Prince Philip:.............0 votes
Prince Charles:..........0 votes
Fergie:........................1 vote
Di:..............................1 vote
The chauffeur:............39 votes
Others ....Abstained

The Queen fired the chauffeur in a real huff and decided that although she was indeed in a bad medical condition she would remain at the meeting as our spokesperson and Head of State and as the most important person.

My strange dream continued with publication in the popular press of the following headlines.

DICK HEAD'S ROYAL FOLLY

Following the publication of Dick Head's latest book, 'The Working Man's Guide To The Galaxy' over 15,000,000 of his graduates voted overwhelmingly for a new Power to the People political party. This new party now holds a 75 seat majority in Parliament and is changing the face of our everyday lives. The day after taking power, the new Prime Minister, Gladstone Churchill (this gentleman changed his name by deed poll from Bert Smith), proposed The Royal Restrictions Bill which ran to 1,675 pages. This Bill was passed without any objections and section 132 sub section 17 stated: In future all members of the Royal family must attend the community clinic in Camden Town for all medical matters.

If Standard National Health Care is good enough for Her subjects then it's good enough for the Royals. Double yellow lines are to be painted on all roads within two miles of the community clinic to be sure of fair treatment for all.

Due entirely to this anti Royal law, the Queen's visit to Iceland has caused a very serious international incident. The Heads of State from all 182 countries were highly offended by the Queen's ugly appearance, embarrassed because she could not hear a word spoken, due to swollen ears, and she could only croak or bark during her speech.

After she sat down she was seen scratching off huge lumps of spotty red skin from her arms and flicking it over the other delegates. By lunch time on the very first day all 182 Heads of State and over 1200 aides had contracted the Tibetian Crazy Fever and were all scratching like crazy.

The meeting broke up in uproar with accusations and threats against the United Kingdom from all sides. This international disgracing of our Queen and country is all because Dick Head wanted to control the Royal Family and make them queue up for medical treatment like everybody else.

We say that Dick Head is a fascist and should be tried for treason, taken to the Tower of London and be beheaded! And then I woke up!

**So, if you intend to criticise Authority,
don't lose your head.**

Chapter 8

INVENTIONS TO XXXXX

"An inventive streak awakens the hidden aspirations of mankind fighting to conquer all and sundry where it is never content unless destruction or disaster temporarily delays this preordained procedure."

Guy Fawkes (1654)

This planet Earth, sustaining so many billions of thriving creatures, committed the unforgiveable sin of allowing our monkey cousins to evolve and develop into the human race. This race, a superior breed of animal has the unique ability of creating anything it so desires without any regard of the consequences of such actions upon the balance of Mother Nature's finely balanced procedures.

Once the steam engine, followed quickly by the internal combustion engine, found its way from the inner thoughts of mankind onto the battlefield of slaughter then we faced only one ultimate conclusion. Until we reach our final destination as a mere dot in eternity, mankind will continue to develop and invent all manner of awe inspiring things for reasons of capital gain, curiosity, fame and sometimes very occasionally for the moral good of mankind.

Often however, these inventions are made essential merely to correct a misdemeanour brought about by other previous inventions of mankind which caused destruction. For Mother Nature, man's destructive stride gives Her no chance now of correcting her sin of allowing the evolution of mankind except by terminating the life of the wayward son and starting over again with this disastrous lesson never forgotten.

Sadly, correcting Her error with the homo sapiens will also necessitate the destruction of most other types of completely innocent life forms.

To fully understand just when and why all of Mother Nature's such well laid plans started to go wrong, we must go back to exactly 17,364,716 BC. We can be so precise about this date following the well publicised series of Borandum carbon tests carried out in 1989 upon human skeletons found below the foundations of the old Coventry Cathedral.

These human remains were found by an archaeological team who dug down to over two hundred feet deep, where those Stone Age remains were discovered as perfect specimens. It established beyond doubt that it was at this point on the earth all those years ago that a Stone Age man, referred to as "Ugh", lived with his ugly toothless common law wife "Err" in a large smelly cave, referred to as "Owm". These people changed the direction of mankind forever.

By today's house design standards, Owm would be rejected out of hand as a disaster area not fit for any car plant worker. This attitude and opinion of the modern car assembly line worker would be further endorsed when he saw the two metre pile of human dung complete with well chewed dinosaur bones chucked on the top of this permanent fixture next to the front door.

This unhealthy practice of storing a big shite heap inside the house, as distasteful as it may seem to us in the luxury of our modern day homes, was the custom in those days and saved a great deal of toilet paper. Modern facilities of sewerage disposal and sit on techniques had not yet been invented - but they would follow on one day in the very near future.

So, Ugh and Err lived at Owm with seventeen exceedingly repulsive children, all named Ahr, together with the two and a half tons of shite and one ton of dinosaur bones. The children were all named Ahr to avoid any confusion that would befall the family by having different names and then forgetting them.

Hospitals were again a thing of the future and any illness within the family was treated as a general part of everyday life and risk. This everyday life and risk managed to kill eleven of the Ahrs before they reached puberty, which was the norm for child mortality in the Stone Age world. If you are a believer and lover of beautiful people then the passing away of these Ahr children was nothing short of a Godsend from Heaven above, even though there still remained six more of the very ugly and aggressive Ahr survivors to haunt the planet for a few more years yet.

Indeed, this same ugly forlorn look can still be seen upon the shoulders of the local people in the same area today, and is referred to as the "Coventry Dumcock Look". God bless the Sky Blues.

The death of our dearest eleventh Ahr was the most tragic and possibly most avoidable one of the lot and this event became the turning point within the recorded history covering the inventive spirit of mankind. I would go even further to say that this disaster became a catalyst that awakened the inventive spirit that would eventually lead us to develop a spaceship for travelling to the moon and create battery operated vibrators built in Taiwan.

Ahr the eleventh, who was only twelve years old at the time of this tragedy, was running at maximum velocity out of Owm, being chased by Ahr the ninth, who was somewhat older at sixteen. As they ran out of the door, they hit each other with flint axes and shouted *Yerbastishitiwanka* and whilst they were so busy trying to kill each other they both bumped into the two metre pile of shite and bones as they fought like a maniac brontosaurus.

The two and a half tons of stinking crappo mix and ton O'bones fell on top of Ahr the eleventh, thus taking him to the blue yonder where all good dead 'ens go.

Ahr the ninth was terrified, because he knew that if he was to inform Ugh and Err of this disaster, then he would very quickly become Ahr the ninth deceased with a flint pick stuck into the back of his head. Self survival being as it was, he kept mum (he called it keeping Err) and the family just assumed that Ahr the eleventh had gone off to fields afar to open up his own Owm. Some six weeks later, whilst eating six foot long spare ribs, Ugh burped loudly, farted six times to the tune of Dixie and shouted "Who moved the family shite pile?!" Nobody replied to this simple question so Ugh hit everybody with his flint walking stick and commanded "Until all the shite has been moved back to where it came from nobody goes out to play!"

So the deceased Ahr the eleventh was quickly found and Ahr the seventh avoided many a boring playless day staying indoors. The dead Ahr was hardly recognisable when uncovered because he had been burnt to solid charcoal by the natural combustion of this crap heap, this burning having taken a grip some few days earlier. When first seeing his black rigid son, Ugh fled outside the cave in absolute panic believing that this black image was a sign from the dark side of evil and indicated bad things were about to happen.

He went to the local mountainside where God appeared as a vision to him alongside a flaming bush and commanded him to mend his ways and rectify the disastrous and evil situation that existed within his family and the local community. So my friends and undergraduates here beginneth the first commandment of inventiveness.

"I am one really pissed off Stoneaged bereaved mother and the wife of a real rock banging prick!" shouted Err after they had found Ahr the eleventh ready for the charcoal burning stove. Despite my feelings for this poor woman having just lost a son, I must say that this was no way for a wife to talk to her breadwinning husband, even if he did persist in storing all that shite in the front room of the family mansion.

Err was not to repeat such abuse, because Ugh, looking totally bemused at hearing such an aggressive comment from his normally passive wife, picked up his flint axe and located it neatly in the centre of Err's forehead at precisely 96.56 miles per hour. In modern terminology this meant that Err was a deceased Err with little concern or worry for the future, let alone that big pile of crap by the front door. Let this be a warning to all wives who are considering any form of criticism of their husbands whilst their loving spouse has a flint axe in his hands. Dead is dead, and it can hurt before the lights go out.

Ugh buried Err in the communal village grave tip and decided to dispose of the crap heap and dinosaurs bones at the same time by tipping them all on top of Err. After selling the few remaining Ahrs to a passing circus, Ugh set about his new life of remorse and dedication to living a better second life than the first. He would become an inventor!

He commenced to build a huge wooden structure resembling a flat roofed shed which covered a massive area of four miles wide by six miles long. The sides were left open except for the support poles, but the roof was constructed and completely covered using two inch thick planks cut from local pine trees. Around this massive structure Ugh built thirty gate houses in stone, complete with pay boxes where, upon the payment of one flint axe, you could pass through the pay gate and reach the roof of this structure by means of wooden stairs.

Once on the roof, the view was a sight for sore Stone Aged eyes because, on top of this huge twenty four square mile platform, Ugh had cut out twelve hundred oval shaped holes in the roof structure. These holes measured sixteen inches across the smallest dimension by nineteen inches across the largest dimension, exactly the right size for the average person. The name given to this marvel of Stone Age construction was "Ugh's Wooden Craphouse" and hence this is the origin of the modern day WC. Ugh became a millionaire in axes overnight and the smell problem in this part of the world was solved forever.

Ugh is the first recorded inventor known to mankind

and this robust gentleman is credited with inventing the WC and laying the foundations for today's Coventry City. Having lived there for a few years I have no doubt as to the authenticity of this fable.

Such a touching and intriguing story from the early days of mankind improves your overall knowledge and illustrates that true human ability can solve any problem that requires solving. All undergraduates should study this hunger of the adventurous spirit within our human make-up as a specialised subject because your knowledge of this will be greatly tested during the final exam. You may even be asked to submit details of your own invention on any subject of your choice.

I consider that your newly found ability to become an inventor of great things is directly attributable to the training and enlightenment that you have received from this book. It is therefore only just and fair that you should share your inventions with me on an equal footing - you retain the satisfaction of being the inventor and I have the intellectual property rights transferred to me.

You don't understand what intellectual property rights mean? Let me explain my friends. It means that once you sign them over to me, then you can continue enjoying life without worry or restraint whilst I am forced to exploit your invention with all the heartbreak that this can cause. I will make the vast investments required to bring your invention to the production stage.

You can have great satisfaction in knowing that all successful inventions earning me in excess of £400,000 in profit over the first two years will result in the original inventors receiving the DikInvent Certificate embossed in gold leaf free of charge. All students sitting the exam must also sign the invention intellectual property transfer rights form. No transfer form, no acceptance of your invention and failure in the exam - quite simple really - got it?

After each year's exam has been marked and assessed, I shall publish a series of Dick Head Graduates

Inventions in which the top 50 inventions from each year's exam papers will be included. This first year's publication will be entitled *Dick Head Graduates Inventions - part 1* and next year's publication will be called *Dick Head Graduates Inventions - part 2,* and so on. I estimate that within twenty years over thirty percent of all patents filed with the Patent Office in London will be under my name.

Becoming an inventor requires an inventive mind and this is a skill not easy to come by even for the experienced original thinker. Having already filed some one hundred and seventy eight different patents, I feel that I am in a position of academic strength to advise you wisely on how to begin on this road to inventing the Disposable Wife or Converting Piss into Petrol inventions. Inventing is very simple once you can identify the problem that needs to be solved. So let me give you some examples of my own inventions to prove this point and to illustrate how clever I am, in addition to being a world famous author.

My very first invention was the DIKWISSAL, which I designed and patented as long ago as 1967 whilst working as an aggressive and good looking young man during my short working period with ALCOHOLICS ACCOMMODATED. This charitable organisation is a modern progressive outfit based in the city of Glasgow and was formed in 1959 by a group of disgraced Lutheran priests to help the many people living in desperate circumstances to survive the evils of drink.

These wonderful saints of the modern age believed in slowly converting alcoholic people into total non drinkers by actually overfeeding them with the very drinks that caused the problem in the first place.

By giving them just too much of a good thing, ALCOHOLICS ACCOMMODATED were practising the policy set down by Professoress Catherine Wodehouse (of Bremerhaven fame) who proved beyond doubt that a monkey forced to eat 50 pounds of nuts per day stopped eating nuts after consuming the first two tons. This theory had been further authenticated in 1963 at PUFFS CLINIC in Putney where habitual cigarette smokers were kept in leg irons for six months and force fed with ten pounds of tobacco every day.

This extraordinary cure was one hundred percent successful as none of the patients ever reverted back to any form of smoking after this drastic treatment. A serious side effect to this otherwise success story is that eight out of ten of these non smoking converts committed suicide within twelve months of release because they could not afford to buy the ten pounds of eating tobacco per day that constituted their new life blood required to satisfy this newly acquired addiction in their lives.

At least they didn't die of lung cancer.

Notwithstanding these sad deaths, PUFFS CLINIC has proved beyond doubt that, unlike smoking it, eating tobacco does not endanger your health. They have issued a new cookery book called *Good Tobacco Eating Habits*, which is given away free of charge with every twenty five pound box of BOGBAK Irish bog grown organic eating tobacco purchased before December 25th this year. BOGBAK is sold in a bright green and brown striped carry home pack, complete with carrying handle, and is available at all good pubs and comprehensive schools.

The government exchequer is highly delighted with this latest tobacco revolution which has allowed them to increase tobacco tax by £1.50 per pound to pay for all local government overspending that is now quietly allowed.

The BOGBAK tobacco company is introducing a new BOGBAKPOKE tobacco product next month which has a powerful hormone additive specifically designed to attract members of the opposite sex to overcome the awful off putting aspects of existing tobacco eating men - more about the results of this product in my book number 35, entitled *Dick Head Prevails*.

Stop rambling Richard and get on with the story

about your inventions!

Yes sirree, my DIKWISSAL invention soon became a necessary worktool for ALCOHOLICS ACCOMMODATED at their Glasgow headquarters where they looked after 15,768 inmates who between them drank no less than 640 different types of alcoholic drink every day.

Before the DIKWISSAL was invented and put into practice, ALCOHOLICS ACCOMMODATED required 158 bartending staff working 24 hours per day to keep all of the inmates satisfied by serving them drinks at the right time and of the right type.

No good making excuses or accusations against these unfortunate piss head inmates like "you piss head, you'll have to wait your turn!" because any unfortunate independently minded customer will just say "bolox to you" and take a hike to the nearest boozer to get pissed as and when he wants to - and what then? Having no customers means having no ALCOHOLICS ACCOMMODATED and no ALCOHOLICS ACCOMMODATED means no jobs for the queer priests in Glasgow and very bad news for the BOGBAK tobacco company.

You've got it! It was indeed the BOGBAK tobacco company that sponsored the development of my DIKWISSAL patented unit - They believed that by curing the alcoholics of drink reliance they could be driven towards eating tobacco.

My God, you must accept that capitalism is such a wonderful system once you can organise for greed to take over and allow somebody else to pay your expenses. You only need identify a need, find an organisation that can profit from that need and hey presto, you have a project paid for by somebody else. So starteth the life of the DIKWISSAL.

It all came to me in a flash one evening whilst I watched a documentary on TV describing how those St. Bernard dogs in the Swiss mountains were trained to transport barrels of brandy around their necks to men in need trapped on the mountain side. This is all very well for the 15.5% of the mountain climbing fraternity that drink brandy, but what about the others that drink whisky, gin and rum?

Why didn't the swiss take the brandy out on the mountainside themselves rather than risk the lives of these beautiful canine saints of mountainside rescue missions? The answer to this question is of course very simple and obvious - it is much cheaper and faster to train a dog to do it than to train a miserable yodelling fool from Geneva.

Voila! The DIKWISSAL was already half way designed and heading towards worldwide production and subsequently to earn me millions of pounds in royalties - all because I identified a need.

Have you understood the invention yet, or shall I continue with this most intriguing of stories covering the build up to when I invented the DIKWISSAL? Ah ha, you want me to continue giving you further background data - this is very good indeed as it shows your true and genuine respect for inventors.

Quite simply put, my DIKWISSAL is a standard type of dog whistle that is fitted with a special multiple dial on the top which allows some 640 different settings to be made. The multiple dial adjusts the air outlet of the whistle so that once blown, each of the 640 whistle settings gives 640 different frequencies of the ultrasonic sound that it emitted. Scientists amongst us are aware that such high frequency ultrasonic sounds can be detected by the canine community but cannot be detected by the human ear. Several of our Indonesian athletes are an exception to this rule.

The DIKWISSAL design took me some eighteen months of part time work, mostly in the evenings whilst not producing meat pies or writing books. Success of this invention was always assured, albeit after causing severe schizophrenia in sixty seven dogs used during the hectic prototype trials. These trials were essential for us to correct the ultrasonic frequency levels that were previously set far too high and continuously perforated the eardrums.

These unfortunate very deaf beasts of wolf descent now run around in crazy circles all day in large cages whining like demented cockroaches in season with large funnel shaped hearing aids sticking out of their ears. Advancement of the scientific world demands that certain sacrifices must be accepted by man and dog alike, working on the principle there is no gain without pain.

My conscience readily accepts that this painful inconvenience caused to the deaf dogs is simply part of a much bigger scenario of achievement which will be judged by future generations as a worthwhile sacrifice. In a further act of kindness I have since supplied each of these hard of hearing hounds with huge circular kennels which has at least stopped them from banging their heads against the wire four times every circuit.

So you've invented a stupid bloody whistle with a knob on top - so what Dick Head?

Lateral thinking is a long lost virtue that all of my undergraduates must acquire as nothing can be achieved by rushing around in circles without a final destination in mind. You must all accept without any question of doubt that Dick Head will only progress your education in the forward direction without shunting you left, right or in reverse. No bullshite from me my students, just positive facts to lead you into a better world of knowledge. Therefore no more piss taking about my DIKWISSAL.

The DIKWISSAL was designed for training golden retriever dogs to recognise a selected number of frequencies emitted from each DIKWISSAL. Therefore if you chose to train each dog to recognise only 32 frequency channels, then you only required 20 dogs to cover the whole 640 frequency spectrum - got it? The ALCOHOLICS ACCOMMODATED organisation in fact trained 640 golden retriever dogs in this way, so that no matter which one of the 640 frequencies the DIKWISSAL was set at, the specifically trained dog would react to such an instruction.

ALCOHOLICS ACCOMMODATED fitted gold embossed leather saddlebags to all 640 of the trained dogs, each saddlebag containing the makings of a specific type of drink to satisfy the patient's requirements. Upon registration into the ALCOHOLICS ACCOMMODATED clinic in Glasgow, each patient is given a drinks list, a DIKWISSAL and instructions for use of the MOBILE DIKBAR which is simplicity itself.

For example, if you require a gin and tonic, you referred to the drinks list which showed that this particular drink was number 14 on the drinks list. Simply dial number 14, blow the DIKWISSAL and the gin and tonic dog will hear the signal together with six different gins, tonic (Schhhhhhh), ice (battery operated ice box) and freshly cut lemon and comes a running. When finished with the dog, set your DIKWISSAL dial 000 to send the dog back to the home base bar.

The record time taken at ALCOHOLICS ACCOMMODATED for delivering a drink to a patient in this new way is a mere 5.8 seconds whereas the longest yet recorded is still a reasonable 9.4 seconds - all timed and verified from the moment the DIKWISSAL is actually blown by the patient until the drink is poured out. A huge success no less!

From the moment that the DIKWISSAL was offered onto the open market the response exceeded all expectations and I have not been able to meet all demands and therefore I have fired my market research company. Manufactured by the CANINE WISSAL COMPANY Plc in Southend, the DIKWISSAL is sold at a price of only £14.90 + VAT and is available at all good pet shops, off licenses, police stations, churches, public conveniences and the Tower of London.

I have so far received over £2 million in royalty payments for the DIKWISSAL from all around the world, with Ireland being the biggest market where over six million DIKWISSALS have been sold within the first twelve months of sale. This is an absolutely staggering figure for such a small country like Ireland, but is even more amazing when you consider that this equates to two DIKWISSALS being sold for everybody, man and canine alike.

Due to the dramatic increase in the demand for beds at the IRISH ALCOHOLICS ACCOMMODATED in Ireland, a special outpatients service is now in operation and has 2,657,897 patients registered so far. Bushmills with water outnumbers all other drinks by a ratio of 6.7: 1.

To maximise my income from this DIKWISSAL project, I employed a new marketing company, Statcom Incorporated of Wigan, to study the world markets for such a unique device. After some three months of study, costing a total of £112,879, they submitted a full marketing prospectus which showed that the largest potential market for us would be in China.

Encouraged by the Irish success, and to take advantage of a market where Statcom Incorporated projected that over one billion DIKWISSALS could be sold, I sent twenty fully trained golden retrievers to Peking for the CHINAPISS exhibition in 1989, together with a hundred thousand sample whistles. This food, wine and spirit exhibition was a huge success, with the exhibition hall doors being closed after only two hours each day, when the maximum 187,000 people that the exhibition hall could hold had packed inside.

After demonstrating the DIKWISSAL to about 25,000 gawking chinky people who were sitting in the gangways eating fried rice, we sold 6,000 whistles to them immediately at $29.99 each. This immediate success made us a huge profit on this first day as the cost price for manufacturing the whistle was only 36 pence each. Boy oh boy, China was our oyster and I calculated that I was about to earn royalties of £234,897,0000 within the first twelve months on the Chinese market.

A small cloud of worry crossed my brain cells when all the golden retrievers rushed off the exhibition stand just after lunch and then failed to return despite much frantic blowing of several DIKWISSALS over a period of several hours. They had all disappeared and in fact were never to be seen by us again.

The next morning we had over 50,000 people causing a near riot in a frantic effort to get near our exhibition booth to buy a DIKWISSAL at the price of $29.99. After less than six hours all the remaining whistles were sold out and we placed a sign up on the booth saying in Chinese, "Velly Solly, Dikvissals solli out" which evoked a great deal of hissing and shouting of "Vloody cafitalisp assfards!"

Sticks and stones may break my bones etc. My capitalist smugness evaporated very quickly when at lunch time the scenes around our exhibition booth became very ugly indeed and violence was on the horizon from which my British Passport would not be protecting me.

About 35,000 of the customers who had purchased DIKWISSALS from us earlier that morning were standing around in riotous mood, blowing their whistles for all they were worth and then shouting filthy abuse. After constant puffing and blowing for some twenty minutes, a tribal chant started up from this mob of, "Ahyom marl behou tar!" which translates approximately to "where the hell are the dogs!"

Rodney Pumpernickel, the British consul, was called as a matter of extreme urgency in an effort for to find out what all the shouting was about and also to get a British gun boat sent to Peking as soon as possible. After explaining my worries to Rodney, he sighed and then showed me the headlines of the Peking English language exhibition newspaper which had the main headlines of:

$29.99 buys a dog and whistle
Buyers claim that they are very tasty!

We immediately telephoned the CRSPCA head office in Peking and complained bitterly about this culinary abuse of our pet dogs. Mr. Sou Yoo Tou a senior representative retorted very curtly to this complaint, "Mr. Head, we never try to give you Europeans a lecture about how you eat your meat in your country and if you think that any sensible Chinese person would pay you $29.99 for a whistle that's worth 50 cents, then you are a prick of the first order and your name suits you - so I suggest you stop moaning and piss off, taking your no noise whistles with you!"

This same gentleman today owns a take away restaurant next to the Battersea dogs home, following his dismissal from the CRSPCA in Peking for verbal abuse against foreign whistle makers. He can often be seen in his back garden blowing one of his DIKWISSALs in the hope of attracting some long lost whistle trained dogs who have fallen on bad times. His meat chop suey is very cheap and makes you frisky.

Without further ado or waiting for your applause concerning the DIKWISSAL project, I would like to move on quickly to explain my second invention, that of the DIKTRAY.

Following a government survey carried out in June 1986, it was calculated using the latest computerised statistical analysis techniques, that exactly 67.45% of all people in this country eat at least one meal a day on a tray in front of the TV set. So my potential inventors, here I had searched out another need which was awaiting fulfilment and hence the DIKTRAY came into being and is now used by over twenty five million people worldwide. Are you starting to learn about the art of inventing my trusty students?

The DIKTRAY is a one piece moulded biodegradable polyurethane tray that is "body moulded" to fit around the average body when it is seated in front of the TV set. No longer will you spill gravy or beer down the front of your clothes if you use a DIKTRAY because the body moulding covers all danger areas of this type. Your plate is moulded into the tray and is fully insulated thus keeping all hot foods hot and all cold foods cold. Similarly you have moulded compartments for soup, dessert and bread and butter. The salt and pepper pots are of unbreakable plastic and fit securely into their location moulding housings, thus avoiding the ever frustrating shout of, "Oh shite I've dropped the bastard salt pot!" Your wine and beer glasses are fitted in a similar way and a three foot long bendy straw is coil wound with spring return for use at any time for any drink.

By including the DIKARM support, you have a floor mounted pedestal onto which the DIKTRAY fits and allows easy movement in or out of the eating position. The DIKTRAY with DIKARM is the modern luxurious way of eating and watching TV, available at the ridiculously cheap price of only £24.99 each. This price is little more than the average cost for one month's supply of condoms, a pure silk tie or five pairs of Y fronts.

After you finish your meal you simply push the leftovers into the garbage bin and wash the DIKTRAY under the tap or place it in the dishwasher - so easy, so very easy, you wonder why nobody has invented it before.

When first launched onto the UK market, our advertising agency arranged a series of twenty second prime time TV commercials which showed the detective Dick Tracy sitting in front of the TV with a DIKTRAY and the commentator saying, "Even Dick Tracy uses a Diktray, see?"

There are some people who search into the most innocently spoken items in order to identify something dirty and this is exactly what happened to us after this particular advertisement was shown on the goggle box. Over 22,000 people managed to be offended by this innocent promotion, thinking that we were indicating a double meaning in our marketing plan, and they complained to the Television Advertising Standards

Committee. In response to such a large public outcry the ASC forced us to withdraw this so called offensive promotion from further TV transmission, but not before over two million DIKTRAYS had been sold.

Exports are leaping ahead to assist the chancellor of the exchequer's daily overspending cock ups, but sales are very slow in Morocco, Uganda, Tibet and Swaziland. In fact, wherever television are not available we find the sales of DIKTRAYS are generally at a very low level, but this is not always the case.

Our overseas sales executive, Joseph Weinstein-Steinhardt recently obtained an order for 50,000 bright red coloured DIKTRAYS from a remote tribe located in a central African country but three months after the shipment we received the following telegram:

"To chieftain of Diktray tribe,

Your excellency, we wish to inform you that the red colour is fantastic and the food fits on the trays perfectly, but we cannot find out how to get a picture to watch. Please send instructions with the next order we are placing now for 75,000 bright yellow DIKTRAYS. Please also send 6 tons of salt, 6 tons of pepper and 250,000 squeezy bottles of Heinz tomato ketchup."

We completed the order as requested and sent 200,000 copies of the SONY brochure advertising their range of TV's. The customer was highly delighted with this brochure and we now sell them this brochure at £18.50 per copy.

McDikalds may not yet be a familiar name to most people, but it may soon be a bigger server of fast food than its famous brother in trade, McDonalds. How can we beat McDonalds at their own game? This answer is very simple because of the new Dikburger which I invented and patented for exclusive use by McDikalds, the future in fast food.

With the ever growing expansion of human knowledge, scientists are now agreed that for a good healthy life, the human body requires a regulated minimum daily intake of several hundred types of vitamins and other elements of the atomic structural range.

After eleven years of research, I have now formulated the DIKBURGER minced meat substitute which is sold now under the brand name of BIG DIK, a product which is guaranteed to build the perfect body. So folks, rush out now to your nearest McDikalds and shout out proudly, "I would like a BIG DIK please!"

Some other inventions of mine include:

DIKBATH for the ultimate bathing experience, fitted with every mod con.

DIKBRUSH for the toothbrush where the toothpaste tube screws into the handle for continuous feeding of toothpaste.

DIKSHOE for shoes with slide on soles and heels to meet all weather conditions and easy replacement.

DIKBOWL for an automatic pets feeding bowl complete with timer for opening and closing of the lid.

DIKDOMMER for an automatic condom warmer and dispenser.

DIKFUZZER for smelling out plain clothed policemen

An inventive mind is an active mind, one which will also search for a better and more efficient way of living through this once in a lifetime opportunity. The subject of this lesson has been to broaden your thinking base to a point where care for all your fellow human beings becomes a major consideration on an everyday basis. In future you will hear people making comments such as, "He's so inventive and considerate all of the time, he really pisses me off". Don't despair at such remarks of envy from your peers because you have now elevated yourself from your old life style into a new world where such sarcastic comments are really just high respect in disguise. Be generous to these people and help them also to progress to a better life by giving them your redundant copy of The Working Man's Guide To The Galaxy which will soon be replaced now by book number 2, *Pilgrims Progress Personified*.

Before I leave this subject until your exam time, I feel that there is one additional patented product which should be explained to you for your intellectual progression. This latest patented invention is called DIKFREE cream and is specifically developed for ladies and their personal protection in this dangerous world.

DIKFREE cream is now available from all good chemists, railway stations and ice cream vans at £6.60 for one boxed tube of cream including detailed instructions for use. This cream is best described as an anti rape deterrent which any female who is worried about a sexual attack can use.

You apply it to the areas of your body which you consider are the most vulnerable to this type of assault, this choice will vary according to one's level of perversity. DIKFREE is totally harmless to the female body as it contains a special hormone which is compatible with the female chemistry, but has the dire opposite effect when even one single male hormone approaches it. It has a most catastrophic effect on the male penis as only the slightest contact with DIKFREE results in terrible agony and excruciating pain far beyond any pain previously experienced by mankind.

Hospital treatment is required urgently within one hour of any male's plonker coming into contact with DIKFREE or else the consequences are most catastrophic and far reaching. After only one hour of a male penis being in contact with DIKFREE the male testicles start to shrivel up like dried walnuts and after a further two hours they drop off with a huge clonking sound as they hit the ground.

Each box of DIKFREE cream comes complete with a bright yellow and red fluorescent self adhesive label which must be used by the cream user. This label is to be applied to the forehead of the cream user as a warning and deterrent to all would be rapists, husbands and boyfriends. These labels read:

I am a DIKFREE person. Touch me and your balls drop off

WARNING: *DIKFREE gives no protection against lesbian attacks but can be used by choirboys.*

Also available, on police instigated prescription only, is the latest antidote FREEDIKFREE cream which requires 24 hours to take full effect, but at least your balls won't drop off whilst you're in prison awaiting trial.

DIKFREEDETEK is an alternative spray-on liquid antidote that turns a bright pink when it comes into contact with DIKFREE and this bright pink colour remains with you for the rest of your life to identify you as a pervert.

Some medical journals have accused me of going too far with the launch of DIKFREEDETEK at £26.70 per aerosol can, but I say that at £13.35 per ball, this is a low price to pay for rapists to remain in this world albeit with a high pitched voice. Better be safe and pinko than castrated.

The Minister of Health, John Pilgrim, recently my praises in the House of Commons by saying, "Since the dawn of mankind, women have been subjected to sexual abuse, but I can now report that Dick Head has achieved another first by using his genius of inventiveness. This time he has astounded medical science by inventing a product called DIKFREE which is today being used by over 94% of the female population and 98% of the members of Parliament and 100% of the church community. Keep up the good work Dick Head, your country is proud of you!"

John Pilgrim omitted to comment upon the large number of 231 M.P's who since the launch of DIKFREE now walk in a strange way and talk like warbling canaries.

Did I dream that a supply of DIKFREE was recently delivered secretly to the city residence of one of our "Royals"? It would be breaking confidence and against my medical ethics to report on exactly who this person is. Suffice it to say that this person's abode is located in London not far from Charing Cross station, has huge iron gates outside and men in red suits marching up and down all day in the front garden. The FREEDIKFREE antidote cream has not yet been ordered from Bucki.........ooops which is a very satisfactory state of affairs.

One of the less than loyal servants employed at the royal pad overheard the recipient of DIKFREE talking to a close relative with regards to the "horrific suffering it could cause to boyfriends, husbands or horses.....and as for losing his balls; what balls!" This royal person refuses to wear the self adhesive label on her forehead, even though I have offered to print a special gold edition saying:

I am a ROYAL DIKFREE person
My husband is an arsehole

This royal person replied by secret letter:

Dear Mr. Head,

Thank you for your considerate thought of sending me the gold labels but after some further consideration, I have decided that they require the following change in the text to suit the current situation that exists within my marriage:

"My husband is a Right Royal Arsehole - Plenty of verbal but has shrivelled balls."

Please print 5000 labels in gold for royal distribution within the palace and to overseas hideaways, plus a further 5,000,000 printed onto Guinness beer mats that I can pass out from my carriage as I look down upon my admirers. Please send the invoice to the Chancellor of the Exchequer, not forgetting to add on my 25% commission, which is to be paid by direct transfer into Panama Bank A/C No:65434653.

Finally, I would like to royally thank you for the tremendous service that you have afforded both the British people and mankind in general with your incredible gift of solving the problems of energy conservation, life on another planet, authority, conscience and thousands more. And now your greatest achievement - DIKFREE. Wherever DIKFREE goes, you will be remembered with gratitude by some and feared by others.

Your knighthood will be just reward in the very near future.

God bless you Dick Head.

Your humble royal admirer,

XXXXXXXX

Some dream!

Chapter 9

FROM OBENFLOOF TO GETTING STUFFED

"To be relaxed is a golden gift not even offered to a headless chicken."

Hennig Olsen (1862)

Hennig Olsen, a giant amongst men, was born on 4th October 1831 in the village of Oben a small township located just a few kilometres outside Oslo in Norway. He was the oldest son of a miserable cheesemaking father and a nutty yoghurt making mother, but other than that the family was very happy. No doubt if Hennig Olsen and his family were alive today then they could now be making real dairy ice cream and frozen desserts for Marks & Spencer.

The Olsen family owned and kept over 3000 goats from whence came the milk from which the famous *Obenfloof Cheese Factory plc* produced the wonderful Obenfloof brand of cheese. This unique cheese was originally developed by the Olsen family over a period of twelve centuries, since its first introduction into Norway some 1200 years earlier.

It is said that around the year 600 AD, Oslo was a tiny village established merely as a stop off point to feed and house the seal and whale hunters of Bavaria during their return trip from the Arctic Circle hunting grounds. These early kraut hunters employed huge sledges pulled by Danish reindeer for transporting their harpooned harvested blubber fat to the German market where it was converted into beer sausage for the teutonic hordes to burp on.

The seal skins were used by the richer Bavarian aristocracy as an early form of Bavarian stop-cock contraceptive device, which was shown to be greatly ineffective in carrying out its true function, but was considered to be the "in thing" to wear at that time and kept parts of the body warm that other skins failed to reach.

By 625 AD Oslo had grown up and expanded dramatically to a point where it boasted some 26 wooden houses, 27 stone built churches and one deeply dug well, complete with a large bucket. You can quickly observe from this data that being a man of the cloth kept you warmer and better fed than being a simple Norwegian serf.

Unfortunately, as the church could not employ all the serfs as priests, then some of the local serfy populace were forced to live in the wooden houses working their Norwegian balls off to pay for the upkeep of all the holy churches. Although in this chapter we refer to the name of this town as that of Oslo in those early days of Bavarian influence, the real name was actually Nowark, but more about this later.

In Nowark they brewed their own local brand of beer which was sold far afield across large parts of Europe, even as far as Castleford in Yorkshire.

Everything was proceeding as normal in Nowark and it appeared as though tranquillity would continue forever, until that fateful day on 23rd June 625 AD when a sailing ship called OZ left the shores of Tibet carrying with it a crew of 354 men, 1200 Tibetian mountain goats, 150 Peking ducks and 3 Chinese cooks on board. This expeditionary ship was heading for the "Oasis of the North" where it was foretold by several circumcised Tibetian wise men with long beards that great riches awaited all brave men who dared to venture to this golden paradise located on the edge of the world.

Were these men from Tibet brave or utterly foolhardy? I will not judge them now as too much water has since passed under the bridge, but one thing is indisputable, set sail they most certainly did, complete with goats, ducks and Chinese cooks. These three Chinese cooks still have a great deal to answer for as they later bred like rabbits and sent members of their families to open up take-away restaurants in most parts of the world.

The Tibetian oracles stated that when you reached this oasis on the edge of the world, "you can climb down the outer edge to heaven" and this explained the reason why 1200 mountain goats were taken along on this epic voyage because they were for riding down this avenue to heaven where "riches beyond a man's dreams" would be found in open abundance. All crew members carried large pick axes, chisels, hammers and booty bags - as it was preplanned for them to return home complete with all those millions of pearls, no matter that the gates would look really tatty and cheap afterwards.

The good ship OZ spent over seven months at sea searching for any part of the edge of the world - whatever edge they found would be used as a starting point to get them to their final discovery. Yes, Sinbad the captain had thought out his task to the last finest detail, once you find the edge, any edge - just keep following the edge in a clockwise direction and you must eventually find the part of the edge where heaven existed. Quite smart really for a slant eyed mariner, but his navigational theory did little to alleviate the sufferings of the 1200 puking sea sick goats and very worried Peking ducks who were having a very rough time at sea.

The seamen were very happy to be alive as they had been given a simple choice by our merry captain Sinbad of either accepting the sufferings without complaint or simply get the fuck off the ship.

Early one sunny morning, the good ship OZ hit a submerged reef just outside the harbour of Nowark and this large inconvenient obstruction decided that the good ship OZ would sail no more; indeed it sank like a stone and its hull settled nice and firmly on the floor of the harbour sea bed where it still sits to this day.

Captain Sinbad, 37 of his motley slant eyed crew, 69 ducks, 693 goats and unfortunately also the three Chinese cooks survived this terrible disaster and reached the shore by rowing boat which they managed to launch in the nick of time just before OZ was lost forever. They all thought that at last they had hit the edge of the world and the OZ had gone over the edge and crashed into heaven.

Without wasting time and space inside this valuable watershed of tutorial literature (pronounced lit-ter-rat-chew-ra) in giving you the lurid and brutal accounts of how the local men folk were all butchered and the women folk were all raped, we shall take this as read and continue with the interesting details of this tale.

Within fifteen years, the memories of the old days of Nowark evaporated as these new occupiers of the territory went about their daily routine of raping the women which helped them to adapt to their new surroundings. They changed the name of Nowark to OZ-LOW, a somewhat sympathetic yet cynical reminder of the disaster that beset their ship and brought them to this place, which they had found out since was a long way from heaven.

For the casual visitor in Oslo today, it is common to see Tibetian features in the faces of many folk in the area, particularly in the village areas located north of the city. In these northern villages, as is the case in many other isolated communities around the world, there is an old feudal saying which simply translates as "keep it in the family" and our Tibetian/Norwegian cousins lived and practised these convictions. It is also very easy to accept that in an area where the outside temperature in the winter drops to thirty degrees below celsius, the task of warming oneself up could be a good reason for this constant family interbreeding as is the norm in most parts of Norway.

This phenomenon of close family interbreeding is nowhere more apparent than in the village of Oben where the subject matter of this chapter, Hennig Olsen, was born. Here, everybody can still speak fluently in the ancient Tibetian tongue which has been passed down through the ages from father to son, normally taught whilst everybody is producing cheese. The Norwegian language is virtually unspoken in this area of the country which is difficult for outsiders to understand, but the Norwegian government is content in allowing this behaviour to go on unchecked, just in case the ancient Tibetan scriptures of Chua Lumpo are even slightly bordering on the truth.

Chua Lumpo was a holy scribe living in the 12th century BC who wrote the famous words, "Yongte arsoo delou vagst poo lau maer geroo" which roughly translated means "Don't piss around with a person's tongue". This logic sound acceptable enough to me as I already speak sixteen languages, plus German guttural talk, to get me by in any situation.

In this same ancient Tibetan dialect the word for goats milk cheese is floof and hence the name Obenfloof was chosen for the very famous goats milk cheese that is the one and only product produced in Oben, and is at the centre of this story.

Once the Tibetan people had completely intermingled with the Norwegian people in the area, they started production of the Obenfloof cheese and very quickly its fame and wondrous taste spread across all of Norway and into other countries within the Scandinavian region. In fact, since 1643, Obenfloof cheese has become the stable diet of all Norwegian armies, leading to such success in battle that the commanders of opposing armies would always demand that their spies went out to find out "If those bastards are eating Obenfloof cheese!"

If the spies returned and said, "Sir, they have tons of the Obenfloof crap," then fear and despair leading to defeatism would be the result. In is a well recorded fact that no Norwegian army has ever lost a battle over the past six centuries, no matter what the odds against them were, providing they had eaten Obenfloof cheese the night before battle.

One of the most famous victories ever recorded was in 1645 when thirty Norwegian Obenfloof eating nuns defended their convent against an army of 3,600 marauding Swedish fiends and beat them with three days to spare. In more recent times, in 1943 to be exact, a much loved son of Germany, Adolf Hitler who happens to be a relation of mine, ordered an airborne invasion of the Obenfloof cheese factory during which raid his airborne forces obtained some 500 tons of the product. Unfortunately for Adolf, all of this cheese was stolen and eaten by an SS regiment in Berlin before it could be sent to the Russian front.

History is controlled by apparently insignificant actions occurring at certain unplanned moments in time, and this action by the SS is the big one that tipped the scales of the second world war on the Russian front. If this Obenfloof cheese had reached the forces around Leningrad, just imagine the difference it would have made. Hitlerburg?, who knows.

Mussolini heard of this coup by Hitler's airborne division where they had obtained the 500 tons of Obenfloof cheese and realised that his spaghetti eating cowards of an army could be made into Roman warriors if only he could get them Obenfloof cheese as well. He sent an urgent telegraph message to Berlin and Hitler replied:

"Dear Il Duce,

I have read with great humour your request for 3 million tons of Obenfloof cheese to help bolster the shitlessness of your arsehole army, but would ask you why you require 3.5 tons per soldier. I appreciate your compliments specifying that German soldiers are 100,000 times braver than your Italian piss heads and I note your calculation that if a German soldier requires 3.5Kg of Obenfloof cheese to win an iron cross then an Italian soldier would mathematically require 3.5 tons.

After speaking to our SS head of dietetic and catering services, Herr Gobbler, he informs me that the human body would have great difficulty in digesting this amount of cheese over the period of a war. He estimates that it would take some 1,732 years for a soldier to eat this quantity and most certainly your soldiers would experience some cholesterol instigated blockages of the heart after they had eaten the first ton.

You may have noticed that the opposing Allied forces are fast approaching Rome and my field commanders are quite confident that you do not have 1,732 years in which to breed bravery and avoid defeat. It is further suggested that you are a short, fat, arrogant and ignorant arsehole that deserves to be strung up by your neck to a lamp post - but I reserve my judgement.

Regards,

Your dominant senior partner in mass murder

Adolf"

Straight to the point our Adolf - never a man to waste words!

Adolf eventually found out that his SS officers had eaten the first 500 tons of Obenfloof cheese so bravely acquired by his airborne forces and in revenge he sent them to a far happier place in the sky via a gas chamber. Another airborne division was sent to confiscate the remaining 350 tons of matured Obenfloof that was stored in underground caves located outside the village for the two year maturing process.

Once bitten - twice shy - this is logic that was well learnt and absorbed by the populace of Oben as they had been expecting another invasion every day since the first one had been carried out. As true patriots they planned a sabotage operation that would do great damage to the mighty German war machine that was now raging across Europe and other parts of the world.

No, they couldn't fight with arms; this was impossible against ruthless super race killers from the skies - but they could use their brains and cheesemaking skills to achieve similar ends.

When the troops landed they indeed found 350 tons of so called "Obenfloof" cheese in the cave storage areas and all was loaded onto six huge Fokker big transport planes that had landed in Oslo that fateful day. "Zis istz vell strangetz becotz zay artz cherringstz utz" spoke the senior airborne officer when he saw the local Norwegians waving swastika flags and shouting out heil Hitler whilst laughing like hyenas.

As these supermen departed for Germany with the 350 tons of Obenfloof cheese on board that could turn the tide for the battle for Europe, little did they realise that the "Obenfloof" cheese on board was in fact a look alike cheese called "Sinenborg". This is a cheap copy which is matured using a herb called "runiie" and this specialised cheese is normally used only as a medical cure for dire cases of constipation, and even then only 50 grams is the maximum dose to be taken within any 10 day period.

Once this cheese was sent to the Russian front, Hitler's problems really started in earnest as it is a very complicated manoeuvre to fire a machine gun with your trousers around your ankles and whilst standing and slipping in a six foot pile of shite. When captured by the advancing army, the Russian soldiers refused to get anywhere near these smelly revolting shitty Germans who were all shouting "bastard Obenfloof!" This is where the name Sourkraut came from.

Back to Hennig Olsen, for God's sake.

He was born at precisely midday on the 4th October, just as 27 sets of bells started to ring out the twelfth toll from all of the 27 churches in Oben. His mother found the previous eleven tolls not quite as pleasant as she did the last, but you only respect pleasure if you experience pain. - no pain, no gain.

This eventful timing should have been an omen in Oben that here was born a boy of uniqueness who was going to rise majestically above the height of normal Obeners. But as usual, the Obeners were all too busy slogging away at making Obenfloof cheese or polishing the church bells to notice the coming of Hennig. If it hadn't been for the three wise men and a shining star, then the same thing could have happened on 0 AD

Hennig lived with his family in their three roomed wooden house on the family farm, where his father quickly taught him all he knew about cheesemaking, and there was nothing his father didn't know on this subject. This teaching included the milking of the goats where for many years Hennig would hear his father shouting out, "Don't squeeze the tits so hard Hennig!" or maybe, "Don't turn the churn so fast Hennig!" and often, "Be careful lifting the cheeses Hennig, they should never be lifted any faster than 17cm per second as variations in altitude ruin the secret qualities."

And so it went on, day after day and year after year until 1876 when Hennig was 45 years old. On 1st of April that year his father passed away at the age of 73, which was a most tragic and mysterious death. Most of the locals put his father's death down to the revenge of the much squeezed tits after he was found stamped to death in the wooden milking parlour with some fifty goats stamping a war dance all over him. He was not completely dead when Hennig rushed over and held him in his arms on that sad Sunday morning.

His dearest father uttered the last words of life, "Watch out for the white headed, big titted one, she'll kill you Hennig - watch out for that Karoline she fu...............ha............" He passed away in Hennig's arms but had a huge beaming smile on his face - now that's the way to go.

When he reached his last gasp, Karoline the milk maid assistant came down the ladder from the loft above and started crying in great despair whilst securing her blouse and brushing her blonde hair away from her eyes. "He was so gooooooooood!" she blurted, without considering the bereaved family's feelings all around her. "He was so Biiiiiiiig" she said smiling at Hennig as she spoke these sensual words. Like father, like son is a well proven saying and Karoline enjoyed the next few hours with Hennig bringing him up to date on how his father had died.

Tragedy and pleasure sometimes get confused, as nine months later Karoline gave birth to quadruplet sons. She had no real way of being sure if Hennig was their brother or father, but it was thought better to assume he was indeed the father. Whatever the truth of the matter might be, this is none of our business as it is purely an internal affair of the Olsen family, and us prying into this any deeper is insensitive and non productive to our case.

It speedily dawned upon Hennig that to support these four children and a hearty wife required an income greatly above what could be earnt by selling Obenfloof cheese. This was not because Norway did not have a common agricultural policy on farm prices, but because the Norwegian government took 60% of all income in taxes to fight the Norwegian/Belgium war that had been raging for over twelve years at this time.

The Belgians occupy the most densely populated country in Europe, with a population split of 6% wanky people and 94% sprouts, and are one bunch of real miserable sods. The war with Norway was caused by the King Alberterano II of Belgium taking his filthy habits of gobbing (spitting with big green lumps) with him when on a state visit to meet Prince Hoppenflurgen of Oslo to discuss the marriage of his daughter Alberina to Prince Dopenfloog of Kristiansand. When it came to discussing just who would be footing the bill for such an extravagant wedding, King Alberterano II shouted out like a crazy man with incensed anti Belgium crabs in his pants, "You are getting the name of our monarchy! for this you must pay the bill!" and then he gobbed a real top class competition winner bonzo directly into the prince's eye and down his beard.

This crass intimidation caused the Prince of Norway to demand that his father declare war upon these Belgium "cretins of culture" and peace would not be declared until a full apology was received for this disgraceful and despicable behaviour. "When we defeat Belgium, we shall execute anyone, particularly a Belgium, who gobs in any public or private place" spoke Prince Hoppenflurgen in uncontrollable anger as he wiped this green ernie from his beard.

Eventually, the Norwegian army, with the benefit of Obenfloof cheese, invaded Belgium and over three quarters of the country surrendered immediately and the Norwegians received their apology as demanded. King Alberterano II had his balls cut off in a successful effort to give him other things to think of, rather than gobbing in the street.

The quarter of Belgium that remained unconquered was left alone and eventually drawn in on the European map as Flemish to ensure that all people should beware of the gobbing if they dare visit this area with such filthy habits.

Hennig worked night and day, seven days a week, but to no avail, because at the end of the first year after the quadruplets were born he was summoned to the local branch of the Cheesemakers Bank by an angry bank manager. "Mr. Olsen, we note that your outgoings are approaching some 25,760 kroners and your income is only 376 kroners over the past 312 days of trading. Your bank overdraft is now, as of today's date, some 57,987.45 kroners and yet your asset value is a meagre 987.34 kroners. Mr. Olsen you are knackered and a bankrupt. Please hand over your factory keys to my secretary and close the door on the way out. Now piss off and don't come back."

You will understand from this conversation with the friendly bank manager that the approach taken by banks regarding customer relationships has hardly changed over the past 150 years. When you've got money, you can borrow more than you require. When you've got assets the bank forces loans down your throat. When you need money under normal business pressures then you've got no chance. Just give them your factory keys and drop yourself in the garbage can.

Here was Hennig with a wife and four young baby sons, all living in a wooden house which he must quit within one month from today, thus leaving him and his devastated family on the streets. In those olden days in Norway, no unemployment money was available for the many poor souls that were thrown out on the streets at the mercy of the unmerciful people.

Unless Hennig switched on his brain box rapido to find a solution to this terminal cash flow problem, then he faced just one simple choice; watch his family starve to death or kill himself. Stop!, stop!, stop!, my friends - I missed out on another option, he could become an inventor and earn millions of kroners and tell the bank manager to get positively and beautifully stuffed - and this is ex act lee what Hennig did.

He designed the OLSEN-OBENFLOOF RAPID CHEESEMAKER which he proceeded to patent successfully in 63 countries throughout the world. This portable unit was a genius of simplicity and engineering, fitted with wheels thus enabling it to be transported to the goats in the hills. It had 36 milking arms, and once these were connected to 36 goats teats everything thereon was fully automatic including pasteurisation, cooling, adding culture and final cooling.

By winding up a spring loaded pump mechanism with a huge two man key and then releasing the "suck/start" lever the whole process was put into fully automatic operation so that six hours later, and untouched by human hand, out came fully moulded blocks of Obenfloof cheese demoulded and delivered onto a packing table.

The real secret of this system was the need to use a special "Obenfloof cheese culture tablet" which looked very similar to a suppository for a giant elephant or for an average Frenchman. This tablet design and make up was part of his worldwide patent and was now sold across the globe together with his automatic machine. With one tablet being required for every 50 kilogram block of Obenfloof cheese, Hennig really coined in the dosh.

By 1877, Hennig retired with his family (now increased to 11 sons) to Kristiansand Kastle, which is located in the Southernmost part of Norway where no Tibetian influence is yet present in the local human bloodstock. The patent royalties had so far earnt him over 65,000,000,000,000,000 kroners which at 10.5 to the pound sterling is an awful lot of money.

If we take the value of money today, this royalty equates to £93,000,000,000,000,000,000 or thereabouts. Royalties for the Olsen family dropped away between 1919 and 1939, but ever since 1945 they have been flooding in from South America, Vietnam, Cambodia, Russia, Afghanistan, Africa and the Middle East.

With all this cash, Hennig first had the manager of the Cheesemakers Bank (the one that took away his old factory) shot and then he became the most relaxed man in Norway, and probably the most relaxed man in the world. He was therefore both very rich and very relaxed - a combination that is impossible today with the multitude of thieves, charity organisations and murderers around us. It is not possible for anyone today to live seven consecutive days in peace and quiet without an envelope being thrust through the letter box, or a jangling box being stuffed under our noses, all requesting money for a cause.

I love any cause that makes me feel a hero, but the most loved cause I have is not to pay any money to the fat cats that run the charity organisations and this gives me a relaxed life.

In my experience, I have found that where there is money there will surely be thieves to steal this money, without the consent of the owners. Where money is given with no receipt required, as is the case with charity collections, then this dosh is treated as heaven handed to them on a golden platter by our criminal fraternity. This haven of easy money with no check or retribution will invite abuse, just like an unlidded honey jar left in the rose garden on a hot summer's day.

Such abuse will be rampant within charity organisations and the church. I respect the small percentage of ordinary gullible people that work night and day in the interest of charity work, but this respect of human endeavour cannot change the natural facts of humanity. I also accept that a proportion of all the cash collected for charity does eventually reach the people in need - but there must be a better way in a civilised society, or do we have a group of people that want to do good whatever other people do?

If this is true, then we would be doing this group of do goodie people a disservice by pressing the governments of the world to eliminate the need for charity. If this happened then what next for these good people who need people to look after?

It is because of the lack of business acumen present within these organisations that the thieves are not rooted out and sent to the bricked up and chained gaol out yonder to become queers at the cost of HM prison services. If you discuss my theory with the charity workers concerned they will go crazeeeeeeeeeeeeeeeee with uncontrollable rage and will shout out wildly to the heavens above, "Dick Head you arrogant prick! why do you even try to accuse the kind charity workers within the Red Rose Organisation of stealing money from the mouths of the people that we feed!"

Calm down people, calm down, you giver of money to the poor, because shouting will only damage your charitable vocal chords and will not have one iota of influence upon my proven theories relating to the thieving class.

My final word on this matter is that I'm right and your stupid and wrong to believe that by wearing an armband and carrying a rattling tin you will turn a crook into going straight. Just leave me alone to relax without your criticism, and you can go about your job of pinching the charitable cash. Deal?

I cannot waste any more time on such a pointless argument in this publication, but if there are still some protesters out there in disagreement with me, I can argue this further with you in my publication No.19 entitled *Give and Take, it's a thieves world,* which is due to be published next year. A price of £176.56 is being charged for this book for all people that support charity workers and only £1.56 will be charged for those that support the thieves.

The difference of £175 per book purchased by the charity workers supporters will be sent to the charity of "Thieves in Need" at Wormwood Scrubbs with your compliments. Now what do you do? Ha, Ha, Ha! Do you ignore the argument and go on holiday to Spain, or do you become a lying crook and get the book at the cheap price of £1.56? You can only order this book from me so we shall soon know how many people are devoted to defending their stupid theory about total honesty in charity work.

For the honest thieves buying this book, you will receive a special six inch diameter badge that says, "Money isn't evryfink, but I'll take it anyway!" For other buyers your badge will say, "I'm a poor honest tosspot"

Back to Hennig

He sat every day feeling rich and relaxxxxxxxxed, this being assisted by his conviction that the world was not flat as thought by his ancestral Tibetian twats (how stupid can you be), but spherical like a Chinese cook's head (those troublemakers again). Hennig decided to pass on his knowledge to the working class and became a writer and wrote many classics, including, *Relaxing made easy* and *Poverty is a real crappy life.*

These writings have placed Hennig into the list of history's top 100 writers over the past 100 years, the list compiled by another writer, Lars Stoppe. Lars Stoppe has himself failed ever to reach the top 100,000 list of all time writers, but he was selected by the Norwegian Literature

Society to carry out this survey and draw up the top 100 list.

How is it that learned people throughout history turn to such fools of no relevance or natural ability for making really important decisions? I will tell you the answer to this previously unanswered riddle, a riddle that has driven men and whole nations to despair over the ages. It is because the decision to appoint an idiot to make the decision is taken by the cleverest men of the land, each one of them wanting the job themselves but refusing to let any of the other clever men take the job if he doesn't get it himself.

All of this group of cleverest men are assembled to vote for the cleverest person who will be the man to make the final assessment on who are the top 100 writers. None of these clever men want one of the other clever men to win the vote and therefore an alternative must be found. If we select a thick prick then he can "never be more famous than me" - they all think the same - so hence the thick prick is voted in and the thick prick selects other thick pricks to win all the prizes. Rather like politics really.

Finally the ultimate accolade - Da! de! da!

On the first of January in the year 1900, Hennig was voted "The most relaxed man in the world" by the 100 most relaxed men in the world. This award consisted of a big leather upholstered armchair, a wristwatch that didn't work and a beautiful bronze sculpture about fourteen inches high depicting two ballroom dancers performing the Vienna waltz. A solid gold plaque mounted onto the side of the polished oak of this sculpture read, "The world thanks Hennig Olsen for perfecting the science of total relaxation".

They had to wake up Hennig to make the presentation, but once awake he walked slowly, yet very precisely, to the podium to make his acceptance speech which he had not yet thought about.

Only an unrelaxed man would write and rehearse an acceptance speech - this was of course forbidden for the most relaxed man in the world. This had been discussed by the 100 members beforehand and a unanimous decision had been made inasmuch that should Hennig be seen to read from notes or present a rehearsed speech then everybody present would hiss and boo until the speech ended. This rather childish behaviour from these relaxed fellows of the relaxed club was found unnecessary as Hennig spoke out fully relaxed and fully unrehearsed for over one hour.

"My Lords, ladies and gentlemen, much as I am unaccustomed to making such speeches (a single small hiss could be heard at this point!), I must say how proud and very relaxed I am to be voted as the most relaxed man in the world, and I an confident that you have made the correct choice. I feel obliged to give a warning to all present this evening; the world is now being run by power mad politicians who are hell bent on passing new laws every day.

These new laws are designed to control our freedom of choice, increase our personal stress levels, destroy any chance of relaxing and keep us all poor. I have even heard rumours that the government will consider passing a law where a proportion of our income will be taxed!

Can you believe this type of imposition upon our freedom to live a free life?

I can also tragically foresee a day when all our lives will be controlled by a small group of politicians and huge industrial monopolies. A day when you will even have to pay for water! (laughing from the audience at this point could be heard). A day when we shall all pay over half of our total incomes to support masses of people who are not prepared to work. Days when our national heritage will be changed forever by the influx of mixed races into our society from all parts of the world. Dark days when governments will take over and nationalise complete industries purely for ideological reasons - yes my friends, maybe even the Bank of England, no less! Sad days when all freedom is dead or at the very best is fully stifled into non existence. Relaxation will exist and die simultaneously at birth."

What ridiculous speculation?

Just before Hennig died on the 17th March 1914, he wrote his final masterpiece, *Searching for freedom in a modern democracy*. This epic in literature covered some 3,675 pages and over 10 million words before his final words were printed, "A modern democracy cannot defend real freedom, only the freedom that democracy brainwashes the people to believe". What a crazy fellow this Olsen chap turned out to be.

Now my cheesemaking buffoons, have you grasped the nettle of this dairy making chapter, or are you still fuming over 'no crooks in charity work'? You think you really understand? Good.

The centre point of this chapter is of course the natural born right to go about our lives in an unhindered and a fully relaxed way in our modern day "free" society. Do we live like free human beings or like government trained robots?

"Of course we are free! - just look at Africa or Russia if you want to argue this stupid point, Dick Head!" Shout all you wish my rampant ignorant low ability and non thinking students, because if you don't listen to argument then you are just acting like the government educated arsehole that you wish to remain. Do you think that I would waste my time discussing the history of some group of stupid Tibetian sailors, a flat earth, Obenfloof bloody cheese and a crazy inventor, if I was just wasting your time?

No my friends, just be quiet for a few more moments, forget your preconceived ideas and listen to your tutor Dickie for a while longer. You have the natural human right to ignore my advice and throw this book into your garbage can, or to punch two holes in the spine and hang it up in your little room. If you do, then you will be marked down on our computer listing as a F.S.D.I.P. The S means Stupid, the D means Democratically and the I means Indoctrinated - work the remainder out for yourselves if you can.

Don't start getting up tight about these other words because it will simply confirm how biased you are about my totally refreshing and clear approach to all working class thinking issues. I could be referring to "Flipping" and "Person", but you are just intent on trying to ridicule and undermine my learned writings.

Please tear out this page and return it to me signed and I will send you your certificate for at least reaching this stage of the graduation course. This is not a full pass certificate, but it is better than nothing (not a lot better), except that we've then finished our dealings with a doubter of crass proportions such as you. For the remainder of non doubters I shall continue.

The point at issue is that it is of little use trying to justify soccer hooligans by pointing to murdering mobs in South Africa - because we are talking about the freedom that we deserve and not making a comparison with freedom, or lack of it, elsewhere. This pointing to other areas of conflict (lack of freedom?) is not our individually thought out assessment of what we actually think, it is the brain washing assessment we receive from that electronic box and as written in our newspapers. We never see the real lack of freedom data from the "bad news" areas of the world - only the "good news" that sells space or improves position in some bloody list or other. You don't agree?

We are never taught our natural born human rights at any time in our lives, because the people teaching us have already been through the modern day system of conforming with the rules set down by civilised government. We are never taught to completely relax our inner being, from birth through to our adult life, as in fact we are taught the direct opposite at all times. "You must do this because..............." we are forced from all sides to do something, no matter if we enjoy it or not.

This indoctrinated habit and ingrained nature is the very basis of all our social ills and explains the aggressiveness that is endemic within modern day society. Society informs us of just what we should strive to achieve and when this achievement cannot be reached or obtained by normal means, then our aggressiveness against society surfaces.

Only a rare lucky individual says, "enough is enough", but if somebody does wish to drop out of this rat race of human greed and uselessness then he is speedily regarded by organised society as an outcast, a weirdo, one not to invite for "drinkies" on a Saturday evening. After all my posh readers, how would appearances look if some smelly weirdo, sporting a ragged beard was to attend the golf club "Captain's Evening" wearing his jeans and smoking pot. Also, imagine him talking to your business associates about the rich capitalistic swine wasting money whilst children starved to death in Africa - No good at all for your future business prospects and a complete knackering of your chances of becoming the next Captain of the golf club.

No matter that this unkempt old mate Tommy was your best friend for twenty years as you grew up together, and that he speaketh only what is the indisputable facts of rich man/poor man life. As you really want to be Captain of your golf club and the wife's sulking - bolox to Tommy and those starving millions - "Another large gin & tonic Rodney and throw that bum out on the street."

Therefore, all Dick Head Graduates must learn to be calm and relaxed and treat this as a naturally born commodity that must be relearnt for incorporation within your basic character if you are to help us rule this land. You must learn to sit, smile and listen, without fear of stress, to all the crap spoken by those fellows in Authority, such as the tax man, bank manager, teachers, poll tax collectors, policemen, parking meter pricks, lawyers, and all other people sent out to degrade us in our lives. When you are approached by that famous wording, "can I have a word with you sir?" which is the standard approach of these people before they then inform you, "are you aware sir that............."

Remember my friends, when all else fails just go out and buy an Obenfloof cheesemaking kit and tell the world to get stuffed.

God bless Hennig Olsen

Chapter 10

UMPTEEN ETHOS TO JOHN BROWN

"The overall length of longitude spanning an extended ostrich's cock is inversely proportional to the size of a diseased dwarf duck with squat legs having his arse hanging a testicle hair's thickness from the ground."

Elizabeth Nightingale (1879)

Have you ever heard of the umpteen ethos characteristic?

No doubt you are more than colossally and ineffably baffled and confused by this teratological way of describing the common human trait of multiple personality, this strange syndrome that both haunts and assists the human mind. A confused and endangered human mind will find its own defence against the stupidity and pressures of modern day enforced slavery which cowers the free spirit that fights for existence within all mankind.

Fence in our kindred inheritance, defended so well by our forefathers with the loss of so many millions of sacred lives, and the human mind will find a different plane by which to fly free with a spiritual self expression that can still exist under today's conditions.

Dependent upon the individual surroundings that effect this self defensive umpteen ethos, will decide the specific plane chosen umpteen ethos for mere existence at any chosen moment in time. A plane for all situations; new worlds waiting in anticipation; lands ready and willing to give sanctuary without question or charge to all lost travellers from our modern life of insanity.

Umpteen ethos man is not to be pitied, but rather to be envied. He is a man with many loving beautiful wives, each one there to satisfy a particular mood and ready to accept him as he is. Each wife awaiting her few moments of shared pleasure, knowing that she will be the only wife during short dramatic and passionate encounters, but happy and content with these majestic moments which far exceed the misery of mere mortal experience.

Jealousy cannot be part of this perfectly orchestrated life where each chosen part of umpteen ethos is a galaxy apart from that of its brothers, yet close enough to form one complete unexplained human being in paradise. Let each of these lives exist undisturbed during their allotted time in eternity, whilst still on this side of the grave, where mere human misunderstandings are transposed into sparkling moments of wonder situated beyond the envious control of the mass hypocrisy embedded into our society today.

My first introduction into umpteen ethos came at the age of only fourteen when a new very short schoolboy named Peter Ivan Slack started at our school. This fellow very soon became universally referred to as "Nutty" Slack because he was born in Wales, was of non-Welsh mixed race, and had the most weird way of behaving that I had ever seen. I was no Greek philosopher sitting in judgement on mankind at this tender age of fourteen, but it was very clear to me during these juvenile days that Nutty Slack was a very strange fellow indeed.

We had many other very strange head banging cases at our school, but Nutty beat them all by several light years and a bit more as a bonus, and his inexplicable approach to life scared us all more than somewhat, because he was weird in a satanic kind of way.

Boys congregating together during their school days quickly gel into a cruel breed of thugs, intent on doing the utmost physical and mental damage to all those unfortunates who are cast outside this mystical circle of hit men dressed in short trousers. So it came about that Nutty was considered, not only a prat of doubtful heritage, but a real short wanker that needed to be punished on a regular basis for such shortcomings (excuse the unintended pun). Apart from being Welsh,

Nutty was also a member of the Slack midget family, of circus and cigar making fame, and stood just 99.67cm whilst wearing his high heeled football boots and reaching for the sky with his fingers uncurled.

"Nutty you're a SLAWB!" would be the regular offensive shout from our super gang every morning as Nutty entered the school playground. His grand and sad entrance was made by walking under the bottom metal rung of the school entrance gate. Nutty tried on many occasions to reach up to grasp the handle of the gate, but it was always just a tiny wee bit too high for him to reach. This indicated that he was not getting any taller on a day by day comparison. We always made sure that the gate was firmly closed a few minutes before Nutty arrived at school so that he had the indignity of actually appearing as the very short midget that he was by being forced to walk underneath.

I assumed that Nutty lived in a shoe box with his midget mother and father where they chose to also install two pairs of size 5A shoes manufactured by Clark's, the famous shoe makers. Clark's, those wonders of modern science, a magnificent company who have tried to undistort the feet of our nation's millions of children who otherwise would be forced to live out their lives as W.C's.

No my students, W.C. is not a nickname for shithouse children, which is such an extremely crude name so often used to describe bow legged children who are forced to wear the cheapo ordinary working class shoes that are too thin for the feet and turn them into semi-cripples. No, W.C. in this context, stands for Without Clark's and covers over 90% of the world's children who are forced by the international order of things to wear non-Clark's shoes and hence to become cripples and impose a very heavy burden upon the economic life-style of their society.

I must give credit to the original shoe designer at Clark's, who in my dayreaming I have seen hobbling to work one day to become disenchanted with the shoe making process that had made him yet another cripple in a world full of cripples.

You can picture my dreams now as he limped into his office in great pain, "Arthur, my bloody feet are killing me and my kids are also starting to hobble!" So he set to work in his dedicated attempt at solving this universal hobbling problem and after years of study, discovered the secret that more than one width of shoe was required to suit all the children of this crippled world. This simple discovery brought about a revolution in shoe design and manufacturing that improved the walking habits of mankind for milleniums to come.

I further visualised that up until the Clark's shoe revolution, the Limpostick Walking Stick Company Limited had experienced 134 years of uninterrupted growth and profits which matched the level of crippleness that inhabited the shoes of the world's population. All this was very quickly about to come to an end after the introduction of the multiple width Clark's shoes and as one could expect, Limpostick's were very unhappy about this development and went bankrupt soon afterwards.

Personally, I would have solved this hobbling problem in a different way by designing new *DikShoe Stretchable Shoes* using leather made from cows hides where the cows had been fed elastic bands and Bostik mixed with their feed. This would have had the huge advantage of requiring only one width of shoe which would stretch to suit the foot itself - quite an advantage over the laborious process of having to produce a full range of non-stretchable shoes.

Don't shout "you cruel bastard!" because you know nothing about how nice the flavours of my elastic bands and Bostik would be if I was to breed cows for this purpose.

With Clark's shoes introduced onto the market, a revolution in walking practice took place in many parts of the world. Millions of happy smiling children could sometimes be seen skipping down the street and singing that famous song, "I'm walking in Clark's shoes to New Orleans". Now we have our children relieved of hobbling feet, but these same millions of sons and daughters still leave our state schools as illiterate idiots unable to read or write, but by Christ can they run fast from the scene of the crime in their multi-width shoes!

When you sit back in your armchair in front of a blazing log fire wearing Clark's slippers drinking a bottle or two of Barolo wine, you may also consider that the condition of our nation's feet is a very important commodity. A great commodity indeed, which has been purposely neglected by all governments of the world since shoes were first invented by the Germans during the great flood of 1786 BC.

Yes my friends, the super race also invented the common shoe, albeit we in Great Britain have now discarded the motorised sole that enabled a million men to march fifty abreast and keep exactly in step from Berlin to Stalingrad. Apparently the motorised control is unreliable over any greater distance and further development ceased following objections from the Kremlin in 1945.

Our super cousins have now diverted their research into a new type of high tech shoe which allows the proud wearer to be a taller person, better worker, better swimmer, blonder, better driver, better smiler, better liar, richer and superior to all other nations. They claim not to have yet fully perfected this new shoe, but I have my doubts about their truthfulness and integrity on this issue.

With the latest emphasis on environmental issues, it will not be very long before the common automobile will be an obsolete method of transport, once we reach the situation where we have insufficient oxygen in the atmosphere to allow the engine to run. To survive NOSS (No Oxygen Syndrome Situation), we must all start walking again instead of using the car and to do this we need reliable non hobbling feet.

I expect the Germans and Japanese to be the first nations to bring in new laws where Clark's shoes will be distributed to all their schools and subsequently to every child free of charge. Within a single generation the Germans will be able to walk faster and more efficiently than the rest of us ordinary folk around the world and have cleaner air to breathe.

Don't ridicule my predictions concerning these new national walking shoes, you gullible undergraduates, that's what the British shoe salesman did when he first tried to sell shoes to the Arab world. After only six months trying to sell to the Arabs he said to his German competitor, "It's all yours Fritz you super race vanker, I'm off home because nobody here wears shoes and it's a waste of time."

The sad result is that the Arabs wear only German shoes, even to this day. Following my revelations in this chapter concerning the British shoe industry, you will now quickly see that Clark's will be the target for an immediate takeover by Deutchenbooten of Munich or Mitsofooti of Tokyo. These are two companies leading the world markets in the high tech footwear field. I have thought of buying shares in Clark's as they are sure to quadruple in value, but my lawyer considers that this would be an illegal act due to my privileged insider information.

Last year after rubbing yet again some DikRub anti hobbling cream onto my poor feet to relieve the pain, I approached the Minister for Walking & Disabled, Mr. Foot, with the question, "How is it that a democratic government can allow shoe makers (Clark's excluded) to manufacture and sell just one fixed width of shoe to the flower of our youth in this great land of ours? You are aware sir, that these obsolete shoes will turn them into a country full of crippled juvenile illiterates not fit to stand (let alone walk) alongside the modern day marching German master race who are all wearing CLARKENFABRIK JAKSTUMPERS issued free of charge by their government?" I fell asleep during his hour long answer, so I must apologise for not being able to take you further along this uninteresting road of learning regarding shoe design or the waffling of government tosspots.

I can tell you confidentially that our Italian war hero cousins from pizzaland issue free of charge a special type of Clarkino fur lined shoe for all children below the age of seventy three, albeit with the toes moulded facing to the rear. The printed instructions accompanying these shoes, instructions which every respectable Italian keeps alongside his condoms in a secret compartment of his wallet, explains the advantage of this rear facing feature quite clearly.

I will translate these instructions into the English tongue to save you ignorant zero-lingual fools the embarrassment of nodding your heads whilst you really haven't a clue what it means. I quote as follows from the Il Instructioni di problemi quando bloodi elli, "Use shoes in reverse to piss off quickly in the event of any sign of a fight or challenge no matter that normal logic dictates otherwise - we are Italian and must live to run away to eat and drink another day."

Our French brothers are different yet again in their choice of shoes for their children. Their children below the age of seventy three are all issued with tight fitting plimsolls produced in bright pink rubber with crepe soles, moulded in the shape of a frog's rectum with multiple warts. These plimsolls do look somewhat strange to non-French speaking people but it is clear that none of their children walk with any sign of cramp or hobbling, but they do persist with their perfected frogs poof wiggle that stands them out from a crowd.

This shoe data all goes to prove beyond any reasonable doubt that our democratically elected fools in Parliament should pass a new law now banning the screwing of mallard ducks in public places and to enforce the sale of children's shoes manufactured in expandable rubber or elastic leather to overcome this shameful neglect of our children's feet.

As I was saying, Nutty was very comfortable living at home.

Apart from his height, Nutty was positively the ugliest person I have ever met (so far) in my lifetime, and I really do mean X stream lee ugh leeeee! His father was a prat midget born in Brussels in 1923 and his mother was an even midgetter midget from the Mongolian hills of Mongolia where her family bred big white rabbits. Needless to say his father's nickname was "Sprout" and his mother's was equalling appealing as "That short ugly rabbit breeder from mongoland".

During his life in the shoe box home, Nutty was forced by the dogma and ignorance of his eccentric parents to learn to speak mongolian on Mondays, Wednesdays and Fridays, and Flemish on Saturday and Sunday mornings, Tuesdays and Thursdays. Sunday afternoons were spent learning Russian because his father believed that when the Soviets moved into Western Europe anyone who spoke Russian would be king of England. "You may be a short ugly shit-head my son, but if you speak Russian you can be the king of England. A very short king, but still a king" expounded his father every week.

Nutty always wore a combination of Flemish and Mongolian national dress, including a big tall grey fur hat, that really did make him stand out from the crowd, even a crowd of midgets. On several occasions the local farmers fired shotguns at him whilst he walked along the footpath to school, mistaking him for a squirrel. This taught Nutty to become the champion midget record holder over the 25 yard dash along the footpath. His fastest time being 23.7 seconds which was achieved with the incentive of a full load of buckshot up his rear end.

Taking all things into account he was lucky to be alive as a midget in England after so many near buckshot misses.

I once told him that I thought he was a very lucky boy indeed to be a midget, to which comment Nutty looked at me in amusement and a little bit confused. I explained that he would really look a real prick in a crowd from a great distance if he had been unlucky enough to have been born seven feet tall and went around wearing his ridiculous mongolian headdress - much better to be a midget.

Nutty, son of Sprout the prat midget from Belgium, was so small that until you approached within a few feet of him he resembled a very tatty and neglected smelly polecat. From this you can understand that Nutty was considered a real weird and strange fellow - not a person that one would normally befriend, except in my case because I took a liking to this little fellow, maybe because he was no competition to affect my personal development as a future writer and gang leader.

Every Friday evening, Nutty was compelled by his parents to attend the International Midgets Association meeting held at the seamen's mission hut in Southend. Up to 300 midgets would congregate there every week to defend the minority rights of the midget community which the government was blatantly ignoring as can be seen from the statistics that not even a single midget has ever been elected as a member of parliament, that is up until last month.

Midgets from ethnic minorities were however better placed to receive government help than other breeds of midgets and this was a main point of contention during many of the meetings. The unemployment rate amongst members of the IMA was running at some 69% during 1991 and was forever rising.

Gone were the days of 1956 when there were six separate films and eight stage plays of Snow White and the seven dwarfs, when there were never enough midgets to go around.

It was at that time that the IMA complained bitterly to the manufacturers of a certain famous branded lemonade drink, claiming the name was being used in very bad taste.

No my students of learning, by 1991 the members of the IMA were getting so mad at the prejudice being shown by society against midgets that they agreed by a massive majority to take further action to bring this prejudice to the attention of the relevant authorities. In an act of haste and instant bitterness, they started their campaign by cutting off half of all the legs of the 600 tables and chairs in the seamen's mission so that they no longer needed to stand up to eat their food. This resulted in their being banned from using this meeting venue and the IMA now meets weekly in the Wendy Dolls House at 5 Cedar Walk Hammersmith.

To qualify as a member of the IMA and to be recognised as a fully established midget, you must be able to walk upright under the bottom rung of the enclosure fencing at Epsom race course without knocking off your top hat - now that is what I call real midget short. This qualifying procedure is insisted upon for the future well being of the IMA to ensure that only genuine midgets are allowed access to their facilities.

It is amazing just how devious some people can be when trying to join the IMA using all forms of cheating during this simplest of qualifying tests. In 1951 a Jewish semi-midget butcher found out that he was 3.76mm too tall to pass the IMA test, so he had a special girdle made with vertical compression screws that applied enough pressure onto his torso to reduce his overall height by 4mm. By cheating in this way, he passed the top hat test but when removing the girdle, he forgot to relieve the spring pressure first when undoing the belt, the springs jumped out and castrated him.

This unplanned castration was such a physical shock to his nervous system that his body survival instincts took over and bent his spine permanently so that he now walks with a distinct stoop that allows him to qualify as a midget without resorting to devious lengths in the future.

The IMA defends the rights of its midget membership and last month had Mrs. Vera Short elected as its first midget member of Parliament for Littlehampton. A new midgets charter has just been put forward as a private member's Bill by Vera Short as follows:

10% of all policemen to be midgets

Postboxes to have ladders mounted on the front.

Public toilets to have safety belts

Puppet & Midget clothes shops in each town

Special midget hats with flashing orange lights to indicate midgets in town

A new midget football league where non midgets must play on their knees.

All pathways to have midget lanes that are one metre higher than normal paths

Compulsory to have at least 100 midget members of parliament, all wearing Noddy hats with bells.

All car manufacturers to produce motorised Noddy cars

Midget pubs to be built alongside all Wendy houses

British Midget Airways to be formed operating radio controlled Airfix Jumbo jets reserved just for midgets

Tall stories to be banned

Jelly Tots sweets to be discontinued

A law to be passed banning anyone taking the piss out of midgets.

The following words are not to be used in the present of midgets: short, squat, brief, inch, centimetre, low, dwarf, duck's disease, little, lack of inches, no height, shrinkage, scantiness, exiguity, scarceness, abridgement, abbreviation, curtailment, cutback, cut, reduction, diminution, contraction, compression, not big, dwarfish, stunted, knee-high to a grasshopper, not tall, squab, squabby, dumpy, stumpy, stocky, stubby, not high, skimpy, scanty, foreshortened, sawn-off, truncated, half-finished, potted, compact, compressed, boil down, reduce, diminish, cut short, dock, lop, prune, shear, shave, trim, crop, clip, bob, check the growth, scrimp, skimp, short ass, short prick, little prick, short wanker or short little wanker.

Any variations on these words cannot be used as an excuse to utter the offensive meaning to our less than fortunate short arsed cousins. In Dick Head, Nutty found his first friendly "tallman", as the midget society refers to the normal height people that inhabit this earth.

When faced with a life of total ridicule, the human mind will either surrender to the surrounding pressures or it will fight back in a variety of ways against these adversities. Nutty Slack chose the latter course, adopting a unique style of Umpteen Ethos as a sure way to equality, fame and satisfaction.

When you're born and are so short of stature
The kids will take the piss right out of yer
Then you grow up to be a little wee lad
The looks you get really make you feel mad
You turn to your saviour that umpteen ethos
To see that height doesn't make you the boss

"The size of the problem" (1978)
Peter Ivan Slack

Peter Ivan Slack C.B.E. (ex Nutty) became one of the famous poets of the twentieth century, writing some of the most disturbing verse one could ever read. He fights for his cause from within his verse, a cause that will survive his mortal death because his umpteen ethos will live on in defence of the shorter man. Here is a true hero for the nation to admire.

> *"The quality of human life is inversely proportional to the advancement of the modern society. A consumer society must by necessity eventually lose its soul"*
>
> *Peter Ivan Slack C.B.E.*
> *"A shortened version of human studies" (1986)*

Nutty was a very religious man and attended church services every day of his life, where he found himself as one with his preordained destiny. Being short was of no disadvantage when praying although he had to remain standing at all times if he wished to see the sermonising and other sales promotional pranks being offered by the church.

He believed that evil was on the increase and the world was near to receiving the second "coming" of the son of God, and who am I to dispute this prediction being made by a close believer who was obviously much more in the know than a heathen writer.

If God one day decides yet again to do something about the terrible evil that is breeding unhindered on this planet then the only solution would be to permanently locate one of His Sons down here to look after His interests on a day by day basis.

Instead of having nails hammered through his Son's hands and feet, God can arrange for his son to take real control of the planet so that the world would be a much better place than it is today and all mankind could live in peace. Of utmost importance with this new Holy administration of government is that there would be no further room for doubt relating to the existence of a "True God", because here would be The Son of the Only God, living as a permanent reminder of our Holy Father, every moment of our mortal lives.

Every so often, this new Jesus would achieve some miracle to re-establish his credibility and to ensure that all doubters were brought back into the fold of the believers.

The frequency of each particular miracle should be timed in such a way so as to receive the widest media coverage, which after all would be the main point of the exercise in the first place.

Each miracle would be transmitted by satellite television across the world to illustrate the power of God to all peoples and animals living aboard this revolving mass of rock floating amongst God's empire in the sky, thus proving once and for all that only God is God and prime ministers are only mortal beings.

The problem of transmitting the miracle information to bats in the Brazillian jungle and to fish living at the bottom of the Atlantic ocean has not yet been solved, but nothing is impossible if He commands it.

Eternity's sun never sets on God's empire.

Indeed, all the starving millions throughout the world could be fed on about 478 fish and 987 loaves every year, thus leaving the rest of us to live without the hidden guilt that we were not helping the poor and needy. This efficient use of fish would put Japanese and Russian factory ships out of business permanently as there would be a glut of fish, unwanted at any price.

God bless the fish.

Familiarity leads to contempt. This well known fact plus the normal human reaction of not knowing when you are well off even when you are well off can lead mankind into dangerous areas of conflict with God and His servants.

A classic example of just how this type of Holy conflict can flare out of control can be related to all you contemptuous students who need to quickly learn respect for the Holy laws to avoid joining those other evil wrongdoers in the furnaces below.

This story refers to a man named "Staa Leen", a one armed shop steward employed at the Basket Weaving

And Doormat Corporation to look after the workers' interests. He lived in absolute poverty in the Wanka Banka village which happened to be the home of the Wanka Banka tribe, situated in the remotest part of North East Africa. Daily you would hear this short stubby aggressive one armed man constantly complaining and whining at the breakfast tribal meetings about how the company, and now God, exploited the workers.

He would spout out of his thin shaped mouth, "It's not right for us to live permanently on fish and bread alone every day of our lives! We Wanka Bankers should demand a better variety of foods; such as chips and vinegar; pickled eggs and pickled onions; gherkins and tomato ketchup; Mars bars and Smarties, plus all the other goodies readily accepted as a natural right by the people of Glasgie in Skootland.

"We Wanka Bankas demand a new miracle from that Jewish fellow in Golders Green to give us all this new food. This should present him with no problems because after all is said and done he doesn't have to pay for it! Until we are granted this equality of eating habits, I propose my brovers that we stop making Wanka Doormats and Banka Baskets, and that's final!"

Just like Herman the German told us earlier in this book, "when one door shuts another one closes", and that is exactly what happened here in Wanka Banka land.

The Wanka Bankas were all killed off the very next week as a direct result of these unreasonable and very unholy demands for better food. Death was brought about by the eruption of a local volcano which has since been renamed "Brimstone" to commemorate this multiple passing away of the entire Wanka Bankas and their baskets.

A mysterious tombstone has been erected upon the burnt piece of land that once stood underneath the house of Staa Leen the biggest Wanka Banka of them all, and it reads:

The Wanka Banka tribe

In times of old when Wanka Bankas were bold
And well fed people were not invented
A man of God brought baked bread and cod
Until all peoples were fully contented
One day a man named Staa Leen
Demanded chips and baked beans
So Brimstone changed them from Bankas to Wankas.

Under this hypothetical way of life with a new son of God running things, God would have banned all scientific research throughout the world as only His Power and Help would be required to solve the problems that He considered should be solved. Even with His daily intervention we would still require much scientific help to advance human knowledge otherwise the earth would still be plagued by suffering and disease.

Diseases which decimated complete generations of people by the great plagues throughout the ages would flare up again unless kept under check. If you are from a third world country, then all of these wondrous scientific advances make no difference to you in any case, so there is no point in worrying about this chapter and you can go now immediately to the next chapter.

People from third world countries are either too uneducated to know that these advanced cures exist, or if they do realise that they exist then they exist as a dream, available only to the rich nations of the West and Japan. Knowing but not being able to get is a sufficient incentive to start a civil war in an effort to topple a corrupt government which does not supply these advanced items to the people in need.

After toppling the corrupt government, you can replace it with another government also unable to supply these items, with all the ministers still wearing the same military uniforms and equally corrupt. Such is the way of life and why only God can help us.

If scientists had not striven to advance human knowledge to the present advanced level, the earth would not be polluted and children would not be fried by napalm whilst thinking of the beauty of life and looking forward to becoming adults. Scientists are the instruments for creating the killing machines but always claim innocence when the children scream.

Does a scientist know best about just how far he should be allowed to progress in his endless search for knowledge in areas of research where many would say these areas are for God alone. Where more is this argument so heated than in connection with research using human embryos. At this very moment world governments are making decisions that will eventually have a most profound effect upon the whole human race. Are we entering the theatre of the Gods where we are forbidden to enter?

Has the human race reached a point in evolution where we are about to meet and comprehend our Creator? Will this information have the backing of irrefutable scientific proof which will effectively destroy all faiths that have been upheld by the human race and has held us together during these few thousand years of modern evolution? What will happen to our peoples when Holy faith is destroyed by scientific proof; proof so strong that only fools would believe otherwise? Can the world survive without a believable Church and God?

The virgin birth can now also be given to us by scientists.

Are we soon going to manufacture a human being in the laboratory; a perfect human being free of any genetic faults, to prove that we were built by ourselves and not by any God? These perfect laboratory built humans will of course replace existing womb produced defective humans because progress knows no other way. The strong will inherit the earth!

Don't shout out, "It's impossible you Dick Head," because this scenario is much nearer to us all than you think my friends, the scientists are obsessed with achieving this aim. Governments may morally object when talking to the ignorant electorate on TV and in statements to the press, but from a political and national security point of view they must allow research to continue. It's no use allowing our enemies to produce an army of super race laboratory produced men to face our army made up of mere ordinary mortals - no competition my friends, the Americans will at last conquer the Earth.

This fear of the enemy, who may be today's friends, will be the irresistible force that will enable research to continue unhindered because eventually we must all own this new race of super humans as it is a weapon just like the atomic bomb. Scientists are but mere tools of governments who do as they are told, even though when being presented with their *Bellnob Prize* they will cry out, "My research is for the betterment of mankind". Bullshite!

Will our new perfect laboratory humans think differently from us "mother born" humans and will they have a holy "soul" like us, or will they be cold hearted perfect humans with no soul? Will God approve of this development or will He, like almost 2000 years ago, take action to correct our misdoings. Sending down a Son to carry out a few miracles will not be enough the next time around because our scientists are ready for him. So what can we expect? I think something very catastrophic will be His answer and we really do deserve our punishment when you look at our track record over the past two thousand years.

No matter how much we object and pray otherwise, the human race will reach its ultimate destination of self destruction as Man knows no other way of going forward except with aggression. If not total physical destruction, then certainly a complete destruction of Man's innermost morality will occur within one hundred years from now. This is an awesome prediction to live with, but like all other bad things we humans adapt to any new degradation that we are thrust into, and we then proceed to manipulate the regulations to our own ends.

This rule applies specifically to our governments that cannot possibly survive this morality revolution in their present form.

When this ultimate achievement of constructing man

made humans becomes a reality, the government of the day will form a nationalised company to avoid, what they describe as, unethical exploitation of such a dangerous and powerful profit making tool. They will of course make a complete cock-up of the whole exercise and manage to increase all costs by 2000% in trying to achieve their aim of increased efficiency in this new area of science. Inefficiency apart, the government will no doubt hold a referendum to decide upon the most suitable name for this new industrial giant that is about to change the direction of mankind forever.

After carrying out a hypothetical market research exercise in the pubs and clubs of Newcastle upon Tyne, I have found out that the winning name of such a referendum is most likely to be CRUMPET INCORPORATED PLC. I would vote for such a name, because it is a name from the people for the people.

All men from the land of Hope & Glory will now be able to obtain by mail order using a major credit card, the woman of their dreams, no matter what characteristics turn them on. I'm no prude but the mind boggles when one considers that every last dreamy detail could be accommodated by CRUMPET INCORPORATED PLC in their mail order catalogue of women for sale. This company has a very good marketing slogan of *Organise for organ eyes* and a TV slogan of *Any shape any time, that's my meanee.*

The TV song is sung by an old ugly fellow holding a glass of Martini in his hand and with 3 young naked women on his lap. At the end of the advert you hear him saying to CRUMPET INCORPORATED PLC on the phone, "Yes, I'll have the new suction model of Margaret Hatchet at £5,700 less £3,600 part exchange for this old model of Betty Banger. My American Express number is........" This may seem an absurd situation, but so was the thought of free love and everyday abortion to our beloved Queen Victoria only 90 years ago. God bless Albert Hall and all who sailed in her.

This new situation will enable the male sex to again

control the world after having lost massive power to the lesbian gang over the past fifty years or so. After natural wastage of the existing race of womb born women, we can revert to using only products from CRUMPET INCORPORATED PLC and then any women that dares to bitch, sulk or say "no" will be sent back for reprocessing. Not bad ha?, and no more women Prime Ministers thank God.

"You're a pervert Dick Head!" shout out all the women now really worried that they will lose their monopoly in one or two areas. To all you worried women out there dreaming of forming a separate company called DICK INCORPORATED PLC, this will definitely not be allowed by any male dominated government. Despite these dreams we should always remember that famous poet, Justin Love, who wrote this note a few moments prior to his death:

Our men of this world are brave and true
Prepared to fight for a decent screw
They would love to order a woman from a book
Decent loving without sulking or a dirty look!

Justin Love was shot dead by his sulking homosexual lover, John Brown, in June 1986, after he found Justin in bed with a blow up female love doll who answered to the name of "Daisy the Blow Job". As requested in Justin's will, he and Daisy were cremated together holding hands. Unfortunately Daisy caused such an explosion during cremation that this type of double cremation is no longer permitted. Justin's left leg and collar bone were recently unearthed by two British Gas workers some half a mile from the crematorium which illustrates just how dangerous these doll cremations can be. Daisy must have been some lover when she was alive.

John Brown was hung for Justin's murder and at his request was then buried on top of where Justin's ashes had been spread.

Love is never ending but his body is a mouldering in his grave.

Chapter 11

COMEDY TO CAPITALISTIC CORPORATIONS

"Deep suffering is but an acceptable inconvenience for the man who smiles at the golden sun and dreams of the deep blue sea."

Admiral Harvey Headbanger (1864)

On the 1st September 1681 in the small village of Share Wood, located just outside Nottingham, a peasant answering to the name of Robin Lumb was about to be hung by his red neck until he was very very dead. Lumb's impending demise upon the gallows was the direct result that followed his reckless audacity in stealing two pigs, one cow and ten loaves of bread.

After these serious offences he also ran off with Lucy "Banger" Bedfellow who happened to be the local Lord Locust's unpaid whore and this was eventually the main reason for his downfall, so to speak. Lord Locust carried the very apt nickname of Bleedin' El because of his habit of carrying out systematic beatings of all the serfs that were under his charge, this savage behaviour carried out in an effort to satisfy his psychopathic tendencies which surfaced whenever he suspected that any of these low class ruffians were enjoying life.

You can imagine his unrestrained fury after being informed that Robin Lumb, a low down serf, had dared to steal goods and crumpet from him, the lord and master himself. Lord Locust worried little about his lost bacon, beefburgers or fried bread, but by God he could not forgive this stinking fellow for taking away his Lucy because this meant that he must go without his nookie until a replacement could be found - and that could take days!

One look at his wife, Lady Locust, would explain to

you in a way that words would fail to achieve, just why he required various relationships with banger Lucy and those before her. Until you had viewed her ladyship in person you could never imagine what the ultimate level of ugliness really was - she was very ugly indeed. How could he go without his thrice weekly Lucy nookie when married to such a horror story?

No, this serious situation must be crushed at birth which meant that he could not show any leniency towards this Lumb bum because to do so would be a green light to every Lumb, Smith, Jones or Birtwistle to follow the Lumb example and steal his nookie providers as and when they felt in the mood. This ungracious behaviour could not be condoned and therefore Lumb must hang as an example to other would be crumpet thieves.

At his very unfair and biased trial, Richard Lumb was pissed on rum when asked if he wished to approach his Lordship's bench to express any mitigating circumstances for his heinous crimes. Lumb approached the bench and replied.

"Me Lord, I nae know any mitty castigated circumstances to talk about, but if this be me punishment me Lord, I would rather be hung. Concerning this 'ere matter of stolen food, me Lord and master of this miserable bleedin' place, I stole it to feed the starving people. I stole the pigs, cow and bread to feed the old folk of me village where already this year we've 'ad over seventy-two of the poor buggers die of Malno bleedin' trition and hypo bleedin' thermia and that my fat Lord ain't right, no it ain't right atall.

"One day in the future the people of this land will rise up and have you rich farts beheaded; democracy will prevail! I wish that I had never taken the old whore Lucy because afterwards she just packed her bags and ran off with a group of real weirdo looking Pilgrim Fathers, all wearing funny hats, to America. Lucy has great plans to be a famous film star and she mentioned somefingk about an Italian git named Porno Grafico who could give her a lift up in diss industry. I've decided that my love for her is dwindling fast me Lord and if she comes back 'ere, she's all yours. Now before you get mad with me, I have a few words for my supporters and you, me Lord and Master Locust:

> "Although I am deep in the shit,
> I gave Lucy my best little bit,
> She said it was far from enuff,
> But better than Lord Locust's stuff,
> When I reach that place in the sky,
> I'll be awaiting for you sweetie pie,
> No matter the importance you claim,
> We're all equal up here, all the same,
> One to one we will meet in fair fight
> I'll cut off your balls, what a sight!

"Anyway me Lord, now go ahead and cut me balls off if you fink this will 'elp you get over this little problem and I will guarantee you my good behaviour in the future. In fact me Lord Locust, I've always fancied meself in the old church choir singing soprano, even though the vicar does behave in a strange way with the little boys."

Our Lord Locust stood up in a terrible uncontrollable temper, shouting "Cut your balls off you stupid git! I'm going to bloody hang you - not by your balls - God knows you deserve it - but by your neck until your are very very dead. Just see how well you can sing in the church choir after that you little wanker."

By this time the crowd were in a festive mood, laughing profusely at Lord Locust and cheering Lumb on to better things in another world. Lord Lucas was somewhat pissed off by such a disrespectful attitude being shown by these damn smelly village serfs, and in anger he shouts to the crowd "See how you laugh when this Bum Lumb is strung up from the old oak tree, yellow ribbons or not he will be a very dead Lumb."

Death has a way of silencing the most objectionable

people and of bringing back reality to their supporters in crime. This was probably the correct penalty to suit the crime because "reality" must be maintained so that Lord Locust remains as the boss in charge and these stinking serfs get back to doing as they are all damn well told.

At exactly 9.00pm that evening, according to the sun dial clock in the church graveyard, Robin Lumb was brought smiling and laughing from the village stockade to meet his maker. Robin had just received a last letter from "banger" Lucy, which came by International Pigeon Post, saying simply,

> *Dear Robin,*
>
> *I thought our jump was well worthwhile.*
> *Have a nice day.*
>
> *Love Lucy.*

Short but sweet, yes? Robin did wonder if the day was going to be all bad because apart from his death sentence, even the carrier pigeon shite upon his head whilst delivering this love letter from Lucy. He could have sworn that the pigeon was laughing at him as it dropped its double load from the sky above.

The sun was shining with a wonderful golden cornlike hue, the trees were so colourful in their autumn shades, the birds were singing in unison and the crowd were chanting "Lumb! Lumb! you're not such a stupid bum!" This united vote of confidence by the crowd made Robin feel really important as he tried to remove the huge deposit of pigeon shite off the top of his head, a task made no easier when your hands are tied behind your back.

Robin felt like a conquering Roman general returning through the gates of Rome with 15,000 captured virgins and 5,000 laughing German slaves - smug was the word, nothing less than smug would suit the feeling that he experienced at that particular moment. He felt so good because of his popularity, that he stood up smiling and started to chant in unison with the crowd - boy was he going to enjoy his only real moment of glory - here was his fifteen minutes of world fame and by Christ was he going to enjoy it.

The short trip to the yellow ribbon emblazoned hanging tree took a full twenty minutes, due to the crowd celebrations and their over exuberance which gave the hanging a carnival atmosphere, which indeed it turned out to be.

The Lumb Festival is celebrated every year to this day and takes place on the first Saturday in July in the same village, now renamed as Sherr Wode, where they traditionally barbecue two pigs and one cow, and bake ten huge loaves for the common people to consume. Free beer is supplied by the Karlene Brown Label brewery who also sell sandwiches at £8.20 each.

As a gesture of good faith by the current Lord Locust, he gives his wife's services to the men in the crowd to do as they will with her for the day. This same tradition applies to all the females with the name of Lucy, although females with the names of Margaret, Ann, Brenda etc are also admitted. In 1989, the number of "Lucys" attending the Lumb festival reached the staggering total of 12,789, of whom 12,645 were from Biggleswade.

No complaints were received from any of the Lucys, but Lady Locust looked far from happy after she was released by the village tug of war team when the last pub closed later that night.

Many complaints were later received from Biggleswade ante natal clinic where pregnancies had increased from 146 in 1988 to 12,644 in 1989. After a further investigation into the circumstances of "Lucy" Brown, the only Lucy from Biggleswade not made pregnant during the festival, it was found that she was a cross breed between a transvestite father and a hermaphrodite mother and only attended the Lumb festival to observe how other breeds did it.

She has recently had all her limbs seriously tied up in tight knots whilst trying to screw herself, and the clinic doctors are deciding whether to amputate an arm and a leg to release her, or just to carry on videoing this historic event for posterity.

We must continue the sad story concerning the fast approaching demise of Lumb. This poor condemned man eventually reached his place of execution where a thousand yellow ribbons were blowing in the breeze. Upon his arrival at this historic place of execution, the celebrations and beer drinking rapidly ceased. Lumb may be a wanker but at least the crowd wished to show just a small sign of respect whilst he be hung by his neck until he be very very dead.

As was the execution custom in Share Wood, he was lifted onto the back of a very tatty brown and smelly donkey answering to the name of "Shit head", and the local executioner, Father Brownfinger, doubling up as the village vicar, approached Lumb to say a prayer. After saying a short prayer of, "Good luck Lumb, you prickhead, I hope you have your balls burnt off where you're going," the noose was placed over Lumb's head.

This sudden indication of imminent departure from his mortal place on Earth instigated a want inside Lumb to sing a rendering (in B flat) of the now famous countryside ditty of:

> *Lord, oh Lord what a farce,*
> *Facing death sitting on me arse,*
> *Some say I should call it me bum,*
> *But I'm so rude when having such fun,*
> *Lord, you've failed in your final request,*
> *'Cos I'm still in the death the bleedin' best,*
> *If only I'd ....ug! ug! ug!"*

God go with you Lumb my son.

My students, my students, what have you learnt from the story about our poor ancestor Lumb

No doubt my clever students are asking their lap top multi-megabyte XLYYTT SUPERPLUS computers for an assessment of this complex thesis, whereas my average student is probably giving his balls a scratch and mumbling, "Christ, just how stupid is this Dick Head?" All abuse and reference to electronic gadgets will get you to a final position of absolute zeer roh my clever clogs students.

The lesson to be learnt in this chapter is of course "laughter in adversity" or as often referred to by the playwright within me as "a comedy of errors".

You must all become experts in the skill of laughter in adversity because nothing is guaranteed to rile somebody more than if you can sit smiling and laughing whilst they verbally throw all the crap they have at you. These Authority creeps are trained to go out and terrorise you, but their training excludes how they should react when you ridicule them whilst they are launching into their infamous death camp speech.

The terrorised working class man has through the centuries crapped in his boots on hearing these execution speeches - but this fear stops as from now my friends! We control the situations that dominate our lives and our right to happiness, not these freaks.

Before progressing further into this current subject of epic proportions as expected from my pen, I must point out that we have two publications for Lumb Lovers to read for further insight into this happy albeit stupid man. These books are, *Lumb's a Plum* and *Laughter with Lumb*. Both have 14% of the entire book directly translated into modern English language from the original text, but you should be aware that the remainder of the text is in swear words which have been left in the original medieval text.

We thought of including a separate reference list to translate these swear words for you, but it was considered that even today the meaning will be quite clear to everyone. eg: Maftabaker, prikball, fannifare and cockterpoke. Available to adults only from: Robin Lumb Trust, Sherr Wode Centre, Sherr Wode, Near Milton Keynes. Priced at £48.02 each, including an artists impression of Lumb's final moments with Lucy in full colour. You'll love it.

After Robin Lumb's death, the Lumb family all thereafter named their eldest sons Robin, even if the sons were born outside of wedlock. This is where eventually the saying of Robin Bastard came from. This particular Robin was born on 1st September 1704, in a barn just outside Stafford on an extremely rainy and cold day. The mother to be, who sold herself under the name of Lucy Hood (a different Lucy than before, albeit still a whore) was being assisted in childbirth by her faithful dummy friend Percy Lumb a plumber.

Thick head Percy was confident that he must be the father of this genius child yet to be born, because after all is said and done, he may have been pissed as a royal parrot but he had managed it twice - or so Lucy said. If that was not a good enough reason, he had paid Lucy two shillings for the pleasure and he certainly was not going to see his hard stolen money go to waste. In for a shilling, in twice for two shillings thought Percy.

The mother to be was known as Juicy Lucy by the entire clientele of the local inn, The Chosen Screw, where she traded her wares seven nights and days per week. This drinking establishment also doubled up as a fee paying marriage guidance office, and had a brothel on one side and a carpenters shop on the other side.

All writers of high repute must beware of making false accusations, even if it's about a proven whore like Lucy and this is why I shall now tell you something more about Lucy. This disclosure has not been printed before because it has not yet been fully proven or backed up with any substantial documentation evidence.

Under the "Rules for Dirty Disclosures Act" brought in by Henry the VIII, the law demands full verification of any such accusations as made in the case of Juicy Lucy.

Because of these strong guidelines, brought in by Henry after his fourth wife's accusations against him, I must emphasise that these details I am about to reveal about Juicy Lucy are only hearsay.

So if you are all clear in your mind concerning this get out CYA clause, we can now continue with the accusations, albeit they are only hearsay - got it?

It was reported from the The Chosen Screw that Lucy was considered to be "Juicy by name and Juicy by Nature". There, I've said it now! - but it's only hearsay remember. With this type of libellous and scandalous hearsay accusation, you can see why it should be Lucy's absolute right by law that I should obtain further proof prior to publishing such filth for working class consumption in these modern days of the 1990's and beyond. She said just before her death, "A whore?, of that you can be sure, but a juicy whore?, of that there is so much doubt" and then she died of a blood haemorrhage during the ill fated childbirth.

To be fully convinced of the authenticity of these Juicy accusations, we would require further positive physical evidence, including personal hygiene humidity readings and litmus tests from the subject matter. Both of these are certainly going to be difficult to unearth after such a long period of time since the alleged accusations were made.

The heirs and successors of Lucy Lumb (nee Hood) could take deep offence at such long forgotten filthy accusations relating to their ancestor Lucy being published in my book. Indeed, they could issue a writ against me for libel; "It is hereby claimed that Dick Head be charged with libel concerning the Juicy Lucy comments..........."

The judge summing up this libel case after the end of a very expensive 32 week libel case would say:

"Dick Head, we find in favour of the Hood libel action and that you have been too clever by half, so sharp that you'll cut yourself and you think that you are as clever as a cartload of monkeys. In fact Dick, you've been a right prick, right Dick? For making such libellous statements we grant damages of some £13,643,785.03 to the Hood family." Some chance of this happening, because as you can see, I've been too clever to make such accusations.

There was no bright star shining over the barn in Stafford when Juicy Lucy (alleged) released the latest Robin of the Lumb family upon an unsuspecting world. Little did the people of 200 years ago realise what danger had just been unleashed. Such was the effort required to eject this little screaming bastard, that Juicy Lucy died during this childbirth.

Her death came as a huge surprise to her friends at The Chosen Screw who all said, "poor old Lucy." Her demise fortunately saved her from the sad experience of raising a lunatic child fated to savage the face of this planet's morality forever. Blonde headed Percy Lumb was amazed that his new born son had bright red hair and chocolate coloured skin, but family is family albeit that the evidence contradicts this.

These paternal feelings, combined with his "value for money" psychology and his love for Lucy convinced our latter day hero Percy to become a one parent family. In memory of Lucy and of the two shillings invested, he named his new multi racial son, Robin Hood-Lumb. What's in a name anyway?

Percy moved north to Trafford Park in Manchester where he lived with his sister Ethel during Robin's growing up days. Since then the family of Hood-Lumb has remained a close knit community, with family intermarriage being very common indeed, and you can't get much closer than that. By the year AD1975, it was estimated that some 50,000 of the Hood-Lumb family lived within 50 miles of Manchester city centre, and all the result of a two bob jump. From little acorns my boys.

Every fortnight during the winter months, the fifty thousand Hood-Lumb family would have a reunion, all wearing stupid red hats, daft red scarves and big leather headbasher boots. They would visit Old Trafford soccer stadium where they would all shout out the same brain retarded tribal song of YOU-NIGHT-TED like demented mad Welsh monkeys with firecrackers up their back sides.

Intermingled with the tribal song would be the clever rendering of THE REF ERR REAS A WANK ERR, whenever a decision went against their team. After the match was over, they then proceeded to spend another hour kicking in the heads of about five thousand equally stupid people wearing equally stupid blue hats and equally daft blue scarves.

Why on earth do we have the good civilised 99% of our population putting up with this idiotic crap behaviour; for what reason? My quick solution to this social unrest would be to send them on a free holiday to Tripoli or inner China - try being a hooligan there my Hood-Lumbs.

In fact overseas the opposite result is true. These dregs of society are treated like the vermin they are when trying to cause trouble abroad - hip hip hooray! No more defenceless policeman to kick in the head - no my bullying cowards, you have battalions of psychotic G-men with batons to reduce your skull to the correct size it needs to contain your brain - straight to prison my lads.

We've all seen these thugs on our left wing run television programmes giving out the news the following day; these innocent angels spouting, "It weren't ous dat started all dis foightin - it was dem - we was jest sitting quietly having a drink mate!"

All this trouble just because Robin Lumb couldn't keep his hands off of Lucy.

"Wo! wo! hold up Dick, you told us that this chapter was all about smiling under adversity, not about a group of idiotic psychopaths". Ok my critical readers, don't get excited, just follow the words of your mentor and control your anger. Certainly do not develop a critical nature towards me at any time as this will lead to an endorsed graduation certificate saying, "Know-all bullshiter full of criticism". Just see how that gets you a job in politics after that my son.

The real lesson to be learnt from Lumb is a very difficult one to understand and absorb, so difficult that it could prove to be an impossibility for any undergraduate who is classified as a *Real Miserable Bastard,* under my self classification system. This system has been expertly incorporated into a new board game called *Dick Heads Humour Pursuit* which is a very interesting way of assessing one's level of humour or level of miserableness.

In this new board game, you select 6 cards at random from the pack and each card has one question with an option of 6 different answers. Depending upon which answer you select, you will be awarded a score of one to six, based upon the humour level (or lack of it) of your answer. Whatever your score is, you move your marker around the Humour Pursuit board the same number of squares as the points that your answer earns you.

Each board square is printed with the exact level of your humour, good or bad, so that at the end of the game, after you have answered all your six questions, you will land upon your final resting place on the board. Just lift up your marker and read your humour level. To reach the centre square which reads, *The funniest fellow in the World,* you must obtain the maximum score of thirty-six points, and if you achieve this you will be treated as really funny by all of us without exception.

To date the only people to achieve this recognition have been Nero, Johm Thomas, Ivan the Terrible, Margaret Thatcher, old uncle Tom Cobley and me.

There are also many other modern day celebrities who would reach my description of being, *The funniest fellow in the world,* but they have all refused to take up my offer of a free assessment on Humour Pursuit.

I sent a free boxed set of Dick Heads Humour Pursuit to an MP who in his married life both loves his wife and another lady of great fame. I cannot name this romeo in the House, due to libel laws that protect such people, but I can tell you that according to newspaper reports, it is alleged he likes to look like a football player, scoring "goals" both in and out of bed.

Now you may think that you know who he is without me having to take the libellous risk of naming him. About three weeks after I had sent this boxed gift (worth over £120 retail - so it was no cheap publicity stunt), I dreamt that I attended the annual "Dick Heads Reunion" party and there he was.

I found out later in my dreams that he didn't understand that only by having the name of Dick Head allows you entrance into this reunion party, but he had attended just in case other qualifications would suffice. Even Dick Heads can vote you know.

In my dream, I approached our lover wonder who was surrounded by a group of deformed inmates from the local hospice for the incurables, and asked gently, "Excuse me sir, I am Dick Head of the Dick Head's Humour Pursuit and Patel's Cheapo Pie Factory fame, have you had chance to use the boxed game I sent you last month?"

He smiled through his massive teeth and replied with a hint of sarcastic politically trained venom, "Yes I have and your chart is all nonsense my friend. Myself and the whole cabinet scored only six points each during the thirty-seven games we played during Prime Ministers question time last Monday. The government ministers of this country were described on your board as, "Very thick, money stupid, devaluation experts, unemployment monsters, conceited, bullies, idiotic, laughing stocks, bullshiters and general arseholes to boot. The conclusion also stated: Self destruct immediately."

I was somewhat taken back and embarrassed by this angry attitude towards me, so I spoke again in a softer voice, "But surely you didn't score only one point on all six questions? Nobody has ever achieved such a low level, not even my pet parrot Betsy or Scrappy Ken, and they really are thick. Indeed Sir, can I refer to card Number 3 which asks:

CARD 3

Question: If you fell over at work because you were completely pissed what would you do?

"To get only one point you must have answered: 'Urinate at the point at which I fell, show my arse to the crowd and fart in tune to God save the Queen."

I further commented, "Sir, as a supporter of the present government, I must ask you all to reconsider your suitability to continue representing us in politics, if indeed this is still your first choice."

At that point he called out, "OK John, I'm ready to go for lunch at Chequers now."

Dick Head's Humour Pursuit is only available from Dick Head's Educational Games Co. Limited, and the first level starter set is priced at only £73.39 including a starter pack of fifty question and answer assessment cards. Progressively advanced cards can be obtained at £9.30 per set with £1.27 allowed in part exchange for your old set, providing they are returned to us in good condition without any sticky finger marks.

Any written comments on the cards such as "bolox" or "you shite head Dick Head" will of course ensure that you are prosecuted as a sender of obscene literature.

The basic starter board is suitable for the average group of miserable working class men, with the centre square (36 points) showing an assessment of *Unhumorous Working Class Man*. Once you can achieve this maximum point assessment regularly then you can proceed to the more advanced level of boards:

up to Unhumorous Working Class Man
up to almost a smile
up to showing teeth like a German
up to basic laughing like a Frenchman
up to understanding your first joke like an Irishman

up to Light heartedness like an Italian
up to Comic of the Month like a Welshman
up to The Funniest Fellow In The World

These new boards are available at only £11.90 each to existing users of the basic set or £67.93 to other people trying to buy on the cheap.

Don't be depressed if your early scores in this game are giving offensive assessments because only through this adversity will you learn to smile and become more humorous. As you read and study my 61 publications, your humour level will either improve dramatically or you will be taken away in a little white van screaming, "No more!, no more!"

We have recently opened our 198th branch of our *Bloody Funny Clubs* group which within the next two years will have a branch open within five miles of every citizen of the British Isles, no matter if you are Welsh or not.

The aim of these Bloody Funny Clubs is to improve the level of humour within each Working class man, until all are at least half as funny as me. This is the aim, but just what results we achieve will be honestly published in our proposed report of *Bloody Funny Or Not,* available free of charge to club members. All members achieving a final classification of *General Miserable Tosser* or below will be expelled from the club without refund of any fees.

Expelled members can still play Humour Pursuit behind closed doors with consenting adults only. Club opening hours are from 9.00am until 12,00 midnight, seven days per week, during which time members can play Humour Pursuit to their own level of achievement with other equally miserable or humorous people. Cross mixing of levels is not allowed, so that for example, a *Real Funny Lad* is never allowed to play with a *Real Miserable Prat.*

Within each level of achievement, we are holding yearly competitions at the Albert Hall in London, in memory of Albert who was considered by many people of his time to be a real comical sod. I'm not amused Mr. Head. The winner of the top level game will be crowned "Champion of Champions - The Funniest Bastard In The World" where the prize will be a complete hand bound set of my 61 publications, all personally signed plus a box of twelve of Patel's Luxury Meat Pies delivered free of charge every week for five years.

A well fed man has a well fed mind. The Champion of Champions can expect to earn in excess of £10 million during his twelve months reign as he travels the world competing in challenge matches with other humorous people.

To date, Humour Pursuit is available in 472 languages and dialects, which allows a peasant from Chile to play a monk from Mongolia, or a pregnant African woman with venereal disease to play the piano at the clinic. This encourages merging of minds on a truly international scale which has thus so far been impossible even for the great United Nations organisation to achieve.

Before Humour Pursuit, the world was obsessed with shooting each other using guns supplied by somebody else; this somebody else helping to incite the shooting in the first place. If only the peoples of the world could all learn to laugh at and laugh with all other peoples of the world, no matter their race or creed, by playing Humour Pursuit, then what an achievement I will have made to world peace. Nobel Peace Prize or not, I'm dynamite!

As from December the 25th in 1992, our new Laughter All over The World international headquarters will be open in Smethwick and all the "Bloody Funny Clubs" in the United Kingdom will have free membership. Once Humour Pursuit becomes the number one board game worldwide, then thousands upon thousands of Bloody Funny Clubs will sprout up all around the world.

To link all these clubs together we shall have? - Yes you've guessed! We shall have the Laughter All Over

The World Centre to coordinate all international competitions and tournaments. So, by fax transmission via our new headquarters, anybody can play anybody else from any part of the Globe. In the event of any dispute over who is the winner then we would have the final decision.

Even Humour Pursuit is down to Robin Lumb.

It is very easy talking about the change in lifestyle and attitude that is needed to change from being a miserable humourless second class fool into a humorous genius like me, but this is more difficult than it sounds. Although it will take a great deal of hard work, it is essential for you to achieve a score of at least 29 on the Funniest Fellow In The World top board during your final exam.

You will not fail your exam by obtaining an inferior mark than this level, but your certificate will be endorsed with the comments as shown on the board square you finish upon. For example, if you achieve a minuscule score of only 8, then your certificate endorsement will read, "More miserable than a German, sick in the mind, sex deviate and hates Christmas". By achieving a higher score of 15 your endorsement will read a milder, "Prefers young boys, laughs at road accidents and breaks wind in church on Sundays".

THESE COMMENTS CAN DAMAGE YOUR WEALTH!

Although it is not absolutely necessary to achieve a pass mark, you can see that a lower mark may force you to become a vicar or a member of the local rowing team.

For students really wanting to get to grips with laughter in adversity, they should purchase my publication Number 38 entitled *Dick Happy*. This book has become the standard reading within this laughter field and is now read by over 400 Members of Parliament at this present moment in time.

It is possible that these Members of Parliament have

confused my book with a book of the same name that illustrates in full colour the 137 positions for homosexuals to participate in the taming of the shrew. My Dick Happy book is available at a special price of only £27.67 direct from my publishers office in Amsterdam. We also have a complete gift wrapped set available containing:

A signed copy of Dick Happy.
A complete boxed set of Humour Pursuit.
Ten different card packs (including the "couples" special pack).
Full set of boards.
Free membership of Southend's Bloody Funny Club.
Free membership of Laughter all over the World.
A Poster of Lucy's last moments with Robin.

All for the unbelievable price of only £130.00 including VAT.

Humour in adversity must not be regarded as another description of taking the proverbial piss! Taking the piss is only appreciated by the pisser and frowned upon by the person being pissed upon, because he is the only one getting wet.

No, my humourless, miserable, debased and thick undergraduates, humour in adversity is an absolute science and is fully appreciated by both parties to the conversation.

Once you have absorbed this lesson into your in depth nature, and you become actually aware of just how important a factor it is for you to incorporate this new science into your character, then your life really changes for the better. Once learnt in its basic form, you must continue to hone up this science to a fine edge.

Make a determined and fully concentrated mental effort to - plan ahead! - to be agreeable and pleasant to all men under any condition approaching adversity. This frame of mind will become your second nature, with friends and Authority alike.

The time will come when you will feel and be fully aware that this science has been perfected to a fine tuning where your inner self will feel smug at all times because you are controlling the confrontations of life. You are in command of other people under all situations, which although in itself is a moral victory over Authority, is little compared with the personal satisfaction of knowing that you are also in full control without inferiority stress that affects and eats away our very well being. You will obtain a fulfilment that you previously thought only existed within a rhesus monkey who was lucky enough to copulate in excess of twenty times per hour without his balls dropping off, so to speak.

During the 1960's, the "flower power" years had their effect on me also and I wrote the book, *If at first you don't succeed then try try again* as my contribution towards peace on Earth. This book was a close study of the rhesus monkeys sexual habits both in captivity and in the outside wild environment.

My study showed that a monkey in its natural wild surroundings is more sexually active than a sober monkey in captivity, where they are only 61% sexually active. However, if both of the partners in captivity are given a bottle of Napoleon brandy and shown a monkey porno film, then the sexual activity increases by 273% for a period of half an hour, and then both monkeys crash out for six hours. Pay close attention when they wake up, because they both look really pissed off with each other and have the most awful fights.

The "Royal No Monkey Business Society" based at Silverstone has made various protests concerning this misuse of monkeys for sexual testing and they recently wrote to the leading laboratory in such research protesting about these experiments. The laboratory sent the following reply:

Your Royal Highness,

Reference your letter dated 21st June from Windsor Castle, I really feel that you have misunderstood the meaning of cruelty to monkeys.

We here at the Monkey Jump Laboratories feed the monkeys on the best food, bring together the healthiest females with the healthiest males, place them in beautiful boudoirs with French music, give them the most expensive Napoleon brandy (by appointment to you Mam) and then let them screw themselves to sleep. In my book this is heaven!

Maybe the porno monkey films are a bit over the top, but even these are tame (so to speak) compared with the Gorilla and Penguin films I've seen from Indonesia.

Please feel free to come and watch at any time.

Your honest servant,

Hank Pankey

PS: Please let me know if you would like a copy of our latest import of "The Gorilla takes the biscuit".

The Haw-Haw-Haw Napoleon Brandy Company from France has recently entered into protracted negotiations with the "Adopt a Monkey" agency of Brixton to make a 45 second commercial which is for international exposure promoting this excellent cognac. They feel that showing a group of monkeys drinking Haw Haw Haw cognac followed by the orgy that will most certainly follow, would increase their sales by a tremendous amount.

Jack Brush, the head of the Adopt a Monkey agency became quite excited about this prospect as he assumed that he would also be starring in this film - a worldwide star at last!!!! He backed up his claim by showing the Haw-Haw-Haw directors a copy of the video film, "The monkey and the Zoo keeper" which proved beyond doubt that he was capable of taking a role in this proposed production. During this meeting in Paris, Jack Brush was so excited and said, "I see no problem with doing my bit and accepting the contract, but I must insist on a few conditions. You see that we have some very ugly monkeys and some very pretty monkeys, and I insist on choosing a good looking monkey for my partner in the film. Also gentlemen I have three further requests before I can sign the contract."

After some weird looks between the directors, they asked him about the three conditions and he answered:

"Gentleman, condition number 1 is that nobody apart from the cameraman should watch me. It would be embarrassing for me if a large crowd were to burst out in applause whilst I reached my final moments." This point was agreed to by the directors, albeit after a great deal of sulking by the one in the pink evening suit.

"Gentlemen, condition number 2 is that I cannot kiss the monkey because although she may be good looking, her breath stinks after eating all of that crappy monkey food that we feed her on. Also just look at those horrible thick blubbery lips Ugh! No, definitely, I cannot agree to any kissing!" After some two hours of fierce argument, with pink suit resigning his position on the board of directors, the directors agreed to forego any kissing in the commercial.

"Gentlemen, now we reach the real stick point number 3. In your contract, a fee of £19,000 is mentioned for this part in the commercial, yes? Well as you know, I am not a rich man, but I have calculated that on my salary at the Monkey Institute, I can pay you this fee over a 5 year period, if that is agreeable to you."

Since this highly successful commercial, which has since been banned from our screens in all parts of the world except Australia, Jack Brush has been committed to a mental institution after he was caught raping a giraffe at London Zoo. Most of the monkeys have been sent to work in a tea bag factory just outside Bristol where they also double up as actors in commercials for the same products.

The remaining monkeys found the mental stress of this work far exceeded their ability and they are now employed as directors for a famous government owned TV station (libel laws etc).

We've gone a long way since Lumb and Lucy got together.

Chapter 12

FROM ARTLESS TO ARTFUL
(every picture tells a story, don't it)

"Translation of our innermost feelings of the soul into a physical representation of these deep personal emotions truly represents works of art. These treasures can only be recognised by a lucky few, but seen as a ghastly confusion by the majority living in this commercialised world. The mistaken belief of acceptable conformity in all fields now classifies art into various levels of greatness, fully influenced by financial considerations. A man without soul can never fully appreciate art, but a man with enough money can buy it."

Laurie Gough(1786)
West Indies Trading Company

WHAT IS ART?

Architecture, fine arts, graphic arts, plastic art, sculpture, classical art, Byzantine art, Renaissance art, Baroque, Rococo, art nouveau, Surrealism, Expressionism, op art, pop art, kitsch, camp, high camp, aestheticism, functionalism, De Stijl, Bauhaus, functional art, commercial art, decorative art, the minor arts, illumination, calligraphy, weaving, tapestry, collage, embroidery, pottery, photography, cinema, paintings, colouring, daubing, finger painting, colourwashing, tinting, draughtsmanship, golden section, pasticio, pastiche, trompe l'oeil, iconography, portrait-painting, portraiture, scenography, scene painting, sign painting, poster painting, miniature painting, oil painting, watercolour, tempera, gouache, fresco painting, mural painting, encaustic painting, impasto, secco, the Primitives, Sienses, Florentine, Venetian, Dutch, Flemish, French, Spanish, Mannerism, Pre-Raphaelitism, Neo-Classicism, Ralism, Romanticism, Impressionism, Post-

Impressionism, Pointillism, Symbolism, Fauvism, Dada, Cubism, Expressionism, Die Brucke, Der Blaue Reiter, Vorticism, Futurism, Surrealism, Abstract Expressionism, Tachism action painting, Minimal art, Minimalism, Conceptualism, Landscape, Seascape, Skyscape, Cloudscape, Scene, Prospect, diorama, panorama, conversation piece, still life, pastoral, nocturne, nude, tableau, mosaic, photomontage, frottage, brass rubbing, icon, triptych, diptych, oleograph, aquarelle, drawing, doodle, cartoon, chad, caricature, silhouette, minature vignette, thumbnail sketch, illuminated initial, old master, masterpiece, study portrait, full length portrait, half length portrait, kit-cat, head, profile, full-face portrait, studio portrait, snap, Polaroid, pin-up, graphic, pictorial, scenic, picturesque, decorative, ornamental, pastel, chiaroscuro, stippled, sfumato, grisaille, ceramics, carving, sculpture, moulding, paper modelling, origami, rock carving, toreutics, statuary, statue, statuette, figurine, bust, torso, head, cast, death mask, waxwork, medallion, cameo, intaglio, relief, basrelief, chase, engrave, emboss, etching, gem cutting, mezzotint, aquatint, xylography and millions of other art forms!

This question is not as simple as it first seemed!

Well my students of total artistic illiteracy, now that you've been made aware of just a few of the fields of art as mentioned above, you must now try to further awaken that soft grey tissue which is located some two inches deep within your egg shaped bone structured thick head and absorb this chapter on artistic wisdom.

Yes my friends, we are now expanding our studies outside the sarcasms of earlier chapters that covered relatively insignificant areas of learning, to enter for the first time the deeper thinking side of my teaching methods. With infinite skill and endless patience I have written this chapter in a most classical fashion, thus guaranteeing to bring you the fantastic results needed for both your basic understanding of true art and its effects upon the behaviour pattern of mankind and those idiotic fools wearing dresses.

We are going to study in depth this long forgotten and much shunned subject that was once in the forefront of teaching methods used so successfully during the past classical eras of history.

Art should be homogeneous with the great periods of history that are most relevant to the progress of the human race within our storybook of wondrous civilisations of the past. Aristwede, the famous Greek tailor turned poet, wrote in 2345 BC, "A bird can fly, a fish can swim, the earth can grow vegetation, the sun can shine, a soldier can fight and mankind will rule the animal kingdom forever, but art far exceeds these minor things because art evolves from the deep soul of mankind and thus from God."

So, what is art?

I'm not referring to just to the pictorial styles offered by the wonderful art galleries, media promotions and art books, but to the real art created by man for the spiritual guidance of man. I want you to soak up and appreciate the true art forms. I want you to develop a creative sense of understanding that has evaded your brain cells ever since you first opened your eyes and saw those idiotic Ovaltini adverts on the TV; including that song about little girls and boys - stop it Dick!

Very soon, your miracle of human optics will no longer be restricted to watching and appreciating a TV receiver and its diet of commercially fabricated sex inspired crap - no siree. In the future you will be digesting the grand works of art that are so awe inspiring that you will need to bang your chest in deep emotion and scream to the heavens, "Thank you Dick Head, I now understand art - I am artful!"

Gone will be those dull days when the highlight of the entire evening was looking forward to watching a gang of Australian pansies appearing on the nightly soap opera television programme talking total gibberish (crap). No more watching crap my students - your future will have arrived in a picturesque and deeply emotional form - a future full of passion that zips open your inner emotions - emotions that will force you by newly released feelings to share this new rich excitement with all others around you.

You will know that true art is not the imitation format that Authority (Media Division) is today forcing down your throats from morning until night as the acceptable status quo of life. How on earth can we believe that there exists a beer that reaches places in our bodies that other beers fail to reach? For me, beer has only one destination and it should reach there as fast as is humanly possible.

Your "finals" exam will cover art as a major subject and for those lucky few achieving honours marks of 87% or above, they can then if they wish proceed directly onto the higher level endorsement study group of Sculpturing Tits Explained.

A full set of chinese chisels, a huge hammer and a forty-five kilogram block of welsh crappy yellow coloured granite is supplied free of charge for all students enrolling on this course. You will be issued with a Randy Mandy blow up doll on free loan as an artists model for helping you to express your own interpretation techniques in sculpturing. Please obtain your own DikBull puncture repair kit from your local sex shop or community centre just in case any pricks should inadvertently puncture Mandy.

A fixed penalty charge of £56.87 will be made against students who return their Mandy dolls showing any damage whatsoever, and the same fixed penalty covers any Mandys not returned at all. Any Mandy found sexually abused will be instantly cremated and the perpetrator reported to the police. Such sex perverts will have their final graduation certificates endorsed with the words , "Keep this graduate away from rubber and moulded items. Unsuitable for working with children's toys or inside balloon factories". These comments will be written in the box headed "Sexual problems and working habits" located in the top left hand corner of your certificate.

If you come under this pervert heading, you may wish to know that you can purchase a copy of Toys for the Big Boys catalogue from Ruby's Rubber Wear and Baby Oil Shop, High Street, Brighton, priced at £67.98 including a surprise packet of assorted Female Crinkles dehydrated ladies. These ladies come singly wrapped and measure only four inches long when supplied in the original dried condition. They are brought back to lifelike appearance and size by soaking them in a bath tub of warm soapy water with a pint of baby oil sprinkled on the top. As lifelike as these ladies appear, you should be aware that they can explode during any misuse, causing severe injuries to various parts of the exposed human body.

For our homosexual friends on this graduation course, we also have a small stock of dehydrated Crinkly Larrys available, but these are not available on free loan as past experience has shown us that severe damage through abuse has forced us to supply on direct sale only at £89.67 for each pack of ten. Please state your colour preference when ordering from, pink, silver, gold or dark brown.

When no further use is required from these Female Crinkles, please pay careful attention to the drying process to avoid serious side effects occurring. Please dry them by hanging them on a standard clothes line, ensuring that they are pegged to the line by using their ears only.

You SHOULD NOT UNDER ANY CIRCUMSTANCES place Female Crinkles inside your tumble drier or airing cupboard for this drying process. We recommend that all abused Crinkly Larrys should be instantly incinerated in the bath tub after use.

Your final art exam will be a very simple test of how

your soul's innermost feelings have developed during this chapter and whether you really do have sympathy with art or if you are in cahoots with the devil himself. To really give you devil lovers a hard time, I have agreed special rental rates with the Archbishop of Canterbury allowing me to hold this section of the final exam inside the cathedral cloisters after morning mass - just in case a prayer or two can help your efforts.

I always encourage my students to take advantage of anything that will give them an extra edge in life, providing that it is for the good of the world at large and does damage to no other man - and sod the women. At exactly 11.00 am during the exam, I have arranged for all students to have an enforced elevenses break where they will be served cloisters cake and black knight tea by a special team of nuns dressed in full evening regalia and singing a beautiful rendering of "Soul Man" in D flat minor.

I have also negotiated with the cathedral management committee that every student taking the exam will be given two free tickets for standing room admittance to the cathedral midnight mass on Christmas eve in 1998. These tickets are for the personal use of the beneficiary and one friend only and it is a criminal offence, punishable by a terrible retribution, to sell these tickets to other people for financial gain.

Homosexual lovers of any of the exam students are banned from the midnight mass in the cathedral but these tickets can be exchanged for entrance to the midnight mass at the Queer Church of Epping's service on new year's day the same year. Proof of sexual deviation will be required before entry, but unfortunately the church vicar will not allow dress style to be used as verification.

Any cathedral tickets that are illegally sold by ticket touts on the day of the performance will be back checked to ensure that students contravening this rule will be identified and punished accordingly. To emphasise our intentions, I must inform all of you cheats that in 1985 three of my students from Zanzibar were found to have sold their tickets to some Afrikaner sheep farmers from South Africa and they received the severest of punishments.

All three were stripped naked and covered in honey taken from the Royal honey pot in Sandringham Palace. When I phoned the palace and spoke to the person on the other end of the line and explained my request and the reasoning behind it, he replied with a horsey laugh, "Bloody good show Dick, take all the honey you need and screw the cheating buggers!" That is real true Royal blue understanding of what we are aiming to achieve and I for one will let them each keep one crown and one of the older carriages when we, the working class, take over this country.

After the three convicts were covered in the royal honey they were nailed to three wooden crosses erected in Kew Gardens and left as a gourmet lunch for the socialist killer bees and the three Russian bears. These three bears had been brought into the gardens to give a more realistic appearance inside the Canadian greenhouse, but after six years they were getting bored with an unknown thief who kept pinching their instant porridge. One of the angry bears was heard shouting at one of these honey bunch criminals just before he ripped off his left arm, "are you the sods who have been snitching my porridge!"

The last one of the three criminals to die of bee poisoning and bear bites repented his evil doings and wished he had gone to midnight mass himself instead of selling his tickets to that bloody Jewish tout. He could be heard praying to the skies, "Please forgive them Dick Head because they know not what.......agh." And so the wicked are punished, Amen.

You have been warned - no cheating.

For your exam, you will be given a set of full colour laser printed copies of paintings produced by one hundred totally unknown artists from all around the world. You must then write a minimum of five hundred words giving your assessment and interpretation of each painting, explaining just what the hell you thought that this fellow was trying to put over to the world. Finally, you must tick the boxes given in the following Assessment Chart for each painting/painter:

QUALITY	OPINION OF ARTIST	ASSESSMENT
Brilliant	*Deep thinker*	*Future master*
Average	*Average*	*Should paint bridges*
Arseholish	*Wanker*	*Lunatic*
Crap	*Mental case*	*Better off in politics*
Real crap	*Sexual deviate*	*Toilet job*

Please remember that your assessments should be based upon what you think about these arty fellows and not how you think that we think what you should think about these painters. Think with your soul totally open - search into each painting until your soul mingles with the soul of the artistic creator himself. Write down what you believe were the innermost feelings of the artist when creating this unique colour tainted canvas.

All souls are not the same and we expect your answers to vary dramatically from the answers from other students in the exam. It is these very differences that help us to interpret your complete innermost make up and sincerity within this subject. I understand that this is asking you to unlock a secret unoiled door within yourself, a door that you may scream to keep closed, but this task must be achieved at all costs even from a deviate such as you.

To help you with this struggle from within, and to fully explain the workings of the innermost soul, you can refer to my publication entitled, *Never tell a Soul* which is available from all good churches and music shops, priced at only $19.99. At today's exchange rate this equates to the very cheap price of only £10.80. A donation of £1.00 from every book sale is sent to *The International Society for Lost Souls,* a fully owned subsidiary company of mine based in New York, which is operated seven days a week to help save the souls of people in dire straits.

To date, no souls have been saved, found or modified, but the company itself made a huge profit of $23,876,546.97 last year whilst employing a staff of only five people. These five huge gentlemen are not yet able to read or write, but do wear some wonderfully attractive leather motorbike suits with the insignia of *Crack takes your Soul* written in gold paint on the back of their black leather jackets. These words illustrate their dedication to our company's cause in life.

God bless America and all who sail in Her.

Because of this close tie up with the American business scene, we were approached recently by the world famous Ghostbusters gang who suggested that we form a joint venture company to be called *Spiritual Spooks.* The deal being suggested was for us to supply the inner spirit and they supply the spooks.

The resultant converted spooks can be used to spread goodness throughout the twilight zone, thus putting an end to further horror films that scare the knickers off my aunt Lottie so much. Our leather bearing staff at the International headquarters in New York objected to this new investment programme because they claimed to be overworked already in running the *Dopey Souls Supplies Division* of the company which is now doing a very big business in needles and special cigarette supplies.

A new *Nostril Relief for lost Souls* aerosol spray has just been launched as a direct sale item onto the streets of New York and sales have increased by nearly 30,000% over the past seven months, adding $5,800,000 to our net profits. No souls are yet being saved, but business is booming and is just great man.

Back to the subject of the exam Dick!

Your exam papers will be marked and graded as follows:

Totally artful
Quite artful
Just artful
Below artful
Above artless
Artless
Completely artless
Arsehole
Wanker
Politician material
Failed exam

Exams apart, even Kings and Queens can get a severe come uppence whilst sitting on their thrones of power lording over a painted empire. One minute they own a masterpiece which for over five hundred years has been recognised as being painted in 1367 by Henrich Einbenflurgen Smith, and the next minute a scientist with micro chips informs them that this painting was painted in 1330ish by Walter Vinegart, a German tosspot who otherwise raised pigs in Hamburg.

One moment a piece of canvas measuring 15.76 square metres is worth $41 million and the next moment it's worth about $23.75. This change around in artistic fortune being brought about simply because a smart arsed scientist with an electronic box of chips proved that Herr Vanker Smith painted this colourful crap and not Henrich Einbenflurgen.

Suddenly everybody in the art world discards this ex famous painting because it was painted by a real prick in 1330ish and not by Einbenflurgen in 1367. Einbenflurgen would have painted a much better picture if he had painted it, wouldn't he?

It was proved that Henrich Einbenflurgen was just a twinkle in the eye of a lusty farm worker at the time this famous painting "Even Germans can smile" was painted in 1330ish or thereabouts. Henrich's father's full name was Banca Adolf Smidtz, a very unfortunate choice of moniker because later in later life he carried the obvious nickname of Banca the Wanka, which is still an appropriate name today. Such a nickname was both embarrassing and unfortunate for him whenever he put his hands into his pockets or went into his local bank to deposit or withdraw cash.

Little did the sarcastic people in the village of Wankburg know that the art master yet to be born to Banca the Wanka was destined to place this village in a prime position on the world map of artistic history. To date, the only thing this village is famous for is flat meat and carrot cakes, so readily eaten by the men of Germany as an aphrodisiac. These flat cakes were originally known as wankburgers but production ceased in 1396 when the Archduke of Jerkoftlingen sued the village factory after he found that the wankburgers did little to boost his sex drive, but made him permanently play with himself.

When Henrich Einbenflurgen Smidtz, the "master", was born at 11.59pm on the 24th December his awful ugly appearance ensured him the name of Einbenflurgen by his appalled drunken parents. Eibenflurgen is taken from the ancient classical Bavarian tongue and translates roughly to "that shitey little ugly bastard" - just how cruel and wrong can a name be, ha? If they could have foreseen the future for their offspring then doubtless they would have christened him Knackerdickpricken as a much more appropriate name.

Knackerdickpricken would have suited perfectly because it translates into "that clever little prick with a paint brush in his hand". But how were they to know that this really ugly snotty nosed brat would soon be creating masterpieces of art that would be world famous until they were burnt to a cinder with everything else in 1999? Conjecture on our behalf concerning the suitability of names for a long dead painter is non productive to the extreme and cannot change history, not even with the assistance of Margaret Thatcher or one hundred tons of wankburgers with cheese.

One minute worth millions, the next minute worthless. Same painting for centuries but today a scientist tells us that a different artist painted it. How can appreciation of art be judged by knowing just who painted it?. Unless of course we are all being conned by the money men and art investors of the world. Can such a devious plot really be possible?

Surely the art experts are not in it for the money?........or maybe........let's think about this some more my simpletons.

So, what is art my students?

To understand a bit more, and to accelerate your little grey brain cells this time, let's look deeper into the life and times of Laurie Gough, the gentleman who wrote the introductory passage quoted at the beginning of this chapter over two hundred years ago. Laurie was the only son of Vanity and Bert Gough, both devoted people in the faith of Rome, as indeed were many millions of misled people throughout the world at that time. They brought Laurie up to believe in the everlasting idea that goodness of heart meant real inner happiness for the soul and took you closer to God your Maker.

On his 14th birthday Laurie was full of goodness in his heart and walking home from the local village school in Paddypatrick, some thirty-five miles west of Dublin. As he approached his dwelling of abode, he witnessed a very personal and tragic event that was to change his direction in life forever.

Here he was a total believer in the Faith, with a life already planned out ahead of him where he was to become a holy Father of the cloth and spread the word of God to fields afar. All these well laid plans came apart at the seams on that fateful moment when he witnessed the bloody death of both his parents.

As he approached his house, both ma and papa were

waiting for him at the front gate with huge smiles upon their faces and his birthday presents in their arms. They walked arm in arm across the muddy road towards him singing, "Happy birthday to you, happy birthday to you, happy birth............Jesus Christ!....Shit!" and both were killed instantly as they were hit by a drunken lout driving a horse and cart full of swedes - the vegetable kind.

Laurie was so pissed off that this drunken bum had broken his birthday present, which consisted of paint brushes and an easel, that he chased him all the way down to Dublin docks. It was here that he broke the killer's neck with a large piece of broken easel, threw him into the docks and shouted "try and stop me becoming a master of art, would you ya bastard!?" The poor drunken man was drowned with an easel support sticking out the top of his head.

Being hung by his neck until dead for the premeditated murder of this poor drunken wretch would inhibit his master of art and church career, apart from hurting his bloody neck. Such a lack of career prospects and fear of pain incited Laurie to leave this place and register as a cook boy on the good ship "Wimpey" which was a dark brown clipper class trading vessel operating between Africa and Dublin. Signing on for 30 years service was shown to be an incredibly stupid act after he quickly found out that living on crappy maggoty food under such awful conditions gave him very little time to become an art master or priest.

This degradation also led him to develop a permanent stomach disorder that was known as *dee crappens,* as named by the teutonic blond gunsmiths, Herr Krieg and Herr Blitzt, who had lived on board the vessel for some twelve years.

During Laurie's fifth year aboard this floating hell, the Wimpey dropped anchor some half a mile off shore of what appeared to be a tropical forested land. A detachment of Welsh Guards left the ship in several beautiful pea green boats which were rowed ashore onto the golden sands of this tropical land in paradise. Welsh Guards?, you may well ask, what the 'ell were they doing on board a crappy merchant ship? you may well further ask. I am not at liberty to divulge such secret information.

I can however assure you that all of these Welsh Guards were of the statutory height of under 5ft tall, dressed in bright red uniforms and led by a Captain Michael Caine. This officer was a real aristocratic gent and told everybody on board in a nice cockney lilt, "My name's Michael Caine."

On seeing the identity of this famous leader of men, Laurie knew immediately they were anchored just off Zululand in Africa. "No singing!" shouted out captain Michael Caine, "just keep those leeky gobs shut and row harder you lazy coal diggers!" he continued to shout as they approached the shore. Once on shore they formed up into single file and marched towards the jungle singing like Cardiff canaries, this despite the shouting from El Capitano to the contrary.

Some two hours later there could be heard the command from Michael, "Steady men, fire only upon my command - and stop that bloody singing!" After ten hours of shooting and drum banging, the drums and guns went quiet and the bugles could be heard blowing a Welsh melody in C flat.

The next morning, as the golden African sun rose above the towering wind fettered jungle where God's brightly coloured beasts of the sky flew and made their home, Laurie witnessed the return of the pea green boats. These vehicles of men over brine contained one hundred and fifty-three dead Welsh Guards and many others with Zulu spears thrust into their chests and other more painful areas of the body.

Chained together in morbid groups, were some five hundred captured slaves, all from the proud Zulu nation but now mere slaves of the white man. Once on board the good ship Wimpey, these brave non-English speaking warriors were loaded into the stinking hold where more than half of their number were destined to die of hunger and disease during the three month trip of horror back to Dublin Docks.

Once in Dublin, these slaves were put to work in the Dublin Brewery where their leader *Pokapontarse* developed a special black liquid tribal brew which he named Guinpiss. This dark brew has over many years become known under a different name by the Irish folk and some thirty million other drinkers around the world.

Due to their excessive drinking habits and awful renderings of the song Danny Boy, the brewery could no longer stand the noise and these slaves were sold to a Dublin sugar merchant with the peculiar name of Granulate Ted Murphy. This same gentleman went on to invent and patent a special sugar processing system.

Eventually, Laurie and the good ship *Wimpey* set sail again, but this time for the West Indies, together with the surviving two hundred and thirty-four Zulu warriors all having fierce hangovers and all excessively overweight following their fourteen months of Guinpiss drinking in Dublin. Once in the West Indies, they were sold at the slave market and put to work on the sugar plantations where Guinpiss was a thing of the past and where they quickly lost weight and also decreased their chance of a heart attack. Slavery was not all bad you know.

It was at this stage in his life that Laurie understood that if he was to become an art master, then had he better get off this bloody ship and start painting some masters - action speaks louder than words. He jumped ship with only one pound, five shillings, two and a half pence in his pocket which was not a lot of money. From this meagre sum, he had to spend immediately four shillings and five pence on an artificial beard as a disguise which he purchased from the *West Indies Artificial Beard Shop*.

This theatrical dress agency was very popular with ship jumpers and was adjacent to "The Southern Fried Chicken Bar" on one side and the "Very Poxy Clinic" on the other side, just off the main town square. After purchasing a long beard and a clap ridden crippled non flying parrot for his shoulder, he proceeded to walk around the town intent on not looking like Laurie Gough. Later he took a job as a stable lad on a sugar plantation estate owned by that famous politician Lord Sutch, thus allowing him to shoot his parrot and burn his false beard which he thought made him look like an unemployed queer pirate.

During the next few years, Laurie wheeled and dealed until he accumulated enough money to buy a forty two acre plot of scrap land which was so poor in quality that everybody thought it was only good for dumping garbage on to - rather like Grimsby on a fine day. He registered this land under his new company name of Tay Limited because he originally thought of starting a tea plantation but found that tea plants would not grow there.

During the next few years he purchased several other pieces of land of a similar crappy ilk which he registered to Tay Limited or to one of his other new companies he had formed, Tan Limited, Lie Limited and Lell Limited. By his thirty-fifth birthday he owned some two thousand acres of land all over the island.

During this time Laurie spent all his spare time trying to cross pollinate a Cuban green turnip with a toffee apple in an effort to find the solution to growing a successful sugar crop on these acres of real crappy ground. In frustration at his endless failures, Laurie eventually threw all his remaining Cuban green turnips into his back field where a swarm of bees returning from Lord Sutch's super quality sugar cane plantation full of pollen settled - yes you've guessed - the bees pollinated the turnips and so was born the sugar beet plant.

Laurie never looked back after that famous point in history and so was born the future of his four famous companies, the Tay-Tan-Lie-Lell sugar conglomerate.

The successful bees got no thanks for their work and died the very next winter, without a prayer or any other form of thanks from anyone. However, the the British bought up all the insect's piss and made petrol from it.

Two years later Laurie was visited by a really strange German idiot from Berlin who answered to the name of "Kraut arsehole" or "Herr Cubitz". This fellow had developed a new flat faced square sugar spoon specifically designed for the teutonic minded people of military fame. These superior people had tried over a period of two thousand years to accept the conventionally shaped spoons like the rest of the civilised world but their nationalistic trait would not let them cut any corners, so it was decided that a square spoon was urgently required.

Some twenty-three million of these flat square spoons had been sold by Herr Cubitz before the German super race understood that these super spoons may be good for an Oxo or for German heads, but they were really awkward when it came to handling the standard Tay-Tan-Lie-Lell sugar processed on the patented Granulate-Ted system from Mr. Murphy.

"Zis spoontz iss verr goodtz butz zee fuckingst sugatz vill snotz stays ontz zee fuckingst spoontz" shouted some 700,000 Germans in the centre of Berlin during the "Screwtz Cubitz Rallitz" held in protest at the forced drinking of unsweetened coffee in the city after all the sugar had fallen off all of the square flat spoons in the city. This crisis is why Herr Cubitz came to see Laurie, the leading expert in sugar, to plead his desperate case. "Pleastz Mienstz Frentz youz mustz helpz meez toos savetz meinst bollaxst - Pleastz givstz mees zee sugartz fors zee squarst flatz spoontz."

Laurie had always been a real soft touch when seeing other people in trouble, but he was just as clever to boot. This combination of softness with brains led to the launch three months later of the world famous Mr. Cubitz sugar lump from Tay-Tan-Lie-Lell. Da, da, da!

Lots of sugar being produced and lots of compliments, but still no time to paint those masterpieces for the world to adore. Lots of dosh but no pretty pictures to admire. All this was acceptable to Laurie as he helped to smooth the life of twenty-three million Germans with flat square spoons and sugar cubes to suit.

In 1738, Laurie became disillusioned with his life as a sugar beet grower and sold his vast plantations to a golden syrup baron from Bermondsey who wanted to invest in the cheap production areas of the West Indies. Laurie moved back to London with some £32 million in liquid assets which he deposited with the Parliament Bank.

At that time the Parliament Bank was the most respected and honourable bank in the world. Bad luck always hits you in the most painful parts when it is least expected, and this was most certainly the case that can now be told concerning the unhappy demise of the Parliament Bank.

The Parliament Bank's head office was situated on a piece of real estate adjacent to the west side of the Houses of Parliament. It was because of this location that the name of Parliament Bank was chosen, and for the most part its reason for fame and honour. In 1778, the Prime Minister of the land was a drunken Cornish sop who mumbled and farted in response to the name of Anthony Caruthers Bedrock, or alternatively responded to "that arrogant pisshead".

This Right Honourable Pisshead banked with The Parliament Bank where he ran up an overdraft of some £478. 13. 3d over a period of only seven months, which I think you will agree is an excessive amount.

Please excuse me expressing the overdraft in the old style of English money but I do like my books to be realistic. This old money was a form of currency invented by Wig lunatics in the twelfth century in an effort to confuse the French in case they decided upon another invasion and occupation. This currency became unnecessary from the eighteenth century onwards when England ruled the world and the French were writing letters. The next William the Conqueror wouldn't find things quite so easy; oh no my froggy conceited, deplorable, unsavoury, garlic stinking, high pitched, homosexual, crazy French fellows joining together with us in one United States of Europe.

The Parliament Bank bank manager sent a carrier pigeon to the Prime Ministers office window with an urgent message strapped to its beak, saying:

> *"Dear Right Honourable Prime Minister - you arrogant pisshead,*
>
> *May I draw your attention to the fact that your current overdraft stands at £478.13.3d as of todays date and we would like you to make settlement of this account within the next 28 days.*
>
> *Your income over the past 4 years has been less than 8d and your overdraft is increasing by the value of 36 pints of gin per week. Please attend to this request as a matter of urgency!*
>
> *Your Servant,*
>
> *M. Thatcher*
>
> *PS: We fed the pigeon bran flakes before it left so that I hope it shites all over you.*

Well, what a cheek!, fancy talking to the P.M. like that, even if your name is M. Thatcher!

Within twelve weeks, the Prime Minister had approved new building plans to pull down the Parliament Bank and build a "Members Bar" on the site so that all the Members of Parliament could drink all day together with the Prime Minister. The plan worked because The Parliament Bank was pulled down, the members bar was built and all MP's became permanently drunk which is now an essential quality if you are going to listen to all that bullshite in Parliament every day.

M. Thatcher died of poverty but his descendants in

the 1980's took revenge upon the Houses of Parliament and are still victimising a man by the name of Fred Bedrock. This poor victimised human being is a coal miner in Derby, who is unfortunately the only living descendant of Bedrock that drunkard Prime Minister from years past. Being vindictive is not of a Thatcher's nature, but revenge for the family's name is a very different matter my students.

On his latest bank statement, this poor guy Bedrock owes Thatcher over £324,768,431, which is the original £478.13.3d owed by his forefather plus interest at 4% over base for those 214 years. The Inland Revenue have confirmed that under sub section 5467/67b paragraph 34/tr6 of the 1956 Finance Act, which covers interest payable on monies owed on debts held by masturbaters and drunkards, the interest payment is non tax allowable unless you are from an ethnic minority group.

Back to Laurie Gough - get off politics Dick Head!

So, Laurie Gough had this vast sum of £32 million, which at today's value would be enough hard cash to buy Great Britain, The Ivory Coast, Kentucky, The Dead Sea scrolls, Kiev, three million chickens, the Queen and any two princesses. Laurie bought none of these, but did have a huge house built only one mile from the Houses of Parliament, adjacent to the River Thames and directly backing onto the Royal Park.

From his back garden he could see King Bertie IV, who was bent as a triple winged coot, changing the guard every day. First Bertie would undress him and then he would redress him in a different uniform. All guardsmen that cooperated with the King during this daily royal exercise had the Royal Charter "By appointment to His Majesty King Bertie IV" tattooed across their backsides plus a pink heart with the words "Love from Bertie" stuck in their hats. Guardsman that refused to cooperate with Bertie's antics were dressed up in feather suits and shot during the daily target practice attended by the whole Royal Family at Windsor Castle.

The nutty Royal Family often sent the Royal Dogs to try and retrieve these huge "birds" and one day Prince Glengorming was heard saying, "My gawd Cecil, just looook at theeeee bloody great size of the bawls on this huge duck I've just shawt."

Laurie now had a great amount of free time to utilise those birthday present paint brushes which at last allowed him to meet his destiny and become the master of his trade. He painted and painted until his fingers were as numb as a woodpeckers pecker eating through Hadrian's Wall. This Irish Woodpecker aside, Laurie eventually realised that his artistic streak was non existent and in disgust he gave all his paintings to Heathrow Airport as a free gift to hang in the departure lounge.

Failure?, you all be commenting too hastily my critical students because Laurie had started to implement plan B - he would become the greatest art collector in the world - da da da! If you can't paint them, own them - very simple really.

Laurie started travelling the world, buying up future "masters" at very cheap prices for as little as 11d (about 5 pence or 10 cents) because these paintings were bought before the art world knew they were masterpieces - got it? Laurie's instinct became so acute that he started buying future masterpieces whilst the paint was still wet on the canvas, and then they were very very cheap indeed.

One particular painting of a weird looking tart named Lisa was bought for only 14d and today this is valued at some £45 million.

He always cheered when the artist of any of his paintings died because then the scarcity theory came into play and the paintings of a dead master doubled in price overnight. In 1746 Laurie had collected some 1,765 masterpieces for an outlay of less than £278, but these paintings were already valued at over £56 million. He did not however own any of the masterpieces being turned out by a famous Austrian artist by the name of Hubbenflubber, so he went personally to visit him in his village of Pumpennickle near Vienna. For only £2,675 he purchased all of Hubbenflubbers paintings to date, but one problem still existed. Hubbenflubber was only 34 years old and his grandfather at 96 years old was still going strong. What if this beer sausage chewer lived just as long as his grandfather?

No, this could not be allowed, so Laurie hired a Japanese lunatic with a big sharp sword to visit and have a little talk with our marching painter from Austria. After chopping off all of Hubbenflubbers fingers, Nagasaki Kashibagi then proceeded to stuff then up his rectum and left him for dead.

Dead artist OK, but a live artist with no fingers and sore rear end is still no problem, right? Wrong my students, because Hubbenflubber survived this ghastly physical attack upon his body and learnt how to paint with a paint brush stuck up his nose. Different style of painting, but equally as famous - Laurie's collection was still not worth any more money - he must take further action.

Nagasaki Kashibagi returned to cuckoo clock valley in Austria and this time cut off Hubbenflubbers head and stuck the remaining body torso onto a tree trunk in the back garden, with a notice on his head saying, "Now very definitely dead," which did the trick. First all his fingers, now a bloody great tree trunk - it was very painful being a master painter in Austria.

At the age of 79, Laurie became a born again

christian and started to pray for forgiveness for all of his past evil doings and other sins that he had purposely committed over his previous greedy unscrupulous years. As is his habit, the Lord forgave Laurie but presented him with a permanent vision of Hubbenflubber appearing every night without his fingers and in a great deal of pain.

Hubbenflubber would always speak out during these horrific visions, "Laurie gough you wanker, the Lord may forgive you but I don't because having all fingers cut off gave me enough problems, but not as much as this tree trunk up my rectum - now that's what I call real pain. However, the Lord has forgiven you, so spend the rest of your days on Earth learning to appreciate art, because one day you'll be coming up to visit me for eternity. I would prefer that you really appreciate art so that we can talk occasionally."

Laurie opened up an art gallery named Tay-tet gallery and gave it to the nation. He then spent the remaining thirty-one years of his life learning to appreciate the innermost expressions of art from the soul, ready for his future discussion with Hubbenflubber.

This is now all part of history, but do you understand what art truly is?

Without the appreciation of art, the human mind cannot express a gentleness in life that would make the world a safer and better place to be in. Governments, churches, armies, etc fight wars and kill people, but artists preach understanding.

So, with this as a proven factor of our deeply set inner make up, why are our children held back and hidden from the wondrous secrets of art? Why is it more important to add up in mathematics when we have electronic calculators, why need we write when we have word processors and why need we read when we have television and tape recorders? All these things are desirable but not a necessity to express oneself as a full human being amongst this planet of so few virgin rocks strewn amongst so much acid sea. Please let our future generations be able to see and live a life free from any commercial pressures of Authority, albeit for a few moments of their lives; but let it enrich their experience.

Art is truly the wonder of free expression of a liberated soul without boundaries.

Every picture tells a story, don't it?

Chapter 13

FROM CHARISMA TO MR. KITHBANG

"Oh to inherit the Earth with charisma and big balls."
Adolf Hitler 1943

Strength of character (balls) apart, every one of us must now enter into the Dick Head Charisma Development Programme where you will not only become fully qualified and ready to assume control of our country's riches, but by just speaking to you for only a few minutes, people on the streets will be saying, "There's another Dick Head graduate with fantastic charisma!"

Have you observed the eccentricity of our university Dons? No?, well my friends this means that you are not very observant. I can tell you that they are highly educated beatniks who apart from being over clever nutters, think that they must act in a bizarre fashion to make them stand apart from us mere products of the British educational fiasco.

Yes!, they are Dons and they are Bohemian salamanders as different from the norm as every Don is expected to be. No good them walking down the street and allowing people to think to themselves, " I wonder if that unorthodox man there is a daft prick or a very clever common or garden Don."

Even the name Don is incredibly stupid, but is acceptable to these aristocrats of wisdom because such a silly name is also very different from any other description that could have been used, such as emeritus, Regius professor, exponent, dominie, pedagogue, prick or twat. No, the word Don is exclusively different and has a quality of its own which signifies that to be a Don is to be full of charisma and demands respect, no matter the level of absurdity of the Don concerned. Therefore my undergraduates of lacklustre charisma and small balls, listen now to the stories and wisdom of Dick Head as we proceed further into our charismatic study lessons.

Do not miss even one digit, do not blink an eyelid, do not scratch your balls - just concentrate until charisma is yours. I realise that some of my undergraduates are harbouring negative uncharismatic thoughts at this crucial moment in their Guide to the Galaxy training and maybe are thinking, "I've already got a lot of that poxy Karizma stuff and much bigger bleedin' balls than that prat Dick Head."

For these aggressive and conceited students I suggest that you retire from the course and revert to getting pissed every night at Willy Wankers Drinking House in Balham where you will find compatible company in which to share your Karizma and probably to stroke your big pair of balls. For those students who continue forward but due to a lack of concerted effort do not progress sufficiently forward in their charisma studies, you will be found out during your final exams and will be marked accordingly using huge capital letters on your certificate, "BIG BALLS - NO CHARISMA!"

So rethink your position and attitudes my sons of the earth before the die is cast and it is too late.

No matter how worldly-wise or talented you actually are, you are considered by other people to be only as scintillating as their opinion of you allows them to think you are, which may be what you are, or indeed what you are not. Therefore, to ensure that we are considered as messiahs in this land, a land containing so few intellectual giants, we must strive with all our mental power to make sure that these people believe with all sincerity that we are what we definitely are not - got it?

We must create an artificially indoctrinated level of mind bending charisma that will have the whole world shouting, "look! it's that charismatic Dick Head, a Giant of a man!" This form of idolatry is something, that after more than 20 years as the leader in this field of total charisma, I can now accept as true recognition of my charismatic powers of teaching even the lowest IQ levels of students.

It is now an established fact that even a Dick Head student with an IQ level equivalent to a golf ball can achieve a charismatic level of 34 on the Bullshite scale if he concentrates and studies this chapter in full. Please see my publication supplement No. 53 of book No. 31 entitled *Bullshite by Numbers* for further details of the Bullshite Scale upon which all of you will be judged in your final examination.

To explain this subject further and to avoid endless fruitless phone calls from people with absolutely zero-zero charisma levels asking, "excuse me Dick Head, but what exactly is the Bullshite Scale and why do you permanently use such shocking language in your so called teachings?" I will explain my reasoning further for these creepy cranky critics. I decided to construct the "Bullshite Scale" in 1970 when I first started to analyse just how the working class man should be educated in a different way, a way in which to bypass Authority which has been established to keep the Working class man in ignorance and poverty since the year dot.

These old rules were set up when the few people possessing all the cash and power had so much to lose and had to take positive steps to protect themselves. Authority has never found reason or logic to establish a standard nationally recognised scale upon which an improving student could and should be judged for any increase in his charisma level. Their aim is to make sure that you do not progress even one iota in the first place and therefore why waste time establishing a scale which would cost a lot of money and would not be used anyway - got it?

My Bullshite by Numbers book could have had the different title of "The General Assessment of Improved Charisma level scale based upon *Dick Head's*

Independent Study of Improved Educational Standards of the Working Class Man, 1970 Edition, but this would obviously defeat the aim of the project. My working class students would be asking me, "What the bloody hell is Dick Head talking about now?"

To avoid a situation where every working class man would have to rush out to buy a children's dictionary from the secondhand bookshop, a Bible from the crippled padre selling matches on Rochester bridge, and a copy of The Socialist Worker sold by that gang of morons strutting about in Coventry town centre, I decided to employ the universally used word of "bullshite" in the title. This obvious choice allows everything to be understood by every one of my standard uneducated undergraduates and I am yet again an anti hero.

Authority hates Bullshite by Numbers in which we have the possibility of accurately (within 0.34%) calculating the charismatic level of everybody by just answering five hundred simple questions. Authority has tried on several occasions to have BBN banned under the Obscene Publications Act, but just before the case ever reaches the High Court we close down the publishing company and transfer publication elsewhere. At the moment it is being published by Clarence The Bullshite Printers (1990) Limited in Peckham, but is due to be transferred again within a few days to Sunderland.

It would take far too long to describe to you all the contents of this blockbuster publication (over 16,4000,000 copies sold so far), but of particular interest is question number 367 which asks:

(a) If you were the Queen, would you keep saving all the money you earn in interest on the money you never worked for, or would you give it away to save young children's lives?

(b) If you were a trade union leader, would you agree to an overhaul of the National Health Service to make enormous savings which could be reinvested in better

services to save more lives, or would you resist these changes to protect your members (and your own) jobs and subsequently allow people to die unnecessarily?

(c) If you had the choice, would you sacrifice the life of one British kidney patient and use the £100,000 not spent on this single operation to save five thousand African children with the same money?

(d) Would you give £50,000,000 to the starving third world or spend this money on British education?

(e) Should everybody in Great Britain pay 5% extra tax to save over 1,000,000 lives per year around the world.?

Answers must be yes or no. You get 10 points for every "yes" and 1 point for every "no". Please see assessment chart on page 589 in Bullshite by Numbers after you purchase your copy. In general, the higher your total mark the bigger the prick you are.

Remember, a man without recognisable charisma is similar to the Royal family without money or with humour. The difference being that you can always develop charisma. P.S.: You cannot improve your charisma by talking to an egg plant.

Unless you study this subject correctly, your search for artificially induced charisma can become exceedingly futile; as happened to my old school buddy Winston Chapelslope who was unfortunately called Boggo by his friends and foes alike at school. Poor old W.C. started to go off the beaten track of life just after he passed his A level exam in biology (grade C), and was accepted as an undergraduate by the *Lagos Burrowing Society* in Nigeria. Here he studied for twelve years the breeding habits of pox ridden rabbits, in which he excelled.

At the end of this fascinating period of study he returned to live with his parents in Brighton carrying his university certificate (printed in eight very bright colours), that specified his qualification as, Mr. Winston

Chapelslope, B.Sc. Lagos (Rabbit Pox Studies). He very quickly found out that this unusual certificate was of little use to anybody in this country, least of all to the rabbits as all the British pox ridden rabbits had been eliminated after the *Clapfree* brand of special antibiotic grass was planted upon Brighton Downs in 1987 by the *No Clap for Rabbits in Great Britain Society.* This heavy expenditure was paid for out of funds given to the society by the left wing local council in favour of ethnic minority rights.

Back here in England W.C. found himself living in the home of his father, complete with this fascinating poxy certificate, but no job. After applying for over two hundred jobs with various zoos, research institutes, lettuce farms and cartoon film studios, the beginning of a serious inferiority complex started to take hold of him, this due of course to the one hundred percent rejection rate from would be employers.

The final straw that broke the pox ridden rabbit specialist's back was when he attended an interview for the position of research chemist with *Nitserbashi Watszikumi Face Powders Plc.* He was interviewed by a very short vicious looking man from Tockeeoh who was wearing a large curved sword on his belt and answered to the name of Mr. Kashiwagi, or alternatively "AyeeeO!" when things got really tough in the factory.

The direct translation of Kashiwagi is in fact "oak tree" so you can only assume that oak trees in Japan are short, arrogant, bad tempered and very anti Mercedes cars.

"Meester Chaheel-Soap, whah youh hink his ha cooh-nehct-hun hoff hour fess pouters an yur ha-work wa-hith de poxy huck-in rabbits?" spoke out our Nipponese industrial diplomat from the land of miracles and unhappy people. In response to this offensive question, our friendly, meek and nutty WC lost his bananas and at the same time lost any chance of a highly paid research position as he answered, "You little chicken shit kamikaze wanker, you think that a few electronic miracles entitles you to rule the world and take the piss out of my twelve years of study? My poxy fucking rabbits, as you describe them, have more kindness in every clap germ than you've got inside your whole miserable shit faced yellow skinned body - arsehole!"

W.C. then aimed a swinging blow at Tokyo Joe's chin and took eight months holiday in the local hospital to recover from a broken neck which he collected as a result of his free flight fall instigated and perfectly executed by Black Belt champion Mr. Kashiwagi. He hit the tiled wall at sixty-three miles per hour and ended up on his back looking at the engraved brass plaque located above the automatic glass exit doors of the building, which read, "Have a nice day - thank you for your visit."

He did not get the job, even though after he left hospital he phoned Mr. Kashiwagi to apologise.

In desperation, an asset encouraged by his oncoming madness and total lack of training in Dick Head's charisma techniques, he placed a 4cm by 6cm box advertisement in the "Rabbit and Foxes Guardian" in big bold letters saying:

Attention Poxy Rabbits

No Need to Despair, get your clap trapped here, Hares seen on Sundays

Phone W.C House Clinic, Freephone 3388664400.

After three months he only had one call from a rabbit, that being from an English speaking rabbit, with an American accent, answering to the name of Bugs Bunny, who phoned every night at just after 11.00 pm to ask him "What's up Doc?"

At last! At last! At last! A friend working for the Local Council put in a good word for him and things looked great.

WC attends an interview for the position of social worker with the Local Authority but even here his lack of charisma immediately becomes a problem. "Mr. Chapelslope" said the weedy and very greasy faced man from Southern Europe answering to the name of Meester Cambiaso, "would you consider that understanding the venereal diseases of sex mad rabbits will help you with this job of looking after sexually abused children in our violent society?" Charismatically zeroed and totally irritated, W.C. scratched his testicles, picked his nose with his well manicured small finger on his left hand and gave his reply.

"Well, Humph!, I accept that rabbits with a good dose of clap are not totally similar or related to the job in question but certainly these infected rabbits suffer in many ways similar to sexually molested children. Pox in rabbits carries similar symptoms as that in the human body, so I feel that with my expertise in this field of medicine, I could quickly identify pox infected children who had just been molested by pox ridden parents faster than anybody else in the area.

"However, to get sufficient evidence for further legal action against the molesters, one must move very fast indeed and you must give me total authority to instruct the children and parents to take all their clothes off as and when I demand, at any time or place. I shall always carry a Polaroid camera to ensure that all the evidence is available to you in full glorious colour." After panting for a minute or so, our Meester Cambiaso whispered, "Mr. Chapelslope, we'll let you know if you have been successful with your application."

W.C is now a traffic warden with the same Local Council.

Being critical of W.C. is as pointless as expecting the tax man to be logical, only in WC's case this is a lot less expensive. Don't sit back crowing, "What do you expect from a wanker like that who studies for twelve years about clap ridden bleedin rabbits in bloody Nigeria!" Your time should be better spent in reading my book Number 17 entitled *Stop Rabbiting And Start*

Charismaticising, available from all good pet shops, tax offices and crappy book stores at only £27.60 including sales tax. This book is not available to any member of the Royal Family, Members of Parliament or tax inspectors. These excluded people are already considered to be perfect for what they are and they cannot be improved in any way. What a wonderful thing to be perfect!

We can all remember as kids that we admired in one way or another, often to the point of paranoiac jealousy, the strength of the school bully and other yobbos who have now grown up to inhabit our overcrowded prisons or to sell drugs to our mentally disorientated generation of young people crying out for our help.

The wonderful vocabulary of, "give it 'ere you bastard" would ring out in class and you always felt obliged to hand over your bag of sweets to retain your straight nose and your milk teeth. "Take it any time Jacko, nothin's too good for you mate" would be your reply whilst at the same time praying for Captain Kirk to beam the bastard to some way off planet inhabited by horrible germ infected human testicle eating Martian football supporters.

Remember also the sixth former, probably the head boy or the school rugby captain, going out with that big built girl that chewed gum - and so on and so on. You didn't like the people themselves but Christ they had charisma - bad charisma it may have been but it was charisma all the same - you have never forgotten them. Do you think that these same people remember you?

Have you ever tried to stand out in a crowd? No?, well don't feel bad about it because most people react in exactly the same way, they shrink into themselves and go out of their way not to be noticed. This was not the case with Herman the German, who acted as the Chief Engineer at Patel's Cheapo Pie Factory. His real name was Herman Ivan Teiser Lorenzo Anzer, born in 1926 to an Austrian army father and a nut head mother from Sicily.

As a bomber pilot in the Luftwaffe he was shot down over the English channel in 1941 but was luckily rescued from the freezing cold North Sea by his own people in an air sea rescue speed boat, but he never really learnt his lesson. Only ten weeks after his sea rescue, we did a better job on Herman the second time around because a Spitfire gave his plane a good old fashioned ten second burst from all cannons to show him that British is Best my son.

He crashed his plane near Ashford in Kent, landing by parachute some two minutes later in the town square of Faversham and spent the rest of the war in a soft hearted prison of war camp located in Scotland. This period of life taught our Super Race Teutonic looking German with blue eyes, blond hair and a standard German smirk, that Britain was to be his home forever more.

After the war, Herman married a Scottish lass named Susan Shayne which pleased Herman greatly as he could refer to her as S.S. without rebuke. He eventually ended up with us at Patel's Cheapo Pie Factory in 1981 as chief engineer and has been a Kraut arrogant pain in the arse ever since - however my friends he has more charisma in only one of his bomb door button pushing fingers than most of us have in all of our bodies.

How so?, you are asking with hate, jealousy and a little curiosity in your evil hearts. How could we at Patel's Cheapo Pie Factory mix with the enemy and the winners of the World cup (and I don't mean for soccer!). Forgive and forget is my motto, let sleeping dogs lie - so to speak. Mostly due to my generous attitude, Herman the German became accepted at Patel's and we quickly learnt that even Germans can have some interesting charisma.

The real fun started when an ex British marine named Paddy O'Callagan was interviewed by Herman in 1983 for the job of maintenance fitter for generally looking after the pie making machines. Our Paddy had spent fourteen years in the Royal Marines, fighting for

Queen, country, and his balls, all around this evil globe where the sun never sets on the Empire we once pillaged. Born in Dublin, he lived there until he was five years old, at which time his father took up a Church position in London where he lived happily as an Englishman until he joined the marines at the age of eighteen.

During his interview with Herman, he was asked all about his experience and qualifications, which he fully disclosed to Herman, including details of his B.Sc. Eng. degree taken at night school over a six year period. He also discussed his life history, including the fact he was born in Dublin, and it was on receiving this piece of information that Herman created the classic saying when he said to Paddy, "Vell, it ish a big problem fors me my Patty to giff you Ziss jobt! You see, vee alveddy haff far toos many foreigners vorking here alveddy!"

Paddy fell over laughing at this statement because here was this Herman the German who had made sixteen bombing raids on London, telling him - Paddy with fourteen years in the British marines - that he was a bloody foreigner! This classical story has survived the test of time in our company. Herman never gave up trying to be "British" and whenever we had a problem he would always, and I mean always, say "Neffer mindt my goot frents, ven vun door shuts, anutter door clozis!" You may ridicule him, but he had charisma - he stood out in a crowd just like a virgin in New York.

Visualise the normal wedding reception with everybody sitting down at the wedding breakfast where the most nervous man there is not the bridegroom, it's the best man because he must come out from hiding under the table and make that traditional bloody speech. No matter how well he rehearses the speech, he will always cock it up and look a complete wanker.

He starts off in the standard way; "I'd first like to fank alls of yous fer comin' and fank the brides parents for puttin' on this smashin' spread." Now panic sets in!, Christ he's forgotten the rest of the speech - poor bastard's sweating so badly that we wished he'd dropped out last week. Trying not to appear quite such a dick as he really is, he stutters on "Fanks to the bridesmaids, great service, lovely day and now a toast to the Bride and Groom." In summing up, we can say that he has just made a complete arse of himself and feels like a crippled blind man with Aids going to the gallows.

If he had taken my charisma course, he would have been the hero of the hour and said something like:

"Hello folks, my name's Bill Loxley, but just call me Billox for short, and I'm full of bullshite and charisma! Ha! Ha! Ha!. It's nice to see Jane and Andy tying the knot before the baby arrives and less than nine months before the divorce - Ha! Ha! Ha!

"We must all suffer for our mistakes, just look at the cake Ha! Ha! Ha! Sorry about the crappy food being served up, but I am informed by the drinks taster - me!, that the booze is great later on. Let's all thank the Bride's Mother and Father who have been very happily divorced for over 10 years, and looking at the mother, I would say the father is an extremely clever man, Ha! Ha! Ha!

"Bottoms up you sex maniacs Ha! Ha! Ha! Well folks I see that even the Man above has made his point by giving us thunderstorms all day and arranging for that pigeon to crap on the Bride's car on the way back from the church, but I'm promised better weather and only constipated doves on the divorce day Ha! Ha! Ha!

"Time to toast the bride and groom folks, but first we should wish them a lot of luck Ha! Ha! for a long Ha! Ha! Ha! and happy marriage Ho! Ho! Ho!

"Finally, I will read you just one of the many telegrams and cards sent to our happy couple on this better late than never day. You can see the rest of the cards behind the bar later in the evening. This particular card is the most touching of the lot as it's from Jane's ex boyfriend Jamey James and it's in the form of a beautiful poem which I would like to read to you now:

Jane was so cool and so terribly tender
Only two double brandies before her surrender
Our time together was like heaven to match
After some three weeks I started to scratch
The doctors' comments put me in a flap
He confirmed a double dose of pure clap
These little green men you gave me my love
Explain this one to Andy my turtle dove!

Great poem folks! Now just a final toast to the bride and groom!"

Some of the more romantic readers will be shouting, "You rotten bastard" or "Filth pure filth!" or "That Dick Head always turns beauty into something dirty." Whatever your feelings about our best man with charisma, absolutely nobody will ever forget Billox. About half will remember Billox with respect and laughter, whereas the other half will remember Billox with disgust. To have half the world respecting you isn't too bad as you can easily think of sticks and stones when you meet the other half who don't know how to take a joke.

By the way, Jane and Andy did divorce a week after the baby was born because Andy would not accept what the doctor told him about the new born child. He was told that he must have had an ancestor from long back who came from China or Mongolia but he shouldn't worry because a dark skinned Chinese looking baby was not unnatural for there are some one hundred and fifty million of them born every year.

Jamey James the poem writer has had all his tablets and injections from the clinic and has since had a sex change operation to become an hermaphrodite. Now he can really screw himself without fear of infection.

How about the stars on TV with "sparkling charisma?" We can all watch and learn a lot from these glamorous film star people. We must take notice of the important charisma bits and separate them from the useless bits that will only lead to a clog up of your memory system and give you an inferiority complex about how ugly you are.

We all remember in 1989 on the "Talk up or Shut up show" transmitted to an audience of twenty-three million people hosted by Walter Sumwhat complete with his highly obvious toupee and very white perfect plastic teeth. When he interviewed Ponco Flowbaker, the lead singer from the pop group Pincos Poncos - how could anybody forget that night - as we all sat bedazzled by Ponco's sparkling shirt with the front slogan of "Thatcher Loves It!"

Remember when he was asked, "Well Ponco, is it true that you take various types of drugs during the course of playing your music at concerts?". Ponco farted loudly and looking through haunted eyes spoke in a strange disjointed language, "Well I won't say that I do and I won't say that I don't but when I'm blitzed out I feel like a cunt." Unquote. This reply, including the fart, made world headlines and a great impression with the young kids because Pincos Poncos sold an extra thirty-two million records worldwide within six months of this episode on TV which became a watershed in television interviewing.

By the way, I'm not too sure that I agree about the Thatcher bit.

The Director General of the television station concerned issued a directive to all management stating:

Gentlemen,

following the foul language and the breaking of wind on the recent programme, Talk Up Or Shut Up show, we must ensure that this behaviour is never again witnessed on our television station. Due to the tremendous publicity given to this disgraceful behaviour, unless we take firm action, guests in the future will all intentionally fart to increase their ratings. This is unfair to our conservative minded audience and the cameramen have issued an ultimatum to us which quite simply says that they will all walk out on indefinite strike if the studio "smells like shit" in the future. So in future gentlemen we must get guests to sign a non farting guarantee form which assures us that they will not use any of the really bad swear words of C...., F.... or P....., but they can say the more accepted words of bloody, damn, bolox (only once) and shit (only twice).

Special airtight plastic undergarments are being made available for those guests we believe are liable to cheat on the farting issue. The transmission will be delayed by ten seconds to allow us to substitute all banned words with "nice" or "nicer" thus ensuring that the television audience is not subjected to such language. We have arranged to install a new Japanese computer synthesiser that will replicate exactly the voice of the guest when making these word substitutions.

The very next night (you remember it well!), when on the Talk up or Shut up show we had Bummer Bill Bates, the President of the Sexual and Deviates Society of Windsor being asked, "What do you think of Margaret Thatcher?" and the TV audience heard him answer, "That nicing nicing needs nicing because she's a nicing nicard!" He then farted like a machine gun and shouted, "Get the nice out of the nicing way you nicing niceards, because I'm nicing well going to shit myself and I need a nicing shit house!"

After that he ran off stage with the audience joining in the mood of the situation and shouting in unison, "This station is a niceard." The camera crews downed tools shouting "No more nicing shit smells" and all TV screens across the country read very clearly, "Normal nicing service will resume as soon as those nicing niceards, the nicing cameramen, will get off their nicing nice holes and get back to nicing work - shit or no shit!"

The Talk Up Or Shut up show was of course forced off the air by Mrs Mabel Brownshack and the television station has some thirty-five thousand pairs of adult plastic pants up for sale at a very cheap rate if you are interested.

The above true stories of life go some way to explain in simple terms how different people develop charisma as can be applied by the working class man. You will have the "Establishment Educated" people and the sons of the rich class poo pooing this idea because they are scared of us obtaining this unique feature that will give us the confidence to talk to them at our level, no matter how they try to talk down to us.

We shall place ourselves in a position of making them talk down to us because the talking down will be controlled by us in such a manner that we shall refuse to talk up to them as this will become as outdated as the backstreet abortionist. Let us stride towards charisma for the working class people who are the backbone of this great country of ours - the future is ours to take. Adding charisma to our other areas of training is yet another stride towards our goal.

All Labour politician must spend at least fifteen months at the Trade Union's school for Destruction of Tory Charisma for Duffs because when entering Parliament it is not enough to mumble all day. Some clever Tory M.P. will shout out, "Will the Right Honourable P. Duff of Merseyside stop mumbling and speak up - does he mean yes or no!" As everybody with brains knows, you must never answer yes or no if you are a Labour M.P. because the Leader of the Party may wish to do another quick change of policy tomorrow, or indeed today. But, after fifteen months training at the reliable DOTCFD school, you'll never say yes and you'll never say no. Despite this training, we should aim for a ten hour TV interview programme on BBC and try to get just one straight answer from these weird fellows.

"Mr Kithbang, where is all the money coming from to finance all these new policies of yours?"

"Well, Dick my boy, the trouble is that you media fellows never understand exactly what our policy is because if you did then you would never have to ask such a question. Have you not yet read our policy document, "Screw the rich it impresses the poor", this explains everything in fine detail.

"That as it may be Mr. Kithbang, but your sums just don't add up. At a conservative estimate, your new policies are going to cost this country some £28 billion more next year and your extra income obtained by screwing the rich will in fact be zero, or less, because all the rich people will piss off to another country."

"That's your trouble Dick Head, always spouting out that the conservatives estimate this or the conservatives estimate that! I can tell you that our comrades from the trade union movement headquarters have quite different figures which not only balance the books, but will allow us to do everything we promise! I'm Scottish and proud of it!"

"So, Mr. Kithbang, you do intend to:

Increase the rate of income tax to 98% for the rich
Reduce the rate of income tax to 4è% for the poor
Free milk for everybody
Abolish company cars
2000% tax rate on pin striped suits
Nationalise all housing
Employ another 2 million miners
All companies run by the unions
Allow anybody to come and live in this country
Build another 7000 hospitals
Give the Russians £50 Billion per year
Send all Americans home
Abolish the Queen
Ban Polo as a game
Pay everybody a minimum wage of £4000 per week
Retire everybody at 45.
Ban the National Anthem
Employ two million more left wing policemen
Ban the German Mark from Europe

Disband the army
Disband the navy
Disband the air force
Dig for more oil in Kent.

And you tell us Mr. Kithbang that this will not cost anymore money!"

"Remember Dicky Head! When we take over government in four years time, we can always produce more money, even if we do devalue the Pound yet again. You must remember that the Pound in your pocket is still worth a Pound no matter how much it costs to buy a Dollar!"

"But with all due respects Mr. Kithbang, all governments around the world, including Cuba and Zanzibar, are very concerned about your proposed policies and believe it will lead to a world recession and even to war!"

"You really are a Dick Head, by saying these stupid things! By the time we sort out the armed forces, there will be nothing for us to fight with, so how can we go to war?"

"Quite so Mr. Kithbang!"

Chapter 14

FROM EARTHLY PARADISE TO SHITE

"Smell is but an advanced skill of the human nostril to accept and tolerate reeks and bouquets with savoir faire leading us all to a stress free life."

> Wally Clapheap (1963)
> Caretaker:Kings Cross Toilets

The human process of discharging unwanted and undigested metabolic products from our bodies leads to the accumulation of millions of tons of smelly waste matter, faeces, stool, crap, excreta, piss, urine, sweat, spittle, spit, gob, sputum, phlegm, mucus, snot, pus and lots and lots of common shite. To avoid having to repeat ourselves over and over and over and over and over again all these words throughout the whole of this chapter, we shall simply refer to all this matter as "shite."

Before the crap experts in our audience start complaining that Dick Head doesn't even know the difference between shite and defecation, I am pleased to put you right on this misconception of yours. I do not confuse this with defecation which, as everybody knows, defecation is the elimination of undigested and unabsorbed food - not shite, but equally as vile and smelly. However your body's digestive system operates, the unwanted matter all ends up inside the same sewerage processing system which must be located alongside somebody's back garden, and hopefully the next one will be built next to your dining room window.

On the 21st May 1978 our planet Earth experienced the greatest thunderstorm that has ever been recorded by the United Nations Meteorological office based in Fukweto, an island located just six miles east off the coast of Bombay. The official report submitted to the UN central weather committee consisted of exactly 1,450 pages of technical data which tried to explain why we had experienced such misbehaviour from our weather God, Fishtail.

The Eternal Power above had decided it was time to drown some 132 poor souls who had been previously living in poverty on this offshore location of Fukweto, where they went about their everyday chores without an evil thought in their minds. I have recently taken the trouble of having this huge report translated from the strange tongue of mother India into the advanced tongue of old England, to be sure that such an awful tragedy can be fully explained to all of my lacklustre students.

In simple to understand terms, on this day of disaster and death of the innocent, it bucketed down hard with rain with a greater intensity than ever before, accompanied by thunder and lightening of drastic proportions. Some 132 ignorant local plebs living on an uncivilised island decided to trust in their Gods and shelter inside the village temple which was built thirty two feet below sea level. Their strong religious beliefs gave then real faith to believe that they could rely upon common prayer to save their poor skins against the terrible force of Mother Nature.

Prayer alone did not unfortunately hold back the rage of the stormy sea for these tragic souls, who became sacrifices to a greater less caring force as they perished with their beliefs still held intact.

If it was not for the ignorance and conceit of the people living in the middle ages, we would today describe this storm as being accompanied by lightning and thunder. After all, it is illogical to have thunder before lightning, or so my physics master Mr. Harrop told us during a physics lesson many moons ago. It is therefore an erratum to say thunder and lightning; but ignorance is a continual affair, encouraged and accepted by subsequent generations of carefree and couldn't care a bolox folk. Therefore, despite the idiocy of the expression, we do say thunder and lightning.

Should this minute point confuse you, please have it explained fully by reading my Meteorological Office publication entitled *Gone with the Wind*, available at The Meteorological Office, all good public toilets and some lower class sailing shops in the Liverpool docks area.

On that fateful day on the island of Fukweto, it was fortunately a beautiful sunny day in England, which just goes to show that you can never be sure where to plan your holiday. At exactly 12.45 pm that fateful day in glorious England, Roberta Roebuck at last achieved her lifelong ambition, an ambition she had dreamed about for all her life (got it?). She was at that wonderful moment being handed the keys to "The Old Rectory", that famous house which Charles I had made his refuge so many years ago whilst trying to keep a head and his balls.

Just why he left such a beautiful dwelling to lose his curls beats me, but royalty does have some strange quirks when it comes to common sense.

Yes, after 35 years of living as a frustrated virgin on this planet earth, Roberta was at last the proud owner of this dream house in the country. I never did get round to asking her whether this was better than the screwing she had missed, because this is not the sort of crude question that one puts to a country girl virgin, even if she did have big knockers and lovely....... Stop!

This country house dwelling of ultimate beauty was the very same building that her dear mother continually romanticised about whilst cradling her children during their formative years. Dearest mother ranted in hysteria about The Old Rectory whilst she lay dying such a prolonged painful death those many years ago. Roberta had adored and loved her mother very much indeed, but at the very moment of taking hold and grasping those keys within her ultra white hands, the excitement had made her temporarily wash away and forget such past grief.

The mystic pull of The Old Rectory was far stronger than any family ties and was indeed a feeling of real being, never before experienced by Roberta. Her new home was far from just mere bricks and mortar; it contained the soul of a bygone age that she felt must be possessed to be real and to give her life a full meaning and completion. "Forgive me mother because I know you would understand."

Located on the outskirts of the twelfth century quaint village of Daftmore on the Hampshire/Surrey borders, this beautiful and extremely well preserved old country house was built in 1688 by Sir Chandery Roebuck II. Constructed from hand hewn Brummy Greystone with Alton Red hand made brick surroundings, it reminded one of past legends of our affluent landed gentry when passion was still a beautiful uncorrupted word. This glorious relic represented a perfect example of England's long lost past, our heritage and soul that is now sadly gone forever, leaving behind a rotting carcase to slowly eat away our national pride.

Sitting in singular triumph amongst its six acres of fully shrubbed and lawned gardens, this glorious structure is still complete with a wondrous Victorian inspired flower bed to remind one of better times past when life was a much simpler and happier task. From the exquisite full length front bayed windows, fitted with leaded panes of coloured glass, constructed in all colours of the rainbow, glittering in the autumn golden sunset. From the front porch you can still stretch your viewing power across uninterrupted fields westwards over a distance of some eight miles, right across to the next village of Daftless.

Daftmore is many times larger in population than Daftless but even so, its inhabitants totalled only a meagre 134 persons of mixed religious beliefs. The majority of this population have Tory leanings and wear the uniform of Marks and Spencers checked sports jackets with striped regimental ties.

Despite the very small number of the local populace, Daftmore sported its own local pub called The Poked

Parrots of May, but from whence this name came I know not. There is however a rather disgusting story derived from local folklore which relates to a very happy gentleman who went by the name of Randy Bird of parrot fame. He was the first landlord of this drinking establishment which was built and established in the year of our Lord 1806.

It is said within the regular whispered conversations which take place in the bar after official closing time, that this thin nosed mein host had been charged in 1808 with twenty seven counts of serious sexual abuse against numerous under aged parrots of assorted colours, size and breed. These alleged poked parrots had all been bred inside his huge covered aviary which was located next to the stable block at the rear of the premises.

In defence of Randy Bird's tainted reputation, I must point out that this story is indeed only hearsay, taken from village folklore and no real proof can be found to fully substantiate these very serious accusations. How would you like to be accused of poking parrots after you're dead and gone? All these stories are to be understood as only bitchy hearsay from local village folk with nothing better to do but gossip. There is no further legal back up of eye witnesses, statements or photographs of the alleged offence being available as definite proof and evidence of this horrible alleged crime against fellow creatures from Australia.

It is however recorded within the village church's notes that after the alleged offence took place, some of the baby parrots born afterwards were of a real strange breed having very large feet with big toes. These animals preferred drinking large glasses of vintage port whilst eating packets of cheese and onion flavoured crisps, refusing all offerings of seed and coconut lumps.

These parrots eventually had to be put down by the local vet because they persistently made romantic approaches to Randy Bird's wife, whom he nicknamed Polly. Rumour has it that she was seen running down the village main street at three o'Clock one morning shouting hysterically, "Randy, you must get rid of these fucking sex mad birds, they're trying to screw me and it bloody well hurts!"

Randy gave each one of his Bird bird family a bottle of the best quality Taylors vintage port and after they had each consumed their bottle, they were sadly put down in the gas oven where he baked his pies. Even when approaching death, you could hear their muffled cries, "get 'em off Polly!"

So, if you ever see a parrot with big feet and toes drinking port, keep it away from your wife, daughter or mistress. No homosexual parrots of this breed have yet been reported, which is a good thing for most of us and a shame for any parrot poking gay gangs and their followers from Aberdeen.

Roberta Roebuck, who had absolutely nothing to do with any type of parrot poking, had spent more than twelve years of her God fearing life working as an expeditionary nurse in the emergency wing of the "executives suicide unit" at the Stock Exchange medical centre in Tokyo. Within this boiler house of capitalistic prostitution the suicide rate amongst its executives increased to its zenith every Friday afternoon, excluding the 25th December (if that happened to be a Friday).

It is a well known fact that Father Christmas does not spend very long in Tokyo every year and generally treats the populace as oriental spoilsports of the Faith. However, during this season of international Christian goodwill to all men, he does always make a gesture towards our Jolly Japanese Joes, normally with one or two fingers. Apart from this busy Friday night self inflicted blood letting period, the Joe's of the stock exchange were far too busy bowing and making money to think of committing "IMABU IGAF" (pronounced "eemarboo eeegarf!").

When counting up the red yens and the black yens at about 8 pm each Friday night, all the Tokyo Joes at the stock exchange started praying very hard to the Japanese God of Yen before daring to push the "consolidated profit" button on their personal computers.

If, after the total came up on the illuminated screen, you heard the roar of "Ohyyyeaaa!", then this indicated a good week at the races. However, if you heard a castrated scream of "IMABU IGAF!" then things were far from fine at the palace and you could be sure that we were approaching impending disaster for that particular individual. It also confirmed without any hesitation or doubt that this particular arrogant yellow skinned slant eyed Tokyo Joe git had just completed a real crappy week and was a very worried individual probably approaching an early passing.

The resultant red yens now flashing away merrily on his gleaming computer screen indicated that the ultimate punishment would very soon be forthcoming. This approaching retribution for the Red Yen failure could only be averted if you could pray very hard and find the luck of Jobsei which could on rare occasions reverse the yen colours on the computer screen before the big boss passed final judgement. It has been found through experience that the luck of Jobsei has been in very short supply since 1945.

My own feeling is that taking into account the fact that being japanese makes you cleverer than the rest of us, then the world is delighted when a few of these clever yellow laddies get into trouble and lose their balls, so to speak.

The chant of "IMABU IGAF!" is the Japanese warriors chant which translates directly into "I Made A Balls Up - I Go Away Forever." This chant was first used by the Irish Kamakazi pilots, pissed up on Guinness, during the second world war when they realised that all was not what it was made out to be during their sixth mission.

The Tokyo stock exchange now has a permanent ban on its executives bringing any guns, knives, swords, broken bottles, ropes, prostitutes, ducks, queers in slingbacks or any other type of harmful weapon into the office. This safeguard in security followed the famous, yet tragic, mass suicide of three hundred and twenty-seven stockbrokers in 1963, which became known in newspapers throughout the world as "Ahsoh!"

This multiple tragedy happened a few minutes after these executives were reprimanded by their president, Panyo Yanyo, for buying 29,000,000 shares at $3.60 each in a British pickle company. This pickle company's name was The Bulldog Nipponprick Pickle Company Limited of Cleethorpes and had been in the same boring business since 1946. The owner, Wally Churchill, who had been a Japanese prisoner of war in 1943, had assisted the friendly Japanese nation to build a very long railroad across Burma, which he did not really enjoy very much.

This feeling of anti Anglo-Yellowface cooperation was the reason for giving such a non patriotic name to the pickle factory. The label on the pickle jars depicted a Japanese soldier laying on the ground begging for mercy with a bulldog wearing a Union Jack coat pissing all over his head. The message below the label read *A British Bulldog pissing is better than a Japanese arsehole begging.* Who am I to dispute this.

It was very sad to watch these highly skilled financial executive wizards excusing themselves by trying to inform Panyo Yanyo that the BNP Company Limited had the fastest growing sales figures and profit/growth ratio of any pickle company in Europe. One very brave short slant-eyed arrogant man about to depart for happier lands, *Glando Plikko,* even suggested that the label could be changed to show *Panyo Yanyo* as the Japanese person on the label - "but of course without the dog pissing all over you sir."

All the excuses given were to no avail as Panyo Yanyo pronounced his sentence, "IMABU IGAF to all of you" as he handed out special happiness tablets to these three hundred and twenty-seven sweaty faced executives.

He demanded that they wait until they got home before they swallowed these sweet and sour (sugar and arsenic) tablets to avoid making a complete mess on his company's floor. These tablets allowed you to die very happily without pain but there was unfortunately an obnoxious and upsetting side effect that resulted in you crapping all over the floor whilst you died singing the company song.

So departed these poor three hundred and twenty-seven human creatures to join our Japanese electronic house in the blue yonder, leaving behind the wonderment of the land of the rising sun. We now only have left 101,987,456 slant eyed untrustworthy yet very competitive guys trying to take away my job here in England!

This single sad catastrophe apart, it was amazing the methods by which the red yen executives chose as their chariot by which to depart our fair land forever. This variation of the heart stopping technique never ceased to amaze our dear concerned Roberta, as she helped collect the various mangled bodies each Friday evening and Saturday morning in her Morris Minor car with a refrigerated trailer towed behind.

One particularly interesting story is that of the ex millionaire Boggai Plonkimu who tried to drown himself by holding his head under water in the toilet bowl. He took this action after he had been informed that his wife had gambled away all his fortune by betting on a single horse on a 200 to 1 outside chance bet. "But Boggai, imagine just how rich you would have been if the horse had won - no pain no gain" she had told him smiling as she left home for good to join a young man in a lovely new Porche.

As is often the case when trying to commit suicide in such sad and unhygienic circumstances, Boggai changed his mind when he realised that he could end up in the same final resting place as the other things that had gone down this bog before him and his Gods would never forgive him. Tragically, when he tried to pull his head out from the toilet bowl, he found that it was very firmly stuck and he could not budge, no matter how hard he tried. As he panicked in a violent frenzy, his feet slipped on the slippery wet tiled toilet floor and he broke his neck, thereby dying instantly of a badly broken neck and smelling very badly indeed. At the inquest which was held the following week, the verdict was that he had died of drowning whilst having his head stuck down a toilet.

Equally bizarre was the sad case of William Teller the bank manager from Biggleswade who had been fired from his executive job at Bartons Bank. This bank had an office located within the Tokyo Stock Exchange where our Billy had held this senior position for the past six years earning some £167,000 per year plus perks and bonuses.

Such a salary is not so high after you realise it costs £12.60 for a packet of biscuits and over £39 for a single condom - and then you find it too small a fit for western guys. These are the same small condoms as supplied in the vending machine installed in the House of Commons wash room, at the request of several famous government ministers. And I thought they were all big pricks.

William's dismissal came very shortly after he openly confessed to stealing the paltry sum of just £4,500 from the bank to buy a secondhand Fiat sports car for his mistress. This big breasted girl, *Greta Bloajobt* from South African, had great ability and technique and had pressurised him for a reward to cover her services rendered.

Despite his lust for Greta, William was filled with remorse and guilt for the shame this would bring down upon his family living in England once this terrible affair became public knowledge, as he knew it most certainly would. After endless days of drinking saki (Harso brand) in an attempt to wash away these wretched thoughts, he realised that hari kari was the most decent exit to escape from such a disgrace.

William therefore decided to end his miserable time on Earth, even though this meant no more of the great Bloajobt who had brought him so much pleasure and ecstasy over the past six months. For the sake of his family he would take the midnight express to heaven with some dignity still left intact and thus allowing the insurance company to pay out the £500,000 life insurance to his dearest beloved wife.

They say you can't take it with you, but you can have a real good try.

William decided to leave this twilight zone whilst hugging a great big stack of the green paper money that he had so loved and adored during his lifetime. He once read a fictional paperback book on a British Airways flight to Cairo, called "God loves a Thief", in which God allowed a christian pilgrim to take his prayer book to heaven with him when he died saving the lives of several thousand African children. If it's OK for a prayer book, then why not a few million dollars.

Billy locked himself inside the huge steel vault of his dearest Bartons Bank, the last thing one Friday night just before the time lock clicked into place. The vault could now not be opened until Monday morning at exactly 9.00am when the time lock went "click" just like clockwork. This would give him a full weekend to achieve hari kari and suffocate to death, which was a sure certainty once all the air ran out.

You could always save air and thus save your life, by holding your breath, but this theory has remained unproven to date. By his calculation he only had another six hours alive on this planet as a living thieving wanker. He was soon to be a very dead thieving wanker without a Bloajobt to his name.

Sitting down smiling on the cold floor of the steel vault, cuddling the £12,000,000 in unused bank notes convinced him that death would not be so bad as he first thought. However, after only twenty minutes of singing the song "money, money, money" and thinking about this idiotic action, Billy Boy realised that suffocation was a horrible death not befitted to a British upper class gentleman. It would be better to steal the £12,000,000 and clear off to Peru with Greta. Unfortunately, the time lock prevented any escape.

When they opened the vault at precisely ten seconds after the "click" on the Monday morning, the head cashier was heard to say in Japanese, "what's that horrible fucking smell?"

On that same suicidal Saturday in London at exactly 4.55 pm in the afternoon, his wife Bertha was watching the telly with a ball point pen and pools coupon in her hand. She screamed in absolute glee, "Jesus Christ, we've won the bloody pools!", boy oh boy was she excited. Yes, she had marked off 24 points on the football pools coupon - the maximum possible - she must contact William with this exciting news because they're gonna be millionaires! By Sunday evening it was confirmed by the pools company in Liverpool, they had won the top prize of £2,675,346.54 - now to tell William, I wonder where he is?

> *I Love, I love my cowboy beans,*
> *Even at night inside my dreams,*
> *Fried for breakfast, boiled for tea,*
> *Billy the Kid's got nuttin' on me,*
> *Eaten once a month with hot pot stew,*
> *My guns then fired so fast and true,*
> *Even John Major chews beans all day,*
> *Before our Norma gave him hell to pay*
> *Cowboy beans make you ever so smart,*
> *Top class brains and a wonderful fart,*
> *Long lost tribes eat tons of beans,*
> *Their favourite is a white human been',*
> *You'll love, You'll love your cowboy beans,*
> *Even at night right inside your dreams.*

This little ditty was written for me by the now long dead Bonking Billy Bonds, a country and western singer considered by many people to be far better than Pavarotti. Most people consider that he was a far better country and western singer than he was ever a poet - what do you think?

I met this drug infested entertainer in Hull during that epic winter of 1975, when the river Humber froze over for the first time since Lloyd George opened his bank. Bondi, as he was known by all his friends, died a tragic death brought about by a massive loss of memory in 1990. His demise happened shortly after he took the wrong turning whilst driving his bright red flashy Pontiac sports car home to his sea front apartment.

Instead of reaching his luxury abode on the sea front and having a good night's trouble free sleep, he ended up driving off the edge of Dover cliffs whilst pissed out of his mind on a mixture of rhubarb juice and home distilled gin.

He was heard, by a blind policeman who was over five miles away at the time, to be singing his favourite ballad of "There will be fucking bluebirds over the fucking white cliffs of ....what the fu...Jesus.......thunk!"

He was buried the following Friday and on his headstone can be read:

Here lies Bonking Billy Bonds
He loved those white cliff of Dover
Took the wrong turn and drove over
Fell down to the sea where he fished
Broke his neck whilst completely pissed

Not very original you may say, but that's easy for you people out there living a life of luxury, no alcohol or drugs - you're the lucky ones. You must allow for the fact that his grieving parents were very distraught and this little ditty was all they could think of in their grief.

I comforted them as much as I could, at the very lively wake held at Bondi's apartment just after the funeral, and complimented them on the ditty because it is the thought that counts. Like father like son. Waste not, want not is a very useful rule for living your life out in a charitable way, so we used up the big bag of dope stored under the floor boards in Bondi's apartment to really make the party swing. Poet or not, Bondi was a great guy who left his mark on this earth!

Back to the story line Dick Head - stop wandering

Two years after buying "The Old Rectory", Roberta met a handsome ex marine, Major Graham Peter Hill, who was a mere 48 years old. Graham was raring to go somewhere and achieve something very quickly in his new civilian role after 28 years in the service of our Country and Queen.

Following a most brief and passionate courtship, of which I refuse to go into any of the intimate details for fear of another libel writ, it became obvious to both of them that here was a relationship created by the powers above, a relationship they had both dreamed of. Graham and Roberta were subsequently married at the village church on the Saturday prior to Christmas in 1981.

Roberta wore pure white (New Persil) and Graham appeared in his full marines dress uniform, and did he look smart and handsome! The wedding was complemented by a full guard of honour from his old regiment, all wearing big shiny swords. The queer vicar wore black with pink shoes and looked very miserable.

Graham was delighted to invest his army gratuity of £57,600 into helping the refurbishment of The Old Rectory, thus allowing it to be returned back to its former glory. Life was just an earthly paradise and just a bowl of cherries for them both. Paradise on earth had been achieved. Just imagine a life within the confines of this type of protected village environment.

Green belt land all around to protect you from the

hordes of working class pricks like us, where you can live with a loving spouse without a worry in the world.

The happy couple bought a bowl of cherries and settled down to live happily ever after. God is very kind to those who believe, but cherries do not last forever.

Nothing changes in Daftmore because it has always been the same and will always be the same, so there you are you doubting donkeys of hope and natural beauty. But what about processing all the shite?

At that time in the life of Graham and Roberta, the local councils were virtually all controlled by the Labour party dimwits and pseudo communist copycats. This idiotic situation arose because the revolutionary brothers promised more things free of charge to the poor and the stupid folk than the plum chewing boys in blue who preferred to remain honest. As usual over 50% of the people who bothered to vote were stupid enough to believe these Lenin followers and vote for them.

The local tax increased dramatically over the following period of two years, to cover all of the broken promises and the unions wage demands. This betrayal of the people came as no surprise to the ruling class people in the village of Daftmore, but what could they do about it? In the confines of the oak panelled parlour in front of a blazing log fire, Graham spoke out confidently "No matter what happens Roberta my love, we have everything we need here in our hideaway heaven despite the cost."

And so the world continued going around and around and around and around - Christ I feel so dizzy. Little did these two little doves in paradise realise that a small imbalance and a great deal of shite was moving in upon them from over the horizon. Well it's got to be next to somebody's back yard, has it not?

One sunny Monday morning in 1984, the 24th April to be absolutely precise, Roberta read her horoscope in the Daily Workhorse (Farmers & Nurses Daily), which read.............

> ***TAURUS:*** *Your life is heading for a change where new winds will bring surprises into your life for you and your loved ones. Welcome these changes so that this fresh approach will give you sparkle and a challenge in your life for the future. Beware of strange faeces.*

Roberta laughed to herself, thinking it was merely a spelling mistake or one of the typesetting staff having a joke. One must never ignore the stars, particularly when their predictions are published in the tabloid newspapers as a warning for all of us to see. My own stars that same morning were very encouraging:

> ***PISCES*** *The power of Mars this month will ensure that you will achieve great things. Beware of those less intelligent people intent on damaging your reputation. You can achieve anything that you decide to do. Go ahead and write a blockbuster book.*

How right they always are.

Just after Roberta read her stars with a laugh and a giggle she saw a young lad of no more than 26 years of age, complete with surveying gear, standing just outside the rear boundary fence of the Old Rectory garden. She quickly called Graham, who was showering in the downstairs bathroom, and informed him of the presence of this curious character.

Graham, being a nosy sort of ex army fellow (because this is what kept him alive) walked slowly at a friendly gait down to the end of his garden where this young fellow was ardently working at his trade. Graham leaned on a fence post, smiled and gently enquired from this zit infested stranger "Good morning my friend, what's going on here then?"

The gaunt angry looking young man hesitated for about 0.05 seconds and replied in a most arrogant tone, that is becoming commonplace within our young society, "None of your bloody business mate!" In his military past thought Peter, a man could have easily died for making such a comment. No matter, he was a civilian now living in the peace and harmony of his country bliss, "Sorry to interfere young man, but I do live here and would like to know what's going on."

The young terrorist inspired governmental employee spat a big green ernie onto the ground, glared at Peter and responded with "I don't give a runny dog's shite where you live mate. You want further details?, then contact the bloody council......sir, but bloody well leave me alone to get on with my job!" At that, our zitty twat faced product of our modern society scratched his backside and strutted away with a superior swagger, feeling quite pleased with himself.

The next morning, Peter drove the 14 miles to the County Council offices in Baldon on Thames, parked his car in the managing director's parking space and entered the front reception hall. He approached a large oak reception desk manned by a blond haired individual who could have been from either sex, except that the big pair of tits gave the game away. "Excuse me young lady, who should I be seeing concerning the reason why a county surveyor has been surveying the back of my property in Daftmore yesterday?"

After a further few chews on the gum in her mouth (probably Wrigleys), and twisting her head at 45 degrees, she responded with a lovely Birmingham accent, "Do What?" Peter repeated the question three more times until the Wrigchew girl improved her answer to, "I'm sorry I don't know love." Peter became agitated, "Then who does Know then" he asked. She replied,"You betta go up an see Arfer on the fiff floor mate."

Peter did indeed go up to see Arfur on the fiff floor who turned out to be Arthur Wills, planning department assistant who was very helpful when asked the same question.

"Yes sir, I do know about this Daftmore business because I have recently seen the plans this very morning. We are selecting a site for the new computerised fully automatic centralised odourless Surrey sewerage processing plant, and your area is one possibility for its location."

"You are of course joking" replied Peter. "No indeed not sir, you see on directive 4532178/hgpy/89/6 dated last May from the Department of Environment, your village site is one of three being considered for this new sewerage plant of modern technology. You see Daftmore is one of the most ideal and cost effective locations in the county. If you draw a line from every WC in the county, Daftmore is at the centre of all this shite - so to speak."

Without boring my readers regarding the total unfairness of such planning decisions, combined with the futility of endless appeals, Peter eventually became reconciled to having this "odourless" processing plant built at the rear of his garden.

He planted 1120 conifers as a screen that would grow to over twenty feet high by the time of the planned completion of this plant. Inconvenient it might be, but it must be next to somebody's back garden and life must go on after all.

Just imagine how terrible it would be if it was not an odourless processing plant; Christ that would be impossible. Peter was a reasonable man and a lifelong democrat.

The new crap plant was completed 14 months late, due to "technical" difficulties but eventually everything was finished, the computers were switched on and the input valves were opened for odourless processing. Yes you've guessed already!

The area for five miles around Daftmore continuously smelt of 100% vintage vindaloo shite on a 24 hour per day basis. In fact after a only a few days, you could smell the VVS on the clothing of anybody that lived in the area, the odour was so bad.

It became very embarrassing when residents of the area were identified in other towns by comments such as "Did you smell the shite of that woman from Daftmore?" Peter complained to the planning department who wrote back after seventeen weeks and said in their letter.

Dear Mr. Hill,

RE: SEWERAGE PROCESSING DEPARTMENT

Following your letter dated the 23rd. June this year, we have investigated your complaint and the results have been studied by the full sewerage plant planning committee.

Indeed, we can see that you have misconceived the description of "odourless", thinking this would mean completely odourless, whereas it has always been accepted that some odour may be present in the local vicinity due to the 5690 tons of raw sewerage processed every day. These plants must be installed next to somebody's back garden and unfortunately on this occasion it was next to yours.

As a good member of society, I feel sure that you understand our position.

Alan L.L. Bull.

Peter had been taught in the marines, fight fire with fire, now he decided to fight shite with shite!

Without more ado, he phoned his officer buddy in the Royal marines, Captain Peter Challis, a man who owed his life to Peter whilst on a tour in Northern Ireland. He requested a supply of BUTA113 explosive which was the latest secret type - small volume, very big bang!

He visited every sewerage processing plant within 100 miles, including the one next door, and blew the processing machinery sky high. This drastic yet effective action put all the plants out of operation for at least two months. During this non operational period, there was an enormous accumulation of some 450,678 tons of unprocessed shite piling up everywhere in the county. In fact the whole county smelt of one big shite heap; yes even worse than it smells today.

The general public took to the streets with barrow loads of human shite and delivered it to the various town halls to show their dissatisfaction. Placards were on sale at all shops and petrol stations with comments such as "Shite here, there and everywhere."

A bogus Doctor Wang was arrested in Maidstone High Street for selling Crapblok tablets that guaranteed to stop the body producing any excreta. "These wonders of ancient Egypt allow the food to be fully used up inside your body. Just one Crapblok tablet a day keeps the shite away!" It was found that these tablets were made from pure cellulose which swelled up within the intestines and blocked up the complete digestive system.

Over 1200 people were later taken ill after using these tablets and were forced to have surgery to rectify this problem. Non treatment would otherwise prove to be fatal or very embarrassing from a social point of view.

To help matters along at a faster pace, Peter highjacked a tanker lorry and personally delivered 10 tons of a well matured variety which he graciously pumped over Mr. Allan. L. Bull's (remember him?) nice new Ford Granada car parked in the front drive of his new four bedroomed detached village house. A note was left on the windscreen, written by Peter on a flag, sticking out of the top of this obnoxious pile, saying "Shite smells nice, don't it?"

The next morning, Peter rang Mr. Alan L.L. Bull to ask if he was interested in buying a large drum of his special "car shite cleaner" that had been developed for motor cars that had been covered in it. He finished off the conversation by saying "Your life will be haunted by shite, shite of every kind, shite from every kind, shite in every kind of condition, wet shite, dry shite, and tacky shite until you close down the processing plant at Daftmore. Now you know what shite smells like my snotty nosed government employee, perhaps you also now fully understand the life we lead. Believe me, Bull my friend, If I continue to smell shite outside my house in Daftmore, then you will continue to smell like shite forever more."

Within 4 weeks, the council announced "Due to insoluble technical problems, the Daftmore sewerage processing plant is closing forthwith"

Never let people shite on you - To go from Heaven to shite is but a processing plant away.

Chapter 15

FROM FREEBEE TO POEMS

"A single word of poetic love is more powerful than an empire's might."
Whitstable Bunfrage (1845)

If only we could correct just half of our earlier wrongs and misdoings in life, imagine how good we would all feel and how nice a place this world would be.

My personal life is littered with long lost relationships that return as grotesque shapes in my dreams, like instant replays of both the past and the future intermingled with the ghosts of deserted friends and broken ideals from such a long forgotten past. The older I become, the more I daydream about how things should have been, had I known then just half of what I know now. I suppose this legacy of conscience, derived from the non caring delinquency of youth is something that sparks recognition within our own inherited sackcloth and ashes burden of guilt.

I make no apologies for retelling personal childhood experiences I now regret which an observer may interpret as the voice of conscience crying out for forgiveness. Such open exposure of my childhood wrongs to the critical world at large illustrates just what an honest fellow I am, which allows me to finally cleanse this guilt completely from my soul. I am forgiven.

I now have no further need for regret, regretfulness, mortification, harking back, crying over spilt milk, soul-searching, remorse, contrition, repentance, compunction, qualms, pangs of conscience, apologies, penitence, disillusionment, second thoughts, deploring, ruing the day, cursing one's folly, never forgiving oneself, blaming oneself, reproaching oneself, kicking oneself, biting one's tongue, wishing undone, wringing one's hands, crying over spilt milk, spending time in vain, lamenting, wanting one's time over again, sighing for the good old days, fighting one's battles over again, reliving one's past, reopening old wounds, harking back, looking back, looking over one's shoulder, sadly missing, regretting the loss, longing for, hankering after, being homesick, expressing regrets, being full of remorse, feeling contrite, feeling remorse, being sorry, asking for another chance, feeling mortified, gnashing one's teeth, having cause for regret, having had one's lesson or generally giving a single shite about what you think about me because I'm more famous than you are.

Logical thought is illogical to a man of dreams.
Ilia Positino (1745)

I have always reserved a deep rooted soft spot for crippled dogs, smoked salmon, vintage cognac and my old school chum Bertie Barry Bannion, who up until his death last week still carried the nickname of Freebee the Hasbean.

This disrespectful *sobriquet* was forcibly engraved upon Freebee's psyche by other less considerate kids attending our Victorian school who considered that such persecution was ample justice against a boy who stood out so dramatically in a crowd and was considered to be a right queer prat. It is amazing how our everyday sense of humour is excited and tickled by acts of tragedy and pain that, after full investigation, are found not to be funny at all.

Freebee once told me that if he could be happy for only one full day in his life, he would change his name to Charlie Chaplain.

I recently witnessed a very pixilated dipsomaniac trying to negotiate his pedestrian route across the main shopping arcade in Gravesend, in his attempt to quickly reach the local railway station, located only two hundred metres away. This semi mobile alcoholic human receptacle managed to reach the first corner on main street before he encountered a Victorian ornamental lamp post which cracked open his head, to such a severe degree that blood gushed forth in rampant quantities upon the pavement below.

Instead of the good and decent folk of this industrial southern town surging forth to assist a man in obvious distress, albeit completely pissed out of his tiny mind, not a single pair of human hands offered anything so charitable. In fact quite the opposite took place, when a group of six young men treated him as a laughing stock by shouting out, "lighting up time's not for another couple of hours mate, Ha! Ha! Ha!" and left him to bleed in peace. Another wonderful example of the progressive teaching methods of our youth where equality at any cost is acceptable.

Comedy for the masses is a bad joke.

This sad and bloodied gentleman persevered with his painful struggle to reach the local station, mumbling continuously, "My god, how do I tell Martha." To cut a long story short, he did finally reach the railway station covered in blood, where a passing taxi knocked him down when he was only a few seconds from the main entrance. Obviously being seriously injured, he was rushed to Gravesend hospital for emergency treatment in an ambulance that had arrived very fast indeed.

From this poor victim's driving license he was identified as George Anderson, a non drinking catholic research worker, who unfortunately died from extensive internal injuries and a fractured skull within a few minutes of being admitted to the hospital. The doctor attending to him in the emergency casualty department exclaimed, "My God, isn't this man the father of those three children killed in the M2 motorway coach crash this morning." Lighting up time was 4.57 pm that day and all was well.

We are now on the threshold of understanding the beginning of the universe which was probably started by naked aggression in another dimension of time and space beyond our human comprehension. Inevitably our world will soon reach a point where the institutionalised church cannot defend its faith, but being bound up by internal self interest, will hold onto the paper tiger until the final disintegration takes place with much disgrace and controversy. Thereafter, who controls the morality of mankind? - certainly not the people themselves. Maybe that will be the time when the universe begins again in yet another dimension in space. God, I truly hope so.

Back to the Freebee story.

Freebee carried an inner hurt with him throughout the whole of his life, being a direct result of this endless mental torture and personal abuse. He gritted his teeth and grimaced whenever he heard people talking behind his back, saying for example "There's that stupid Freebee the hasbean, isn't it?"

I became Freebee's caring protector during his tortuous childhood years at the Canal End Secondary School in Wapping where about 87% of all burglars and 78% of all Labour left wing M.P's were spawned and occasionally educated. Only one Tory M.P. has been born in Wapping since 1865 but the Conservative party has high hopes for the future, or some time later than that.

To improve upon this dismal record of Conservative fornication in this unemployed constituency, the latest Tory candidate for Wapping for the next election has pledged himself to screw anything that moves, at any time and in any place, if it will assist him to get elected. Now that's real dedication to the Tory party, far beyond the normal call of duty. He should do very well.

Freebee was positively very thick having an IQ going off the bottom level of the DikFik Scale for thickness. Even worse than being of ultra low intelligence was his tremendous height that topped seven feet five inches (2.2 metres), meaning that he was definitely not a midget like Nutty Slack.

He was so tall that he could see over the top of a standard height door whilst standing on tip toes and only wearing Woolworth's slippers. Height alone should be of no disgrace in a fair world, and for some professions it can be a tremendous asset. Freebee tried to use his height to maximum advantage by taking up basketball and he joined the local junior club, but never made even the ninth reserves due to his inability to jump more than a few inches from the ground.

The team trainer was very sympathetic towards Freebee, but eventually the day of truth had arrived, "Barry my friend, I've never had a team member who tried harder to make the grade, but unfortunately your body weight at over twenty one stones (200lbs/135Kgs) makes it impossible for you to jump the correct height for basketball. This alone would not force us to eject you from the club, but so far this year you've knackered up the sprung loaded gymnasium floor on six occasions, costing us over £800 in repairs.

The Basket Ball Floors Insurance Company inspector has just written to us saying, and I quote, 'If that fat bastard Bannion stays, then we leave'. As this is the only insurance company in the world that is prepared to insure basket ball court floors, I must ask you to leave the club". This gave Freebee an inferiority complex that made him think of himself as being that fat bastard Bannion. Insurance companies can be so cruel in their decisions.

This gigantic stature really pissed Freebee off, because he had always wanted to follow in his uncle Jock's footsteps and become a Peeping Tom, for both the variety of view and because no formal qualifications were required for this exciting trade. It soon became obvious, even to Freebee, that a real fat tall geezer carrying a step ladder around at the dead of night would definitely look suspicious and attract some attention from the ever watchful community police. "Excuse me sir, but why are you standing on top of this step ladder at 1.47am in the morning looking into the bathroom of the nurses accommodation here at the hospital?" You could try telling the officer that you operate a night time window cleaning service, but this is really skating on very thin ice.

Freebee also tried out a pair of stilts which he hid down his trousers whilst walking to the scene of peeping, but on each occasion of use, his weight forced the stilts into the soft back garden earth where he had to abandon them at the scene of his crime. Freebee then quickly sold his step ladder to a real midget who used it for posting letters. This peeping tom failure further increased his phobia of being a big fat tall failed basket ball non playing peeper.

Freebee eventually managed a single grade F pass in his CSE examination in the subject of Cooking and became highly proficient at preparing fried eggs with chips, peas and brown steak sauce. Cooking was indeed a strange subject for a boy to study, but Freebee took to this culinary profession with tremendous enthusiasm just a few days after he visited Wandsworth prison and spoke to his brother Yul who was serving twelve years for fraud which he committed whilst he was working as chief accountant for Casandra's Casino in Southend on Sea, a town famous for its whelks, beer and puke.

Freebee misunderstood the simple conversation that he had with his brother during visiting hours, an error fully highlighted during subsequent cooking lessons when he made a real mess of cooking his history books in the pressure cooker.

Yul was instantly dismissed from his job at the casino, after the fraud was uncovered, with no compensation for loss of office. He is suing them now for unfair dismissal and is expected to win the case.

Taxes on alcohol and tobacco must be carefully balanced to appease the health lobby and yet maintain the same total income for the exchequer. Banning of these commodities would lead to a thriving black market where no tax would be collected and even more products would be sold. Nothing to do with Freebee, but an interesting observation.

Some people, even before they are born, never have a real chance of achieving their full potential in life, this normally due to the lack of moral guidance given by parents during their informative young childhood days. I will in full defence of Freebee's anti social behaviour and dirty habits suggest that it was this very lack of moral guidance from his parents that was the root cause of his ingrained problems.

With different Tory voting parents, the world could have been blessed with a second coming of Einstein, but this is all a matter of relativity and playing with yourself. Indeed, if his father had been a carpenter, who knows what could have been the result. Me a disciple?, the hat would certainly fit.

Freebee was the youngest son of a huge and violently aggressive non English speaking Mongolian father and a beautiful young mother originating from the *Boobob tribe* of Peru. The Boobob tribe is situated within the inner regions of the Peruvian Jungle where total isolation from the outside world for over two thousand years has kept their unique cultural heritage intact and uncontaminated from our western filth.

His mother's name was *Nok-Nok* and she spoke only very basic English, even after living in Wapping for over 25 years. She could however speak a fluent native Boobob dialect which is now virtually extinct, except within the Boobob home village itself or inside Freebee's council house at breakfast time. "Bunya togis pertog bufez" was her favourite shout whenever Freebee acted stupidly, which was more the case than not. After a few years it became clear to Freebee that this native chant meant "shut up you stupid little bastard", although I argued with him and said that it may have meant "Shut up you shitey little wanker."

This argument has never been resolved.

Fortunately for Freebee, Nok-Nok spent most of her evenings at the local ballroom learning how to dance like an angel, which she partially achieved with the assistance of a wide variety of partners; in fact she had a different partner for each dance. It never occurred to Nok-Nok that it was mighty strange that she always had to ask for a dance as no one had ever asked her.

This unusual scenario never worried Nok-Nok because apart from being unintelligent, the people of the Nok-Nok tribe were also famous for being very rude and greedy people that grabbed whatever they wanted, as and when they wanted it. Being short of stature was a slight problem to Nok-Nok because she could never talk to her partners whilst dancing, owing to her head being at least two feet lower than theirs. Her almost total lack of the English language, combined with her chanting of boobob war chants during the exciting parts of the music, did little to encourage people to be seen with this import from Peru a second time around on the floor.

This is not race prejudice, it's simply a self survival case of not wanting to look a prick twice in one evening.

Her choice of dress for these dancing lessons was very colourful as she had hand made a wonderful native dress of all colours, adorned with great numbers of beads and cats teeth, all as used by the Boobob tribe for tribal dancing. The best description that I can think of is that she resembled a disfigured African Rainbow Parrot during the mating season with cats teeth around her neck.

Every time she returned home after these dancing lessons, the same upsetting routine would take place at the front door of the council home. She would lightly knock on the door (to avoid waking up her miserable spouse) and Freebee would come downstairs and whisper, "Who's there?" to which she would always reply, "Nok-Nok, who's there?" This really pissed Freebee off no end.

His grandfather was the ninth son of a mongolian sheep herder and a fanatical watcher of American films at the local village Mongoland cooperative television shop, which he partly owned. So fanatical was he about Hollywood films that he named his sons, Bert, Frank, The Vikings, How the West was won, The Bible, Alexander the Great, Hollywood, and South Pacific.

His grandfather's original surname was Chunk-ee-git, which has been the family name ever since 1378 AD, when the very first Chunk-ee-git won the Mongolian weightlifting gold medal at the eleventh oriental games by lifting six pregnant goats above his head and holding them there for two hours without wavering. This great achievement won him the gold medal, but sadly five of the goats were forced to have abortions the following day.

The King of Mongolia, being always present at these games, became so excited because a mongolian had at last beaten those bloody Tibetans, that he shouted out in uncontrolled excitement, "just look at that bloody marvellous Mongolian Chunk-ee-git", and from that day forth the family name has been known as thus.

At twelve years of age, Chunk-ee-git (South Pacific model and soon to be Freebee's father) was sold by his mother for a crate of Vladdington vodka to a Jewish/Russian circus owner, to be trained as a circus boy. After spending six years shovelling up elephants crap, he was trained to perform Russian sword dances on top of bears heads whilst the bears walked around the arena and jumped through large flaming hoops.

Chunk-ee-git found this work very exciting during his wild formative teenage years when danger was the adrenalin of life to seek out. At the age of twenty three he was drafted into the Russian airforce and spent three years at the Commoblinsk Training School in Siberia, training to fly military supply aircraft of all shapes and sizes. This prestigious career was an easy challenge to his high IQ and he became the star pupil of that year's student intake into the flying academy.

On finishing training he was placed in charge of flying a huge Bigbastdi multi-engined freighter plane, used for flying arms, flags and bribes to idiotically dressed dictators located all around the world. On the 10th March 1961, whilst transporting guns, flags, gold bullion, one hundred million roubles and two hundred tons of tinned Heinzki baked beans to a South American general, his plane flew into a huge flock of Icelandic Geese.

These beautiful geese from Toronto were innocently flying south with their families for a vacation in Chile when they were hit by this communist silver bird. Some twenty of these beautiful animals, all from the same unlucky family, were sucked into the air intake of the jet engines, and down, down, down, went this gigantic plane from Karl's Kingdom, code named "Red Red Red", heading for the desolate rain forests below.

Meanwhile, down below in the Boobob village, all five hundred and sixty-five members of this undiscovered tribe were sitting in the village sun-baked square paying homage to a miserable wrinkled medicine man who was chanting a Mad Hatter's prayer for the Gods of Harvest Time to deliver to the Boobob tribe a better harvest. This better harvest was now critically overdue to relieve the starvation that had beset the village for over two years. He promised to sacrifice his life to the Gods if only the famine would end today, even though he was lying through his ass because he was the first one to be fed every day from the meagre village pantry.

Well my critical socialist left wing students, it's no good if the man having direct contact with God dies, is it? It's all very well saying that everyone should share and share alike like all good socialists, but if the old wrinkle face dies of starvation, how can he continue making a deal with the Powers above to give the village the food it needs? Cleverness is my middle name.

Whatever your opinion is on such difficult political and religious issues, we have no time to discuss it further now because at that very moment the Boobob medicine man was hit by one of the huge wings from Chunk-ee-git's aeroplane as it came down and crash landed just outside the village square. The medicine man was no more in one piece because the plane's wing transformed him into a Boobob pancake covering some fifty square metres of the village square.

Even a Holy man finds difficulty recovering from such a traumatic change in the body pattern and he was pronounced very dead without the need of medical assistance. A postmortem was not carried out.

Catastrophe thought the Boobobs!, not only are we all starving to death, but now our Holy One has been killed by a silver Satan from above. The whole tribe wailed and cried like demented yuppies finding out that their Porsches had been scratched and their filofaxes had been stolen. Hark! my Boobob tribe members, a more powerful replacement Holy Man is at hand, a replacement bearing gifts of food, food in the form of twenty huge mangled geese which is food of the highest order, plus magical food in small silver containers produced by the Gods above.

And what do we have here?, they all thought in wonderment and with a little Peruvian trepidation as Chunk-ee-git climbed out of his wrecked plane looking like a giant alongside these midget tribes people. He shouted at the tribe, "Kesog Berondif byredp nutyrs" (which in Liverpool English means "What the fuck was that!), and immediately all members of the tribe fell to their knees thinking that this was a Mighty command from this God of all Gods who had just landed from the skies. How they were to eventually regret this mistaken identity.

Being a God, a certain Prime Minister once told me, can give you a feeling of complete power and Chunk-ee-git lost no time in realising that here was definitely a group of people ready and very willing to be exploited. From being sold for a case of Vladdington vodka to dancing on bears heads whilst his balls were being singed, and now being made into a God; not bad for a sheep herder's son. He took command of his opportunity immediately and shouted out in his best quickly learnt dialect, "I want to cook my goose!" and sure enough this was the result.

Following the ceremonial eating of the roast geese, our new God, renamed as "Smart Ass" by the tribe, opened up one hundred tins of Heinzki baked beans with sausages plus 100 bottles of Vladdington Vodka, which he handed out as a further show of kindness from their God of the silver bird from above.

As has been the custom in the Boobob tribe for over eight hundred years, all virgin maidens at the age of fourteen spend three nights with the Holy One to forfeit their virginity and Smart Ass really enjoyed this part of his official duties. Unfortunately in such a small tribe, this treat was a very rare occurrence, but Gods can change rules, can't they?

He therefore called a village meeting and looking extremely sullen and forlorn, told the tribe in a sermon like voice,

"My people, during a long walk in the wilderness last night, I have been informed by our Father of all Fathers that I must sacrifice my body even further to ensure that all the females in the village are protected by the gods. I have been instructed from above that all females between the ages of fourteen and forty-five must have full cleansing of their souls every tenth night of the year and on all other nights when our moon is hidden from view.

"By giving this sacrifice of my body and soul, our spirits from above promise a village full of female purity and male happiness, guaranteeing a wonderful harvest every year. Yes my people! I am prepared to make this sacrifice for my beloved people that I have been sent to protect! I shall post a list of all the ladies to be cleansed outside my hut every morning and if the moon cannot be seen during any night then all the women must come to my hut immediately and remain there until the moon appears again.

"I pray to our Father for moral courage and strength to carry out his wishes"

Pretty good, Huh? He then opened two hundred tins of corned beef and one hundred bottles of Vladdington vodka to thank the village for their understanding.

Some two years later, the tribe had an extra sixty-eight children, the majority of whom were not of the midget variety, but a new breed of giant kids that went around the village calling our Holy man "Dada". This type of playing house and families is definitely very bad for the conning business because it started to really piss off the menfolk who began to wonder why Clever Ass had parties every night and sexual orgies in the village water reservoir before breakfast.

Only last night he was seen drinking that fire water and singing a noisy song called "If only Karl Marx was here, I'd shoot his balls off!" No, something was definitely amiss and the menfolk had become more than a fraction agitated about these tall children, so they called a meeting to ask Clever Ass to give them a further sign to prove his Holiness to disperse the doubts now creeping into their minds.

During this meeting one of the villagers actually said to him, "Excuse me your Holy Clever Ass, but for all we know you might just be a dirty old bastard only interested in screwing all our women folk every tenth night and every night during the eight month monsoon rain period, rather than to please the Holy Spirits in the sky as you claim. Also, you promised us good harvests and since you brought in this new tribal custom of screwing all of our women, not one drop of rain has fallen and we are all getting really fed up with eating baked beans and corned beef."

Things were now surely turning for the worse, but at least the over indulgence had taught Clever Ass that he had now had enough to last a lifetime and maybe he had better get out whilst the going was good and before his balls were removed. He selected his favourite nuptial partner, her tribal name being Bukadsercher Domercokyut but renamed as Nok-Nok based upon her prowess over the past two years, and made his plan to escape from this village of doubting and ungrateful men and grateful women.

Ecstasy becomes boring after a while.

The next morning he prayed to the spirits and convinced the tribe that all would be well within one hundred risings of the sun, providing they all worked together to build a huge boat as an tribute to the God of Water (still pretty good, huh?).

The menfolk were finally convinced to build this boat when he told them that the great spirits now commanded that Clever Ass go out into the wilderness to discuss the cleansing of the women and whilst he was away this custom would be suspended. After walking in the wilderness, with six bottles of Vladdington Vodka, for three days, he returned with a very thick head and spoke out heartily, "My people, God has spoken! He indeed now can see that your woman have been permanently cleansed by the wonderful Clever Ass and the custom can now cease. However the Water God's ship must be your only priority to ensure that the rains will come, and in simple terms He has told me, no boat means no water. Peace, love and prosperity to all of you."

Yes indeedee, this thirty foot boat, designed from God's Drawings given to Clever Ass whilst he was out in the wilderness was completed in no less than 89 risings of the sun - ready to go now Clever Ass?

"God has told me that in tribute and thanks of your success in building this Water God's Idol, a tribal party will now take place over the next ten days and ten nights and all the men must cleanse all the women in a huge tribal orgy!" And so started the biggest piss up ever seen south of the North Pole since the Irish discovered America.

Everyone was completely in the land of the Vodka

nod, all that is except for Chunk-ee-git (now reverted back to his real name ready for his new life). The Water Gods boat was loaded with all the remaining food, fifty cases of Vladdington vodka and the one hundred million roubles in bank notes which was much lighter to carry than the gold bullion, and off Chunk-ee-git and Nok-Nok sailed to a new world and life of luxury.

Yes, they set sail down the river from the innermost part of the Peruvian jungle, setting a course for England, the home of democracy, the country with no racist policies, where Chunk-ee-Git could settle down and marry this sex maniac midget from Peru and live happpily ever after.

Some nine months later after an amazing number of unbelievable exploits, they arrived at Westminster Bridge Quay in London where they began their new life. The new life started in poverty after the banks in London and at the Hilton hotel refused to accept or change any of his two tons of useless roubles.

After some desperate times in central London, they moved to Wapping where they were allocated a council apartment on a nice multi cultural high rise estate overlooking the canal and railway track. After applying for several jobs, but never being successful, he took the advice of his 21 year old communist social worker to change his name from Chunk-ee-git to Gareth Osterley Bannion by deed poll; Gareth being such a nice Welsh name, don't you think?

By now you will understand that the disadvantaged position of Freebee in his life had begun even before he was born, but as I have tried to teach you all time and time again, everybody has his day, yessiree indeedee.

During our final day of school at the prize giving ceremony, Freebee was presented with his CSE certificate in cooking and as he walked up onto the stage to collect this hard earned award, the whole school became a lunatic asylum. A great roaring chant went up, "Freebee, Freebee, Freebee" followed by howls of laughter, which was no way of encouraging additional confidence in the mind of the thickest guy ever to have attended this school. The result of this uncalled for barracking was to disorientate Freebee to such an extent that instead of walking back to his seat via the stairs, he walked directly off the edge of the stage and fell into the school orchestra, which was ready and willing to offer a screeching of "God save the Queen".

Broken drums, bent trumpets, Freebee's broken wrist, pissed off headmaster and a roaring crowd - what a way to go. This final disgrace on his last day at school became the ultimate straw that broke his back; he decided then that he would spend the rest of his days showing these clever smug bastards just who was Barry Bertie Bannion. So began ten years of high stress to be followed by ten years as a guest of Her Majesty's prisons.

Freebee's first full time employment was with "Honest Jack's Garage" under a Government youth training scheme (Cheap labour), supposedly to train as a motor mechanic, but instead he spent two years polishing cars on the secondhand car forecourt. Despite this blatant exploitation of Freebee's labour and dormant talents, Freebee had the everyday opportunity of driving all these lovely vehicles whilst moving them on and off the forecourt in the morning and afternoon. Driving quickly became his love and joy.

He decided that driving would one day make him famous, from the very first moment he felt the mechanical power and raw energy that could be created by fossil fuels being converted into mucho speedo. He spent his third year with Jack being taught how to adjust the speedometer mileages on old bangers from 120,000 miles back to 37,235.1 miles and how to respray a rusty old car to look exactly like new. Jack really liked Freebee because he was cheap to employ and did exactly as asked, without realising or worrying how legal were the requests he made.

Freebee was now fully trained and ready to bring

down his main childhood tormentors, that smug creep, Walter Ivan Tomlinson, the six foot giant who was now a police officer with the C.I.D. at Wapping police station. Dear Walter, the boy who used Freebee as a football and punch bag several times per day was now practising this same art with the police.

Freebee visited Walter's four bedroomed detached house on "Blossom Avenue" one delightful morning at 3 am and gave Walter's beautiful BMW car a nice wash down with "Dynamic Paint Remover and Paint Thinners", and then completed his night's work by slashing all four of the very expensive low profiled tyres. He then posted a visiting card through the letter box that read, "To a Turd from a Nurd - have a nice day. PS: your car looks great!"

Freebee carried out this operation with absolute precision in just under thirty-five seconds and awaited excitedly for Walter's reaction which he read in the "Wapping Weekly News" the following Friday, where on page eleven in a corner was a modest headline "Policeman's car damaged" followed by only a brief description in sixty-five words of roughly what had happened.

Not enough! thought Freebee, so he had one thousand new visiting cards printed "Have a nice day - Officer Tomlinson C.I.D." and then proceeded to carry out carnage on a grand scale all around the area, each time leaving this new visiting card to be sure of a more positive reaction from Turd. Firstly, he slashed the tyres of all four hundred and eighty-nine luxury cars (not touching ordinary less expensive cars) that were parked in the Canal Walk car park, leaving cards on the windscreen of the unfortunate ones.

He followed this up by buying a supply of ice lolly sticks and magic glue, which used together put every one of the six hundred and thirty-four parking meters in town out of action, with this visiting card stuck onto the protruding stick end. He then systematically spent one hour ordering taxis to take Walter home from the police station; yet he hardly needed sixty-seven of them.

He then wrote to Walter's superior officer, acting as a supergrass, to inform him that Walter, not being satisfied with his normal £5,000 per month to keep quiet about drug pushers, wanted more and was now dealing in drugs himself. Just to push home this story, he phoned the police station to complain that an officer from their C.I.D. had sold drugs to his fourteen year old son. "No officer, I cannot give you his name because he has been warned that if he talks, then he never walks."

Following a blood test, dear Walter was transferred to Aberdeen as a clerical officer in the traffic control department and has since had a mental breakdown. The good news is that he is no longer thumping innocent people under the protection of his fellow police pugilists and Freebee was very pleased at the outcome.

Now I have a question for my law and order students: what is your assessment of this action taken by Freebee? Did the downfall of this thug justify the means used by Freebee to bring about his demise? My own assessment is given in book 26, entitled *Screwing Your Enemies By Unconventional Means,* which will be published next year for students of my graduate course. No fixed price has yet been set for this publication, please await a further bulletin.

Freebee now bought his first vehicle, a seven year old Mercedes G Wagon (the Jeep type) and he immediately felt the power of driving his own transport from the moment he sat behind the wheel. Here was a tool which would allow a minion such as Freebee to express himself with the same power as any other human being. Inside his power palace, complete with four wheel drive, Freebee was in control of his destiny for the first time in his life; no more taking the crap, no more being bullied, here was his destiny in life.

Life could be so goooood! Four wheel drive in such a vehicle can take you virtually anywhere, and this ability was exactly the cause of Freebee's further downfall in life.

"I don't need maps, all I need is a compass!" shouted Freebee, dressed in a boy scout's uniform, as he set out on his voyage of terror and revenge on that sunny day on the 21st August 1987. In hindsight I realise now that his mind had already flipped and he was being controlled by his subconscious with revenge on society as its only objective. Freebee sped away from home for the last time, to spend five weeks driving across country and dale on a trip of carnage that included so many offences that it took over three hours to read out the full list of charges in court.

The complete story is to be told in a non fictional novel I am writing to be entitled, *Nurds, Turds and Freebee's Revenge*.

In court, Freebee pleaded guilty to all of the charges, but commented that "Sir, I do not regret anything I have done, except that I did not intend to drive over the favourite corgis at the Windsor garden party, nor did I intend to offend any working class people that were present at this party."

When asked if he had any further points to make as mitigating circumstances, he answered, "Yes sir!, I regret that I could not get all of those rich bullying bastards from my school days, and I regret that you were not present during the Epsom race meeting when I ran over all the stewards and other rich bastards. Yes sir, you can be sure that the next time I go driving then you will be included as numero uno on my target list."

This was not the way to ask for clemency after putting into hospital sixteen old school bullies, thirty-five people of the aristocratic section in our society, killing two race horses and two corgi dogs. He was sentenced to ten years in prison. Freebee looked at me as he was about to be taken down and said, "Dick, at last I'm being treated normally like anybody else."

It was only ten days ago today, as I was loading

mysterious meat carcases into a barrow at Patel's Cheapo Pie Factory during the late evening shift, that Pusher Jack called me to an urgent telephone call. Pusher Jack obtained his name, not from drugs, but because he spent all his living hours in the office writing and writing and writing.

No matter when you saw him, he was like a little beaver, scratching away with his Kwink pen which he told me his mother had given to him as a birthday present some thirty-four years ago on his seventh birthday. If I ever have the need to buy a pen to last thirty-four years, I shall certainly buy a Kwink model because Pusher Jack and his Kwink pen have proved to me that Kwink pens are the best value that money can buy.

I took the telephone call by saying "Hello" and a crying sobbing voice said, "Dixie Ed, dis Bally vel orfool cos e ded an nek by skol tie!" Are you confused? Certainly I had to dig very deeply into my "understanding twats dictionary" and still all was confusion until I heard the same crying voice carry on and say, "Dixie Ed, you Bally nummer one pal, pleece elp me get him place in hunting ground!" The penny clicked and I came over very cold as I asked, "Is that you Nok-Nok? Has something bad happened to Freebee - sorry I mean Barry?" She screamed in pain down the phone, "Dis vot sesh me cos Bally ded buy fucked neck!"

Eventually I learnt the full sad story after telephoning the prison warden who informed me "Yes Mr. Head, Mr Bannion has passed away, but beyond that I have no further comment except that he has left a letter marked for your attention." I did not collect this letter personally but after attending the funeral, Nok-Nok (of who's there fame) came over to me and with tears in her eyes said, "Dixie Ed voo Av dis papa pleece" and she handed over a grubby envelope that was marked on the front:

"To Dick Head, the only man that ever believed in me," and when I opened up this letter and read its contents, I sat down and cried for the first time for over

20 years. God, how I cried.

Dear Dick,

After spending the last three years in this hell hole, I now realise that my life on this Earth never going to improve for me because in here, I live with two queer psychopathic killers that make the Canal End Secondary school seem like a happy kindergarten in spring time. In fact if I had been born in this hell hole, I could have coped with school life as a doddle - such is the unfairness of my life. I am daily assaulted by these two macho homos and by anybody else who pays them for the privilege, so you can imagine the situation that exists. Nobody cares and the warders just laugh or give me a thump for fun if I complain.

To keep any form of sanity, I have trained myself to go into trances and to remember the many times that you and I would go fishing together down those old gravel pits in Kent, on our own from early morning daybreak until late at night when the sun went down like a golden halo of the angels. You would quietly listen to my rambling dreaming thoughts about how one day the name of Freebee Bannion would be remembered amongst the greats of history. Yes Dick, despite all what has happened, I really liked being called Freebee by you because from you it was different; you meant no disrespect like the other guys.

You remember when you won the special "school colours" tie for captaining the school football team and winning the Kent Cup, and then giving it to me during one of our fishing trips. Well my friend, I've kept that tie by me all for all of my life and now I've kept it by me for all of my time in eternity. This tie will be the instrument for me to leave this life of total hell and send me to a better life elsewhere. Don't feel bad for me Dick, just feel joy at our past closeness and memories.

Over the past two years, I have started to write

poetry and in my locker I have left you all the poems that I hope you can remember me by. Thanks a lot for your support and love over these so few years; see you in the next life.

All my love,
Freebee the Hasbean

> *My life's end on this earth is almost nigh*
> *All my years here are going without a sigh*
> *This world will never miss my final breath*
> *At last a winner at this moment of death*

God, did I cry!

It took me several months to come to terms with the life and death of Freebee and the injustice of this modern world of ours toward people with such insecure characters. If only in early schooling someone could have nurtured this poetic ability of Freebee to give him a reason to carry on living, then we could have enjoyed a new creative form of poetry. Should I have protected him more from the bullies? Should the teachers be ostracised for not protecting him? Should the prison service be reformed to save other people from the same fate?

My conclusions are very critical of all sides of society, but equally we are all aware that society cannot accept a man such as Freebee without casting him outside normal society as a reject. I have to believe that Freebee is now in a better place, a place where all people are ugly and all of them write beautiful poetry. Oh, I forgot to tell you that I reclaimed Freebee's manuscripts and next month they are being published under *Freebee Bannion's Look at Life and Death.*

Freebee was a real man

Chapter 16

ENGLISH LANGUAGE TO CONDOM TESTING

"Swear words are only effective if they are found offensive. Regular use breeds a familiarity leading to ineffective offensiveness and therefore subsequent obsolescence of the swear word. With present day usage, all swear words should be obsolete within twelve months".

Professor Henry Wisenbach (1976)
University of Utah - Wasterbach Literary Prize Winner

Dick Head Health Warning.

This chapter expresses some very radical views relating to the Japanese and Swiss nations, plus giving advanced information of a proposed new law now going through the House of Lords to abolish all swear words from the English language.

If you are easily shocked or disturbed by today's current acceptance of foul language and rampant race prejudice, you should bypass this particular chapter and move on directly to chapter 17 where the subject matter gets back onto a level keel and you will be shocked no longer.

Neither Dick Head nor his publishers can take any responsibility for mental health problems, utmost disgust, wilting plants, upset bankers, disappointed racing drivers, pissed off racing drivers' wives, misquoted seamen (or semen), unsatisfied Eskimo women, executed Welsh choirs, Oxford or Cambridge yuppies complaints, two moaning postmen or any other general complaints no matter how or from where they originate.

You have been positively warned that the reading of this chapter has been shown to damage the health of some sane people under laboratory conditions, so imagine the tremendous damage that can be done if you read this chapter under the idiotic conditions present in our everyday lives.

English is exquisite amongst all languages of the world, allowing linguistic perfection to be achieved by romantics and poets alike, giving full personal expression under all situations in life. Descriptions perfected with luxuriant literary selection, transmitting the author's deepest emotions felt whilst his pen sweeps gracefully across the manuscript.

Whether we refer to creative writing, belles lettres, classics, humanities, literary genre, fiction, metafiction, faction, non fiction, lyricism, poetry, plays, drama, classicism, neo-classicism, Sturm & Drang, Romanticism, symbolism, idealism, expressionism, surrealism, realism, naturalism or writing of The Holy Bible, it is so much better expressed in the English language.

William Shakespeare once told my great great great great great great grandfather's brother, "without the English language I would be knackered but with it I am famous." Criticism of the Baird's reckless use of the English language is feckless and foolhardy because we all know what he managed to achieve in the literary world. It is only an ignoramus or a Welshman who would thus ask "are we not better off with it than without it, so to speak, that is the question."

Did you know that William Shakespeare's writings have not only stood up to the pressure and test of time, but these classical masterpieces have been able to leap across continents where translated versions of his wonderful books are today even available in the Japanese language. I personally would not go to see Macbeth at the Hari Kari Theatre in Osaka if ever I visited the Land of the Rising Sun (and raw fish, sharp swords, slanted eyes and expensive scotch), but then I'm not Japanese, am I?

Just imagine listening to Shakespeare in Japanese,

"Weng Klodo bora nar dejong!" If you are a Baird lover going on holiday to Tokyo, I proffer you a word of warning: don't laugh during the performance even if it is supposed to be funny. The Nippons have a history of cutting off your clever little heads for much less significant offences than you taking the piss out of a Japanese Macbeth. Pearl Harbour was nothing in comparison. To be or not to be?, that is a bloody stupid question.

News flash!

"A Japanese cargo plane carrying Japanese car spares from the Tokyo factory to the motor show in London, blew up in mid air over Dover this morning. Mr. Smythe-Jones, a farmer located within the crash zone complained that his farm labourers refused to work in the fields today because they claimed it was raining Datsun cogs."

The whole industrialised "free world" has allowed the Japanese to completely destroy or severely damage home based manufacturing industries, including electronics, cameras, watches, cars, ships, and radio controlled condoms. Successive governments in countries throughout the world have allowed these wonders of the east to rape their industries by standing quietly on the sidelines whilst an endless number of huge ships bring in these Japanese products that were previously manufactured locally.

In Great Britain we previously used products manufactured by British craftsmen even though these products were in short supply due to these same craftsmen being on strike and drinking hot cocoa whilst sitting around the picket line coke fire in the middle of a cold wintery night in Crewe.

No trade agreement with these Karate Kids in striped suits will ever be honoured because to the Japanese, any agreement is taken as a sign of weakness by these slaves to mass production perfection who have one single master plan: to dominate the industrial world whilst smiling like masturbating hyenas.

The world has allowed them an entry in all markets, free of any real controls, thus permitting them to complete successfully the invasion that was first started in 1945. This latest yellow invasion is far better planned and uses the rules of the international game to guarantee success.

This time we cannot fight back and knock seven bells of shite out of these yellow invaders although the danger is even greater than before. We are actually financially helping them to screw us into financial slavery.

Just try exporting products to Japan; Ho Ho Ho!, you've never seen brown tape (mixture of red and yellow) like it since Hitler applied for membership of the South Walton and Weybridge Jewish Stockbrokers Club in 1937. The Nippons have a book of rules that need to be seen to be believed; hence very few western consumable products are ever available in Japanese shops, and you think that homosexual dolls are rare?

Now that the Japanese share the world's money supply together with the Swiss, they are rich enough to start buying up complete countries, using the money our governments helped them earn in the first place. Pretty neat hu? Got it, my economic wizards? It's called "How to screw yourself twice without really trying."

> *"The Japanese drive on the left hand side of the road so that our cars don't suit their market"*
>
> *Willy Steinbacher*
> *President - USA Export Agency (1990)*

The Swiss are also amazing people, having everything arranged in logical order with nothing out of place, even the holes in their cheese are drilled ten millimetres apart. Did you see that TV programme of "60

Minutes" relating to the Swiss drug problem? Well if you did not see this my Red Cross fanatics, then you will be amazed to hear about "Needle Park" in Zurich which was set up by the Swiss as an organised way of getting drug taking people away from the nice city areas to avoid upsetting the local bankers. All the human drug garbage was invited into this park where they could buy, sell and take drugs with no problems or interference from authority guaranteed. A safe haven for the drug barons, drug pushers and drug takers alike.

As one would expect, Aids was naturally rampant among the vast number of young people rotting away inside this wonderful paradise on earth which quickly became a home for the living dead where they shared both needles and arseholes at will. In a belated but useless effort to hold back this uncontrollable spreading of Aids, a special arrangement of "new needles for old" was carried out on a daily basis, but little good was really achieved.

This free supply of needles was available to all without even the need to rub the lamp, so efficient were the Swiss at getting rid of their horrible problems. Despite urgent requests from the park inhabitants, the same Swiss authorities refused to meet demands for them to also issue new arseholes for old Aids infected ones.

How on earth can a civilised nation condone free and open drug taking to be openly allowed with the express approval of their authorities? What's the use of trying to fight drugs when a few hundred yards away from the city centre, you can buy them and take them with immunity? How about the protection that these poor kids in the park once expected and deserve from their parents and government alike?

What's happened to all the money that was earnt from this government sponsored drug taking racket? It's with the Swiss banks of course, together with all the other dirty money that is deposited into those underground vaults of evil. Before any of my bank employed students start having epileptic fits over these accusations, I would ask you to tell me the reasons why anyone deposits money with a Swiss bank.

Anyone that says, "Dick Head, it's not as simple as you are saying because many people around the world like the Swiss banks for their efficiency and friendship." Friends, wankers and countrymen, lend me your ears, I do declare that during my working class lifetime I have met no man, woman, or queer in slingback shoes, that likes the Swiss people in any way whatsoever. Indeed I would go as far as to say that the Swiss don't even like each other, even at Christmas time because they have to spend money.

I further declare that people investing money do not invest it with the people they like but they invest it with people that give them the most in return and if necessary to keep their mouths shut when black money is being deposited. The swiss live, sleep and die thinking about money and gold, this being why they even manufacture cakes that look like a roll of bank notes.

Absolute precision is a way of life for them which was perfectly illustrated some two years ago on a flight due to leave from Geneva for London: the pilot apologised for a four minute delay in our departure time! Just try discussing that with my favourite world airline.

Do you prefer a bottle of gin "half empty" or "half full"? Your choice I am told will be the single clue required by Dr. Zambesi Zuo Zilch of the Psychiatrist Centre in Singapore for him to produce a full report on your past and future life. His assessment would include just how greedy you are and how long your liver will hold out under present consumption rates of this wonderful victorian inspired liquid of the masses.

This 3Z report will be typed out on an Amstrad word processor using English language only, as perfected by the one and only modern day scribe, Simon Oxford (1531 to 1641). This genius of the written word was held in such high esteem by the literary world during the latter part of the sixteenth century that the government of the day decreed that his works should be recorded for all time in a small bulky book called Simon's Oxford Dictionary.

This made Simon Oxford and his Dictionary famous in all lands and he was considered to be so very very clever that his initials are still used even today in that well used phrase of "Clever S.O.D." for describing somebody of exceptional academic ability. It goes without saying that Dick Head is a clever sod.

At the age of 108, Simon Oxford was presented with the Pope's Popelitzer prize for literary achievement which was the premier accolade during the reign of Henry VIII. Due to some political and religious upheavals relating to the sexual habits of our monarch and his pet rabbits at that time, the Pope was unable to visit England to present this prize for fear of being boiled in oil. He therefore sent a personal holy carrier pigeon with a message to the Archbishop of London (roman catholic brand), requesting that he, or one of his clergy, present the Popelitzer prize to Mr. Oxford.

This presentation ceremony (or lack of it), started to take on embarrassing proportions when it was found that all the archbishop's clergymen had died by mysteriously losing their heads, or they had left for a very long holiday across the channel. The Archbishop wrote a letter of apology to the Pope explaining that he could not present the prize as requested because all of the faithful roman catholics had been beheaded and that he was now living in hiding with a sheepherder in Wales.

Simon Oxford's family have since built a large town to the west of London, A circus with its own tube station, a trouser factory, a shoe factory and a university that turns out thousands of prats every year.

These darling boys of Oxford University can at least beat those equally yuppie ponces from that other university built by the industrialist, Cambridge Oliver Kennedy.

During the 1794 university boat race, the Cambridge crew were so completely pissed up on expensive rum punch that the whole crew climbed into the back of the boat at the same time and catapulted the front of this splendid vessel straight up into the air, killing an innocent swan that was otherwise heading towards Windsor Castle for his lunch. This rare accident badly ruptured Mr. Oliver Kennedy by throwing him up in the air where he made a dramatic false landing on top of Barnes bridge railings. The landing saved his life but sadly caused him some permanent medical problems that made him less important and more impotent.

The common folks expression of "A complete C.O.K. up" became a favourite way of describing such stupid mistakes thereafter, in remembrance of this boat race accident.

During the Second World War, a famous royal Royal Navy officer, whilst inspecting one of His Majesty's ships of the line, asked a seaman about the condition of one of the guns that appeared badly damaged. This gun had received a direct hit from a bomb dropped by a German dive bomber (flown by a lunatic blond haired and blue eyed pilot answering to the name of "Fritz") on the ship's return holiday fishing trip from Russia. In a beautiful cockney lilt, our man of the salty sea spoke out politely but firmly to our Royal personage, "Sir, the fucking fucker's fucked!"

Without blinking, this member of our Royal family replied "that's fucking bad fucking news." This true story (including the very shocking language) is just to confirm that even members of the Royal family have been recorded throughout history as frequent users of certain swear words under arduous conditions. A man in wartime uses swear words to release tensions from within.

The F word is used today as just another word within our vocabulary, in an effort to add colour or obscenity to the subject matter being discussed. That dying breed of yuppies use swear words to emphasise their very stupid pointless points and sometimes in an attempt to be comical (and I thought they were all funny sods).

The working class man uses swear words because of his lack of vocabulary or for when he is really very mad at something, somebody, or a rival football fan. Why is it that some people become very indignant when swear words are used on the television, which is normally in some third class crappy American film about a misused hero who fights back to beat all the mafia and queers single handed, despite the crooked policeman involved. Have you noticed how heroes never eat, sleep, shower, shite or shave?

Words are only words, invented by man, for use by man and spoken by man: they were not invented by the Devil to be banned by God and His followers. If you say "Bolox you fucking pervert" to any Eskimo, he will most certainly give you a big smile, followed by a plate of raw fish and then for good luck he will invite you to screw his fat ugly and very generous wife. So my stuck up nosed readers, not everybody gets upset in the same way about swearing as you do. God bless the Eskimo and his friendly habits.

Just after the Indianapolis 500 race was shown live on TV last week, I had a horrific dream concerning a member of the Royal family of ours making a live television appearance on the "Corgi & Friends" chat show. When asked by Wally Stringfellow, "Your Royal Highness, is it true that you have a steering wheel from a grand prix racing car hanging over your bed in your Royal bedroom and this steering wheel has twenty seven notches carved on it?" Her reply shocked me greatly as she shouted, "Mind your own fucking business you conceited prick because as a member of the Royal family

I am allowed to choose my own notching mates and whatever number of grand prix I fancy. In any case it's none of your fucking business!"

What a way for Royalty to speak to one of the upper class television interviewers who after all was only trying to enlighten the public about the habits of our Royal family. The same dream included a look into the Houses of Parliament, just after the Labour party had helped defeat (by only one vote) a "Hang Welsh Singers" motion. One of our idiotic Conservative Ministers spoke out in great blue arsed anger at losing this important vote, "You bloody Welsh wankers are all the same, always wanting the best teaching jobs, always singing like cockroaches with a dose of the shites and now you think that these bloody awful choirs from the valleys should be left alone. They are a bloody menace to the sanity of all Englishmen and I say we should hang all those sodding welsh sods!"

From the back benches came the mob retort of "Shame, fucking shame!"

Thank God it was only a dream.

Smoked salmon is only great to eat if it's very expensive to buy and when you are only served a minuscule portion of it - just like at every Christmas lunch. In the same way, champagne is fantastic when you are poor enough to drink it only at weddings (if it's somebody elses) or after rich aunt Bess has just taken her last trip to the happy hunting grounds above and she has left you a few bob and the family grandfather clock. Just imagine if every morning you were forced by law (I don't mean the mother-in-law) to eat lashings of smoked salmon and drink as much champagne as you could consume without being too sick.

For a week this gorging would be absolutely fantastic and the immediate result would be that the whole nation of working class people would be be pissed every day and swim the one hundred metres in less than forty seconds - so much for Mark Spitz and the dolphins. But how would we all feel after six weeks? After six weeks, smoked salmon would sell for five pence per pound, champagne would be cheaper than beer and at breakfast time you would hear the complaints of, "I want some lovely toast and marmalade, you know where to stick that awful bloody fish and that poxy bubbly crap!"

Most people get fed up with almost anything if they get too much of it, except for life itself.

Petrol prices increased, inflation zooming, big hole in the sky causes hurricanes, Chelsea win the cup, Labour party win the election, Italians still singing crappy songs, more mercury in our drinking water, salmonella in our chickens, lamb and beef makes you go crazy, more traffic wardens than police, more civil servants than crooks, banks get richer, we get poorer, another boring royal birth and another million regulations to control our daily lives.

Whatever our feelings of indignation are when hearing these miserable facts about our everyday life, the human brain can always absorb further bad news so that after a while all bad news is accepted and becomes integrated into our life style.

The same rule of acceptance applies to swearing, so that if all swear words were legally made non swear words and officially became part of the Queen's English then we would never hear a swear word again, because all old swear words would now be non swear words by law. Obscene language immediately solved with one stroke of the pen, all because of some additional deep thinking from Dick Head.

Life after conversion of swear words into non swear words would not be straightforward because objections would be received from the righteous toss pots in Weybridge and Guildford. In this wondrous free country of ours we must allow freedom of speech to all, even if unreasonable use of this freedom leads to many killings whilst the author of this free speech earns millions by doing it. Personally, I would allow somebody like myself to decide what is published or not, because you know that you can trust me.

"But Dick Head, if you make all existing swear words non swear words, then all the working class fellows working at the mill will stop swearing and may be treated the same as educated people like us upper class executives from Oxbridge."

To avoid this happening, we must have a new set of even worse swear words created and then taught to the working class kids by those long haired militant queer teachers in the comprehensive schooling system; the working class must know their place in society. This rebalancing of the class system is inevitable and is will be further discussed in greater detail in book number 29 due out next year, *Swearing Totally Bleedin' Rewritten.*

I am holding a competition to select the best and most innovative new swear words for inclusion within this exciting new publication; please sent me your suggestions on a postcard and the best 10 new swear words will win a prize of a "Black Mamma" vibrator complete with "giant ram" extension piece and twenty-four replacement long life batteries. So far, we have received the following suggested swear words: Clapdicking, Browning, Clitdip, Rambo and Crabcreep.

During a recent discussion on swearing with the Reverend Arthur Turnley of the "Church of the True and Non Doubting Believers" from the Falkland Islands, we discussed a different approach to solving this problem. We agreed that a swear word is chosen for effect and impact and therefore we could all use just one swear word that would be easier to remember. We can then simply add a different prefix in front of this only swear word which would give us the ability to emphasise the impact of the only swear word. After a few bottles of holy wine we decided that a perfect word for the only swear word would be *Shitfukuntit.*

This could then be prefixed by "a little", "quite a bit", "a lot", "fully blown!" and "to the Devil". Everything was accepted by Rev Turnley, apart from the final prefix referring to the Devil and he is awaiting comments from Canterbury where it is now being considered by the Archbishop and we hope to hear his comments very soon - you will be kept fully informed and updated you "to the devil Shitfukuntit" readers.

I am investigating the effect that the use of non swear words (words that were swear words before my new law came into being) will have upon the growing pattern and general health of flowers and carrots in the royal gardens. There is real fear within royal circles that a new breed of plant should be cultivated to survive this new era of royal talk that will most surely follow. Already the royal plant nurseries in Windsor are playing an endless tape recording of the new non swear words (sung by the royal family) twenty four hours a day to a full range of these new species of plants.

After a worrying initial period, during which there were serious signs of wilting and sulking, it is reported that all plants are now taking it well. This new progressive indoctrination programme is now being described as "an outstanding success" from Buckingham Palace but they refuse to allow their flower song to be available on general release.

For the moment, until the full changeover of swear words to non swear words takes place, the royal nurseries must label the various species very carefully indeed, one species marked "Shite and Bolox OK" whereas the other label says "Shite & Bolox not OK".

No more complaints about swearing. No more bad language on TV. No more kids being whacked for saying "Fuck you mate." All in all Dick Head, your ideas are now likely to be accepted worldwide, or maybe condemned by less forward thinking and adventurous people.

In for a penny, in for a pound, that's what I fucking think anyway.

History is full of geniuses (genii?) that were centuries ahead of their time, so why should I be any different.

I've often wondered how the really posh people get nasty with each other. When Lady Edith Smythe-Phillippe and husband Lord Chatterly reach such a point in an argument where the ordinary working class guy would start pulling his plonker the resultant conversation is intriguing.

"James, I think you are a bonking large penis, no bonking good to any bonker in any bonking place - so why don't you just bonk off you bonking parent less bonker!" Talking without real swear words really doesn't have the same effect does it?

At this same end of the language scale, we reach the tongues of perfection and total class superiority that has been inbred for centuries into our upper class. No amount of education or money can qualify you as a member of this aristocratic elite that controls the old money here and around the world. These "backbone of the country" elite are so bound up by their understanding of tradition, honour, class, money, morality and pride, that there is no room for any other opinion to be absorbed; if you don't agree with them, you are wrong and they have enough money to prove that you are wrong.

All doubts have been taken away by generations of successful predecessors that have helped to make this such a proud and powerful nation. During the glorious days of the empire, when our armies raped the earth, these "Whato's" were the officers in charge.

Did you see that fantastic film of "Ghandi" where our troops massacred hundreds of Indians? This approach never changes, except that today it is the ordinary guy who is being massacred but still by the "Whato's". They control our Civil Service, Banks, Stockbrokers,

Diplomatic corps, etc. which means that in effect they control our lives in virtually every way. Your job is safe for as long as your company is not taken over by a "Whato" who decides to asset strip the plant and make a killing or a tax loss - either way mate you are now UNEMPLOYED.

Try talking to a "Whato"? You will firstly find that this is more difficult than getting a tax rebate or a full set of screws in a self assembly kitchen unit. If you are unlucky enough to eventually get to see him, you will experience for yourself the class gap that generations of these "Whatos" have created as a barrier to protect their gold and class position.

"Sit down my dear fellow, how can I help you?" You sit down nervously in a soft low chair whilst Reginald Percy Windsor looks down upon you from behind his desk as you start your prepared speech. "Well, I 'av come 'ere today to see why you took my job away from me. I fink it's disgustin and you should be ashamed of yerself".

After puffing on his pipe for a few minutes and nodding his head in sympathy, he responds in a sombre well trained manner, "Yes, Mr Wally, I can see that you have been personally affected by expansion plans at Frenchies Original Condom factory, but our growth plans required the building of a modernised plant that could cope with the wonderful increase in the demand for condoms ever since the Aids epidemic arrived on the scene. It is our duty to society Wally to supply what the public demands."

You fidget in your chair for a few seconds and say, "Excuse me sir, but my name's not Wally, its Jacko, and what you are really saying is that I'm unemployed because the Aids scare increased demand for condoms?" "Well, yes Wally, that's right in a way, but don't worry, I will speak to my people at the new factory in Belgium, I'm sure I can find you a job there using your expertise as a condom tester. All's well that ends well Wally."

You will be totally lost for words as he walks you to the door, patting you on the back as you walk out of his office. Our Whato had really screwed you without you knowing it, you the unemployed condom stretcher; unemployed because of a band of queers in San Francisco. The company is now moving to Belgium and the farthest you've ever been is to see Manchester United at a home match. And in any case you can't speak the Belgian language!

No my working class friends, as usual the Whatos have yet again made money out of a tragedy, just as they have done throughout history. Whilst our boys were dying in France during two world wars, the Whatos were getting richer.

I wonder how they actually test condoms, because I'm now starting to worry about this a lot lately.

Chapter 17

DEATH'S KNELL

Oh this world of pure triumphant wonder,
Floating serenely on a pirouetting course,
Gigantic force of interstellar splendour,
Spinning like a fire dragon up in the sky,

Transporting huge oceans as leaves in the wind,
An aqueous pulsation of ebbing and flowing,
In synchronised step with each lunar gyration,
Flaming residue spun from the gold mother sun,

Each child reaching out for its true destination,
Earth charges unseen to a man made destruction
Dame fortune can never change this end that is nigh
No saving reprieve from our Lord of redemptions

Bright shining lights reflecting as black centred hearts
Finality takes innocence and goodness away with it all,
With the devil's execution of evil in Satan's satirical way,
This Earth incredibly covered in endless living vegetation,

Miraculous colours and functions unique to each species
Each masterpiece blending with God's intricate construction,
Support and sustenance for all creatures great and small,
Creatures and vegetation delicately balanced for survival

A single mass evolved by milleniums of natural selection,
So long for mankind, but a mere glimpse in all of our time,
Blending all together in absolute harmony with Mother Nature,
Alas, now the greed of mankind destroys this balance of life,

An industrial revolution producing all filth and destruction,
Leads us down an endless road to our ultimate extinction,
Did God plan this lunatic race of man's inevitable evil?
The final tool by which Mother Earth would reach her tomb,

Just a cloud of atomic dust floating away in outer space,
Within endless bounds of long lost souls swaying so gently,
Massed souls of the past within the Galaxy of the dead,
Will this finale of our greed end us all in this place?

Transmitting our warrior species uncontrollably away,
To lands across the endless barriers of space and of time,
Past black holes and stars and further to another land,
To reach other virgin soils eagerly awaiting our spores

Where God will create this world in six days of His life,
This spinning new world linked by its gentle rotation,
With its brothers and sisters and a red warming sun,
Ignited by God to support this rebirth of man's life

Is Earth's demise just a prediction of God's promise
For His children's lost souls so intent on such greed,
Installed from Heaven's watching creed up above?
Tempting us to follow where lust takes our hands,

Were our ancestors from another star in the regions above?
From a destructive galaxy separated by unknown energy and time,
Did they live and die through this same preordained agenda?
Are we space dust from another dead world destroyed far away,

Organisms retaining memory chromosomes of that other life,
Are we following this identical course of death and rebirth,
Each world's end signalling another's beginning of life,
Just like the life cycle of the Canadian red salmon,

Living lives followed by sure death after their job is done,
This harvest of human existence can disappear any moment,
God! can a return to goodness give us a stay of execution,
Or will death's knell toll when we reach that level of evil,

That tips the switch thus finally sending us all on our way,
Did Jesus only delay our final and ultimate destruction?,
But we fools let greed and evil take over quickly again ,
No chance God of us changing again, of this we are so sure,

Please God be kind and rethink your choice at the last,
But if man's greed makes survival a thought of the past,
Please, my God, make it good, quick and really bloody fast.

Amen.

Paul Rockford III (1992)

Chapter 18

DIKHED'S 20 QUESTIONS

How the time has flown by for both of us during this first book of learning, when you have been able to experience a self determination that you once thought was beyond you, only given to those high and mighty upper class clever dicks (so to speak). I hope that The Working Man's Guide to the Galaxy has done its job well and already your future horizons have been expanded to offer new opportunities yet to unfold.

Like making fresh popcorn, you waited in anticipation for the very first "pop" to awaken those long dorment thinking capsules embedded so deeply inside your brain. From this beginning followed the sense of real adventure, becoming more exciting as the subsequent "pops" finally became a champagne cocktail trail of learning.

Don't keep repeating to me those embarrassing words of "Thank you Dick Head" because I'm getting so accustomed to such appreciation that any more of this same boring acclaim will start to really piss me off. It makes me feel so 'umble, so very 'umble.

So endeth your first learning session with The Working Man's Guide to the Galaxy, now for your concentrated weeks of revision for when you are ready to sit your exam paper to achieve your first degree in life. You will then feel as confident as though you were indeed a Dick Head yourself, when you can then head for the next book of even greater learning. *Pilgrims Progress Personified*.

You must complete your revision and sit your 20 Questions exam before you attempt this second book.

Good luck to all of you, your future is nigh.

This DikHed's 20 Questions exam paper is for the B.Sc. (DikHed) degree which is now accepted and recognised amongst the majority of leading institutions throughout the world as an important Dick Head qualification.

Students obtaining a 65% or higher pass mark will be awarded a 1st class degree (part 1) whereas a score of over 85% will result in an honours degree being issued. Scores below 65%, but above 25% will achieve a 2nd class degree, whereas scores below 25% will result in a failure certificate being issued.

All DikHed 20 Questions exam papers should be submitted, together with a certificate issuing fee of £15.00 made payable to DikHed Promotions . Marking and issuing of certificates will be carried out within 28 days of receipt of such completed papers. The DikHed Examination Board's decision on the degree level issued is at its absolute discretion and no correspondence can be entered into with wankers who consider that they deserve a higher or lower grade than the one issued to them.

The personal identification page plus the DikHed 20 Questions exam page should be removed from this book and returned to us for marking. This is to ensure that nobody can enter the exam on the cheap by not purchasing their own copy of this book.

All B.Sc. DikHed exam certificates will be personally signed using my famous pen and original verdant ink. I have sufficient ink reserved for the signing of over sixteen million certificates. Other ink colours can be used at a surcharge of £11.80 per signature - so you will see just how much I prefer using my own green ink.

Any obscene remarks written on any part of your 20 Questions exam paper will result in instant rejection and failure. All failure certificates issued to obscene writings of this kind will be heavily endorsed with "obscene prick" stamped in the top left corner for all the world to see.

You are allowed to make reference to The Working Man's Guide to the Galaxy at any time during your DikHed 20 Questions exam and this will not be classified as cheating.

Good luck to you all!

B.Sc. DikHed 20 Questions

Name: ....Date:............................

Address:..

....

....

....

Date of birth: ....

Sex: Male/Female...

Marital status: ....

Party you vote for (optional declaration):

....

Are you a heavy drinker?: ....Yes/No

Do you swear a great deal?: ....Yes/No

Order Details

QTY.

.............B.Sc DikHed exam fees and certificate £15.00

.............Additional certificate copies.......................£12.00 each

.............Additional cost for non green signature............£11.80*

.............DIKHED special one size tee shirt ....£15.00 each

* Please specify colour.

**Please enclose cheques made payable to DIKHED PROMOTIONS.
Credit card payments can be made by ACCESS or VISA**

Credit card type: ACCESS/VISA Card No:. ....

Expiry date: ....Name on card:....................................

Signature of Cardholder..

Daytime contact phone number:...

**Return all exam papers, order forms and payment to:
DikHed Promotions, P.O. Box 102, Rochester, Kent ME1 1NS.**

DikHed 20 Questions

B.Sc. DikHed Multiple Choice Exam
All questions must be answered. Where appropriate tick the answer you think is correct. All students have ten DikHours to complete this exam paper.

1. Would you buy a BigDik from McDikalds?...........yes/no/maybe
2. Do you approve of Banger Lucy?............................yes/no/maybe
3. Do you sympathise with Watcher Will? ....yes/no/maybe
4. Do you like Mr. Bolox Toyou?................................yes/no/maybe
5. Are you offended by the language used herein?.....yes/no/maybe
6. How many swear words are used in this book? ...none/lots/a few
7. Do you think Randy Bird was guilty? ....yes/no/maybe
8. Do you like art? ....yes/no/maybe
9. Would you use a dishwashable condom? ....yes/no/maybe
10. Would you like me to be Sir Dick Head? ....yes/no/maybe
11. Was Lord Al Mytee guilty? ....yes/no/maybe
12. Was Dr. Kenya guilty? ....yes/no/maybe
13. Is a bent copper worth anything? ....yes/no/maybe
14. What is your favourite Dik invention?..
15. Should DikFree be banned?....................................yes/no/maybe
16. Please give your new swear word ....
17. Was Testiscrotum a nice guy? ....yes/no/maybe
18. Do you still eat meat pies? ....yes/no/maybe
19. How much would you pay for a 1937 Hitler cuckoo clock?..
20. Was pussy treated nicely? ....yes/no/maybe

Chapter 19

BEAT THE BAN!

Unfortunately, following a recent world marketing survey, DIKSHOP goods have been banned from sale in all areas of the world except for:

Abidjan, Alderney, Andorra, Antipodes Islands, Azerbaidjan, Azores, Baku, Bangladesh, Beirut, Belorussia, Belize, Benin, Bouvet Island.

Bolivia, Bulgaria, Bujumbura, Burma, Cameroon, Cambell Island, Chile, China, Colombia, Congo, Cook Islands, Corsica, Cuba, Dominica, Ecuador, Elba.

Equatorial Guinea, Fujeirah, Futuna Islands, Gabon. Ghana, Haiti, Honduras, India, Isle of Wight, Kampuchea, North Korea, McDonald Islands, McDikalds Islands (all 327 of them), Mahe Island.

Moldavia, Monrovia, Muscat, Nepal, Paraguay, Pitcairn Islands, El Salvador, Somalia, Swaziland, Uganda, Ukraine, Uzbekistan, Zaire and Zanzibar.

We are exploiting this situation and feel confident that the full range of DIKSHOP goods will be on open sale in all the above countries within a few weeks. We are also frantically translating this book into these languages so that citizens of these progressive countries are able to rise up with us, taking control of their lives by purchasing The Working Man's Guide to the Galaxy in their own language.

For citizens of banned areas wishing to purchase the goods mentioned in this book, you must await the following advertisement that will be placed in various newspapers in the near future:

DIKHED UNDERGRADUATES
All goods now available from:
(an address and phone number will be shown here)

A different address will be shown every week to fool the police authorities who have tried so very hard to slow down the DikHed march to power. Just phone in your order with credit card number. Nothing stops us!

A recent Government ruling now allows us to openly offer the DikHed Tee Shirts and you will find your order form on page 419 of this epic publication.

DikHed Promotions, P.O. Box 102, Rochester, Kent ME1 1NS.

DikHed supporters always Beat the Ban!

Chapter 20

MASTERFUL QUOTATIONS

I must compliment all undergraduates on your trials and tribulations of completing the course work and exam as set out in The Working Man's Guide to the Galaxy. Your next challenge is to read my next course book *Pilgrims Progress Personified* to obtain your DikHed Masters Degree. As a prospective post graduate, you should complete some extensive study during your vacation prior to commencing this more difficult course.

During my endless search for knowledge, I occasionally come upon special words of wisdom written by men of a brotherly ilk which is ideal study material for all postgraduates striving to complete the Masters degree course. I have great pleasure in sharing these words of wisdom with you all. For students wishing to specialise on this subject of famous quotations and short poems, please see my book number 84 entitled *Words of a feather stick together.* OK folks, let's get to it and go for it.

Snowmen should not await the summer sales before buying a Fridgidair.
Joseph Weatherby (1975)

I would love to share everything I have, excepting for the things I like best or with the people I don't like.

Lord Bunting (1875)

Oh master! give me some water, I'm dying of thirst.
Oh slave! who will save me when the water runs dry?
Oh master! I will save you when the water runs dry
Oh slave! You are so understanding - goodbye.

"An ode to Samuel" by Waynwright Birtwhistle (1845)

We care not for the blessed aged heroes who created this good green land of free men and liberty. We leave them to fade away in their twilight misery without friendship, dignity or love. This accepted but hidden degradation of our nation's strength is tolerated simply by the unspoken word, but what of when I inherit their shoes?

Bartram Mulligan (1984)
Chairman of the Retired Rights Society

Churches continue becoming richer whilst the needy become poorer. Maybe God is just another capitalist after all.

Andrew Dickens (1959)
Committed suicide outside St. Pauls Cathedral

We salute the inventors of modern things which reduce our lives to boredom and weakness in the false belief that we need a better standard of living. Will we salute these same people for the moral corruption and pollution that their efforts have produced and will surely destroy this world?

Professor Heinrich Dortfield (1990)

If I was an angel, I would drink large vodkas every day to wash away my feeling of utter hopelessness whilst looking down upon the self destruction taking place below.

Angelo Bono (Milan 1990)

Please give my people some food to survive this famine,
Please give us just the leftovers that you throw away,
Please give us a small portion of your western caring,
Please give as you would for other richer nations,
Please don't turn this into another pop concert fiasco,
Please just help your fellow man who is starving today,
We can only say please, we have no oil with which to pay

"Somebody who cries and cares" (1987)

The generosity of a rich man is only tempered by his bank balance.
Colombo Justine (1911)

Darwin's theory of evolution is never open to doubt and is now a positive fact. My mother in law is directly related to an anthropoid ape and a jabbermouth woodpecker full of bullshite
Wally Bird (1975)

If there is such a thing as reincarnation, then I would like to come back as a tin of evaporated milk.
Nez Laihytin
Indonesian Ambassador to God in Zurich

An airport lounge is where demented, fat, ugly and boring housewives believe that they are famous and beautiful film stars. With this misconception in mind, they strut around, looking like demented, fat, ugly and boring housewives thinking that they are famous beautiful film stars.
Adam Whunce
"Ortewice" travel magazine (1990)

The characteristic of an arsehole is a man who is only happy when he makes somebody else unhappy. A complete arsehole is a man who is unhappy even when he is making somebody else unhappy. The rest of us are unhappy all of the time.
Nick Singh
"Unmittigated arseholes are aliases" (1975)

Eventually computers will inform us when to laugh, cry, piss and die. This is acceptable to the man who writes the programmes.
Sofia Ware
A mechanical pissing robot toy
(born in Cardiff 1971)

An Englishman's house is his castle that guarantees to keep him in poverty until he dies, at which time his children sell the castle to an Asian immigrant and bugger off to Disney World to see Mickey Mouse.

Norman Forte (1975)

Let there be lite, and there was lite   *Bud Weiser*

Neutrality in Switzerland is a profitable business.

Father Toblah Rhone de Zurigo (1745)

Albert Einstein was relatively clever but suffered from piles.

"Bridges Knocked Down"
Bill Bailey (1953)

Having a whale of a time involves frying fish in Tokyo.

"I'd rather be a Martian"
Randy Deptford (1990)

Given the choice of being tall and ignorant, or short and a genius, I would choose to be the King of Switzerland.

"Success is an adjective"
Bertram Boffermoose

I'm not a pacifist, I just want to see my twenty first birthday, get married, have children, play golf, buy a house, and believe in God. The alternative offer is to get my balls blown off defending a pile of sand inhabited by people that hate our guts. To save oil, I'll walk to work.

Johne Emlyn Wayne II (1973)

Education elevates superiority but degrades sensitivity

"Heated Arguments"

All letters should be thrown away unopened, thus bringing back a sense of old fashioned sanity and thrift into our mundane lives. If it's that urgent they can come and see us, and if it's not then why bother to write.

"Shoot the postman"
Mervyn Stamp (1938)

Dictators are evil, but what this country needs is a strong man with the powers to force this government to do the right things to make this nation a great world power again.

"The New British Empire"
Rustin Bernard Waterhouse (1974)

You are what and who you are, which is different than whom and what you were, a far cry from who and what you will be.

"Personality Blips"
Warren Hare (1933)

ISympathy is a facet of our social conscience which cannot survive in our world of self pity and self centred greed. A sympathetic world would not act audience to millions of our brothers withering in the African sun.

Joe Jean Bloggs (1978)

An act of lust in old Bangkok
Dragged away and now I'm lost
I'm only an innocent poxy germ
Cruelly passed from sperm to sperm
My fear of dying now coming true
This penicillin kills more than flu.
Now sweating so much in utmost fear
Goodbye my friends, I'm a gonorrhoea

"The talking pox germ"
Dick Clapper (1976)

Technological murder overrides individual guilt.

Airmarshal Kersuto (1975)

The pig is more upset than the chicken at breakfast time.

Francis Bacon (1756)

Instant dislike is a foolhardy assumption comparable only with immediate favour. Judge and respect the value of your fellow humans in the fullness of time when you will be presented with many surprises. Loving to hate and hating to love are very similar indeed.

"Love hate relationships"
Taylor Goodfellow (1975)

One moment of true goodness following a lifetime of greed gives some redeeming of the soul. One moment of greed following a lifetime of goodness is a simple human weakness.

Duchess Nancy Ray Gorn (1889)

The progressive advancement of a developing state allows for cruelty as integral to reaching its final goal.

Ivan Polankitani (1927)

Who are we to criticise other nations carrying out actions far less cruel than those carried out within our own empire less than one hundred years ago - does time change right from wrong?

Wilmott Peters - Novelist (1986)

Beyond reasonable doubt is a lottery that has hanged many doubtful people in a reasonable way sending them to the beyond.

"Spoodervane's Solutions"
Stanley Spoodervane (1958)

Social science is to analyse the evil of mankind and then talk about it forever without suggesting any realistic solutions.
Harry Osmand Worth (1968)

Toilet paper is a foul habit not intended for human consumption.
"Bog Stories"
Lotti Gretano (1942)

Perjury is a far better thing than allowing the guilty to go free.
Justice Clayton - retired (1934)

Habits are for boring holy folk who keep repeating themselves in a boring way over and over and over again, which makes them very very very boring holy folk all of the time.
"Repeat Business"
Gabriele Ekko (1978)

Athletes should now be handicapped as horses, based upon the level of drugs being consumed. A midget health freak is now a possible 100 metres champion.
"Blind Dopes"
Ben "Muchopillo" Giovanno

Tax inspectors are the bowels of satan; a generous reputation they fully live up to with enthusiasm.
(Name & address supplied)

Heroes are for wars that peace cannot afford.
Sergeant Bill Smith V.C.

Ethics forever change to accommodate the advancement and degradation of civilisation, whilst God remains unmoved.
Archbishop Ferdinando Volenti (1973)

If all liars were struck down, this country would have 49,657,346 wheelchairs, of which 12,876,098 would have personalised number plates.

Winstone Wonkall (1990)

The man from Mars detested chocolate.

Clarence Cadbury (1987)

Stop Press!

The Italian minister of defence surrendered to the boy scouts this morning.

"Italian war heroes"
Gucci Gucci (1987)

Lufthansa flight LH34876 from Frankfurt to Tokyo arrived 3 minutes and 53 seconds late this morning. A spokesman wearing a steel helmet confirmed after the pilot had been shot that this was an isolated event which would not be repeated in the future.

"Airborne Kings"
Orwell Nemesis (1988)

Blessed be the man who truly believes in morality and queer priests.

Angelo Paddypoke (1975)

If I could convince the bank to let me buy Arsenal football club, I promise to find a non wanking referee.

Richard Rubbins (1983)

Ambition is a curse encouraged by the freedom dreamers who lead us into captivity and chains. A man with no ambition experiences very few disappointments but always achieves his dreams.

"Sitting and playing with my plonka"
Luciano Zilchetto (1975)

I would like to be a pumpkin
Growing so big and fat
Admired by all the people
Including old postman Pat
Pat used to eat green apples
Now prefers sweet pumpkin bits
This poor sweet innocent pumpkin
Is a boiled up vegetable git!

> "Talking to the vegetables"
> Beatti Potta (1976)

Never trust a green skinned alien with a forked tongue and a knife in his belly button.

> "When they arrive say hallo"
> Sam Witherstall (1943)

After a lifetime of ambition and searching for a dream, the only worthwhile thing on this planet is to eat fish and chips with malt vinegar.

> "The Big Con!"
> Lucy Bennet (1971)

I'd rather be a donkey than an ass but would choose to be an ass than being a woman.

> "The Superior Sex"
> Graham Letcher (1964)

Tax inspectors must not accept suicide as a factor when assessing tax evasion and they must continue to vigorously pursue the surviving spouse with extra venom during the weak moment of grief thereafter.

> Inland Revenue Official Memo (1985)

Financial Times are very hard for the majority but pink for the few.

> "Paper Chase"
> Ed Eatorr (1949)

If you've never worn a pin striped suit, congratulations!

"Funny Business"
Joseph Tailor (1941)

Some like it hot, the rest of us read The Times

"Quaintly Done"
Peter Duckworth (1959)

Time waits for no man, unless it's on a watch made in Italy.

Mezzo Volta (1990)

Queenie, queenie, oh rich little queenie
How much do your riches grow
Two million a day makes you feel gay
What goodness your taxes will sow
Oh no dear sir, I pay no dues
As one of the privileged few
But how this cash would help oh so much
Helping poor subjects with a royal touch
Oh no dear sir, you must tell your friends
My family and friends, they must spend, spend, spend
And also the corgis too - up you!

"What's mine is mine!"
Liz Buckingham (weekly statement)

God, I hate women. The only thing to be said about them is that they stop us from all being queer.

Archie Poofter (1964)

Oh that bloody phone
Rings night and day at home
No moments of true peace
The rings they never cease
But when I'm dead and gone
Will the rings go on and on?

"Dead Ringer"
Telly Compton (1965)

A true nationalist justifies murder as a glorious way to his ultimate victory - but this victory will surely lead him to the furnaces of hell where his rhetoric and his gun no longer prevail.

Thomas Beatty (1931)

Clockwork oranges require winding up before breakfast.

"The Cock Crows"
Simon Winters (1987)

Most people find it difficult to boil an egg and yet we allow them to vote.

Sammy Thompson (1961)

The perfect staple diet is the fixing of my wife's tongue to her chin.

"Office Planning"
Wilfred Penn (1968)

Biting the bullet requires very quick reactions.

"Queer Quirks for Quislings"
Lee Enfield Jnr (1916)

When a lawyer smiles, protect your balls and check your wallet, then run like hell.

"Legal Screwing"
Nick Bailey (1961)

Cash flow is a problem on the way out and interesting coming in.

Lloyd Barclay (1911)

Dying without creating is a crime against humanity

Alex Stephenson (1864)

Whenever I think of parrots, they make me puke

"Sick as a Parrot"
Wetherall Flintstock (1914)

One should never worry about relaxing but should try to relax when worrying

Ostell Backwith (1398)

A Big Mac is more powerful than the sword

Donald A Berg (1987)

Endless white silk, gently caressing the earth
Soft whispering clouds, billowing far down below
Harmoniously carrying man's sleek silver birds
Witnessing the magic of God's wondrous sky
A flaming red sea now carrying the bright dawn
The glitter of diamonds now moving from view
Such power, such beauty, such hope for mankind
But sadly we come downwards to face the real truth
Where filth, greed and envy are killing our planet
Oh how I yearn for my next journey up in the sky
To see but for an instant how it really should be.

Wing Commander "Blue" Smythe-Hommerstone (1991)

At least a sewer rat knows just what he's getting into.

" It's a Crappy World"
Digona Bugatti (1969)

All murderers should be given 10 years hard labour of selling double glazing.

"Smash & Grab"
Jimmy Barlow (1991)

I've never yet pissed upon a Frenchman, but I promise you all that this serious defect in my nature will be gloriously rectified as soon as the pub closes.

"The Wanking Frenchmen"
Bertram Mulligan (1987)

Rudolf the reindeer was an alcoholic

Father Cross (1956)

I've tried for 20 years to train my parrots to put the kettle on but they have all died of broken necks.

"Songs are for the Birds"
Jim Hawkins (1959)

A mouse working in a cement factory will never know the difference between chalk and cheese.
"Concrete Yogurt"

Whilhelm Mortari (1979)

Giving a false impression really annoys American Express.

"False Images"
Viktor Visanker (1990)

Whenever I can't sleep, I drink strong coffee to wake myself up

"Saucy Samuel"
Lee Perrin (1875)

Our scientists will soon visit other planets where a virgin birth and magical tricks will lead another world into a history of bloody conflict.

Bjorn Sundell (1990)

Artificial insemination is very boring,
I prefer the real stuff.

"Back To Nature"
Judith Summers (1969)

Understanding class envy explains why conflict exists but also further convinces both sides that the class gap should be even further widened.

Harold Bateman (1990)

Bluntness is not an acute problem, just a sarcastic comment from a sharp talker.
                                   Leandro Cassalini (1910)

He used to be a very calculating person, before he ran out of batteries.
                                   "The Forceful Porpoise"
                                   Everard Reddie (1986)

Boredom is never experiencing want.
                                   Jordan Pedersen (1854)

The electronic bleep is today's permanent itch.

                                   "Scratching the byte"
                                   Calvin Kulata (1984)

Natural confidence afforded by self esteem is an invaluable, albeit rare human asset, overshadowed by that devil vanity, a synthetic arrogance causing massive destruction since the birth of mankind.

                                   "I am the greatest!"
                                   Jack "Wonderman" Smith (1964)

Chapter 21

BECAUSE

During the writing of my early manuscript for this book, I intended to have a dedication printed in the front to thank just a few of the people who have inspired me to such heights of personal achievement. My publisher considered this as too weepy for the casual buyer to accept during the normal instant view of the first few pages before buying. As a compromise to the wishes and needs of my publisher I have agreed to have this dedication placed as the final words in this publication. For me, nothing has altered because my feelings remain the same.

I dedicate this book to:

My wife Shirley who for more than 25 years has believed in me and has coped with my unreasonable behaviour and the eccentricity which slowly overwhelmed me as a natural defence against accepting too quickly the real truths of life.

My sons Gary and Sean, of whom I am so proud have both grown up to be part of a new caring generation of thinkers and givers, intent on making this earth a far better place when they depart than it was when they arrived. This gives me great hope for the future of mankind.

My father from the green of Ireland who left wonderful memories with untold numbers of us some 26 years ago. Even now we find that our respect for him and his intelligence increases every day that the sun rises over the horizon.

My mother who left us more recently, the one responsible for that obstinate streak and the endless verbiage that has seen me through a colourful life of many obstacles.

Doctor Clive Layton of Upper Wimpole Street, London, who is the best plumber I have yet to meet, who so skilfully cleared the pipes of my heart in 1990, thus to extend my short stay here with you all.

Terry Freeman, Who as my real school friend has spent a life risking his life to save others in distress, then returning with humility to become the funniest man I have yet to meet.

Keith La Rondie who was my partner in business for many years and died so tragically in a pub fire with his teenage daughter alongside him. Keith brought a new dimension of ambition to my life and his memory is greatly responsible for driving me on through these latter years to greater heights.

Finally to my recently departed canine friend Henry, who showed the human race how life really should be.

Thank you all

Richard Head.